USA TODAY bestselling author **Heidi Rice** discovered she loved romantic fiction at about the same time she discovered boys and she's been adoring both ever since. With this in mind, her first brilliant career plan involved marrying Paul Newman. As she was thirteen, Paul was pushing fifty and there was the small matter of Joanne Woodward, that didn't quite pan out. Brilliant career plan B involved a job as a film reviewer for a national newspaper, but one wonderful husband, two beautiful sons and a lot of really bad B-movies later and she was ready for a new brilliant career plan—so she branched out into the wonderful world of romance writing. Her first novel was published in 2007 and she hasn't looked back since. She lives in London but loves to travel, particularly in the US, where she does a Thelma and Louise road trip every year with her best mate (although they always leave out the driving-off-a-cliff bit). And she's having so much fun, she's almost not sorry that first brilliant career plan didn't work out.

Heidi loves to hear from readers—you can e-mail her at heidi@heidi-rice.com, or visit her website: www.heidi-rice.com

P.S. I'm Pregnant

Heidi Rice

Mills & Boon, an imprint of Harlequin (UK) Limited,
Eton House, 18-24 Paradise Road, Richmond, Surrey TW9 1SR

PS I'M PREGNANT! © Harlequin Enterprises II B.V./S.à.r.l. 2012

Originally published as:
Hot-Shot Tycoon, Indecent Proposal © Heidi Rice 2009 and
Public Affair, Secretly Expecting © Heidi Rice 2009

ISBN: 978 0 263 90178 8

024-0712

Printed and bound by
CPI Group (UK) Ltd, Croydon, CR0 4YY

Daisy

To Bryony, for knowing when the Elvis impersonator needs to be kicked out of the manuscript.

With special thanks to Eilis, who made sure Connor didn't sound like an extra from *The Quiet Man*.

CHAPTER ONE

'You can't do this. What if you get caught? He could have you arrested.'

Daisy Dean paused in the process of scoping out her neighbour's ludicrously high garden wall and slanted her best friend, Juno, a long-suffering look.

'He won't catch me,' Daisy replied in the same hushed tones. 'I'm practically invisible with all this gear on.'

She looked down at the clothes she'd borrowed from her fellow tenants at the Bedsit Co-op next door. Goodness, she looked like Tinkerbell the Terminator decked out in fourteen-year-old Cal's sagging black Levi's, his tiny mother Jacie's navy blue polo neck and Juno's two-sizes-too-small bovver boots.

She'd never been this invisible in her entire life. The one thing Daisy had inherited from her reckless and irresponsible mother was Lily Dean's in-your-face dress sense. Daisy didn't do monotones—and she didn't believe in hiding her light under a bushel.

She frowned. Except when she was on a mission to find her landlady's missing cat.

'Stop worrying, Juno, and give me the beanie.' She held

out her hand and stared back up at the wall, which seemed to have grown several feet since she'd last looked at it. 'You'll have to give me a boost.'

Juno groaned, slapping the black woollen cap into Daisy's outstretched palm. 'This better not make me an accessory after the fact or something.' She bent over and looped her fingers together in a sling.

'Don't be silly.' Daisy shoved her curls under the cap and tugged it over her ears. 'It's not a crime. Not really.'

'Of course it's a crime.' Juno straightened from her crouch, her round, pretty face looking like the good fairy in a strop. 'It's called trespassing.'

'These are extenuating circumstances,' Daisy whispered as a picture of their landlady Mrs Valdermeyer's distraught face popped into her mind. 'Mr Pootles has been missing for well over a fortnight. And our antisocial new neighbour's the only one within a mile radius who hasn't had the decency to search his back garden.' She propped her hands on her hips. 'Mr Pootles could be starving to death and it's up to us to rescue him.'

'Maybe he looked and didn't find anything?' Juno said, her voice rising in desperation.

'I doubt that. Believe me, he's not the type to lose sleep over a missing cat.'

'How do you know? You've never even met the guy,' Juno murmured, wedging the tiniest slither of doubt into Daisy's crusading zeal.

'That's only because he's been avoiding us,' Daisy pointed out, the slither dissolving.

Their mysterious new neighbour had bought the double-fronted Georgian wreck three months ago, and had managed to gut it and rehab it in record time. But despite all Daisy's overtures since he'd moved in two weeks ago—the note she'd posted through his door and the message she'd relayed to his cleaning lady—he'd made no attempt to greet his neighbours at Mrs Valdermeyer's Bedsit Co-operative. Or join the search for the missing Mr Pootles.

In fact he'd been downright rude. When she'd dropped off a plate of her special home-made brownies the day before in a last ditch attempt to get his attention, he hadn't even returned the plate, let alone thanked her for them. Clearly the man was too rich and self-centred to have any time for the likes of them—or their problems.

And then there were his dark, striking good looks to be considered. 'All you have to do is look at him,' Daisy continued, 'to see he's a you-know-what-hole with a capital A.'

Okay, so she'd only caught glimpses of the guy as he was striding down his front steps towards the snazzy maroon gas-guzzler he kept parked out front. At least six feet two, leanly muscled and what she guessed most people would term ruggedly handsome, the guy was what she termed full of himself. Even from a distance he radiated enough testosterone to make a woman's ovaries stand up and take notice—and she was sure he knew it.

Not that Daisy's ovaries had taken any notice, of course. Well, not much anyway.

Luckily for Daisy, she was now completely immune to men like her new neighbour. Arrogant, self-absorbed charmers who thought of women as playthings. Men like Gary, who'd sidled into her life a year ago with his come-hither smile, his designer suits and his clever hands and sidled right back out again three months later taking a good portion of her pride and a tiny chunk of her heart with him.

Daisy had made a pact with herself then and there—that she'd never fall prey to some good-looking playboy again. What she needed was a nice regular guy. A man of substance and integrity, who would come to love her and respect her, who wanted the same things out of life she wanted and preferably didn't know the difference between a designer label and a supermarket own brand.

Juno gave an irritated huff, interrupting Daisy's moment of truth. 'I still don't understand why you haven't just asked the guy about that stupid cat.'

A pulse of heat pumped under Daisy's skin. 'I tried to catch him the few times I spotted him, but he drives off so fast I would have had to be an Olympic sprinter.'

She'd suffer the tortures of hell before she'd admit the truth. That she'd been the tiniest bit intimidated by him, enough not to relish confronting him in person.

Juno sighed and bent down, linking her fingers together. 'Fine, but don't blame me if you get done for breaking and entering.'

'Stop panicking.' Daisy placed a foot in Juno's palms. 'I'm sure he's not even home. His Jeep's not parked out front. I checked.'

If she'd thought for a moment he might actually be in residence the butterflies waltzing about in her belly would have started pogoing like punk rockers. 'I'll be super-discreet. He'll never even know I was there.'

'There's one teeny-weeny problem with that scenario,' Juno said dryly. 'You don't do discreet, remember.'

'I can if I'm desperate,' Daisy replied. Or at least she'd do her best.

Ignoring Juno's derisive snort, Daisy reached up to climb the wall and felt the skintight polo neck rise up her midriff. She looked down to see a wide strip of white flesh reflecting in the streetlamp opposite and caught a glimpse of her red satin undies where the jeans sagged.

'Blast.' She dropped her arm and bounced down.

'What's the matter now?' Juno whispered.

'My tummy shows when I lift my arms.'

'So?'

Daisy frowned at her friend. 'So it totally ruins the camouflage effect.' She tapped her finger on her bottom lip. 'I know, I'll take off my bra.'

'What on earth for?' Juno snapped, getting more agitated by the second.

'The material's catching on the lace—it won't rise up as much.'

'But you can't,' Juno replied. 'You'll bounce.'

'It'll only be for a minute.' Daisy unclipped the bra and wriggled it out of one sleeve. She passed the much-loved concoction of satin, lace and underwiring to Juno.

Juno dangled it from her fingertips. 'What is this obsession you have with hooker underwear?'

'You're just jealous,' Daisy replied, turning back to the wall. Juno had always had a bit of a complex about her barely B-cups in Daisy's opinion.

She put her foot in Juno's sling and felt her breasts sway erotically under the confining fabric. Thank goodness no one would get close enough to spot her unfettered state. She'd always been proud to call herself a feminist, but she was way too well endowed to be one of the burn-your-bra variety.

'Right.' Daisy took a deep breath of the heavy, honeysuckle-flavoured air. 'I'm off.'

Grabbing hold of the top, she hauled herself up, her nipples tightening as she rubbed against the brick. Throwing her leg over, she straddled the wall with a soft grunt.

She peered through the leaves of a large chestnut tree and scanned the shadows of their neighbour's garden. Moonlight reflected off the windows at the back of the house. Daisy let out the breath she'd been holding. Phew, he definitely wasn't in.

'I still can't believe you're actually going to do this.' Juno scowled up at her from the shrubbery.

'We owe this to Mrs Valdermeyer—you know how much

she adores that cat,' she whispered from her vantage position on the wall.

The truth was Daisy knew she owed her landlady much more than just a promise to find her cat.

When her mother, Lily, had announced she had found 'the one' again eight years ago, Daisy had opted to stay put. She'd been sixteen, alone in London and terrified and Mrs Valdermeyer had come to her rescue. Mrs Valdermeyer had given her a home, and a security she'd never known before—which meant Daisy owed her landlady more than she could ever repay. And Daisy always paid her debts.

'And don't forget,' Daisy said urgently, warming to her subject, 'Mrs V could have sold the Co-op to developers a thousand times over and become a rich woman, but she hasn't. Because we're like family to her. And family stick together.'

At least Daisy had always felt they ought to. If she'd ever had brothers and sisters and a mum who was even halfway reliable she was sure that was how her own family would have been.

She looked back at the garden, gulped down the apprehension tightening her throat.

'I don't think Mrs Valdermeyer would expect you to get arrested,' Juno whispered in the darkness. 'And don't forget the scar on that guy's face. He doesn't look like the type who can take a joke.'

Daisy leaned forward, ready to slide down the other side of the wall. She stopped. Okay, maybe that scar was a bit of a worry. 'Do me a favour—if I don't come back in an hour, call the police.'

She could just make out Juno's muttered words as she edged herself down into the darkness.

'What for? So they can cart you off to jail?'

* * *

'Forget it, I'm not conjuring up a fiancée just to keep Melrose sweet.' Connor Brody tucked the phone into the crook of his shoulder and pulled the damp towel off his hips.

'He went ballistic after the dinner party,' Daniel Ellis, his business manager, replied, the panic in his voice clear all the way down the phone line from New York. 'I'm not joking, Con. He accused you of trying to seduce Mitzi. He's threatening to lose the deal.'

Connor grabbed the sweat pants folded over the back of the sofa and tugged them on one-handed, cursing the headache that had been brewing all day—and Mitzi Melrose, a woman he never wanted to see again in this lifetime.

'She stuck her foot in my crotch under the table, Dan, not the other way around,' Connor growled, annoyed all over again by Mitzi's less-than-subtle attempts at seduction.

Not that Connor minded women who took the initiative, but Eldridge Melrose's trophy wife had been coming on to him all evening and he'd made it pretty damn clear he wasn't interested. He didn't date married women, especially married women joined for better or worse to the billionaire property tycoon he was in the middle of a crucial deal with. Plus he'd never been attracted to women with more Botox and silicone in their body than common sense. But good old Mitzi had refused to take the hint and this was the result. A deal he'd been working on for months was in danger of going belly up through no fault of his.

'Come on, Con. If he backs out of the deal now we're back to square one.'

Connor walked across the darkened living room to the bar by the floor-to-ceiling windows, Danny's pleading whine not doing a damn thing for his headache. He rubbed his throbbing temple and splashed some whiskey into a shot glass. 'I'm not about to pretend to be engaged just to satisfy Melrose's delusions about his oversexed wife,' he rasped. 'Deal or no deal.'

Connor savoured the peaty scent of the expensive malt—so different from the smell of stale porter that had permeated his childhood—and slugged it back. The expensive liquor warmed his sore throat and reminded him how far he'd come. He'd once had to do things he wasn't proud of to survive, to get out. The stakes would have to be a lot higher than a simple business deal before he'd compromise his integrity like that again.

'Damn, Con, come off it.' Danny was still whining. 'You're blowing this way out of proportion. You must have a ton of women in your little black book who'd kill to spend two weeks at The Waldorf posing as your beloved. And I don't see it being any big hardship for you either.'

'I don't have a little black book.' Connor gave a gruff chuckle. 'Danny, what era are you living in? And even if I did, there's not one of the women I've dated who wouldn't take the request the wrong way. You give a woman a diamond ring, she's going to get ideas no matter what you tell her.'

Hadn't he gone through the mother of all break-ups only two months ago because he'd believed Rachel when she'd said she wasn't looking for anything serious? Just good sex and a good time. He'd thought they were both on the same page only to discover Rachel was in a whole different book—a book with wedding bells and baby booties on the cover.

Connor shuddered, metal spikes stabbing at his temples. No way was he opening himself up to that horror show again.

'I can't believe you'd throw this deal away when the solution's so simple.'

Connor heard Danny's pained huff, and decided he'd had enough of the whole debate.

'Believe it.' He put the glass down on the bar, winced as the slight tap reverberated in his sore head. 'I'll see you the week after next. If Melrose is bound and determined to cut off his nose to spite me, so be it,' he finished on a rasping cough.

'Hey, are you okay, buddy? You sound kind of rough.'

'Just fine,' Connor said, his voice brittle with sarcasm. He'd caught some bug on the plane back from New York that morning and now there was this whole cluster screw-up with Melrose and his wife to handle.

'Why don't you take a few days off?' Danny said gently. 'You've been working your butt off for months. You're not Superman, you know.'

'You don't say,' Connor said wryly, resting his aching forehead against the cool glass of the balcony doors and staring into the garden below. 'I'll be all right once I've a solid ten hours' sleep under my belt.' Which might have worked if he hadn't been wired with jet lag.

'I'll let you get to it,' Danny said, still sounding concerned. 'But think about taking a proper break. Haven't you just moved into that swanky new pad? Take a couple of days to relax and enjoy it.'

'Sure, I'll think about it,' he lied smoothly. 'See you round, Dan.'

He clicked off the handset and glanced round at the cavernous, sparsely furnished living room in the half light.

He'd bought the derelict Georgian house on a whim at auction and spent a small fortune refurbishing it, thanks to some idiot notion that at thirty-two he needed a more permanent base. Now the house was ready, it was everything he'd specified—open, airy, clean, modern, minimalist—but as soon as he'd moved in he'd felt trapped. It was a feeling he recognised only too well from his childhood. And he'd quickly accepted the truth, that permanence for him was always going to feel like a prison.

He turned back to the window. He reckoned a therapist would have a field day with that little nugget of information, but he had a simpler solution. He'd sell the house and move on. Make a nice healthy profit—and never be stupid enough to consider buying a place of his own again.

Some people needed roots, needed stability, needed for ever. He wasn't one of them. Hotels and rentals suited him fine. Brody Construction was all the legacy he wanted.

He dropped the handset on the sofa.

His shoulder muscles ached at the slight movement. Damn, he hadn't felt this sore since he was a lad and he'd woken up with the welts still fresh from dear old Da's belt. He squeezed his eyes shut. *Don't go there.*

Forcing the old bitterness away, he lifted his lids and spotted a flicker of movement in the garden below. He blinked and squinted, focussing on the shadowy wisp. Slowly but surely, the wisp morphed into a figure. A small figure clad suspiciously in black, which proceeded to crawl over one of the flowerbeds.

He jolted upright and braced his palm against the glass, his head screaming in protest as he strained to see. Then watched in astonishment as the intruder stood and dipped under one of the big showy shrubs by the back wall—a light strip of flesh flashing at its midriff.

'What the…?' The whisper scraped his throat raw as fury bubbled.

Damn it all to hell and back, could this day get any worse?

A surge of adrenaline masked his aching limbs and exploding head as he stalked across the living room and down the wide twin staircase. Whoever the little bastard was, and whatever they were about, they'd made a big mistake.

No one messed with Connor Brody.

For all the trappings of wealth and sophistication that surrounded him now, he'd grown up on Dublin's meanest streets and he knew how to fight dirty when he had to.

He might not want this place, but he wasn't about to let anyone else nick a piece of it.

CHAPTER TWO

'HERE, kitty, kitty. Come to Daisy. Nice kitty.' Daisy strained to keep her voice to a whisper as sweat pooled in her armpits and the coarse wool of the beanie cap made her head itch.

She scratched her crown, pulled the suffocating cap back over her ears and peered into the pitch dark under the hydrangea bush. Nothing.

Why hadn't she brought a torch? She huffed. And gave up. This was pointless. She'd almost broken her neck getting over the wall and had then spent ten long minutes searching the garden, gouging her thumb on one of the rose bushes in the process, and she still hadn't seen a blasted thing.

She crawled out from under the bush, her fingers sinking into the dirt as she tried to avoid squashing any of the plants in the flowerbed.

Raucous barking cut the still night air like a thunderclap. She clasped her hand to her throat and swallowed a shriek.

Her heartbeat kicked in again as she recognised the excited yips. Trust Mr Pettigrew's Jack Russell, Edgar, to give her a flipping heart attack—it had to be the most annoying dog on the planet.

She puffed out her cheeks and sucked on her sore thumb.

Well, at least she could go back home now knowing she'd done her best to find the invisible Mr Pootles. Wherever he'd got to, it wasn't Mr Hot-Shot's back garden.

She stood, ready to walk back to the wall when the yapping cut off. The sound of a soft pad behind her had her glancing over her shoulder. She spotted the dark silhouette looming over her and had a split second to think. 'Oh, crap.'

A muscled forearm banded around her tummy and hauled her off her feet. Her breath whooshed out as her back connected with a solid wall of hot, naked male.

'Gotcha, you little terror,' muttered a deep voice.

She sucked in a quick breath ready to scream her lungs out, when a large hand slapped across her mouth—smothering her with the scent of sandalwood soap.

'No, you don't, lad,' the voice murmured, the hint of Irish in it only making it more terrifying. 'You're not calling your mates.'

She struggled against the band around her waist. It didn't budge.

Lifting her as if she weighed nothing at all, her captor hefted her back towards the house. The soap smell overwhelmed her as she listened to the grunts of her own muffled screams through the powertool now buzzing in her ears.

Daisy's head began to spin as tomorrow's tabloid headlines flashed across her mind. WOMAN SMOTHERED TO DEATH OVER MISSING CAT.

She kicked clumsily, connecting with thin air, and the baggy jeans slipped off her hips. Then the arm released and she landed hard on the ground, pitching head first onto the grass. As she scrambled up a hand grasped the waistband of her jeans and yanked.

'Hey, what's with the satin panties?' came the shocked shout from behind her.

She gasped, blood surging into her head as she lurched round and hauled the jeans back up to cover herself.

'Who the hell *are* you?' he yelled.

Silhouetted by the porch light, all she could make out of her captor were acres of bare chest, ominously black brows, waves of dark hair and impossibly broad shoulders.

Her whole body vibrated with fury as embarrassment exploded in her cheeks, but all that came out of her mouth was a pathetic yelp.

He reached forward and whipped the beanie cap off her head. She tried to grab for it but her hair cascaded down.

'You're a girl!'

She swiped her hair out of her eyes as outrage overwhelmed her. How dared he manhandle her and scare her half to death? She snatched the cap back. 'I'm not a girl,' she snapped, her voice returning at last. 'I'm a fully grown woman, you big bully.'

He took a step forward, towering over her. 'So what's a fully grown woman doing breaking into my house?'

She stumbled back, now holding the trousers in a death grip. Outrage gave way to common sense. What on earth was she doing arguing with the guy? He was twice her size and not in a very good mood if that threatening stance was any indication.

Forget standing her ground. Time to get the hell out of Dodge.

She turned to bolt. Too late—as strong fingers clamped on her arm.

'I don't think so, lady. I want some answers first.'

The forward momentum pulled her off her feet. 'Let me go,' she squeaked, tugging on her arm. His grip tightened as he dragged her backwards up the porch steps.

Panic welled up as he marched her through sliding glass doors into a massive open-plan kitchen. The smell of fresh varnish assaulted her nostrils and light blinded her as he snapped on a switch.

He hauled her past polished oak work surfaces and gleaming glass cabinets to a sunken seating area and shoved her, none too gently, into a leather armchair. 'Take a seat.'

She went to leap up but he grabbed the arms of the chair, caging her in. Heat radiated from his naked chest like a furnace, as did the heady scent of soap and man. She flinched at the fury in his face, which was now illuminated in every shockingly masculine detail.

A drop of water from his damp hair splashed onto her sweater. She shrank into the cool leather as the moisture sank into the fabric and touched her naked breasts.

Ice-blue eyes dipped to her chest and her traitorous nipples chose that precise moment to draw into excruciatingly hard points. Heat flared in her face. Why had she taken off her bra? Could he tell?

'Stay put,' he snarled, his laser-beam gaze lifting back to her face. 'Or, so help me, I'll give you the spanking you deserve.'

She began to shake, her heart wedged in her throat. Up close and rather too personal, the stark male beauty of his face was staggering. Dark slashing brows and angular cheekbones rough with stubble did nothing to detract from the cool, iridescent blue of his eyes, nor the livid white scar twitching against the tensed muscles of his jaw. As his gaze swept over her she noticed he had the longest eyelashes she'd ever seen.

They ought to have made those arctic eyes look girly. They didn't.

'You can't spank me,' she whispered, then wished she hadn't as his eyes darted back to hers.

'Don't tempt me,' he rasped.

Daisy's heartbeat sped up to warp speed. *Do not antagonise him, you silly cow.*

He straightened and raked a hand through his hair, pushing the thick black waves back from a high forehead. His gaze slipped to her chest again.

Her cheeks got several crucial shades hotter.

'You can stop shaking,' he said at last. 'You're in luck. I don't hurt women.'

The contempt in his voice was too much. Her temper flared, destroying the vow she'd made moments before. 'You just scared the crap out of me, Atilla. What the heck do you call that?'

'You were in my garden. Uninvited,' he sneered. Not sounding anywhere near as apologetic as he should. 'What did you expect, a red carpet?'

Before she could come up with a decent comeback, he turned and stalked over to the kitchen's central aisle. She noticed a curious hitch in his stride. Why was he walking as if he were on a swaying ship?

He bent over the double sink. Her eyes lifted to his back and she stifled a gasp, the question forgotten. A criss-cross of pale ridges stood out against the smooth brown skin of his shoulder blades. Daisy swallowed convulsively.

Whoever this guy was, he was not the rich, pampered, narcissistic playboy she'd assumed.

Coupled with the mark on his face, the scars on his back proved he'd lived a hard life, marred by violence. Daisy bit into her bottom lip, clasped her hands to stop them trembling and dismissed the little spurt of pity at the thought of how much those wounds must once have hurt.

Do not make him mad, again, Daisy. You don't know what he might be capable of.

He filled a glass with water, then turned back to her. Propping his butt against the counter, he crossed his bare feet at the ankles and stared. She shivered, suddenly freezing in the heat of the late-July evening.

He downed the water in three quick gulps. Daisy swallowed, realising her own throat was drier than the Gobi Desert. Probably the result of the extreme emotional trauma he'd put her through. She wasn't about to ask him for a glass, though. Keeping her mouth firmly shut at this juncture seemed like the smart choice.

He put the glass down on the counter. The sharp snap made her jump. He coughed, the sound harsh and hollow as it rumbled up his chest, and rubbed his forehead against his upper arm. Bracing his hands against the counter, he dropped his chin to his chest, gave a weary sigh.

Daisy let a breath out between her teeth. With those broad shoulders slumped he looked a little less threatening. When he didn't speak for a while, or look up, she wondered if he'd forgotten her. She eased out of the chair. The treacherous leather creaked, and his head snapped up.

'Sit the hell down,' he said, the huskiness of his voice doing nothing to disguise the snarl. 'We're not through.'

She sat down with a plop. He still looked enormous, and she suspected he was doing his level best to intimidate her, but she could see bruised smudges of fatigue under his eyes.

She ruthlessly quashed another little prickle of sympathy. Whatever was ailing him, he'd terrified her, threatened her and quite possibly let poor Mr Pootles die a long and painful death.

She'd be better off reserving her sympathy for the Big Bad Wolf.

'What exactly do you want?' she asked, pleased when her voice barely wavered.

He crossed his arms over his chest and cocked an eyebrow, saying nothing.

Completely of their own accord, her eyes zeroed in on the dark curls of hair on his chest, which tapered down a washboard-lean six-pack and arrowed to a thin line beneath the drooping waistband of his sweat pants. The worn grey cotton hung so low on his hips, she could see the hollows defining his pelvis. One millimetre lower, and she'd be able to see a whole lot more.

The errant thought had Daisy's thigh muscles clenching.

Her gaze shot back up to find him watching her. The heat flared across her chest and up her neck. Did he know where her thoughts had just wandered?

He rocked back on his heels, still studying her in that disconcerting way, and tightened his arms over his magnificent chest. Her heart gave an annoying kick as his biceps flexed, and her eyes flicked to a faded tattoo of the Celtic cross on his left arm.

She gulped, struggling to ignore the long liquid pull low in her belly. What was wrong with her? The guy might have the tanned, sculpted body of a top male model, but Daisy Dean did not get turned on by arrogant, self-righteous bullies, however buff they might be.

'So let's hear it,' he said, his soft, but oddly menacing tone cutting the oppressive silence at last. 'What were you about in my garden?'

She thrust her chin up, determined not to feel guilty. Her mission had been innocent enough, even if it now seemed somewhat suicidal. 'I was looking for my landlady's cat.'

He coughed, the dry rumble making her wince. 'How much of an idiot do you think I am?'

She bit back the pithy retort that wanted to pop out of her mouth.

'His name's Mr Pootles. He's a large ginger tom with a squinty eye,' she hurried on, despite the sceptical lift of his eyebrow. 'And he's been missing for two weeks.'

'And you couldn't come to the door and ask me if I'd seen him? Because why exactly?'

'I did, but you never answer your door,' she said, righteous indignation building. If he'd answered his damn door in the last two weeks she wouldn't be in this predicament. In fact, now she thought about it, this was all his fault.

'I've been out of the country this past week,' he shot back at her.

'Mr Pootles has been missing for two. And anyway I left messages with your housekeeper—and brownies,' she added.

His eyebrows shot up. Why had she mentioned the brownies? It made her sound like a stalker.

'Look, it doesn't matter.' She stood up, forcing what she hoped was a contrite look onto her face. 'I'm sorry I disturbed you. I didn't think you were in and I was worried about the cat. It could have been starving to death in your backyard.'

His eyes swept her figure again, making her pulse go haywire. 'Which doesn't explain why you dressed up like a burglar to come look for it,' he said wryly.

'Well, I…' How did she explain that, without sounding as if she were indeed a lunatic? 'I really should be going.'

Please let me get out of here with at least a small shred of my dignity intact.

'The cat obviously isn't here and I need to get back…' She stumbled to a halt, edging her way round the chair.

'Not yet, you don't,' he said, but to her astonishment his lips quirked.

She blinked, not believing her eyes. Was that a smile?

'I got the brownies, by the way. They were tasty.' He rubbed his belly, his lips lifting some more. The smile became a definite smirk.

'Why didn't you answer my messages, then?' And what was so damn funny all of a sudden?

'They probably got lost in translation,' he said easily. 'My cleaner doesn't speak much English.'

He straightened, swayed violently and grabbed hold of the work surface.

'What's wrong?' Daisy stepped towards him. His face had drained of colour and looked worn and sallow in the harsh light.

He put a hand up, warding her off. 'Nothing,' he growled, all traces of amusement gone.

She could see he was lying. But decided not to call him on it. After the way she'd been treated he could be at death's door for all she cared.

He let go of the counter top, but didn't look all that steady. 'I know what happened to your cat.'

It was the last thing she'd expected him to say. 'You do?'

'Uh-huh, follow me.'

Gripping the edge of the centre aisle, he made his way across the kitchen. He moved with the fragile precision of someone in their eighties, his bare feet padding on the floor.

Daisy tramped down on her instinctive concern as she followed him. She hated to see people suffering, and for all his severe personality problems this guy was obviously suffering. But he'd made it clear he didn't want her sympathy, or her help.

He shuffled to a small door in the far wall and opened it. Leaning heavily on it, he beckoned her over with one finger.

As she stepped forward he pulled the door wide. She heard the soft mewing sound and glanced down. Gasping, she dropped to her knees. Nestled in an old blanket beneath a state-of-the-art immersion heater was Mr Pootles—and his four nursing kittens.

Make that Mrs Pootles.

'The cat showed up after I moved in.' She glanced up at the husky voice, saw the hooded blue eyes watching her. 'She had no collar and didn't want to be petted so I took her for a stray.'

Daisy studied the cat and her kittens. A saucer of milk had been placed next to the blanket. She reached out a finger and stroked one of the miniature bodies. The warm bundle of fluff wiggled. Daisy sat back on her haunches.

Maybe the Big Bad Wolf wasn't as bad as he seemed.

A little of Daisy's anger and indignation drained away, to be replaced by something that felt uncomfortably like shame.

'She had the kittens ten days back,' he continued, the hoarse tone barely more than a whisper. 'The cleaner's been looking after them. They seem to be doing okay.'

'I see,' she said quietly.

Daisy stood, resigned to eating the slice of humble pie she'd so cleverly served herself by climbing over his garden wall in the middle of the night.

Still, she took a few seconds to collect herself, brushing invisible fluff off Cal's jeans and then folding down the waistband so they'd stay up without her having to cling onto them. Humble pie had always been hard for her to swallow. Having delayed as long as possible, she cleared her throat and made eye contact.

He was studying her, his expression inscrutable. She might have guessed he wasn't going to make this easy for her.

'I'm awfully sorry, Mr…?'

'Brody, Connor Brody,' he said, a penetrating look in those crystal eyes. Her pulse skidded.

'Mr Brody,' she murmured, her cheeks flaming. 'What I did was unforgivable. I hope there are no hard feelings.'

She held out her hand, but instead of taking it he glanced at it, then to her astonishment his lips curved in a lazy grin. The slow, sensuous smile softened the harsh lines of his face, making him look even more gorgeous—and even more arrogant—if that were possible.

Daisy held back a sigh as her heart rate kicked into overdrive.

How typical. When Daisy Dean made an idiot of herself,

it couldn't be in front of an ordinary mortal. It had to be in front of someone who looked like a flipping movie star.

'So are your cat burgling days behind you, now?' he said at last, the roughened voice doing nothing to hide his amusement. He tilted his head to take in every inch of her attire, right down to Juno's Doc Martens. 'That'd be a shame, as the outfit suits you.'

She dropped her hand. Make that a movie star with a warped sense of humour.

'Enjoy it while you can,' she said dryly, trying hard to see the humour in the situation—which was clearly at her expense. She knew perfectly well she looked a complete fright.

'And what would your name be?' he asked.

'Daisy Dean.'

'It's been a pleasure, Daisy Dean,' he said, still smirking as if she were the funniest thing he'd ever seen.

'I'll come back tomorrow to get the cats, if that's okay?' she said stiffly, clinging to her last scrap of dignity.

'I'll be waiting,' he said. The hacking cough that followed wiped the smirk off his face, but only for a moment. 'I've a question, though, before you go.'

'What is it?' she asked warily, the teasing glint in his eyes irritating her.

Honestly, some men would flirt with a stone.

He didn't say anything straight away. Instead, his gaze roamed down to her chest and took its own sweet time making its way back to her face. 'Did you lose the bra on your way over the wall?'

Colour flared in her cheeks and her backbone snapped straight. That did it. 'I'm glad you find this so hilarious, Mr Brody.'

'You have no idea, Daisy,' he said, coughing out a laugh, his pure aquamarine eyes sparkling with mischief.

'I'm off,' she said through clenched teeth, not even trying to keep the frost out of her voice.

She might have been wrong about the cat, but she hadn't been wrong about him. He was an arrogant, overbearing, insufferable, full-of-himself—

A hissed expletive interrupted her cataloguing of his many character flaws.

She turned, watching in astonishment as he stumbled and then collapsed. The thud of his knees hitting the laminated floor made her wince.

She crouched beside him, her resentment fading fast as she took in his pallid complexion and the tremors racking his body. 'Mr Brody, are you okay?'

'Yes,' he hissed, a thin sheen of moisture popping out on his forehead.

She pressed the back of her hand to his brow, felt the scorching heat as he jerked back. 'You're burning up, Mr Brody.'

'Stop calling me that, for Christ's sake.' His head snapped up, the headache clear in his bloodshot eyes. 'The name's Connor.'

'Well, Connor, you've got yourself a very impressive fever. You need to see a doctor.'

'I'm okay,' he said, gripping the work surface. She offered her hand, but he shrugged it off as he struggled onto his feet, the muscles in his arms bulging as he hauled himself upright.

She could see the effort had cost him as he stood with his hands braced on the polished wood. His chest heaved in ragged pants and the fine sheen of sweat turned to rivulets running down his temples.

'You can leave any time now.' He grunted without looking round.

She came to stand next to him, could feel the heat and resentment pulsing off him. 'What? When I'm having so much fun watching you suffer?'

The tremor became a shake. 'Get lost, will you?'

She rolled her eyeballs. Men! What exactly was so terrible about asking for help? Propping herself against his side, she put an arm round his waist. 'How far to your bedroom?'

'There's a spare room across the hall.' The words had the texture of sandpaper scraping over his throat. 'Which I can get to under my own steam.'

She doubted that, given the way he was leaning on her to stay upright. 'Don't be silly,' she said briskly. 'You can hardly walk.'

To her surprise, he didn't put up any more protests as she led him out of the kitchen and across a hallway. The spare room was as palatial as expected, with wide French doors leading out into the garden. She eased him down onto the large divan bed in the dim light, his skin now slick with sweat. He shivered violently, his teeth chattering as he spoke.

'Fine, now leave me be.'

He sounded so annoyed she smiled. The tables had certainly turned. She didn't have long to savour the moment though as brutal coughs rocked his chest.

'I'm calling the doctor.'

'It's only a cold.' The protest didn't sound convincing punctuated by the harsh coughing.

'More like pneumonia,' she said.

'No one gets pneumonia in July.' He tried to say something else, but his shadowy form convulsed on the bed as he succumbed to another savage coughing fit.

She rushed back into the kitchen, spotted the phone on the far wall and pumped in the number for her local GP. Maya Patel lived two streets over and owed her a favour since the mother-and-baby club fund-raiser she'd helped organise a month ago. Her friend sounded sleepy when she picked up. Daisy rattled out her panicked plea and Connor's address.

'Fine,' Maya said wearily. 'You need to get his temperature down. Try dousing him with ice water, open the windows and take his clothes off. I'll be there as soon as I can,' she finished on a huge yawn and hung up.

Daisy returned to the bedroom armed with a bowl of ice water and a tea towel. The hideous coughing had stopped, but when she got closer to the bed she could feel the heat pumping off her patient. He'd sweated right through the track pants, which clung to his powerful thighs like a second skin.

She flipped the lamp on by the bed to find him watching her, the feverish light of delirium intensifying the blue of his irises.

'The doctor said to try and get the fever down,' she said.

She took his silent stare as consent and dipped the cloth in the water. She wrung it out and draped it over his torso. He moaned, the sinews of his arms and neck straining. She wiped the towel over his chest and down his abdomen. Her heart rate leaped as he sucked in a breath and the rigid muscles quivered under her fingertips.

The cloth came away warm to the touch.

'Dr Patel's on her way,' she said gently. 'Is there anyone you want me to call? Anyone you need here?'

He shook his head and whispered something. She couldn't hear him, so she leaned down to place her ear against his lips.

Hot breath feathered across her ear lobe and sent a shiver of awareness down her spine. 'There's no one I need, Daisy Dean,' he murmured, in a barely audible whisper. 'Not even you.'

She straightened, looked into his face and saw the vulnerability he was determined to hide.

He might not want to need her, but right now he did and

Daisy had a rule about people in need—you had to do your best to help them, whether they wanted you to or not.

She rinsed the cloth, wrung it out and placed it on his forehead. He tensed against the chill, his big body shivering.

'That's a shame, tough guy,' she said as she stroked his brow. 'Because I'm afraid you're stuck with me until you're strong enough to throw me out.'

Connor closed his eyes, the blessed cool on his brow beating back the inferno that threatened to explode out of his ears. Every single muscle in his body throbbed in agony but those cool, efficient strokes, over his cheeks, across his chest, down his arms, doused the flames, if only for a short while.

He'd always hated it when his sisters had fussed over him as a kid, trying to tend the wounds their father had inflicted in one of his drunken rages. Even then he'd hated to be beholden to anyone. Hated to feel dependent. But as his eyes flickered open he was pathetically grateful to see his pretty little neighbour leaning over him. He stared at her, taking in the clear, almost translucent skin and the serene, capable look on her face as she soothed the brutal pain. She reminded him of the alabaster Madonna in St Patrick's Church, which had fascinated him as a boy, when he'd still believed prayers could be answered.

But then his Virgin bit into her full lower lip and shifted on the edge of the bed to dip the cloth back in the water bowl. His gaze dropped, taking in the enticing movement of her breasts and the outline of erect nipples against her skintight top. Despite the heat blurring his senses and the pain stabbing at his skull, Connor felt the rush of response in his loins.

He shifted uncomfortably and she turned towards him. Flame-red curls outlined her head like a halo and the vivid jade-green eyes grew larger in her gamine face.

She placed gentle fingers on his forehead, pushed back the

hair that had fallen across his brow. 'Try to get some sleep, Mr Brody. The doctor will be here shortly.'

The desperate urge to take back what he'd said, to ask her not to leave, overwhelmed him. He opened his mouth to say the words, but nothing came out other than a guttural murmur. He grasped her wrist, grimacing as his shoulder cramped. He had to get her attention, make her stay, but however hard he tried he couldn't make a coherent sound.

'Don't talk, you'll only tire yourself out.' She took his hand in hers, folded her small fingers round his palm and squeezed. 'It's okay, I won't leave you,' she said, as if she'd read his mind.

He shut his eyes, let himself fall into the fiery oblivion, his mind clinging onto one last disturbing thought.

Would wanting to see his angel of mercy naked send him straight to hell?

CHAPTER THREE

DAISY placed Connor's hand carefully by his side, listened to the harsh pants of his breathing as he fell into a fitful sleep and then ran all three of Maya's instructions back through her mind—one of which she'd been pretending she hadn't heard.

She nipped over to the room's French doors, unlocked the latch and flung them wide. Maybe two out of three would do the trick. But the evening air was suffocatingly still, creating no respite from the heat.

Daisy sat back on the bed. She chewed her lip and concentrated on wiping the cloth over the contours of Brody's upper body. She applied the cooling linen to his arms and shoulders, and listened to the low groans as he struggled with the fever.

After five agonisingly long minutes, it was clear the fever had no intention of abating. If anything it seemed to be getting worse, the ice water now lukewarm in the bowl. Daisy wiped her own brow, cursing her smothering outfit for the umpteenth time that night.

Where was Maya? Shouldn't she have been here by now? But even as she registered the thought she knew it was a delaying tactic.

Brody shifted on the bed, his movements stiff and uncomfortable.

What was her problem? She should just take off Brody's sweat pants and be done with it. She was being ridiculous, behaving like a silly schoolgirl, when she was a mature, sensible and sexually confident woman.

Good grief, she'd seen naked men before. She'd lost her virginity at nineteen, to sweet, geeky Terry Mason. She wasn't exactly prolific when it came to partners and some of them had definitely been more memorable than others. But none of her relationships had been disastrous enough to give her a complex about nudity. Hers or anyone else's.

Until now.

Okay, Brody was a stranger, and his physique had affected her rather alarmingly already. But she could hardly let the poor bloke suffer because she'd had a sudden, inexplicable attack of modesty. And anyhow, this wasn't remotely sexual, she was only trying to get his temperature down until Maya arrived. Plus, he probably had underwear on. There was absolutely no need to worry.

That vain hope was crushed like a bug when Daisy peeked under his track pants and spotted the dark, springy wisps of hair.

She let go of the damp waistband so fast it snapped back into place. Brody moaned, sweat beading on his forehead in the lamplight.

Calm down, Daisy, stop being a ninny. You can do this. You have to.

She'd just ignore her pounding pulse and her quivering ovaries.

Right. She got up to look for some fresh linen, reasoning she'd need a sheet once she got the sweat pants off, to preserve his modesty. Not that she thought he had a great deal from his cheeky remark about her bra, but it seemed she had more than enough for both of them.

It took her approximately two seconds to find the brand-new bed linen in the dresser drawer. After spending a full minute undoing the packaging and snapping out the sheets, she was all out of time-wasting tactics.

Perching on the edge of the bed, she shook Brody's shoulder.

'I have to take your sweat pants off, Mr Brody. They're soaked and we need to get the fever down.'

No response, just another hoarse groan. Fine, she wasn't going to get his permission. She'd just have to hope he didn't sue her when he woke up and found himself naked.

She hooked her fingers in the waistband, pressed her thumbs into the damp fabric and sucked in a breath. She turned her face away, heat pumping into her cheeks as she eased the garment over his hips. Almost immediately, something halted its progress. She tugged harder, he grunted and the fabric bounced over the impediment.

A few moments more of give, and then the sweat pants got stuck again.

She fisted her hands and tried the same trick twice, but this time the pants weren't budging. Anchored, she guessed, under his bottom. She huffed, not ready to look round. Whatever that bump had been a moment ago, she knew she'd got the pants far enough down now to afford her more of an eyeful than was good for her blood pressure.

She squeezed her eyes shut, gripping the band of elastic harder, when he mumbled something and rolled towards her. As the trousers loosened Daisy sent up a quick prayer of thanks and gave them a swift yank. They slipped down before he flopped onto his back again. She was leaning so close to him now, she could feel the heat of his skin against the side of her face, and smell the musky and oddly pleasant scent of fresh male sweat and sandalwood soap.

Do not turn round. Do not turn round and look at him.

Daisy repeated the mantra in her head, staring at the open doorway and trying not to picture long, hard flanks roped with muscle as the silky hair on his thighs tickled the backs of her fingers. She gave a huff of relief as she peeled the sweat pants over his knees, inching along the edge of the bed as she went. The effort to keep her balance and resist the urge to look at him had sweat beading on her own brow. Concentrating hard, Daisy nearly toppled off the bed when her patient groaned again.

Daisy noticed the difference in sound immediately, her ears attuned to even the slightest change in tone. This groan didn't sound like the others, more a low, sensual moan than a painful grunt. Daisy puffed out a breath, damning her overactive imagination as her thigh muscles clenched and the sweet spot between them began to throb in earnest.

Get serious, woman. This situation is not erotic. Pretend you're undressing a sick child.

But however hard she tried, Daisy couldn't think of Brody as anything other than a man. A man in his prime. An extremely sexy, naked man who had something nestled between his thighs that had produced that resilient bounce.

As she was busy conjuring up some extremely inappropriate images to explain that damn bounce Daisy's luck ran out. The heavy, confining folds of the track pants locked around Brody's ankles. No matter how hard she tugged and pulled and yanked she couldn't unravel the sodden fabric and get the pants the rest of the way off.

Blast, it was no good, she'd have to look to sort out the tangle.

Keep your eyes down. Remember. Eyes on toes.

Muttering the new mantra, she swivelled her head and her

eyes instantly snagged on something they shouldn't. Something that had her jaw dropping, her eyes widening and the liquid between her thighs turning to molten lava.

Wow!

She'd found the source of her bounce. And it was more erotic than anything she could have imagined on her own. Brody, it seemed, despite his fever, his delirium and his earlier exhaustion, was sort of turned on. His partial erection sat proud and long, angling towards his belly button.

Daisy swallowed past the rock lodged in her parched throat. She'd always been a firm believer that size didn't matter, but that was before she'd seen Connor Brody naked. Everything about the man was quite simply magnificent.

The sudden urge to run her fingertip along the ridge of swollen flesh was so all-consuming, Daisy had to fist her hands and force her gaze away. She stared at the ceiling and gritted her teeth. Utterly disgusted with herself.

How could she have admired his private parts like that? How could she have even considered touching them? How had she gone from frightened schoolgirl to raging nymphomaniac in the space of a few minutes?

What she'd almost done was unconscionable and unethical, a gross invasion of his privacy and against everything she'd ever believed about herself. She had absolutely no right to take advantage of the poor man when he was delirious and burning up with fever and needed her help.

She grabbed the sheet she'd laid out at the bottom of the bed and whisked it over him. It settled in a billowing wave over his lower half, but did nothing to disguise what was underneath. If anything, veiled in the expensive linen—the stark white standing out against his tanned skin—Connor Brody's naked body looked even more awe-inspiring.

She spent several seconds grappling with the sweat pants,

finally freeing his feet, struggling to forget what she'd seen. But she couldn't.

Her eyes drifted back up and she noticed the small scar on his hip, which disappeared beneath the sheet. Her breath gushed out.

She'd always thought Gary had a beautiful body. Fit and perfectly proportioned, with that tantalising sprinkling of hair that had made her mouth water. Of course Gary had always thought he had a beautiful body too, which had taken the shine off a bit. But there was no getting round the fact that Gary compared to Brody was like Clark Kent compared to Superman.

Brody's long, lean limbs, toned muscles, the deep and, she now knew, all-over tan and that arresting face made quite a package all by themselves—not to mention his actual package, the memory of which was making Daisy feel as if she were the one with a fever—but even more tantalising was the hint of danger about him, of something not quite tame.

One thing was for sure, Gary naked had never had the physical effect on her Brody was having right this instant—and the man wasn't even conscious.

She couldn't catch her breath. Her skin felt tight and itchy and nothing short of a nuclear explosion had detonated at her core. And her ovaries weren't just quivering, they were doing the rock-a-hula—with full Elvis accompaniment.

Daisy frowned, contemplating what her unprecedented reaction to a naked Connor Brody might mean—none of the options being good—when the doorbell buzzed.

She leaped off the bed so fast she tripped on the carpet and almost fell flat on her face.

Brody must have heard her, because his eyelids flickered and he grunted before turning onto his side. Unfortunately, he took the sheet with him, flashing Daisy the most delicious rear end she'd ever set eyes on. She yanked the sheet back to cover his bare butt before her blood pressure shot straight through the roof.

Her heartbeat racing and her pulse pounding in her ears, she headed down the corridor to the front door. She took several deep breaths as she fumbled with the latch.

Get a hold of yourself. He's just a good-looking bloke and, from his rough, arrogant behaviour earlier, not a very nice one at that.

She tugged the door open to see her friend and local GP Maya Patel on the other side.

'This had better be good, Daze.' The harassed doctor marched past her with a loud huff, toting her black bag under her arm, her usually immaculate hair falling in disarray down the back of a two-piece track suit. 'I hope you realise I can't actually treat this guy as he's not registered with our practice. I could end up getting sued if any—'

She stopped in mid-sentence to gape at Daisy. 'Blimey, that's a new look for you. What are you? In mourning or something?'

Yes, for my nice, sensible, discerning libido, Daisy thought wryly.

'It's a long story,' she said as she led the way down the hall. The less Maya knew about the situation, the better.

'Who is this bloke anyway?' Maya asked, following Daisy into the darkened room.

'I told you, my new neighbour.' *And the harbinger of nymphomania.* 'I called round to ask about Mr Pootles and he collapsed in front of me.' *Sort of.*

'Let's take a look at him.' Maya sat on the edge of the bed, and plopped her bag on the floor. 'What's his name again?'

'Connor Brody.'

Maya touched his shoulder. 'Connor, I'm Dr Patel. I'm here to examine you.' She moved her hand to his brow when he failed to reply. 'He's certainly got quite a temperature,' she said, lifting her hand. 'How long has he been out?'

Daisy glanced at her watch, and realised he'd only collapsed about fifteen minutes ago, even though it felt like a lifetime. She relayed everything she knew to Maya, who began rummaging around in her bag.

'Would it be okay if I popped next door while you examine him?' Daisy asked. 'I'll be right back as soon as I tell Juno what's going on.'

'Sure, it shouldn't take long,' Maya replied, fishing a thermometer and a stethoscope out of the bag. 'Looks like this nasty twenty-four-hour flu bug that's been doing the rounds to me, but I'll check his vitals to make sure it's nothing more serious.'

Daisy high-tailed it out of the room. She did not want any more flashes of Connor Brody's anatomy just yet. She'd had enough already to keep her in lurid erotic fantasies for weeks.

'Have you completely lost your marbles?'

Daisy ignored Juno's pained shout as she walked past her down the corridor to her bedsit, the towel wrapped tight around her freshly showered body. 'I've got to go back there. He's really ill. I can't leave him to fend for himself.'

'Why not? You don't know the first thing about him.' Juno followed her into her room and slumped down on the bed. Her brows lowered ominously. 'What if he gets violent?'

'Don't be melodramatic. I told you, that was a misunderstanding,' Daisy said, riffling through her wardrobe. Connor Brody getting violent was one of the few things she wasn't worried about. 'He looked after Mrs Valdermeyer's cat. I think I've misjudged him. He's not a bad guy.' *Well, not in that way.*

She pulled out her favourite dress, a simple bias-cut cotton sheaf printed with bright pink blossoms. 'Once the fever's broken and I'm sure he's okay, I'll leave.' She certainly didn't want to be around the guy when he had all his faculties back. Brody unconscious was quite devastating enough, thank you very much.

'But it's the middle of the night, he's a stranger and you'll be in the house alone with him,' Juno whined.

Daisy paused in the act of slipping on her hooker underwear. 'I'll be perfectly safe. Apart from anything else, he's unconscious.' She presented her back to Juno after tugging on her dress. 'Here, zip me up. I told Maya I'd be back straight away.'

Juno continued to grumble about personal safety as she zipped Daisy into her dress. Daisy tuned her friend out as she spritzed patchouli perfume on her wrists, put on her bangles and brushed the tangles out of her newly washed hair.

She knew why Juno was a pessimist, why she hid behind baggy dungarees and a scowl, and why she always saw the cloud instead of the silver lining. Juno had been hurt badly once, very badly. She didn't trust men. Which really was rather ironic, Daisy thought as she stared at herself in the mirror. After Daisy's grossly inappropriate behaviour in their neighbour's spare bedroom, Brody wasn't the one who couldn't be trusted.

'Why are you getting dolled up?'

Daisy stopped dead, her lip gloss in mid-air. 'What?' She met Juno's censorious gaze in the mirror.

'You're all dolled up. What's that about?'

'I am not,' Daisy replied, mortally offended. But as she focussed on her reflection she could see Juno had a point. The figure-flattering dress, the sparkle of bangles and beads, the signature scent of patchouli, not to mention the make-up she'd been applying, made it look as if she were planning a night on the town, not a night spent nursing a sick man.

Shocked and a little dismayed, she shoved the lip gloss back in her make-up bag.

She most definitely was not dressing up for Brody's benefit; the very thought was ludicrous. She didn't even like the guy.

Daisy slipped on her battered Converse, forgoing the beaded Indian sandals she'd already pulled out of the closet. 'I'm not dressed up—this is me getting comfortable,' she said lamely.

She pretended she didn't hear Juno's grunted, 'Yeah, right,' as her best friend trailed after her.

'Don't wait up,' Daisy said, closing the door to her bedsit. 'I'm not sure when I'll be back.'

'Be careful,' Juno said, giving her one last considering look.

The crooked banisters of the old Georgian house creaked as Daisy made her way down the stairs. She noticed the peeling paint as she opened the front door, the patched plaster on the stoop. The house's imperfections had always made her feel comforted and secure. As she walked the few steps to Brody's door she couldn't help comparing Mrs Valdermeyer's cosy wreck of a house to the sleek, impersonal perfection of its neighbour.

Daisy sighed as she walked in.

The sight of Brody's naked body might have short-circuited her hormones, but she was not going to allow it to short-circuit her brain cells too. The very last thing she needed was for anything to happen between her and her arrogant new neighbour. He might be dishy, but she'd only needed to spend a few minutes in his company—and his home—to know he was so not right for her it wasn't even funny.

'He'll probably drift in and out until the temperature breaks,' Maya Patel announced, slinging her black bag under her arm.

'Keep dousing him with ice water. And if you can, get some more paracetamol down him in four hours' time.'

Daisy nodded, the butterflies having a ball in her stomach at the thought of the long night ahead.

'Are you sure it's not serious?' Daisy asked. Like most doctors, Maya didn't seem to think anything short of double pneumonia was worth getting excited about.

'I'm sure he'll be fine once he's sweated it out of his system. His temperature's hovering around one hundred and two, but that's to be expected. If it gets any higher give me a call. But his breathing's okay and he's a young, healthy guy.' Maya smiled at Daisy. 'Actually, if I wasn't here in a professional capacity, not to mention married and a mother of three children—I'd say he was a total hunk.'

Daisy dropped her head to concentrate on undoing the front door latch, her cheeks boiling.

'He's been in the wars a few times,' Maya continued. 'But he seems to have come through them surprisingly well.'

'You mean the scars on his back?' Daisy asked as she yanked the heavy door open.

'Yeah, do you know where he got them?'

'No, I hardly know the guy,' Daisy replied. Then her curiosity got the better of her. 'What's your professional opinion?'

'Old, probably from before he hit puberty would be my guess, but I'm no expert,' Maya said matter-of-factly, then chuckled as she stepped onto the stoop. 'And why, might I ask, do you care if you hardly know the guy?'

Daisy struggled to come up with an answer that wouldn't sound totally suspicious. She might as well not have bothered.

'Ah-ha.' Maya pointed an accusing finger at her. 'I thought so. Seems I'm not the only one who thinks our patient is a hunk.'

'He's okay,' Daisy replied flatly, praying her rosy cheeks weren't a total giveaway.

Maya jogged down the front steps. 'Let me know how he's doing tomorrow if the fever still hasn't broken.' She turned by the kerb and wiggled her eyebrows at Daisy. 'And keep an eye on your own temperature, Daze. Being in a room with a guy that hunky and that naked all night long can be hard work.' She winked. 'But I'm sure you're up to the job.'

She laughed as Daisy's cheeks shot from rosy to beetroot, and climbed into her car.

Daisy locked the front door and leaned back against it, focussing on the room down the hall where her hunk of a patient awaited.

A platoon of butterflies dive-bombed under her breast-bone.

Hard work indeed. Maya didn't know the half of it.

CHAPTER FOUR

CONNOR awoke with a start to the dazzle of morning sunlight. The shadows from the long, traumatic night still lingered at the edges of his consciousness.

He squinted, threw his arm up to ward off the glare, and noticed several things at once. The hammer in his head had quit banging, his muscles had stopped throbbing in time with it and he was no longer sleeping in a sauna. He eased his arm down as his eyes adjusted to the light, gazed out at the leafy old chestnut in his back garden, and the last of the dark disappeared.

Hell, it was good not to feel as if he'd gone six rounds with the champ any more.

How long had he been out? He didn't have a clue. He caught a whiff of perfume: flowery, spicy and wildly erotic. Recollections from the night before washed over him: the pain, the heat, the terror. But more vivid was the recollection of calm words, of whispered reassurances, of firm hands soothing him back to oblivion when the cruel flashbacks had wrenched him to the surface. And all the good memories were wrapped in that enticing scent.

She'd stayed with him. Just as she'd promised.

He pushed up on his elbows as panic sprinted up his spine. *Where is she? Has she left?*

His heartbeat slowed when he spotted her curled up in the armchair across the room. He drank in the sight of her—like the icy water she'd made him sip through the night—then felt like a fool.

When had he turned into such a girl? The nightmares had stalked him on and off throughout his life, always catching him at a weak moment, but he'd learned to handle them a long time ago. They didn't bother him now the way they once had. It was good of her to stay last night, to see him through the fever and the familiar demons it had brought with it, but he didn't need her here.

But as he gazed at her a smile curved his lips. He might not need her, but she was still grand to look at in the daylight.

He folded his arms behind his head, relaxed into the pillows and indulged himself.

She'd changed her cat-burglar outfit, which was kind of a shame. The creased summer dress did amazing things for her figure, but the hint of satin at the plunging neckline, which he guessed matched her panties, meant her nipples were no longer clearly visible. Still, the pale, plump flesh of her cleavage was some compensation.

Her rich red hair, which had been springing out all over her head last night as if she'd had an electric shock, fell in soft unruly curls to her shoulder, framing high cheekbones. His lips quirked as his gaze wandered to her feet, which were folded under her bum, and he spotted a pair of battered blue basketball boots tied with lurid green laces.

The funky mix of styles suited her. From the little he could remember of last night, before he'd passed out, she'd been headstrong and prickly as hell—with a surprisingly soft centre when her angel-of-mercy tendencies had come charging to the rescue.

He sat up and swung his legs off the bed, glad that they didn't even wobble as he stood up. He wrapped the sheet around his waist, and his smile widened as he spotted his sweat pants neatly folded at the end of the bed. She must have stripped him. The smile became a grin. What he wouldn't give to have been conscious at that moment.

He stretched, yawned and rubbed his throat—pleased to discover the rawness gone—but kept his eyes on his angel of mercy.

Jesus, but she was pretty, in a cute, off-the-wall way. Not his usual type for sure, but then he considered himself very flexible where women were concerned.

Despite the horrors of the previous night, desire stirred. Then his stomach growled, interrupting the erotic direction of his thoughts—and reminding him all he'd eaten in the last twenty-four hours was her brownies.

The memory of the rich chocolate squares—crusty on the outside with a luxuriously moist centre—had his senses stirring again and his stomach giving another loud rumble of protest. She didn't move, her breasts rising and falling in steady rhythm. Connor's heart stuttered. She really had exhausted herself on his behalf. No one had ever done that before.

Once you factored in the gift of the brownies and her mad mission to save her landlady's cat, it occurred to Connor his sweet and captivating neighbour was quite the little Good Samaritan. Definitely not his type, then. But he still ought to thank her for being so neighbourly. At the very least he should show her there were no hard feelings for sneaking over his garden wall.

He chuckled. What he'd like to do was scoop her up and give her a long, leisurely kiss to show his appreciation. He resisted the urge. He doubted she'd thank him for the attention until he'd had a shower.

He strolled to the French doors, and closed the drapes.

He'd let her sleep a while longer. Once he'd cleaned up and staved off starvation he'd wake her. He could offer her breakfast and then maybe they could get to that thank-you kiss if she wanted. No harm in seeing if they couldn't celebrate his recuperation together before she took the cat and its kittens and headed home. If he remembered correctly she hadn't been completely immune to him before he'd fallen on his face.

He began to whistle softly as he left the room. He felt a little shaky, probably from lack of food, but his other symptoms were as good as gone. It looked like another scorcher of a day outside, the morning sun making the garden's showy blooms look bright with promise. He'd call the French deli round the corner, get them to send over some fresh pastries and coffee and they could eat on the terrace. He fancied finding out a bit more about the intriguing Miss Daisy Dean before he sent her on her way.

All the stresses and strains of the last few days, the torments of the night, lifted as he bounded up the wide sweeping staircase to his bedroom suite. It felt good to be alive and back to his usual self. Anticipation lightened his steps, making him feel like a kid let loose from school on the first day of summer.

An hour later, Connor had indulged in a scalding hot shower, pulled on his favourite worn jeans and Boston Celtics T-shirt and stuffed down the last two brownies and a cup of steaming black coffee.

He peeked into the spare room and frowned. Angel Face hadn't moved. He padded into the room and squatted in front of her. Thick lashes rested on her pale cheeks and her breath scythed out in the gentlest of snores.

He caught a curl of hair that had fallen over her face, breathed in the spicy scent and then tucked it behind her ear. He skimmed his thumb over her cheek, felt the soft downy skin as smooth as a child's and fought the urge to kiss her awake. Still she didn't budge.

He cocked his head. Damn, but that position had to be uncomfortable, she'd have a crick in her neck when she came round and probably wouldn't thank him for it. She'd be better off sleeping in his bed. The sheets were fresh and she could lie down flat. It was the least he could do after all she'd done for him.

Never a man to second guess himself, Connor threaded one hand under her bum and the other beneath her shoulders and hefted her into his arms. She murmured something, then cuddled into his chest, her flyaway hair tickling the underside of his chin. Her scent drifted up and he breathed it in. She smelled delicious. So delicious he had a hard time controlling the rush of blood to his groin as he walked from the room.

She was surprisingly light, even in his weakened state it took him less than a minute to carry her up to his bedroom. As he placed her gently in the middle of the deluxe king-size bed it struck him how tiny she was. Probably no more than five feet two or three. Funny he hadn't noticed that the night before—no doubt the indignant scowl on her face had made her seem taller. He grinned again, his hands braced on his hips. He certainly hadn't managed to intimidate her much—and he'd been in a bad enough mood to give her a very tough time.

She stirred, squinting in her sleep. He strolled to the large floor-to-ceiling windows, where sunlight flooded the room, to close the curtains.

'Where am I?'

He turned at the soft murmur, to find his guest propped up on her elbows. She gazed at him out of those large mossy eyes, looking confused and wary—and good enough to eat.

'You were out cold,' he said as he finished closing the curtains. 'I figured you'd be better in bed.'

Her eyes popped wide. 'Mr Brody! What are you doing up?'

He sat on the edge of the bed, and smiled, touched by her concern. 'I'm right as rain, thanks to you.' He traced his thumb over the pulse in her throat, resting his fingers on her collarbone, and felt her shiver of response. 'And seeing as you've seen me naked, Daisy Dean, I think you best be calling me Connor, don't you?'

Colour flooded her cheeks, giving her pale skin a pretty pink glow. He chuckled, desire stirring again, but a lot more forcefully this time. No, she wasn't immune to him at all.

What the hell? Why not let breakfast wait until after that thank-you kiss?

Daisy blinked, the last of the sleepy fog clearing from her brain. Goodness, those eyes, that face were even more devastating spotlighted by the shaft of daylight beaming through the curtains.

And his comment had brought back dangerous memories: of how delicious he'd looked naked—and just how thoroughly she'd assessed all his assets.

She pulled back, sat up. Did he know about that? Maybe he hadn't been as delirious as she'd thought.

'I'm so glad you're feeling better,' she said. She breathed in the scent of freshly washed male and was hit by another alarming jolt of memory. 'Sorry to pass out like that but it was a long night.'

'It was,' he said, the confidential curve of his lips doing very strange things to Daisy's heart rate.

'Right, well…' she edged back '…I should shoot off. You obviously don't need me here any more and I—'

He leaned over and grasped her upper arm, halting her retreat in mid-scramble.

'You'll not be running off,' he said, 'before I've a chance

to thank you.' The mesmerising blue gaze dipped to her lips as the Irish in his voice became more pronounced. 'Properly.'

Heat flooded between her thighs. But instead of saying the polite denial her mind was screaming at him—something else entirely popped out of her mouth. 'How do you intend to do that?'

His eyes flared and he cradled her cheeks in his palms. His hands felt rough but unbearably erotic as he threaded his fingers through her hair, pushed the heavy mass back from her face. 'How about we start here?' he murmured, still smiling that devastating smile, his breath feathering her cheeks.

Then he slanted his lips across hers. The warm, wet heat was so shocking, and so unexpected, Daisy gasped. His tongue probed, firm and possessive, and her mind disengaged completely as the reckless thrill, the spike of adrenaline shimmered through her bloodstream.

He tasted of coffee and chocolate and danger. Forgetting everything but the feel of his lips on hers, Daisy sank shaking fingers into the silky black curls at his nape and drew him in as a drowning woman draws breath.

He didn't need any more encouragement. The kiss went from coaxing to demanding as he hauled her against him, his palm sweeping down her back. The weight of his long, strong body pressed her into the mattress as he pushed her down. She gave a staggered moan. This was madness, supreme folly and she couldn't summon the will to care.

As his lips stoked her into a frenzy she heard the hiss of her zipper. He reared back, breaking the kiss. Their eyes locked, his stormy with passion, the gleam of desire so intense she felt as if she'd been branded.

'You're beautiful, Daisy Dean,' he said, his thumbs stroking her nipples through the fabric as his eyes met hers. 'I want you naked.' The gruff statement was both question and demand.

She drew in ragged breaths, her arousal painful, as he tugged down the bodice of her dress, unsnapped the hook of her bra and bared her breasts.

She should have been shocked; she should have pushed him away. This was all wrong and she knew it. She'd been telling herself all night, she didn't even like this man—that he was not her kind of guy. But the time spent tending him, caressing fever-drenched flesh, hearing the broken cries of his nightmares, had formed a strong bond of intimacy that she couldn't seem to shake.

She'd looked into his soul last night, was looking into it now. They'd connected on some primal level and this was the only way to break the spell.

She wanted him naked too. She wanted him inside her.

His legs straddled hers and she looked down to see the ridge of his erection pressed against faded denim. Her fate was sealed as all her common sense dissolved to leave nothing but raw need clawing at her gut.

She shifted, but couldn't budge, pinned to the bed under him.

'You'll have to get off me if you want me naked,' she said.

'Good point.' His grin dazzled her. 'I'll race you,' he said, bounding off the bed.

She lurched into a sitting position, and watched mesmerised as he whipped his T-shirt over his head and his six-pack rippled. She looked away, determined not to be distracted from the task at hand by the muscular chest she'd spent most of the night memorising by touch. Anticipation surged through her. She was going to win this race.

She grappled with her shoelaces, cursing her choice of footwear. If only she'd stuck with the sandals. Finally she freed her feet, toed off the boots and flung them off the bed. She heard the thud as his jeans hit the floor, concentrated on wriggling her dress over her hips.

Heat blasted through every nerve ending as she looked up to see him standing before her, gloriously naked and his erection looking even more magnificent than she remembered it.

She bit into her bottom lip; her breath clogged her throat as excitement and trepidation seared her insides like a flashfire. He mounted the bed, grasped her ankle and gave a sharp tug. 'Come here,' he said, dragging her beneath him.

'Wait.' She braced her hand on his chest. 'I want to touch you.'

'Same here,' he said, cupping her chin. 'Let's negotiate.'

Then he kissed her, moulding their mouths together and crushing her body into the mattress. The coarse hair of his chest abraded swollen nipples. She dragged in a breath, let it shudder out as his lips trailed over her collarbone. His tongue slid fire across the swell of her breast and then his teeth nipped at the rigid peak and tugged. Rough hands kneaded her buttocks as his lips found hers again, the kiss so wildly erotic she thought she might be consumed by the flames.

She reached down, shaking with suppressed desire, and cupped his powerful erection in her palm. He shuddered as her fingers wrapped around the pulsing length.

She revelled in the feel of him, everything she'd imagined and more. His forehead touched hers, his whole body vibrating, his breathing harsh as she stroked and caressed him, learning the shape and texture as she had yearned to do all through the night. Velvet over steel. So solid, so warm, so responsive to her touch.

She ran her thumb over the thick head, felt the tantalising bead of moisture. He cursed softly and grasped her wrist, jerking back.

'You'll have to stop, or this'll be over before it's begun,' he rasped.

'I don't want to stop,' she cried, desperation edging the words.

Don't make me stop. Don't make me think, her mind screamed.

I don't want to think, I just want to feel.

'Are you sure?' he asked. 'I don't want to rush you.'

She'd never been more sure of anything in her life.

'I want to rush. I'm ready,' she said, alarmed, need overwhelming her. She had to do it now, before the delicious fog of sensation cleared.

'Let's see how ready, then,' he murmured.

Before she could figure out what he meant, his fingers delved into the curls at her sex. She shuddered as he circled her clitoris and probed. She cried, gripped his shoulders, slick juices flooding out as she bucked against those knowing fingers, primed to explode.

He chuckled. The sound deep, husky and self-satisfied. 'Hell, you're incredible.' His fingers pushed inside her, his thumb grazing the hard nub. She moaned, clinging to the edge of control. 'But you're a bit tight, Angel Face,' he said, sounding regretful.

'What?' The question shuddered out on a breath of need— and confusion. Why was he still waiting?

He groaned, holding her buttocks as he pressed his erection against the slick folds of her sex. 'I don't want to hurt you.'

'You won't,' she gasped. 'I want you inside me.' How much more encouragement did he need? 'Now.'

'You're sure?' he asked again, making her want to scream.

She nodded, lifting her knees, angling her hips to accommodate him, so frantic she'd lost the power of speech. If he didn't get on with it, she'd die of need.

She was about to tell him so when he stilled, cursed under his breath and then, to her complete astonishment, pulled away from her and climbed off the bed.

She bounced up on her elbows. Horrified.

'Where are you going?' she cried out on a thin wail of exasperation. Had he lost his mind?

He bent to get something out of his bedside table. 'What's the hurry, angel?' he murmured.

Her eyes drifted down to that perfect rear end. Lust and frustration surged through her. She wanted to scream the house down. He'd worked her up to the point of meltdown and now he'd decided to rearrange his dresser!

'What's the hurry? Are you joking?' she squeaked, embarrassed by the desperate quiver in her voice.

He turned back gripping a telltale foil packet between his fingers and heat flooded into her cheeks. Even in her rampaging nymphomania, how could she have forgotten about protection?

'No joke,' he said, sounding ever so slightly smug. 'We wouldn't want any surprises.'

He knelt back on the bed, grinning at her as he ripped open the packet with his teeth and rolled the condom on. He put his hands over her shoulders, forcing her back on the bed, caging her in.

'Hasn't anyone ever told you, patience is a virtue, angel?' His eyes dipped to her tightly peaked nipples. 'Although, it should be said, there's not a lot of virtue in what I'm thinking right at the minute.'

Daisy's caustic reply caught in her throat as his lips covered hers. She rose up to kiss him back, letting the need, the sensation take over. But as she wrapped her arms round him, her fingers found the ridges on his back and tenderness welled up right beside the need.

His fingers gripped her hips and in one smooth move, he thrust inside her.

She sobbed, the fullness shocking her, the fury of sensations making her cry out. Then he began to move. Slow,

heavy, insistent strokes that had the orgasm coiling ruthlessly inside her.

A staggered moan wrenched from her throat as the intense
pleasure sent shock waves rocketing up from her core. She
anchored her legs round his waist, sweat slicking her skin as
she moved to meet each of his deep thrusts with thrusts of
her own, and he drove deeper still. Her high-pitched pants
matched his harsh grunts. Everything clamped down, her
whole body glowing and pulsating as it rode the crest of a
magnificent wave. The broken sobs echoed in her head as she
burst free and exploded over the top—and heard his muffled
shout as he crashed over behind her.

'That was amazing. You're amazing,' Connor murmured,
stroking Daisy's cheek, then winced at the cliché.

But what else was he to say? Hell, if he hadn't been hori-
zontal already he would have fallen over. He'd never had a
stronger, more satisfying orgasm in his life. The experience
had been literally mind-altering.

Using every last ounce of his strength he braced his arms
to stop himself from collapsing on top of the woman responsible and crushing her. Her eyelids fluttered open as he
stared down at her. He grinned as she focussed on his face.
She looked as shattered as him, those round expressive eyes
wide with amazement.

Then her vaginal muscles squeezed around him in the
final throes of her orgasm.

'God, sorry,' she whispered as the pink in her cheeks darkened to maroon.

She looked horrified.

He had no clue what the problem was—but with her still
wrapped tight around him he was finding it hard to give a
damn. Feeling the blood rushing back to his groin, he did the
decent thing—with not a small amount of regret—and lifted

off her. The next round would have to wait. Something had spooked her—and he didn't want to scare her off.

Propping his elbow beside her head, he leaned over her. His gaze swept her lush little figure and came to rest on her face. The flush of afterglow warmed her skin and dilated her pupils, darkening the deep green of her eyes, while the sprinkle of freckles across her nose defined those impossibly high cheekbones. She really was gorgeous.

She coloured even more, then looked away and tried to scoot out from under him. He locked his arm round her waist. 'Now where would you be going? We're not half finished yet.'

She wiggled, he held firm. Finally she looked at him, her cheeks now a deep and very becoming shade of scarlet. 'There's no time for anything else. I really have to be going, Mr Brody.'

His eyebrows shot up at the formal address. Then he simply couldn't stop himself. He threw back his head and roared with laughter.

When he finally got his amusement under control, she'd stiffened like a board, her bottom lip puffed up in a defiant pout as she glared at him.

He grinned. What *was* she about?

Women! He gave his head a rueful shake. They really were a whole different species. But didn't that make them all the more fascinating?

'Angel Face,' he murmured, loving the way her eyes narrowed, 'as we've just made love like a couple of rabbits, I think you'd best be calling me Connor.'

CHAPTER FIVE

DAISY was utterly mortified. But she couldn't decide if she was more annoyed by her own behaviour or the patronising look on Connor Brody's face as he held her trapped by his side.

'I don't feel comfortable calling you by your given name,' she blurted out. And then realised how prim and ridiculous it sounded.

Thank goodness he didn't bust a gut laughing at her again. But the twinkle in his eye made it clear it was a struggle not to.

'Should I make you more comfortable, then?' He pulled the sheet over her, flattening his open palm on the expensive linen and lifting his eyebrow as if willing her to share the joke.

Daisy felt the warm weight of his hand on her belly and turned away, feeling so exposed she wanted to die on the spot.

When she'd surfaced a moment ago to find him gazing at her, his face flushed, those sexy blue eyes intent on hers and his erection still gloriously firm inside her, the hideous truth had dawned on her.

She'd ravished a complete stranger. Had as good as begged him to make love to her.

Which meant she was her mother's daughter after all. Her mother, who had spent her whole life latching on to any guy who could give her a decent orgasm.

Daisy didn't know the first thing about Connor Brody. And he knew nothing about her. For all he knew she could be the sort of woman who made rabbit-love every chance she got. He couldn't possibly know she'd never ravished anyone before in her life.

The fact that the orgasm they'd shared had been the most incredible she'd ever had only made the situation that much worse.

When the muscles of her sex had clenched in response to the feel of him inside her, she'd been mortally embarrassed. Knowing she'd been tricked by her pheromones into believing they shared an intimacy, a connection, that they actually didn't.

Whatever way you looked at it, she'd used this man and his mouth-watering body to slake a temporary physical thirst— and fallen victim to her own libido. In so doing she'd broken the solemn promise she'd made to herself as a teenager, that she would never be like her mother. That she would never let her libido rule her life.

A calloused thumb skimmed down her cheek. 'What's the problem? Tell me and we'll see to it.'

Daisy swung round to face him. The tenderness in his eyes surprised her, but the lazy, confident, let's-humour-her smile on his lips contradicted it rather comprehensively.

Daisy felt her misery being replaced by irritation.

It really was a bit much of him to find the biggest identity crisis of her life so hilarious.

She sat up abruptly. She had to stop wallowing. Letting a total stranger witness her having a breakdown was not going to help matters. 'I'm absolutely fine,' she said, her voice as matter-of-fact as she could manage.

She grasped the sheet to her breasts, pushed her hair behind her ears, and felt a tiny bit better. She'd always been a woman of action. Once she saw a problem she set about fixing it. She'd have more than enough time later to analyse her wanton, irresponsible behaviour and what it all meant. Right now she needed to get the heck away from her studly neighbour before anything else happened.

The way he'd been studying her—all that smouldering intent in his gaze—suggested he was planning a repeat performance. And she wasn't entirely sure she could trust her body not to take him up on his offer. Given what this little liaison had already cost her, another frenzied encounter with Mr Sex-On-A-Stick was the very last thing she needed.

'This is a little awkward,' she said. 'But could you pass me my dress? I need to be off.'

He made no move to get her dress, so she scooted down the bed, intending to lean over him and get it herself.

But as she did so he stroked a hand down her hair. 'What's the rush?' he murmured, his voice husky but firm. 'Let's talk about it. Whatever it is, we can fix it.'

She gaped at him over her shoulder. Would you credit it? The only time in her life she'd rather gnaw off her own tongue than talk about her feelings and she'd found the one man on the planet willing to share and discuss.

'Mr Bro…' She paused when his eyebrow lifted again. 'Connor, we had sex. It was great sex. So thank you. But I don't think there's anything else to say.'

Both his eyebrows lifted at that one. Clearly, her no-nonsense approach had shocked him but she soldiered on. 'We have absolutely nothing in common,' she continued, slipping off the bed. 'We're obviously totally wrong for each other.'

She dropped her end of the sheet and whipped on her dress. 'This was strictly a one-shot deal after a difficult night.'

They both knew the score here, and if he thought they were going to have another quickie for old times' sake he could forget it—the first one had been quite devastating enough to her peace of mind.

She pulled on her knickers, scouted around for her bra, grabbed it off the floor and shoved it into the pocket of her dress. 'So why don't we call it quits and leave it at that?'

She straightened, holding one baseball boot as she scoured the luxurious deep-pile carpet for the other.

'Are you serious?' he asked. He hadn't moved, the sheet resting tantalisingly low on his hips as he stared at her.

'Absolutely,' she said, forcing a smile.

Noticing the way the thin wisps of black hair curled around his belly button, she swallowed and averted her eyes. To her immense relief she spotted the other boot peeking out from under the bed. She grabbed it and stood up.

He'd propped himself up on the pillows, and was still studying her, looking stunned.

No doubt with those dark, dangerous good looks and the masterful way he made love, having the woman do a runner was a new experience for him. Daisy couldn't muster much sympathy. He'd have to learn to deal with it. She had her own problems.

He slid his feet to the floor, the sheet now barely covering him.

Daisy threw up her hand to stop him going any further. 'Please don't get up. I can see myself out,' she squeaked. The last thing she needed was another full-frontal view of that mouth-watering physique.

Before he could say another word, she dashed out the door, barefoot.

* * *

Connor gaped at the open bedroom door and listened to the pit-pat of Daisy's footsteps as she hightailed it down the stairs.

The muffled slam of the front door echoed at the bottom of the house.

He flopped back on the bed, stared at the ceiling and frowned at the fancy light fixture his interior designer had insisted on shipping in from Barcelona.

What the hell had that been about?

He might as well have set her tail on fire, she'd shot out of the room so fast. Either he'd been hallucinating, or he'd just been treated to the female equivalent of the 'wham-bam thank you, ma'am' routine.

He guessed he ought to be hurt, but first he'd have to get over the shock.

Not that he hadn't been dumped before, mind you. Of course he had. He could still recall Mary O'Halloran, slapping him down in front of all his mates when he'd been thirteen and full of the carelessness of youth. He'd snogged her and forgotten to call her the next day so he figured he'd deserved it. In fact, he still felt a little guilty whenever he thought about Mary.

But even Mary, riled to the hilt, hadn't dumped him without chewing his ear off first for twenty minutes about all his shortcomings. And he'd never met a woman since who wouldn't talk you to death about 'the state of the relationship' as soon as look at you. God, when he thought about all the times Rachel had insisted on 'having a little chat about where they were headed' his stomach sank.

So why should he care that Daisy had brushed off his offer to talk? Sure, he hadn't really meant it. All he'd wanted to do was calm her down, get her to stick around.

He lay on the bed, the ripples of sexual fulfilment making him feel lethargic, and tried to convince himself it was all for the best. He should be overjoyed. It made things a lot less complicated. He wasn't looking for anything serious and neither was she.

He rubbed his belly, stretched his legs under the sheet, contemplated taking another shower, then caught the heady whiff of her scent. Heat surged into his crotch. He frowned and sat up, staring at the tent forming in his lap.

The damn problem was, he wasn't pleased. Because he wasn't finished with her yet. Okay, they had nothing in common, and their one-night stand, or one-morning stand or whatever the hell it was didn't have any future. But still, he hadn't wanted it to end, not yet. He'd had plans for today. Fine, so them getting naked and having mind-blowing sex hadn't been a definite part of it, but he didn't see why they shouldn't go with the flow there. They might not be compatible out of bed, but they sure as hell were in it. In fact they were more than compatible. She'd been as blown away as he had by the intensity of…

He stopped, his brain finally catching up with his indignation. Had she been spooked by how good they were together? He relaxed back into the pillow, the pounding heat in his groin finally starting to subside.

That had to be the problem. Daisy might be the most pragmatic, forthright woman he'd ever met, but she was still a girl. And wasn't it just like a girl to analyse everything to death? To worry about what great sex meant instead of just enjoying it while it lasted.

He huffed out a laugh.

And now he thought about it, he didn't have to feel hard done by either. Little Daisy might turn out to be his ideal woman. Someone sexy enough to turn him inside out with lust and smart enough to know he wasn't a good bet for the long haul. Hell, they'd only just met and she'd already figured that out. Now all he had to do was show her that just because they weren't going to spend the rest of their natural lives together, didn't mean they couldn't spend the next little while exploring their potential in other areas.

He whipped back the sheet and leaped out of bed—his faith in the wonder of womankind restored. He'd have that shower after all, get dressed and then head to her place and invite her back for breakfast. Whatever she had planned for the next couple of days he'd persuade her to drop it.

Daisy seemed to be remarkably susceptible to him— whether she liked it or not. Getting her over this little hump so they could finish what they'd started shouldn't be too tough. He strode into the bathroom, his whistled rendition of 'Molly Malone' echoing off the tiles.

CHAPTER SIX

CONNOR was feeling a lot less jolly two hours later as he stood on Daisy's doorstep. He braced the box under his arm, heard the furious feline hiss from inside and stabbed the door buzzer, impatient to see Daisy again and get at least one thing sorted to his satisfaction.

It had taken him an eternity to chase her landlady's cat down and get it in the box—and he had a criss-cross of scratches on his hand for his trouble. Unfortunately the cat wasn't the only thing that had mucked up his morning. After a panicked call from the architect on his Paris project, he'd had to book a Eurostar ticket for this afternoon.

As soon as he'd put the phone down to his PA, Danny had been on the line from Manhattan, begging him to bring his trip there forward a week to stave off the now apparently imminent possibility of the Melrose project going belly up. He really hadn't needed another conversation about Danny's ludicrous 'fake fiancée' solution so he'd ended up agreeing to fly over there from Paris at the end of the week.

All of which was going to stall his plans to get the delicious Daisy Dean back in his bed any time soon. But once he'd finally wrestled the cat into the box, he'd made up his mind he wasn't prepared to write the idea off completely. Not yet.

He glanced at his watch. He knew a cosy little four-star restaurant in Notting Hill where he and Daisy could discuss their next moves over a glass of Pouilly Fumé and some seared scallops before he grabbed a cab to St Pancras International. He didn't see why he shouldn't stake his claim before he went. A three-week wait would be a pain, but he could handle it if he had something tangible to look forward to when he got back.

He pressed the buzzer again. Where the hell was she? It was ten o'clock on a Saturday morning and she'd been up most of the night—surely she couldn't have gone out?

He noticed the ragged paint on the huge oak door and glanced up at the house's elegant Georgian frontage. Crumbling brickwork and rotting window sills proved the place had been sadly neglected for years. She really did live in a dump.

The thought brightened his mood considerably.

Maybe he could persuade her to housesit while he was gone. He'd had a call back from the estate agent while he was having his spat with the cat. Even if he got an offer straight away as the guy seemed to think, it would take a bit to do all the paperwork. And he liked the idea of Daisy being there, waiting for him when he got back from his trip. He was just imagining how much they could enjoy his homecoming when the door swung open.

'Well, if it isn't the invisible neighbour.' The elderly woman standing on the threshold stared down her nose at him, which was quite a feat considering she was at least a foot shorter than he was. The voluminous silk dressing gown with feather trim she wore looked like something out of a vintage Hollywood movie. Her small birdlike frame and the wisps of white hair peeking out of her matching silk turban would have made her look fragile, but for her regal stature and the sharp intelligence in her gaze. Which was currently boring several holes in his hide.

'What do *you* want?' she sneered, eyeing him as if he were a piece of rotting meat. 'Finally come to introduce yourself, have you?'

As Connor didn't know the woman, he figured she must have mistaken him for someone else. 'The name's Connor Brody. I've a cat with me belongs to the landlady here.'

He put the box down in front of her, the screech from inside making his ears throb and the slashes on his hand sting.

She gasped and clutched a hand to her breast as her face softened. 'You've found Mr Pootles?' she whispered, tears seeping over her lids. She bent over the box—the anticipation on her face as bright as that of a child on Christmas morning.

He stepped forward, about to warn her she was liable to get her hand ripped off, but stopped when she prised open the lid and a deep purr resonated from inside. He watched astonished as she scooped the devil cat into her arms. Lucifer rubbed its head under her chin, gave another satisfied purr and slanted him a smug look. The little suck-up.

'How can I ever thank you, young man?' The old woman straightened, clutching devil cat to her bosom as if it were her firstborn babe. 'You've made an old lady very happy.' The joyful tears sheening her whiskey-brown eyes and the softening of her facial features made her look about twenty years younger. 'Wherever did you find him? We've been searching for weeks.'

'The cat's been bunking in my kitchen,' he said, stuffing his hands in his pockets, not sure he really deserved her thanks. 'I should warn you. There's more than one cat now.'

The elderly lady's eyes popped wide. 'Oh?'

He nodded at the creature, who was gazing at him as if butter wouldn't melt in its mouth. 'Your Mr Pootles became a mammy eleven days ago. I have four kittens at mine.'

'Four…' The lady gasped and then giggled, sounding for all the world like a sixteen-year-old girl. She held the cat up in front of her and nuzzled it. 'You naughty cat. Why didn't you tell me you were a girl?'

Connor figured it probably wasn't his place to point out the cat couldn't talk. 'Here.' He pulled out a spare set of keys from his pocket. 'You'll want these to get the kittens now, as they're too little to be on their own for long.'

'Why, that's awfully sweet of you,' she said, taking the keys.

'They're in a cupboard in the kitchen,' he added. 'Is Daisy around?' he asked, awkwardly. 'I need to speak to her.'

The old lady's eyes widened as she put the keys in the pocket of her gown. 'You know Daisy?' she asked, sounding a lot more astonished about that than she had been about her tomcat's kittens.

'Sure, we're friends,' he said, colour rising in his cheeks under the old woman's scrutiny. It wasn't a lie. If what they'd got up to that morning didn't make them friends, he didn't know what did.

'Well, I never did,' she said. 'After all the nonsense Daisy's said about you in the last few weeks.'

What nonsense? She hadn't even met him until last night.

'Daisy's such a dark horse.' The old woman gave him a confidential grin, confusing him even more. 'I always thought she might have a little crush on you, the way she could not stop talking about you. Little did I know she'd been fooling us all along. So, did you two have a lovers' tiff? Is that why she said all those awful things?'

'No,' he said, totally clueless now. And not liking the feeling one bit. 'What things?'

The old woman waved her hand dismissively. 'Oh, you know Daisy. She's always got an opinion and she does love to voice it. She told us all how you were rich and arrogant and far too self-absorbed to care about a missing cat. But we know that's not true now, don't we?'

Connor's lips flattened into a grim line. So she'd bad-mouthed him, had she, and before she'd even met him. Wasn't that always the way of it? As a boy it had driven him insane when people who barely knew him told him he'd never amount to a thing. That he'd turn out no better than his Da.

But Daisy's bad opinion didn't just make him mad. It hurt a little too. Which made him more mad. Why should it bother him what some small-minded, silly little English girl thought?

Was that why she'd bolted? Because she'd decided he wasn't good enough for her? If she thought that she was in for a surprise.

'Is Daisy in her room? I need to speak to her.' *Make that yell at her.*

'Of course not, dear,' the old lady said quizzically. 'Daisy and Juno are working on The Funky Fashionista.'

'The what?'

The woman gave him a curious look. 'Her stall in Portobello Market.'

'Right you are,' he said hastily. Not knowing what Daisy did for a living probably made his claim to be a friend look a bit suspect. He took a step down the stairs, keen to get away.

Portobello Road Market was round the corner. It shouldn't take him too long to track her down—and give her a good piece of his mind.

'But, Mr Brody…' The elderly woman called him back. 'How will I get your keys back to you?'

'Don't worry about them,' he said, a smile playing across his lips as the kernel of an idea began to form. 'You keep them. If I lock myself out, it'll be useful for you to have a set.'

He waved and hopped down the last few steps to the pavement.

He mulled his idea over as he strode down the street towards the Bello. And the more he mulled, the more irresistible the idea became. Sure what he had in mind was outrageous, and Daisy wasn't going to like it one bit, if her disappearing act that morning was anything to go by. But if ever there was a way to kill two birds with one stone, and teach a certain little English girl how not to throw said stones in glass houses, this had to be it.

After the shoddy way she'd treated him, it was the least she deserved.

Daisy Dean owed him. And what he had in mind would make the payback all the sweeter.

CHAPTER SEVEN

'NO WONDER you're knackered. It's called compassion fatigue.' Juno scowled as she placed the last of Daisy's new batch of silk-screen printed scarves at the front of the stall. 'You didn't need to spend the whole night there looking after him. You don't owe that guy a thing. And I bet he didn't even thank you for it.'

Oh, yes, he did.

The heat suffused Daisy's cheeks as she recalled how thoroughly Connor Brody had thanked her. She ducked behind the rack of cotton dresses and prayed Juno hadn't noticed her reaction.

'Why are you blushing?'

Daisy peeked over the top of the rack to see Juno watching her. Did the woman have radar or something? 'I'm not blushing. I'm rearranging the dress sizes.' She popped back behind the rack. 'It never ceases to amaze me how out of order they get,' she babbled, shoving a size fourteen in between two size eights.

'Daze, did something happen I should know about?' Juno asked quietly, appearing beside her. She placed her hand over the one Daisy had clutching the rack. 'If he did something to you, you can talk to me—you know that, right?'

The concern in Juno's eyes made Daisy's blush get a whole lot worse as embarrassment was comprehensively replaced by guilt.

It had taken her less than twenty minutes of angst after bolting out of Connor Brody's house that morning to get over her panic attack. She wasn't even sure what she'd got so worked up about now. Okay, so she'd jumped him, but who wouldn't in her situation? She'd been exhausted. She'd spent the whole night in close proximity to that beautiful body of his. She'd seen him at his most vulnerable plagued by those terrible nightmares and it had created a false sense of intimacy. So what? He hadn't exactly objected when she'd demanded he make love to her. And she'd never be idiotic or delusional enough to fall in love with a man like Connor Brody. A man who was so totally the opposite of the nice, calm, settled, steady, average guy she needed.

All of which meant she could rest assured that what had happened in Connor Brody's bed that morning hadn't suddenly turned her into her mother. Because that had always been her mother's mistake—not the pursuit of good sex, but the belief that good sex meant you must have found the man of your dreams. Daisy knew that good sex—even stupendous sex—had nothing whatsoever to do with love.

The relief she'd felt had been immense.

But the one thing Daisy hadn't been able to get past—or to justify—was the scurrilous way she'd treated Connor Brody. Not just after they'd made love—but before she'd ever met him. Was it any wonder Juno thought something bad had happened at Brody's house when Daisy had spent the last few weeks assassinating his character to anyone who would listen?

And on what evidence? None at all. She'd judged him and

condemned him because he was rich and good-looking and, if she was being perfectly honest with herself, because she'd fancied him right from the first time she'd laid eyes on him and she'd resented it.

She'd broken into his home, all but accused him of killing a cat he'd actually been looking after and then—after trying to make amends during the night by nursing him through his fever—she'd ruined it all by seducing him first thing the following morning and then freaking out and running off.

Thinking about the way she'd brushed off his perfectly sweet attempts to calm her down made her cringe. He'd been a nice guy about the whole thing—had even offered to talk about it, and how many guys did that after a one-night stand? And what had she done? She'd told him to get lost. The poor guy probably thought she was a total basketcase and frankly who could blame him?

Daisy gave a deep sigh. At the very least she owed the man an apology. What was that old saying about pride going before a fall? She might as well have hurled herself off a cliff.

'Daze, you're really starting to worry me.' Juno's urgent voice pulled Daisy out of her musings. 'Tell me what he did. If he's hurt you, I'll make him pay. I promise.'

Daisy gave a half-smile, amused despite everything at the thought of Juno, who was even shorter than she was, going toe to toe with Brody. She shook her head. 'He didn't hurt me, Ju. He's a nice bloke.'

She paused. Maybe *nice* was too tame a word to describe Connor Brody, but it served its purpose here. 'If anything, it's the other way around—I hurt him.'

She knew she hadn't done more than dent his pride a little, but that still made her feel bad.

Walking round the stall, Daisy pinged open the drawer on the antique cash register. She lifted out the rolls of change and began cracking them open.

'How?' Juno asked, picking up a five-pence roll and ripping off the paper wrapping.

Daisy blew out a breath. 'I've been a complete cow to him. All those things I said to you and Mrs V and everyone else, all the assumptions I made. They all turned out to be a load of old cobblers.' The tinkle of change hitting the cash drawer's wooden base couldn't disguise the shame in her voice.

'What makes you think he'd care?' Juno scoffed, but then she'd always been willing to think the worst of any good-looking guy. Daisy wondered when she'd started to adopt the same prejudices.

'That's not the point,' Daisy said. 'I care.'

'All you really said was that he's rich and arrogant. What's so awful about that?'

'He may be rich, but he's not arrogant.' As she said it Daisy recalled the way he'd kissed her senseless before she'd even woken up properly. 'All right, maybe he is a little bit arrogant, but I expect he's used to women falling at his feet.' She certainly had.

'So what? That doesn't give him the right to take advantage—'

Daisy pressed her fingers to Juno's lips. 'He didn't take advantage of me. What happened was entirely consensual.' Just thinking about how consensual it had been was making her pulse skitter.

'What exactly *did* happen?' Juno's eyes narrowed. 'Because it's beginning to sound as if more than rest and recuperation were involved. You're not telling me you slept with him, are you?'

Daisy's flush flared back to life at the accusatory look in Juno's eyes. How on earth was she going to explain her behaviour to Juno when it had taken her so long to explain it to herself? She opened her mouth to say something, anything, when the rumble of a deep Irish accent had both their heads whipping round to the front of the stall.

'Hello, ladies.'

Daisy's heartbeat skipped a beat. He looked tall and devastating in the same worn T-shirt and jeans he'd stripped out of that morning—and amused. His lips twitched in that sensual smile she remembered a little too vividly from the moment she'd woken up in his bedroom.

'While I hate to interrupt this fascinating bit of chit-chat—' he gripped the top of the stall's canopy and leaned over the brightly coloured scarves and blouses '—I'd like to have a word, Daisy.' His forefinger skimmed her cheek. 'In private.'

Daisy swallowed, feeling the burn where the calloused fingertip had touched.

'Daisy's busy. Buzz off.'

He dropped his hand and shifted his gaze to Juno, still looking amused. 'Who would you be, then? Daisy's keeper?'

'Maybe I am?' Juno blustered, standing on tiptoe and thrusting her chin out—which made her look like a midget with a Napoleonic complex next to Brody's tall, relaxed frame. 'And who the hell are you? Mr High and—'

Daisy slapped her hand over Juno's mouth.

'It's all right, Ju,' she whispered, desperate to shut her friend up. 'I'll take it from here.'

All she needed now was for Brody to get an inkling of what she'd said about him to pretty much the whole neighbourhood. This apology was going to be agonising enough, without Juno and her attitude wading in and making it ten times worse.

'I'll explain everything later,' she said into Juno's ear, holding her hand over her friend's mouth. 'Can you look after the stall on your own for half an hour?'

Daisy took Juno's muffled grunt as a yes and let her go.

'Fine,' Juno grumbled. She shot Brody a mutinous look. 'But if you're not back by then I'm coming after you.'

Daisy gave Juno a quick nod. Great, she guessed she'd owe Juno an apology too before this was over. She picked up her bag and rounded the stall to join Brody. Right at the moment, though, she had rather bigger fish to fry.

'I know a café round the corner in Cambridge Gardens,' she murmured, walking through the few milling shoppers who'd already made it up to the far end of the market under the Westway where The Funky Fashionista was situated.

He fell into step beside her but said nothing.

'Why don't we go there?' she continued, not quite able to look at him. 'They do great cappuccinos.'

And Gino's cosy little Italian coffee house was also off the tourist track enough that it shouldn't be too crowded yet. The last thing she wanted was an audience while she choked down her monster helping of humble pie.

It took them less than five minutes to get to Gino's. Not surprising given that Daisy jogged most of the way, clinging onto her bag with both hands and making sure she kept a couple of steps ahead of Brody's long stride. As soon as they'd walked away from the stall she'd been consumed by panic at the possibility that he might touch her or speak to her before she'd figured out what she was going to say to him.

And how ridiculous was that? she thought as they strolled into Gino's and she grabbed the first booth by the door. He'd been buried deep inside her less than three hours ago, given her the most earth-shattering orgasm of her life and now she was scared to even look at him.

She slid into the booth and hastily dumped her bag onto the vinyl-bench seat beside her, blocking off any thoughts he might have of sitting next to her. Casting his eyes at the bag, he slid his long body onto the bench opposite. As he rested his arms loosely on the table she noticed the Boston Celtics logo ripple across his chest.

Her eyes flicked away.

Don't even go there, you silly woman. Hasn't that chest got you in enough trouble already?

She raised her hand to salute Gino, who was standing behind the counter. 'Would you like a cappuccino?' she asked as she watched Gino wave back and grab his pad.

'What I'd like is for you to look at me.'

The dry comment forced her to meet his eyes.

'That's better,' he said, the low murmur deliberately intimate. 'Was that so terrible now?'

Daisy decided to ignore the patronising tone. She supposed she deserved it.

'Look, Mr Brod... I mean, Connor. I've got something to say and I...' She rushed the words and then came to a complete stop, her tongue stalling on the apology she'd worked out.

Then Gino stepped up to the booth. 'Hello, Daisy luv. What'll it be? The usual?'

Daisy stared blankly at her friend, struggling for a second to remember what her usual was. 'No, thanks, no muffin today.' She'd probably choke on it. 'Just a latte, not too heavy on the froth.'

'As always, my lovely,' Gino said as he jotted the order on his pad, his broad cockney accent belying the swarthy Italian colouring he'd inherited from his mother. 'What's your poison, mate?' he asked, addressing Brody.

'Espresso.'

'Coming right up,' Gino replied. Then to Daisy's consternation he tucked his pad under his arm and offered Brody his hand. 'Gino Jones, by the way. This is my place,' he said as Brody shook it. 'Haven't seen you in here before. What's your name?'

Daisy rolled her eyes. She'd forgotten what a busybody Gino could be.

'Connor Brody,' Brody replied. 'I moved in next door to Daisy a few weeks back.'

Gino frowned, releasing Brody's hand. 'You're not the bloke who—'

Daisy coughed loudly. Good God, had she blabbed to Gino about Brody too? Why did she have such a big mouth? 'Actually, we're in a hurry, Gee,' she said, slanting Gino her 'shut up, you idiot' look. 'I've left Ju alone on the stall and the market will be heaving soon.'

'No sweat,' Gino said carefully. 'I'll go get your drinks.' Then he shot her his 'don't think I won't ask you about this guy later' look and left.

'You know, it's funny,' Brody said, although he didn't sound at all amused, 'but people around here don't like me much.' The statement sounded slightly disingenuous, but Daisy suspected that was wishful thinking on her part.

Her stomach sank to the soles of her shoes as guilt consumed her.

Time to stop messing about and give the man the apology she owed him. And she better make it a good one.

'Mr... Sorry, Connor.' She stalled again, forced herself to continue. 'I've behaved pretty badly. Climbing into your garden, accusing you of...' She paused. *Don't say you thought he killed the cat, you twerp.* 'Of not helping to find Mrs V's cat. And then...' The blush was back with a vengeance as he watched her, his face impassive. 'This morning I forced you to make love to me. And then I ran off without saying goodbye. I feel completely ashamed of my behaviour... It was incredibly tacky and I'm awfully sorry. And I'd like to make it up to you.' She stumbled to a stop, not sure what else to say.

His expression had barely changed throughout her whole

rambling speech. Maybe he'd looked a little surprised at first, but then his face had taken on this inscrutable mask.

'Hmm,' he said, the sound rumbling up through his chest. For some strange reason, Daisy's knees began to shake. She crossed her legs.

He cocked his head to one side. 'That's a lot of sins you've to make up.'

'I know,' she said, hoping she sounded suitably contrite.

To her surprise, he reached across the table and took her hand in his, threading his fingers through hers. 'What makes you think I was being forced, Daisy Dean? Did it seem to you I wasn't enjoying myself?'

She gulped past the dryness tightening her throat. How had they got onto this topic? 'No, it's not that. It's just. I was rather demanding. I don't think I gave you much of a choice in the matter.'

She ought to tug her fingers away, but somehow they'd got tangled up in his. Just as her stomach was now tangled in knots.

He rubbed his thumb across her palm, making her fingers curl into his. 'You'd be wrong about that,' he said. 'You gave me a choice and I took it. With a great deal of enthusiasm.'

His thumb began stroking her wrist, doing appalling things to her pulse rate. She was just about to muster the will to pull her hand away when he let her go and sat back.

Gino cleared his throat loudly and slid their coffees onto the table.

'Here you go, folks.' Gino sent Daisy a searching look, raising his eyebrows pointedly, before leaving them alone.

No doubt Gino was as confused as she was. Why had she been holding Brody's hand? Letting him caress her like that? It wasn't as if they were intimate. Well, not in the proper sense.

She wrapped her hands around her coffee mug to keep

them out of harm's way. 'I'm so glad there are no hard feelings,' she said.

At least she would be glad, once she'd got away from that penetrating gaze.

'Not about making love to you, no,' he said, the Irish in his voice brushing over her like an aphrodisiac. 'There are no hard feelings about that. I enjoyed it, a lot. And, I think, so did you.' It wasn't a question. 'But as to the rest,' he continued. 'There you've more explaining to do.'

Her cup clattered onto the table and coffee slurped over the rim. 'I do?'

'Why did you run off?'

'I don't know,' she lied, and then felt guilty again when he lifted one dark brow. He wasn't buying it.

'It was a bit too intense,' she said. 'And I don't usually jump into bed with men I hardly know.' She clamped her mouth shut. Half the truth would have to do. Because she was getting the weird sensation she was being toyed with, lured into some kind of a trap. Which was preposterous, of course, but Daisy never ignored her instincts.

'That's good to know,' he said.

She took a gulp of the hot coffee and then reached for her bag. 'I'm so glad we got all this settled. I'd hate for us not to be friends. Especially as you live right next door.'

Which made the whole thing even more awful. How was she going to face him every day if her hormones went into meltdown every time she looked at him? She'd have to get that little problem under control and quickly. But for now she decided distance was probably the best medicine. Slinging her bag over her shoulder, she slid out of the booth and offered her hand. 'I'll see you around. The coffees are on me. I'll tell Gino to put them on my tab. Thanks for being so understanding.'

He clasped her hand, the warm, rough feel of his palm

sending little shivers up her arm—and held on. 'Sit down. We're not finished.'

'We're not?'

He nodded at the booth seat. 'There's still the matter of the making up to settle.'

'What?' She plopped back in her seat, not at all sure she liked the commanding tone.

'The making up.'

Finally he let her hand go. She tucked it under the table, her fingers tingling.

'You said you wanted to make up for what you'd done,' he said calmly. 'And we're going to have to sort it now, because I don't have much time.' He looked at his watch. 'I'm catching the Eurostar to Paris in a little over an hour. I've got eight days there and then I'll be two weeks in New York.'

Daisy's shoulders slumped with relief. Thank you, God. She had no idea why he was telling her his itinerary, but at least she'd have over three weeks before she had to see him again. She should be well over this silly chemical reaction by then. 'That's wonderful. I'm sure you'll have a lovely time. I'll miss you,' she added, a tad concerned to realise it was the truth.

'Not for long, you won't,' he said, the predatory smile that tugged at his lips concerning her a whole lot more. 'Because when I get to New York you'll be meeting me there.'

She choked out a laugh. 'You lost me,' she said, but she could have sworn she heard the sound of a trap snapping shut.

He relaxed back in his seat, the picture of self-satisfaction. 'You want to make things up to me,' he prompted. 'It so happens I need a girlfriend in New York for those two weeks. It has to do with a business deal.' He tapped his fingers on the table in a rhythm that sounded like the tumblers of a lock clicking into place. 'And that girlfriend's going to be you.'

He could not be serious? Was he insane? 'Don't be ridiculous. I'm not going to New York. When I said I wanted to make things up to you, I was planning to bake you another plate of brownies. Not take a two-week trip to New York as your fake date. Are you nuts?' He was still looking at her with that cocksure, you'll-do-as-you're-told expression on his face. It was starting to annoy her. 'Even if I wanted to go.' Which she most definitely did not. 'I couldn't possibly. I've got my stall to run.'

He sighed. 'If your little bodyguard friend can't run the stall on her own you can find someone to help her. I'll pay any wages due. My PA will sort out your travel plans.' He looked pointedly at his watch again, as if to say, *I don't have time for this.*

Daisy's temper kicked up another notch. 'You're not listening to me, Brody. I'm not doing it. I don't want to. You'll have to find someone else.' She did not want to spend two weeks alone with him in New York. She already knew how irresistible he was—what if she had another lapse in judgment brought on by extreme hormonal overload and jumped him again? Things could get very complicated indeed. 'I don't owe you that much,' she finished, indignation seeping from every pore.

'Oh, but you do, Daisy Dean.' He leaned forward, those icy blue eyes chilling her to the bone. 'You told half of London I was selfish, arrogant and not to be trusted. That's known as slander.'

The blood seeped out of her face. How did he know about that?

'There happen to be laws against that sort of thing. So unless you want me to be calling my solicitor, you'd best be on that plane.'

He got up from the booth. She drew back, but he caught her chin in his fingers and tilted her face to his. 'And, Daisy,' he murmured, the warmth of his breath making her heart go into palpitations. 'Who said anything about a fake date?' he finished, his lips so close she could all but feel them pressed against hers.

'But I'm not your girlfriend,' she managed to say as her heart pounded in her throat. 'I certainly don't love you. And right now I don't even like you.'

His gaze swept over her, making her notice the length of his lashes again, before his eyes fixed on her face. If she'd hoped to wound him she could see by his expression she'd failed.

'Make no mistake. This is only a two-week deal. I'm not in the market for anything more and neither are you.'

She thought she could hear a tinge of regret in his voice and cursed her overactive imagination. She doubted he had the emotional capacity for regret. The rat.

'But we don't have to love each other for what I have in mind.'

With that, his lips came down on hers in a hard, fast and sinfully sexy kiss. She tried to twist away but he held her firm until she felt the pulse of response, the throb of heat. And before she knew what was happening, she was kissing him back.

He pulled his mouth away first and straightened. 'You like me right enough, Daisy Dean.' He brushed his thumb across her bottom lip. 'And we both know it.'

She jerked back, mute with anger and humiliated right down to her knickers—which were now soaked with need.

'There will be lots we can see and do in Manhattan—and I've a mind to show it to you,' he continued, that devil-may-care charm not the least bit fazed by her furious glare. 'So, you can spend the two weeks in your bed alone, or make the most of the experience. The choice will be yours.' He gave her a mock salute. 'I'll see you in New York, Angel Face.'

Daisy glared at his back as he strolled out of the café,

heard him whistling some off-key Irish ditty as he disappeared down the street.

The overbearing, conceited, blackmailing jerk.

She flung her bag on the seat. How dared he steamroll her like that?

She glowered at the booth opposite, sure she could feel smoke pumping out of her ears. To think she'd actually felt sorry for what she'd said about him. He wasn't just arrogant. He was a megalomaniac—with an ego the size of his precious Manhattan.

If he thought she was going to step into line, he could forget it. And whatever happened she was not going to sleep with him again. No way, no how.

But even as she made the promise she knew it was going to be next to impossible to keep.

CHAPTER EIGHT

BY THE time Daisy had packed up the stall with Juno that evening and trudged back to her bedsit, she'd decided the conversation with Brody in Gino's café had been his crazy idea of a joke. Either that or she'd been dreaming.

He couldn't be serious about blackmailing her into a trip to New York. This was the twenty-first century—people didn't do that sort of thing. Well, not people with any semblance of decency.

She turned on the light and toed off her shoes, every cell in her body weeping with exhaustion after a virtually sleepless night and ten solid hours on her feet—not to mention the day's emotional trauma. Thank you so very much, Connor Brody. Pulling off the bangles on her wrist, she dropped them into her jewellery box, then sat on the bed and unclipped her silver ankle bracelet. She'd just forget the whole ridiculous episode.

She hadn't even told Juno about Brody's threat. She'd forced herself to calm down before returning to the stall—her lips still red and puffy from Brody's goodbye kiss—and had put a few things in perspective. Brody could not possibly have been serious. So why bother Juno with the details?

Edging her curtain back, Daisy peeked at the windows of

Brody's house. Pitch black. Thank goodness. He must be in Paris. She huffed. Good riddance.

She let the curtain drop, lay down on the bed and stared at the fairy-tale motif she'd painted on the ceiling last winter. A blue-eyed, black-haired cherub winked at her cheekily from behind a moonbeam.

She shifted onto her side and tucked her hands under her cheek—the damn cherub reminding her of someone she did not want to be reminded of.

Sunday and Monday flew by in a flurry of work and other related activities. Daisy manned the stall, ran a class on silk-screen printing at the local community centre, got stuck into her latest clothes designs and did her regular slot at the Notting Hill Arts Project—happily getting neck-deep in tissue paper, glitter and PVA glue as she helped her group of five- to ten-year-olds make their costumes for this year's Notting Hill Carnival. Just as she'd suspected, there had been no word from Brody. By Tuesday night, the events of the weekend had been as good as forgotten—give or take a few luridly erotic dreams.

Bright and way too early Wednesday morning, her three days of denial came to an abrupt end.

'Daisy, Daisy, open up, dear.' Mrs Valdermeyer's excited voice was punctuated by several loud raps on the door. 'A package has arrived for you. Special delivery no less.'

Daisy rolled over, blinking the sleep out of her eyes. Stumbling out of bed, she checked the Mickey Mouse clock on the mantelpiece and groaned. It was still shy of seven a.m.

She pulled the door open and her landlady whisked past, holding a small brown-paper parcel aloft like a waiter on silver-service duty. She laid it ceremonially on the bed. Then turned to Daisy and bounced up on her toes.

'Isn't it exciting?' She clapped her hands. 'It's from that handsome young man next door—it says so on the front.'

Daisy felt a much louder groan coming on, but bit it back.

'What's going on?' Juno stood in the doorway, wearing her Bugs Bunny pyjamas and a sleepy frown.

'Daisy has a package from a gentleman admirer. Isn't it exciting?' Mrs Valdermeyer plopped down on the bed and patted a spot next to her. 'Come in, Juno, and let's watch her open it.'

Daisy felt the groan start to strangle her. Fabulous. When had her bedroom become package-opening central?

'What gentleman admirer?' Juno asked. Walking into the room, she glanced at the package. 'Oh, him,' she scoffed.

Daisy opened her mouth to speak—and start ushering her audience out the door—when Mrs V interrupted her. 'Don't be such a grump, Juno dear.' She whisked a pair of scissors out of her dressing gown with a flourish. 'The man is positively delicious and he saved Mrs Pootles from a fate worse than death. Daisy could do a lot worse.' She offered Daisy the scissors. 'In fact Daisy did do a lot worse—remember that awful Gary?'

'Do I ever,' Juno replied, sitting next to Mrs Valdermeyer. She caught Daisy's eye. 'But I'm not sure this guy is that big an improvement.'

'Well, he's certainly a lot better looking,' Mrs Valdermeyer shot back.

'We're not dating, Mrs V,' Daisy interceded, before her landlady got totally the wrong idea. 'So there's no need—'

'Why ever not, dear? He's loaded, you know. Which, I might add, comes in very handy if the passion fades.'

Daisy grabbed the scissors, resigned to opening the package as quickly as possible before the conversation deteriorated any further.

She snipped the string and folded the paper back carefully, aware of the two pairs of eyes watching every move she made. Her heart pummelled as she opened the lid.

Please don't let him have put crotchless knickers in here. Or something equally tacky.

But as she upended the box she was surprised to see three envelopes of varying sizes and a slim, black velvet case bounce onto the bed.

'How marvellous. Jewellery. Open that last, Daisy,' Mrs Valdermeyer said, thrusting the first of the envelopes into Daisy's hand. 'Jewellery needs to be properly savoured.'

Once Daisy had opened all three of the envelopes, Mrs Valdermeyer was practically doing cartwheels around the room and Juno's frown had turned into the San Andreas fault.

Daisy slumped onto the bed, stunned. In her lap she had a first-class return ticket to JFK dated for twelve noon that coming Sunday, a carefully typed itinerary of her travel arrangements signed by someone called Caroline Prestwick and a gold credit card in her name.

Her hand shook as Mrs Valdermeyer thrust the jewellery case into her lap on top of the other booty. Daisy picked it up, and found another envelope attached to the bottom of the case.

She ripped it off, stared blankly at her name scrawled on the front in large, block letters and then tore it open. Inside was a sheet of thick textured white paper with the Brody Construction logo stamped across the top. As she scanned the contents of the letter her fingers began to tremble.

Angel Face,

I found the sparkles in Paris and thought they would suit. Get anything else you need with the card—and don't spare yourself. I want you to look the part.

There's a car booked for the airport. See you at The Waldorf.

Connor
PS: I've my solicitor on speed-dial if you don't show.

'It's all so wonderfully romantic,' Mrs Valdermeyer crooned over her shoulder. 'Two weeks at The Waldorf *and* a gold credit card. You're going to have the time of your life, Daisy.'

'What does he mean about his solicitor?' Juno said.

'I'm not going.' Daisy folded the letter and shoved it back in its envelope. She couldn't possibly go. Okay, somewhere in the last few days she'd got over her anger, and for a moment Mrs Valdermeyer's industrial-strength enthusiasm had almost blinded her to the truth. For a split second she'd seen herself on Connor's arm decked out in glitters and her best posh frock. She'd never been further than Calais on a school trip so she felt she was entitled to get momentarily carried away. But she couldn't do it. And what had he meant by 'I want you to look the part'—as if she were his personal mannequin? The cheek of the man.

'Of course you're going, my dear. Don't be absurd,' Mrs Valdermeyer said.

'I really don't think she should,' Juno piped up. 'She'd be totally at his mercy and—'

'Stop right there, Juno.' Mrs Valdermeyer got up and took Juno's arm. 'I want you out of here. Daisy and I have to talk about this in private,' she said, dragging Juno to the door.

Before Juno had a chance to say anything else, she'd been shoved over the threshold and had the door slammed at her back.

Mrs Valdermeyer brushed her hands together. 'Right, now the most unromantic woman in the Western World has gone, let's discuss this properly.'

She sat down next to Daisy, laid a hand on her knee.

'You don't understand.' Daisy fisted her fingers on Connor's perfunctory letter. 'It's not romantic at all. He just needs a girlfriend to hang on his arm for a couple of weeks. We're not even dating. It's a business thing. Or something.' She let out a trembling breath. The truth was, he thought so little of her, he hadn't even had the courtesy to tell her why exactly he needed her there.

Daisy shoved Connor's letter and the jeweller's case back in the box—ignoring the cold fingers of regret gripping her stomach.

How pathetic that she felt depressed she couldn't go. She was her own woman, she didn't need a man to complete her and she certainly didn't need some too-sexy-by-half egomaniac sweeping her off her feet only to dump her back down to earth again two weeks later.

'He may very well think that,' Mrs Valdermeyer said gently, resting her knarled hand over Daisy's. 'But I suspect there's a bit more to it.'

Tears pricked Daisy's lids—and made her feel even more pathetic. 'Like what?' she said, cynicism sharpening her voice.

'Daisy, dear. Men don't ask a woman on a first-class, all-expenses-paid trip to New York just for the sake of a business deal.'

'He didn't ask me,' Daisy said, the tears she was busy ignoring clogging her throat. 'He told me. And I think he's expecting some pleasure mixed in with his business to justify the expense.'

Mrs Valdermeyer chuckled fondly. 'He is a scoundrel, isn't he? Just like my third husband, Jerry.' She patted Daisy's leg, still chuckling. 'But once you've tamed him, my dear, you'll see they're the very best kind. Both in bed and out.'

Daisy tried to smile at the old lady's irascible tone, but

somehow she couldn't muster more than a strained grimace. 'I don't want to tame him. Believe me, it would involve far too much work.'

Mrs Valdermeyer took Daisy's hands in hers. 'Look at me, dear.' Daisy lifted her eyes, saw that the old woman wasn't smiling any more. 'Don't you think you're taking this a bit too seriously? Surely, this is about a man and a woman having a marvellous adventure together. Nothing more. And you've had far too few adventures in your life to let one as spectacular as this pass you by.'

Daisy huffed. 'That's where you're wrong. I had enough adventures to last me a lifetime before I ever came here.'

'No, you didn't. Those were your mother's adventures. They don't count. This is going to be your adventure and you're going to enjoy every minute of it. You need to get out there and experience life before you can think about finding love, you know.'

A flutter of butterfly wings began to beat under Daisy's breastbone. She tired to ignore them. 'I really don't think…'

Mrs Valdermeyer held up her finger to silence her. 'Don't think, Daisy. You're a dear sweet girl who thinks far too much, mostly about everybody but herself. For once, don't think, just feel.' She patted Daisy's knee. 'Take it from me, I'm an old woman and there are a few things I've learned. You've got the rest of your life to plan things out, to do the right thing, to be cautious and careful and responsible. That's what you have to do when you start a family—that's what your mother should have done and didn't. And if you find the right man to do it with it won't be boring, let me tell you. But you're young, and free and single and you get to be spontaneous now, to live life as it comes and take whatever fun and excitement you can grab.' She picked up the velvet jeweller's case. 'Now, I want to know what sparkles your handsome scoundrel picked out for you in Paris. Don't you?'

Mrs Valdermeyer placed the case back in Daisy's lap.

Daisy stared at the embossed gold lettering on the top, ran her finger over the textured velvet. She sighed. What the heck. What harm could it do to take a quick peek? She lifted the heavy case in one hand and opened the lid.

The sight of the emeralds winking on a lattice of silver chains had her heart leaping into her throat and threatening to choke her. She took an unsteady breath and touched the precious stones.

The butterflies went haywire as the fanciful, fairy-tale images that had been hovering at the back of her mind came into sharp, vivid and all-too-real focus.

She could feel the beautiful necklace warming her cleavage, see the luminous satin of a ball gown she'd once designed in her dreams shimmering in the glow of a thousand tiny lights and sense Connor, tall, dark and far too dangerous, his blue eyes bold with appreciation as he held her close in his arms.

She slammed the lid shut like a frantic Pandora with her box.

But the giddy beating of her heart and the heat coiling in her belly told her she was already far too late to seal in the ridiculous dream.

CHAPTER NINE

IF THE days prior to the arrival of Connor's package had gone by in a flurry, the ones afterwards went by in a blur. Once Daisy had faced the fact that she'd have to go to New York—or spend the rest of her life wondering what she might have missed—she became determined to make the absolute most of the opportunity, and avoid all the pitfalls at the same time.

Daisy being Daisy, the practicalities had to be handled first. So she lined up Jacie to help Juno on the stall, finished as much merchandise as she could, rearranged all her community and charity activities and then spent every other spare minute she had working on her wardrobe for the trip. Whether this turned out to be the grandest adventure of her life—or the biggest disaster—she intended to look fabulous. She had her own distinctive style, and whether Connor approved of it or not, she planned to look the part. That would be her part—not his.

As she drew patterns and cut fabrics and stitched and pleated and hemmed and appliquéd late into the night she worked out a basic survival strategy to go with her amazing trousseau.

Whatever happened in New York she would not lose

sight of what really mattered. Her life, her career—such as it was—her hopes and dreams for the future did not depend on two thrill-seeking weeks spent in the City That Never Sleeps with a man who had twice as much sex appeal as Casanova and half the depth. As long as she kept her hormones under strict supervision—and didn't succumb to any delusions about true love—she would be absolutely fine.

But despite all Daisy's preparations and pep talks, when Sunday morning arrived, and a black Mercedes with a liveried driver parked in front of the bedsit, the nerves kicked in.

While the chauffeur loaded her suitcase into the boot, she clung onto Mrs V and Juno in a goodbye hug. But as she climbed into the plush leather interior the smell of money and privilege overwhelmed her and the nerves got worse. She wound down the window and gave her friends a shaky wave as the powerful car purred to life and swept away from the kerb.

Once the only home she had ever known was out of sight, she wound the window back up, pressed the button for the air-conditioner and listened to the deafening thumps of her heartbeat over the quiet hum. What on earth had she let herself in for?

She dropped her head back and sighed.

She would be walking into a world she knew nothing about. And throwing herself on the mercy of a guy she knew even less about—not to mention her own surprisingly volatile libido.

She forced herself to take a series of steady breaths as she smoothed the bias-cut sheath dress she'd finished the night before over her knees and felt the pearly silk whisper under her fingertips.

She watched the terraced houses of west London whisk past.

Fine, maybe this would turn out to be the stupidest thing she'd ever done—but at least she'd be doing it in style.

Daisy Dean had never coveted the lifestyles of the rich and famous. She'd never worried about how much money she had, only that she had enough—and she'd been more than happy to work as hard as she had to have the stability she'd always craved.

But as she stepped out of the royal blue limo onto Park Avenue and gazed up at the art deco frontage of The Waldorf Astoria, its gilded-gold filigree glinting in the mid-afternoon sunshine, Daisy had to concede that being rich beyond your wildest dreams might have its uses.

For a girl who'd only ever been on the cheapest of short-haul flights, the journey across the Atlantic—in a leather seat that folded down into a bed bigger than the one she had at home—had been like a dream. She'd cruised above the clouds at thirty thousand feet, sipping champagne and snacking on cordon bleu cuisine—or as much as her nervous tummy would allow—and made herself savour the experience and enjoy it for what it was—a once-in-a-lifetime adventure.

'Ma'am.' The Waldorf's doorman interrupted Daisy's thoughts to hand her a blue ticket. 'Give this to the desk clerk when you check in and we'll have your luggage sent right up to your room.'

'Thank you.' Daisy pulled a ten-dollar bill out of her purse, glad she'd changed some of her own money. But as she offered the tip to the doorman he simply shook his head.

'No need for a gratuity, ma'am. You're Mr Brody's guest. He's already taken care of it.'

'Oh.' Daisy slipped the money back into her purse, her cheeks colouring.

In the last few days she'd been careful not to dwell on her

position as 'Mr Brody's guest'. But somehow not even being able to tip the doorman made her feel a bit cheap.

She pushed her uneasiness aside as she made her way up the carpeted stairs to the lobby area. Brody needed her here for his business thingy. She was doing him a favour, so why shouldn't he foot the bill? And she hardly needed to create more problems—she had quite enough on her plate already.

Her breath caught as she took in the huge chandelier hanging over The Waldorf's marbled forecourt and heard the tinkling strains of a Cole Porter song being played on a grand piano in the cocktail bar.

Portobello Road and the Bedsit Co-op suddenly felt a lot more than half a world away.

All leather sofas, vaulted ceilings and dark wood panelling with an ornate carriage clock as its centrepiece, the reception area was no less intimidating. Feeling hopelessly out of place, Daisy approached the desk.

A woman with perfect make-up and an even more perfect smile greeted her. 'What can we do for you today?'

'My name's Daisy Dean. Mr Connor Brody has booked me a room.' The minute the words were out of her mouth, the blush coloured her cheeks again. At least she'd assumed he'd booked her a room. In all the hurried preparations of the last few days and the glamour of the flight, it hadn't even occurred to Daisy to wonder about it. The thought of the kiss they'd shared in Gino's came blasting back to her and the crack he'd made about this not being a 'fake date' and she realised she should have contacted him and clarified their sleeping arrangements. She tried to ignore her pummelling heartbeat. *Don't be silly, Daze, he couldn't possibly be arrogant enough to assume you'll be sleeping together.*

The receptionist tapped a few buttons on her console and smiled. 'You're booked into The Towers Suite with Mr Brody.'

The bottom dropped out of Daisy's stomach. 'Are you sure?' she stuttered.

'Why, yes, of course, Mr Brody made the arrangements personally,' the receptionist continued, apparently oblivious to Daisy's distress. She handed Daisy a thin plastic card in a paper envelope. 'The Towers Suite is on the twenty-first floor,' she said chirpily, pointing to the lifts at the end of the lobby. 'You have a special penthouse elevator for your exclusive use. Mr Brody left a message to say he's in meetings downtown this afternoon, but we're to contact him when you get here and he'll be back at about six o'clock to escort you to dinner.' She smiled again, her teeth so white they gleamed. 'If you have the ticket for your luggage, I'll have it taken to the suite.'

Daisy reached into her bag and handed over the ticket, her mind whirring. She wanted to demand the receptionist get her another room, but how the heck could she do that when she had a grand total of one hundred dollars in her purse? She'd have to have it out with Brody first, and then insist he get her another room. But the thought of that altercation filled her with dread. She hadn't seen him for over a week, but just the mention of his name had made her thigh muscles clench and her nipples pebble beneath the thin silk of her dress.

'Thanks for your help,' she said, taking the key card in shaking fingers.

She walked to the lift lobby, keeping her back ramrod straight.

Forget feeling cheap, she might as well have had a huge scarlet letter A pasted on her breast.

When Brody finally turned up, she was going to have serious words with him.

After having inspected The Towers Suite, Daisy felt even more intimidated—and like a naive fool.

Taking up most of the twenty-first floor, the suite's rooms were all enormous and luxuriously appointed. Daisy walked through it, her eyes widening until they were the size of dinner plates. Leading off the palatial entrance lobby was a sitting room which boasted a grand piano, a plasma TV the size of a small cinema screen and a lavish balcony with a breathtaking view of the Upper East Side. There were also two walk-in wardrobes and a dressing room, but—surprise, surprise—only one bedroom.

Done out in cream silk wallpaper and matching upholstered furnishings, the bedroom had an en-suite bathroom containing a circular whirlpool tub big enough to house an entire rugby team. Daisy had particular trouble breathing though when she got a load of the obscenely large bed. Raised on a dais and covered in a gold satin quilt, it had enough pillows to put a harem to shame.

Of course Brody had just assumed they'd be sleeping together. Why wouldn't he? The man obviously had more money than God, and the arrogance to match. And when you factored in his devastating good looks and that bad-boy Irish charm, she'd bet her bottom dollar no woman had ever said no to him.

She strode back into the bathroom, her annoyance choking her. Twisting the gold-plated taps, she watched the steaming water gush out. Sprinkling in a generous helping of flakes from a heavy glass jar on the vanity, she breathed in the lavender mist and tried to focus on the scent's calming properties. She had a few hours till he arrived at six o'clock. She'd soak out the kinks from the flight, try to relax a little and go over exactly how she was going to handle Brody when he showed up.

CHAPTER TEN

Daisy glanced at the clock on the wall. Still only four-thirty. She closed her eyes, slid into the lavender-scented bubbles and let her mind drift over the classical music coming from the state-of-the-art console in the wall. Despite the battle that loomed large in her future, all the muscles in her body melted into blissful oblivion. When was the last time she'd been able to indulge herself like this? In a place as luxurious as this? Never, that was when.

Ten more minutes of nirvana, that was all she asked, then she'd get ready to face Brody.

She heard a small clicking sound beneath the music and frowned.

'Welcome to New York, angel.'

She shot upright, her eyes flying open as water cascaded onto the floor. 'What are you doing here?' she yelped, wrapping her arms around her naked breasts.

'I live here,' Connor Brody said, the lazy grin spreading as his eyes drifted down.

He stood by the tub, looking tall and gorgeous and intimidating, his hands sunk into the pockets of a charcoal-grey designer suit, a few wisps of chest hair visible above the open collar of his white shirt. She'd never seen him in anything but sweats and jeans and a T-shirt before now. The formal business-wear should have made him look tamer and more sophisticated, but somehow the perfectly tailored fabric had exactly the opposite effect—accentuating the rough, raw masculinity that lay beneath the veneer of civilisation.

And to make matters worse, she was stark naked.

Daisy swallowed heavily, the blast of heat flooding through her coming from more than just the hot bath. She was in serious trouble here.

Those deep blue eyes wandered to her bosom. 'Glad to see you made yourself at home.'

Daisy sank down sharply, splashing more water over the rim, until her chin hit the bubbles. Keeping one arm tight across her breasts, she used the other to shield her sex.

'If you don't mind,' she squeaked, equal parts outrage and mortification, 'I'm having a bath.'

'So I see.' He grinned some more. Then, to her astonishment, he took off his jacket, flung it on the floor, rolled up his shirt sleeves and perched on the edge of the tub.

'What are you doing?' she cried, still squeaking, as he picked up a bar of hotel soap.

Those piercing eyes fixed on her face as he ripped off the soap wrapper, dipped his hands into the water and began lathering the soap in long, tanned fingers. The glint of mischief in his gaze did nothing to diminish the desire.

'Giving you a hand,' he said casually, too casually. The deep husky tone of his voice reverberated across her nerve endings.

She pressed her palm into her sex, struggling to hold back the surge of heat that had made the muscles loosen. 'I don't want a hand.' The breathlessness of the words meant the statement didn't sound as definite as it should.

His lips quirked, as if she'd said something amusing.

He dropped the soap into its bowl and threaded soapy fingers through the hair at her nape. 'Are you sure?' he murmured, reminding her of their first night.

She gasped as his thumb stroked the rapid beat of her pulse and his hand cradled the back of her neck. She braced wet palms against his chest. Water splashed onto the floor as she soaked the front of his shirt. She could see the dark shadow of his chest hair through the damp linen, feel the hard muscles beneath and her arms shook.

He simply laughed and pulled her easily to him as his lips covered hers.

He devoured her mouth, exploring with the strong, insistent strokes of his tongue. The heat geysered up from her core as her fingers curled into the wet fabric. She wanted to shove him away, she really did, but his tongue, his lips were making her light-headed, and every single nerve in her body was throbbing with need. He let her go abruptly and stood up. She could hear the pants of her own breathing, ragged against the melodious tones of the concerto, as she watched him strip off his shirt and kick off his shoes. He reached for his belt and suddenly sanity came flooding back.

What was she doing? What was she letting him do? She wasn't his mistress. Maybe she wasn't going to be able to resist him for long, but she would not be treated like some convenient sex toy—at his beck and call whenever he felt like it.

'Stop it. We're not making love,' she said, but the words came out on a barely audible croak.

He glanced up, his hands stilling on his belt. 'What was that, now?'

She shivered under the intensity of his gaze as he stared at her, sure she was about to catch fire. 'We're not making love until we've got a few things sorted out,' she said, her arms clasped so tightly around her breasts she could hardly breathe.

'What things?' he said, sounding mildly interested.

She gulped, spotting the impressive erection tenting the loose pleats in the front of his trousers. The muscles in her thighs went liquid and her sex throbbed painfully, an instinctive reaction to the memory of how good he'd once felt inside her. It seemed absence had only made her more of a nymphomaniac.

'I'm not your mistress. You may think I'm bought and paid for. But I'm not.' She babbled to a stop. He was looking at her as if she'd taken leave of her senses. 'You don't own me,' she soldiered on regardless. 'And I won't be treated as if you do.'

He shrugged. 'Right enough,' he said, then pulled down his zipper. The crackle of the metal teeth unlocking drew her gaze down. 'Move over. I've a mind to join you in the tub.'

'I most certainly will…' But her indignant reply backed up in her throat as his trousers and boxers dropped to the floor and her eyes fixed on his groin. Unfortunately, he hadn't got any less beautiful, any less magnificent than the last time she'd seen him naked. Her whole body began to shake.

She gulped, her mouth bone-dry, and forced her eyes back to his face as he stepped into the tub. The sensual smile made it obvious he was very well aware of the effect his nakedness had on her.

He settled beside her, his big body making the water and her temperature rise. 'Now, where were we?' he said.

She lay transfixed by her raging hormones as he reached behind him for the soap.

She opened her mouth but no coherent sound came out as he lathered the soap then, nudging her arms to the side, placed his hands on her breasts. Her breath gushed out, sensation overwhelming her as he lifted the heavy orbs, his thumbs teasing swollen nipples. She arched up, closed her eyes, and groaned. Those demanding, purposeful fingers felt so good. She wanted him to touch her all over, everywhere. Her eyes jerked open, heat spiralling down to her core, when he captured her nipples and tugged.

'This is such a bad idea,' she whispered, swaying towards him and gripping his lean waist for balance as he continued to concentrate all his attention on her breasts.

He laughed, a raw, dominant chuckle that told her he knew exactly how good an idea her body thought it was. 'I know,' he rasped as she felt his erection nudge her thigh. 'I left the damn condoms in the other room.'

She flattened one hand on his chest, felt the silky resilience of smooth flesh over bunched muscles and tried to find the will to stop him. But then his palm glided down her abdomen and found the swollen flesh of her sex under the water.

His fingers explored, brushing her clitoris with the tiniest of touches and she bucked against him, crying out. He sealed off her cries with a harsh, demanding kiss, dragging her against him with one arm as his other hand continued to play havoc, stroking and caressing, pressing her sweet spot and then retreating. Her hips moved in a siren's rhythm, her fingers clutching at the back of his neck. He fastened his lips on the pulse in her throat, suckled as she threw her head back and gave herself up to the sensations exploding up from her core, only dimly aware of the water soaking the floor.

The orgasm roared through her, each wave pulsing over her body with greater intensity. The broken sobs of her release echoed as she collapsed against him, limp and shuddering, his embrace the only thing that was keeping her from sinking into the bath water and drowning.

She felt the insistent outline of his erection against her hip as his breath whispered across her ear lobe. 'Let's finish this in bed.' The words had barely registered when he stood up, hefted her in his arms and stepped out of the tub, splashing water everywhere.

'Put me down.' She struggled, the serene moment of afterglow wiped out by acute embarrassment.

Why had she let him march in and take over like that? Why had she succumbed so easily? She was more at his mercy now than ever.

He set her on her feet and threw her a towel before grabbing one for himself. She wrapped it around herself. The drenched bathmat squelched beneath her feet and the remnants of his suit lay sodden on the marble tiles. 'Look what you've done,' she cried, knowing she wasn't talking about the mess.

He smiled, rubbing the towel across his chest, the relaxed grin casting a seductive spell. 'Don't worry, I intend to do a lot more—and soon.'

Heat scorched her insides as she realised just how far out of control things had become. He threw his towel away, then covered the fists she had anchored on hers with one large palm. 'Let go, angel. You don't need it.'

'I'm cold,' she murmured as she trembled, but she knew she wasn't.

'You won't be for long,' he said. Her fingers released of their own accord and he dragged the towel away. Lifting her against his chest, he carried her into the bedroom.

Her mind struggled to fight the sensual lethargy as he tumbled them onto the bed, trapping her beneath his body. She could feel every single inch of him, all firm muscle and lean masculine strength. She flattened her palms against his chest. 'Don't. I don't want you.' Her body screamed 'liar' as her mind struggled with the feeling of powerlessness, of being under his control.

He stiffened and something flashed in his eyes. 'I think you do,' he said, his voice strained. He took a condom from the dresser.

'You can't make me.' Her voice rose as she watched him sheath himself with single-minded efficiency.

'Make you?' He raised his head, one eyebrow bobbing up as his hand swept into her hair, cradled her head. 'I would never make you,' he said carefully, his thumb brushing her bottom lip. 'You must know that. But you're lying to yourself as well as me if you say you don't want me, angel.'

Strong hands gripped her thighs, angling her pelvis. 'Tell me again you don't want me and I'll let you go. I'll not force you,' he said.

She could feel the heat pulsing at her core, her chest heaving with longing, and knew she couldn't lie a second time. Couldn't bring herself to say the words that would deny her the pleasure he would give her.

The huge head of his erection probed. The pressure was immense as the slick folds of her sex tightened around him, but then he stopped.

The yearning to feel that one strong thrust that would force him deep, impale her, consumed her. But he didn't penetrate any further, the sinews in his neck taut as his eyes locked on hers.

'Ladies' choice, angel,' he murmured. His lips touched hers in a mocking kiss, tension vibrating through him. 'Now you tell me what it is you *do* want.'

Her hips flexed instinctively, and the delicious heat speared through her as he sank a fraction deeper. His fingers tightened, holding her still. She bit hard into her bottom lip, trapped and tortured by her own desires. Her own weakness.

'I want to hear you say it,' he said.

Her whole body clamoured for the release, for the blessed joy that only he had ever given her—and he knew it, she realised. She groaned, desperate to force the yearning back. Why was he making her beg? Hadn't she admitted enough? Hadn't she given him enough power? If she begged him now she'd be no better than a mistress—and maybe a great deal worse.

'Tell me you want me,' he demanded, his raw pants matching her own.

A staggered moan of surrender escaped her lips. 'Please... Do it. I want you. You know I do...'

A sharp dart of shame pierced her heart, but her mind disengaged as he thrust fully into her at last. He drove in up to the hilt, spearing through the tight, tender flesh and hurtling her over the edge. The orgasm burst free so much faster and stronger than before. She cried out, clutching his shoulders, clinging on as her legs locked around his waist. He pumped in and out in a furious, frenzied rhythm, filling her with an intensity, a ruthlessness that dragged her back with alarming speed and forced her over again—and again.

Finally, as she shattered into a million tiny glittering pieces, drained and exhausted from the relentless waves racking her body, he shouted out his own release—and shattered too.

CHAPTER ELEVEN

CONNOR collapsed onto his back, flung his arm across his face and struggled to draw a steady breath as his heartbeat battered his chest like a heavyweight champ's punching ball.

Where the hell had that come from?

One minute he'd been teasing her, enjoying the way her eyes darkened with desire, and the next he'd been gripped by a possessiveness, an intensity he didn't understand.

His affairs with women were always casual and fleeting. Sex was fun, fulfilling and must never be taken too seriously. He didn't do intense. So why had he turned into such a caveman when she'd told him she didn't want him?

The minute she'd said the words, he'd known she was lying. He'd seen the desire in her eyes, known all he had to do was touch her and she'd respond. But even so, he should have backed off, left well enough alone. Instead, something had welled up inside him, a bitterness, a resentment, a feeling of inadequacy he recognised from his childhood—and he'd been overwhelmed by the need to prove her wrong, to make her admit the truth.

He glanced across at her. She'd curled away from him, her

shoulders trembling. He rose up on his elbow. Hell, was she crying? His heart clutched in his chest.

He pulled the quilt up to cover them both, smoothed his hand over her hip. She shifted away.

'Daisy, are you all right?'

'Of course,' she said, but her voice sounded small and fragile. He studied the sprinkling of freckles across her shoulder blades, the way her damp hair was already springing up around her head. She looked so delicate to him all of a sudden. He winced. She'd been so tight around him and yet he'd taken her like a man possessed. Had he hurt her?

'Are you sure?' he asked, not sure he wanted to hear the answer.

She didn't reply, just sat up with her back to him, and pulled the thin cotton shift she'd left beside the bed over her head. He watched her movements, jerky and tense. The urge to hold her, to comfort her, to make up for what he'd done, blindsided him.

He stiffened. What the hell was happening to him? He didn't even recognise himself. She'd done something to him. Come to mean something he didn't understand.

In the last week he hadn't been able to stop thinking about her. Getting her to New York had been a game—a way of showing her the error of her ways, and enjoying some great recreational sex into the bargain. Or so he'd tried to tell himself.

But if it was all a game, why had he bought her a ten-thousand-euro necklace without a thought when he'd been window-shopping in the Marais? Sure he was usually generous with the women he dated, but not that generous after only one date. Why had he spent over an hour outlining his plans for her trip with his PA? Why had he called the airline first thing that morning to check she'd boarded the flight? And why had he cancelled the rest of his meetings and raced back to The Waldorf as soon as he'd got the word she'd checked in?

He'd been behaving like an over-eager puppy begging for scraps. It made him feel vulnerable in a way he hadn't since he was a lad. But he hadn't been able to stop himself.

And then, to make matters worse, when he'd walked into the bathroom and seen her lush body covered in soap suds, her soft flesh pink from the heat, the expected sexual charge had been swiftly followed by a blast of euphoria and bone-deep satisfaction that made no sense at all.

Given all that, was it any surprise that when she'd told him she wanted no part of him he'd been bound and determined to prove her a liar? To prove that she did want him—because he wanted her so damn much it was starting to scare him.

'Daisy, will you look at me?' he said, his patience stretching. 'I want to see you're okay.'

She glanced over her shoulder.

Relief washed through him when he saw no evidence of tears.

'Why wouldn't I be okay?' Green fire flashed as she faced him. 'You gave me what I wanted, right? What you made me beg for. You should be pretty pleased with yourself, all things considered.'

An unreasoning panic seized him as she turned away and he leaped forward to catch her arm.

'Wait.' His fingers clamped on her wrist.

Whatever had happened, they'd have to sort it out, because he wasn't ready to let her walk—not yet. Not until he sorted out what the hell was happening to him. She'd triggered something inside him and he needed her here to make it stop.

'Let go of me,' she said, her head bowed as she tried to wrestle her hand free. 'I'm not staying. You'll have to find another fake date. The sex is great, but the subservience I can do without, thank you.'

He dropped his feet on the floor, sat on the edge of the bed and pulled her to him when she tried to resist. 'Daisy, I'm sorry.'

He'd never apologised to any woman before her—he'd never needed to—and the words burned like acid on his tongue. He figured they'd been worth it, though, when she stopped struggling and looked at him. Anger still simmered, but behind it was something much harder to fathom.

'What are you apologising for?' she asked, her voice flat and remote. 'For giving me my first multiple orgasm?'

He had hurt her. He could see now he'd humiliated her. He knew a lot about pride and what it felt like to have it beaten out of you. Enough to know how much it hurt.

He took her other wrist and tugged her towards him, pressing his knees into her thighs, to keep her near. 'It wasn't meant as a punishment,' he said. He rested his hands on her hips, blew out a breath as he touched his cheek to the soft cotton covering her breasts. Her hands remained limply by her side, the muscles of her spine rigid beneath his fingers as she arched away from him. Lavender, underlaid with the scent of her, made blood surge into his groin, he hoped to hell she couldn't see it beneath the thick folds of the quilt. He raised his head, saw the flush of unhappiness and something else he didn't recognise on her face.

'Why did you make me beg for it, then?' she asked, accusation weighing every word. 'It was cruel and humiliating. What were you trying to prove?' Her frankness and vulnerability stunned him—and made him feel like a worm.

He shrugged, keeping his hands on her waist so she couldn't pull back any further.

'I wanted you to stay. And it seemed like a good way to persuade you.'

It wasn't the whole truth. In fact it wasn't even half of the truth. But he could hardly tell her how desperate he'd been to see her, how much he'd been looking forward to her coming over. It would make him look like a besotted idiot—and give her entirely the wrong impression.

Women always tried to romanticise sex—especially exceptional sex. And that was all this was really about. No woman had ever responded to him as she did, no woman had ever affected him quite like her before. But once he got her out of his system things would be fine.

Obviously his desire to stamp his claim on her had been brought on by sexual frustration. He'd never been this attracted to a woman in his life. But that would pass soon enough, he was sure of it. Romance had no part of it. Not for him.

'Why did you have to make me say it?' she asked, the words more confused than angry.

He choked out a half-laugh. Christ, why had he? 'I don't know.' And he was pretty sure now he didn't want to know. Best to leave that can of worms well enough alone. He'd just have to make damn sure he didn't lose his cool with her and open it up all over again.

Her eyes sharpened and he could see she didn't believe him. But then she sighed and her shoulders slumped. Finally she looked back at him and what he saw, to his amazement, was guilt.

'I know you paid a lot of money to get me here. And you didn't force me, not really. I wanted to come. I've never been to New York before.' She glanced round the room. 'And this place is incredible. But it's all so overwhelming. And I can't stay here as your mistress. It's demeaning.' Her brow furrowed. 'If you still need someone to pose as your girlfriend you can get me a cheap room, somewhere else, and I'll still do it. Then you won't be out of pocket. Okay?'

His heart contracted at the seriousness on her face. Damn. He'd known she was a Good Samaritan but this was stupid. He couldn't care less about her 'posing' as his girlfriend or the money he'd spent getting her here. Truth was he'd been showing off a little, wanting to dazzle her, trying to make sure she came. Who would have known his attempts to impress her would backfire?

He sighed. He should have guessed she'd be the first woman to be turned off by the money instead of turned on by it. She was so contrary.

But how could he tell her how much he wanted her with him and not make it sound as if there were more going on than there actually was? He needed to lighten the mood, get things back on their proper footing, not make them more intense.

Then a vague recollection of what Danny had said about the whole Melrose problem came to him and he had his answer in a flash of divine inspiration.

'You'll stay here with me, Daisy. You didn't just come for New York or The Waldorf. You came because you want me and I want you. And after what just happened there'll be no more denying it.' That at least he intended to make very plain.

She stiffened. 'I don't care. I told you I won't be your—'

'Shush now,' he said, feeling the flutter of her pulse as he pressed his thumb into her wrist. 'I've a solution to the problem that should satisfy your pride.'

He gave her a friendly pat on the rump. 'Go get some clothes on. We've a lot to do before we can have supper and I'm famished.'

Instructing her to meet him in the lobby in twenty minutes, Connor left Daisy to get dressed in the private dressing room. As she prepared herself for the evening ahead Daisy got the distinct impression she'd just been railroaded, but she felt too bewildered to worry about it now. She needed some time alone, to make sense of what had happened. Of what she'd let happen.

She'd been so angry and humiliated after they'd made love—correction: after she'd begged him to make love to her, again—that she'd wanted to hate him.

But then he'd apologised, and she'd been forced to face the truth. He'd been honest about how much he wanted her and she hadn't. And then she'd been doubly humiliated. Not only could she not resist him, but she couldn't even claim the moral high ground now either.

As she dabbed on make-up and slipped into the vintage satin halter-neck dress she'd made she admitted that her protests that afternoon had made her seem like the worst kind of hypocritical prude. Had she really pretended to herself when she'd got on that plane—with a dazzling array of hooker underwear in her suitcase and the memory of their last sexual encounter still vivid in her mind—that she wasn't going to sleep with him?

She'd been deluding herself all along and all he'd done was point it out to her—in a rather forceful manner. The fairy-tale fantasy that had lured her onto the plane didn't just involve the glitz and glamour of a luxury fortnight in New York. She'd also been enthralled by Connor Brody and the incredible sexual chemistry they shared.

She stepped out of the penthouse lift, her pulse skittering as she saw Connor walking towards her, looking devastating in another of his designer suits. She wanted him, more than she'd ever wanted any man, and, however disturbing that might be to her peace of mind, she would have to stop denying it if she was going to learn to handle it.

Connor ushered her into the limo, and the small of her back sizzled under the warm weight of his palm. She sat back as the car sped off, watched the dizzying sights and sounds of Park Avenue roll by, and attempted to revise her survival strategy. Okay, staying out of Connor's bed was not going to be a viable option for the next two weeks. But her basic theory was still sound. All she had to do was make sure she didn't let her heart follow her hormones.

She watched as Connor leaned forward to give the driver instructions. Jet-black hair curled against the light-blue collar of his shirt; she clasped the purse in her lap and resisted the urge to run her fingers through the silky locks. Connor Brody was a dangerous man: dangerously attractive, dangerously desirable and dangerously single-minded. When he wanted something he went after it. And at the moment he wanted her.

She gazed back out of the window, tearing her eyes away from him.

But he'd already told her this was strictly a two-week deal—and that suited her too. She wasn't going to start looking for her happy ever after with a guy who wasn't remotely interested. She wasn't her mother and this was her chance to prove it once and for all.

After their two weeks were up she would make sure she walked away from this relationship with some enchanting memories to savour and her heart one hundred per cent whole. The next fortnight would be a grand adventure that she intended to make the absolute most of, but it was not real life.

'We're here,' Connor said, taking her hand and stepping onto the sidewalk.

Daisy stared at the iconic jewellery stall as he tipped the driver. 'What are we doing here?'

'It's all part of the solution to our problem.' He cupped her elbow in his palm. 'By the way,' he said, his eyes sweeping her frame, 'that dress is deadly.'

Although the compliment pleased her, probably more than it should, she ignored the little leap in her pulse rate. He was railroading her again. And it was about time she put the brakes on. He'd called enough of the shots already.

'What solution?' she asked as he pushed the revolving door and stepped in behind her.

He settled his hand on the nape of her neck, his thumb stroking the sensitive skin. 'I'm buying you an engagement ring.'

And just like that, her senses went haywire and her calm, measured, practical approach to the whole situation went up in flames.

'I'm not wearing it. This is ridiculous.' She tried to tug her hand out of his grasp, but he simply lifted her fist and brushed his lips across the knuckles.

'Stop sulking, angel.' He sent her a teasing smile. 'Maureen will think you don't like the ring.' He nodded towards the sales lady, who was pretending to stack some of the store's signature blue and silver boxes.

'It's not that and you know it,' she snapped, hoping Maureen couldn't hear them. 'I can't wear it.'

Having endured the ten-minute charade as he and Maureen had ummed and ahhed over a selection of engagement rings until he'd finally picked out a delicate silver band studded with diamonds, Daisy wasn't sulking, she was in a state of shock.

She didn't want to wear the heartbreakingly beautiful ring.

She'd once dreamt of the moment when a man she loved and who loved her in return would put an engagement ring on her finger. Connor wasn't that man, would never be that man and this definitely wasn't that moment. She knew that. But she still didn't want him to put that ring on her finger.

'Why can't you wear it?' he asked, flattening her hand between his palms, turning it over. 'You don't want to be my mistress. Fine, I understand that. So we put the ring on. You become my fiancée for the next two weeks. Problem solved.'

She looked at him, saw the confidence, the arrogance and that devilish determination and wanted to kick him—not to mention herself. How could she explain her objections without coming across as a romantic fool? And why had she objected to being his mistress in the first place? When the alternative he'd found seemed a thousand times more disturbing. She felt as if she'd sashayed out of the frying pan and crashed headlong into the fire.

'But I'm not your fiancée. It would be a lie. I don't think it's right. To lie, that is.' Great, now she sounded like a self-righteous prig instead.

He chuckled. 'Angel, don't take this so seriously. It's only for two weeks.' He brushed her cheek. 'We have some fun, my business deal is settled and no one's pride is compromised. Fair enough?'

It sounded so reasonable when he said it like that. Was she blowing this out of proportion? Making a big deal about nothing? Hadn't Mrs Valdermeyer also accused her of taking things too seriously? If she wanted to enjoy the next two weeks, make the most of them, didn't she have to learn to relax first?

She sighed. 'Fine, but you'll have to do all the introductions. I'm not good at lying to people.'

He smiled. 'It won't be a lie, just one of the shortest engagements on record,' he said and slipped the ring on her finger. But as the cool silver slid down she felt another band tighten around her heart.

Connor felt the slight tremble as he held her wrist to push the ring home. He steadfastly ignored the answering jump in his pulse. Sure he'd never put a ring on any woman's finger before, and never intended to again. The strange surge of pride, of satisfaction as he did it, didn't mean a thing. Not a blessed thing.

CHAPTER TWELVE

'I'VE GOT to tell you, it's been fabulous meeting you, Daisy,' Jessie Latimer said, her bright face brimming with enthusiasm. 'Monroe and I always knew the woman to capture Connor's heart would have to be very special. After all, he's quite a handful.'

'Yes, he is.' Daisy clutched the stem of her champagne glass and forced herself to smile back—not easy when her face ached and she felt as if she were about to throw up. Connor Brody wasn't just a handful, he was quite possibly a dead man after putting her in this excruciating predicament. Especially as it had come totally out of the blue.

The last week had gone by in a whirlwind of sights, sounds and activities. Daisy had never been anywhere as full on as New York before or with anyone as full on as Connor. And, despite all her misgivings, they'd had a wonderful time. They'd managed to pack in the Metropolitan Opera, the Met, Coney Island and the Circle Line tour, and in between times had had the best sex of Daisy's life. Because Connor was as full on a lover as he was a tour guide, but she'd soaked up every amazing sight and mind-blowing sexual experience and found she still wanted more. They'd both been determined to keep things light and non-committal. They didn't talk about the future and they didn't delve into each other's real lives and, as a consequence, she'd had very little time to dwell on the whole 'fake engagement' thing.

She thought she'd been handling it really well.

In fact, in the last six days, she'd only had two major hurdles to overcome. The worst had been the first night, when she'd tried to take the ring off in the bathroom of their suite and Connor had asked her to leave it on. He'd given her some excuse about not wanting to buy another if she lost it, a cocky smile on his lips, but when they'd made love that night and she'd spotted the ring winking at her she'd felt that funny clutch in her heart again. And it had taken her over an hour to fall asleep, despite the jet lag.

She'd handled the second hurdle much better. Being introduced to a group of Connor's business associates at an exclusive cocktail party the previous night had been a cinch in comparison. She'd decided that she'd settled into the charade now and it would be plain sailing from here on in. All she need do was think of herself as an actress playing a role.

But then they'd arrived at the opening of the brand-new Latimer Gallery twenty minutes ago, and Connor had introduced her to Monroe Latimer—a world-famous artist whose work Daisy had admired at the Tate Britain only a few months ago—and his wife, Jessie. And the subterfuge of pretending to be Connor's fiancée had become a thousand times tougher.

It had been obvious as soon as they'd been introduced that the couple were close friends of Connor. As he'd given her no warning, Daisy had assumed that Connor would simply tell them the truth. But when Jessie had spotted the ring and got excited, Connor had lied without a qualm, even talking about their wedding plans, before Monroe had dragged him off to find a beer.

Consequently, Daisy had been stuck lying through her teeth to a woman she'd warmed to instantly. A fellow Brit, Jessie Latimer had been friendly and funny and welcoming from the get-go; she'd been gracious and not at all big-headed when Daisy had gushed about the gallery and her husband's work and told Daisy some sweet and charming anecdotes about the couple's three daughters and what it was like to be an Englishwoman in New York. But the instant they'd got onto the subject of Daisy's impending nuptials, Daisy had felt as if she were being strangled by her conscience.

She wasn't a dishonest person—and she was fast discovering that she was a rubbish actress too.

'You're so different from the other women he's dated,' Jessie said. Her eyes widened and she touched Daisy's arm. 'God, I'm sorry, that sounded really gauche. But I mean it in the best possible way. Monroe and I have known him for three years now—ever since we started this project.' She glanced round the loft-style space in Tribeca which housed some of New York's most prestigious modern art. 'We hit it off with Connor right away, not just as an investment partner but as a friend,' Jessie continued. 'But Monroe and I could never get over some of the bimbos he dated.' She gave an easy laugh. 'I'm so glad he's finally found a woman who can match him. It's what he's always needed in his life, I suspect. Although it's taken him a hell of a long time to figure it out.'

Daisy felt her fake smile crack. Why had he lied to his friends like this? It was awful. The diamond ring felt like a lead weight on her finger as she lifted the champagne flute to her lips and took a fortifying sip. Her heart pounded so hard in her throat it threatened to cut off her air supply.

'Is there something wrong, Daisy? You're looking a little pale.'

Daisy's stomach took a swooping drop. This was the moment of truth. She couldn't continue lying to this woman.

No wonder she looked pale—she was definitely going to be sick any moment.

'I don't know how to say this,' she said, her fingers shaking on the glass and making the champagne slop to the rim.

'What is it?' Concern darkened Jessie's eyes, making Daisy feel like even more of a fraud.

'We're not engaged. Connor and I.'

Jessie's eyebrows shot up. 'You're not?'

'No.' Daisy stared down at her hands, the glint of diamonds on her ring finger only adding to her shame. 'We're not getting married. We only met two weeks ago. He's my neighbour. He paid for me to come here so I could pose as his fiancée.'

God, the whole thing sounded so unbearably sordid. She looked up, steeling herself to deal with the disgust she expected to see on Jessie's face.

But she didn't see disgust. Jessie's shoulders trembled and then, to Daisy's complete astonishment, she started to laugh.

'You're kidding?' Jessie blurted out at last, when she could finally draw a steady breath.

Daisy shrugged, acutely embarrassed. 'No, I'm not. It's dreadful, I know. He's deceived you and Monroe. I've deceived you...' She trailed off, not sure what else to say when Jessie had to clasp her hand over her mouth to hold back her giggling fit.

As she stood there, listening to Jessie's muffled laughter and watching the beautiful people nearby craning their necks to stare at them, Daisy began to wonder what was worse—being Connor Brody's scarlet woman or a complete laughing stock.

'I'm so sorry. Don't be embarrassed.' Jessie squeezed her arm, managing to subdue her mirth with an effort. 'It's just, you have no idea how ironic this is.'

'Thanks for taking it so well,' she said tentatively.

'Don't mention it,' Jessie said, still grinning. 'Look, I hope you don't mind me asking this. But it's obvious you're not comfortable with this whole set-up. Why did you agree to do it?'

Daisy blew out a breath. 'That's a good question. And it's sort of complicated.'

'I'm sure it is,' Jessie said. 'And I don't mean to pry. But Connor's a good friend, and I'd love to know what's going on between the two of you.'

'It might take a while to explain it, from my point of view anyway,' Daisy said, realising to her surprise she didn't mind giving Jessie her answer. After all, she'd given the question a lot of thought over the last week and it was about time she came clean about her motives—to herself as well as Jessie.

'Honey.' Jessie smiled. 'We've got all evening, or at least until Monroe and Connor find a beer, which could take a while seeing as the caterers only stocked champagne for this event as far as I know.'

'All right,' Daisy said, taking a deep breath. 'First off, I should tell you I live in a bedsit in West London. I work six days a week on my stall in Portobello Market. And this whole scene…' she did a circling motion with her glass to encompass the glittering crowd of Manhattan's movers and shakers surrounding them '…is about as far from my real life as it's possible to get. I help out at the local old people's home once a week. I run the Carnival Arts project for the kids on a nearby council estate. I mentor and volunteer and I'm totally committed to my friends and my community.'

'Now I know why I liked you instantly,' Jessie said easily.

Bolstered by the appreciation she saw in Jessie's face, Daisy smiled. 'Don't get me wrong. I love my life. I love the stability and the purpose and the sense of belonging it gives me and I intend to build on that when I have my own family one day. And I'm not interested in becoming rich or anything.' She hesitated for a moment, stroked the stem of her glass. 'But I've spent my whole life being cautious, and practical and responsible until I find my Mr Right.' She looked at Jessie, saw the compassion in her eyes, but decided against bringing up her mother's misbegotten love life—that seemed a bit too personal. 'Connor, like the world he lives in, is the complete antithesis of my Mr Right. He's exciting, sexy, charming, completely spontaneous and totally unreliable.'

And the best lover I've ever had, she thought, but decided not to mention that either. After all, she didn't want Jessie to think she was a total slut.

'He's the opposite of what I'm looking for in a life partner. He's not dependable or interested in settling down and I totally understand that. So I'm not under any delusions.' Thank goodness. 'But right here, right now, I guess he's a guilty pleasure that I couldn't resist. I decided when I got his plane ticket, these two weeks were going to be my Cinderella fortnight and so far they've worked out really well.' Give or take the odd heart bump. 'But once this is over I'll be happy to go back to my real life and my real dreams.'

'I see,' Jessie said, giving her a considering look.

'I guess that sounds as if I'm using him,' Daisy said quickly, realising how it sounded now she'd spelled it out so succinctly. She started to feel a little queasy again. This woman was Connor's friend, after all, not hers, however much she might want her to be. 'But as he's using me right back,' she continued, 'I don't feel guilty about it.' Or she was trying hard not to.

'I don't think you're using him,' Jessie said staunchly.

'You don't?' The knots in Daisy's stomach loosened.

'No, I don't,' Jessie said firmly. 'And even if you were, it would serve him right.' She sent Daisy a quick grin. 'The words *hoisted* and *petard* springing to mind.'

Daisy's breath gushed out in a relieved huff. Maybe Jessie's approval shouldn't mean so much to her, but somehow it did.

'But I've got to tell you,' Jessie continued, 'I do think you might be selling Connor a little short. At least as far as you're concerned.'

Daisy's heartbeat kicked hard in her chest, her breathing becoming uneven again. She wasn't sure she liked the wistful look in Jessie's eyes. 'How so?'

Jessie stared at her for a long moment. 'The Connor you described—the handsome, reckless, unreliable charmer—is only the Connor you see on the surface. That's the face he shows to the world and that's the way he likes everyone to see him. Especially women.'

Jessie paused to pick up a canapé from the tray of a passing waiter, but her eyes barely left Daisy's. 'It's the way he came across to Monroe and I when we first met him.' Jessie bit into the salmon puff, took her time swallowing it. 'In fact when we got involved with this project we were both worried about him. He'd come recommended, but still we thought, Can we count on him? Will he bail out if the going gets tough? We were putting a lot of money on the line and as much as we liked him personally we weren't sure about him. Precisely because he seemed so relaxed, so easy-going, almost overconfident.'

'So why did you risk it?' Daisy asked, intrigued despite herself. She'd never asked Connor about his work, just as he'd never asked her about her stall. It was all part of that unwritten agreement they had that this wasn't a serious relationship, but, still, she wanted to know more.

'Originally we went ahead because I got my brother-in-law Linc, who's a Wall Street financier, to do a thorough check on Brody Construction. The company's still young, even now, but it came out with flying colours, so we signed the partnership deal with Connor.' Jessie huffed. 'Almost straight away things started to go wrong on the project. The permits took much longer to come through than originally forecast. One of the suppliers went into receivership out of the blue. The building had a structural problem that hadn't come up on the survey. Talk about a money pit. Frankly, the whole rehab was a complete nightmare.' She grinned. 'Connor, though, turned out to be our knight in shining armour, and the exact opposite of what he had first seemed. He was dedicated, conscientious, incredibly hard-working, inventive and one hundred and ten per cent reliable. He even put on a tool belt himself a couple of times towards the end of the build to get things done.'

Daisy felt her chest swell with pride at Jessie's praise— and then felt ridiculous. After all Connor wasn't even her proper boyfriend. She began to wonder if she really needed to know about this side of him. It had been so much easier to dismiss him as a feckless charmer.

'It's nice to know he's so good at his job,' she said, trying hard to sound non-committal. 'He must enjoy it, which is probably why he's so successful.'

'He does enjoy it. But I'd say what he enjoys most is the challenge. Which brings us to the fascinating subject of Connor's love life. Which has never been remotely challenging.'

Daisy sipped her champagne, but the bubbles did nothing to ease the dryness in her throat. She really didn't need to know about his past relationships with women. Especially as their relationship had a sell-by date that was fast approaching. Now would be a good time to change the subject.

'What were they like?' she asked. 'The other women he's dated?' Blast, where had that come from?

'Interchangeable and shallow,' Jessie said, before Daisy could take the question back. 'I was being a bit unfair calling them bimbos, though. Some of them have been very shrewd.

The last one he dated, Rachel, being a case in point. I wasn't at all surprised when she told Connor she was pregnant.'

Daisy bobbled her glass. 'Connor has a child?'

'Of course not,' Jessie said. 'She wasn't pregnant. It was what you might call a very convenient scare. Just when he was trying to end the relationship.'

'What did he do?' Daisy asked, riveted by the topic despite everything.

'To everyone's astonishment he offered to marry her, to support the child. Even though Monroe and I both knew it was the last thing he wanted to do. When he told us she wasn't pregnant after all, he looked like a guy who had escaped the executioner's block.'

'He didn't want to be a father?' Daisy said, feeling strangely depressed, even though she already knew Connor wasn't the family man type.

'I don't think it's quite that simple. I don't know for sure, but I think he had a really tough childhood and his attitude to kids and family is very confused because of it. But one thing I do know is that he is petrified of commitment. He's a property developer but as far as I know the place he's rehabbed in London, the house next door to yours, is the first home he's ever bought for himself.'

'I see,' Daisy said, feeling even more dispirited.

Jessie sent her a knowing smile. 'Which makes it all the more bizarre that he's put his ring on your finger less than two weeks after meeting you.'

Daisy glanced at the ring, which seemed to have got even heavier while they were talking. 'Yes, but I've told you it's not a real commitment. On his part or mine.'

'Are you sure?' Jessie cut her off.

Daisy blinked. Swallowed. Of course she was sure, because anything else didn't bear thinking about. But somehow the denial got lodged in Daisy's throat.

'There are several things about this situation that don't add up, Daisy,' Jessie continued. 'First off, it's very noticeable how different you are from the other women Connor's dated. You're not shallow, or stupid, or shrewd. Second off, he treats you differently from the way he treated them. I mean, he walked in here with you on his arm and basically staked you out as his for everyone to see. He's never done that before. He's not the possessive type. Not till now anyway.' Jessie took Daisy's hand and held up the ring. 'And this whole fake engagement thing. It seems a bit extreme. Why does someone like Connor need a fake fiancée? That I'd really like to know.'

'He hasn't said, not specifically,' Daisy replied, and decided then and there she was never going to ask him. Because everything Jessie was saying was making her feel very uneasy.

'Fine,' Jessie said. 'But I guess what I'm really saying is, I know Connor. And I think there's a lot more going on here than either he or you realise.'

Daisy gulped in a breath, felt her heart pound against her chest wall like a battering ram. Now she really couldn't breathe. This she definitely did not want to hear. Because she could see a great big chasm opening up at her feet.

One she had no intention of jumping into.

She pulled her hand out of Jessie's grasp. 'I'm really flattered that you'd think I'm special, or different,' she said carefully, 'but I'm not.'

'To which I'd have to say,' Jessie countered, 'that if you really think that, you're selling yourself short, as well as Connor.'

Daisy lifted her glass of champagne, ignored the way it trembled as she took a sip.

She couldn't do this. She couldn't afford to think for even a moment that this thing with Connor could be anything more than it was, because that way lay serious danger. She couldn't afford to fall in love with a man who was petrified of commitment, for whatever reason. And she didn't want to.

Jessie, she decided, was just a hopeless romantic, who clearly cared deeply about Connor and wanted him to be happy. But whatever Jessie might think about their so-called relationship, it wouldn't change the outcome of their two-week fling. And Daisy was far too practical and well grounded to think it could.

'There's no big romance here, Jessie,' she said, but her voice wasn't quite as firm as it should be.

Jessie simply smiled and said, 'Don't be so sure.'

'Right, spill it, buddy, what's between you and that cute little redhead?' Monroe Latimer slanted Connor his 'you're busted' look and slugged back the last of his beer. 'And don't tell me she's your fiancée.' He dropped the empty bottle onto the bar. 'You may have got Red fooled, but I happen to know wild horses couldn't get you to propose.'

'Fair enough.' Connor lifted his hands in surrender, knowing when he'd been rumbled. He'd planned to tell Monroe the truth straight away, but, well, what with one thing and another, they'd been at the bar for twenty minutes partaking of Monroe's secret stash of beer and he hadn't quite got round to it. 'She's not my fiancée. She's my new neighbour in London. She's smart and pretty and, for reasons too boring to mention...' and way too transparent to mention to Monroe '...I needed a girlfriend while I was here and she fitted the bill. No strings attached.'

'Hmm,' Monroe said, keeping his eyes on Connor as he signalled the barman for a fresh beer. 'Which does *not* explain why you told Red and me she was your fiancée. Or why you bought her what has to be a real pricey ring.'

Connor took a gulp of his own beer. 'It's complicated.'

'I'll bet,' Monroe said, looking at him as if he were a bug under a microscope.

'And not the least bit interesting,' he countered.

'Humour me.'

Connor gave a half-laugh, although he wasn't finding being a bug all that amusing any more.

Monroe was a mate, a good mate. They'd even got drunk together one night and told each other more about their pasts than either of them was comfortable with—and their friendship had survived it. But there was one thing they'd never agreed on. And that was the subject of love and family.

That same night, when they'd been legless and overly sentimental, Connor had told Monroe that he would never fall in love. And Monroe had told him right back that he was talking a load of bull. Monroe had said that a guy didn't get to pick and choose those things, which Connor had thought then, and still thought now, was even bigger bull. Maybe Monroe had been blindsided and fallen in love with Jessie, and once Connor had got to know Jessie he could see why, but Connor knew that would never, ever happen to him.

Because what Monroe didn't know, what no one knew, was raising a family, having a home, was Connor's idea of hell. And no woman would ever be able to change that for him. Christ, when Rachel had told him she was pregnant, his whole life had flashed before his eyes—and not in a good way.

He knew Monroe and Jessie thought his reaction had been down to the fact that Rachel wasn't the right woman for him, but he knew different. He knew it had nothing to do with the woman. It went much deeper than that, and much further back. He'd offered to marry her, to support the baby, because he couldn't live with himself and know a child of his had been left to fend for itself. But that hadn't changed his gut reaction. He didn't want the child and he didn't want a wife. Any wife. And he was fine with that, fine and dandy.

He could tell by the way his friend was looking at him right now, though, that Monroe thought this little charade with Daisy was somehow significant. Sure he'd enjoyed her company in the last week. He'd got a thrill out of showing her the sights, and seeing her wide-eyed, enthusiastic reaction to everything. And in bed? Let's just say she'd exceeded his wildest expectations. He'd even got an unexpected kick out of showing her off as his fiancée. But that was all there was to it. A week from now they'd go their separate ways and that would be that. So Connor intended to head his friend's misconception right off at the pass.

'All right,' he sighed. 'I should have been straight with you and Jessie. But after all the matchmaking advice I've had to endure from your lovely wife over the last three years, Roe. You've got to know, I couldn't resist when she spotted the ring.'

'Fair point.' Monroe saluted him with his bottle of beer. 'I'll grant you Jessie is pretty damn persistent. But I hope you realise your little joke is going to backfire on you.'

'She'll forgive me,' he said, feeling his confidence returning. He raised his eyebrows. 'After all, she can't resist my irresistible Irish charm.'

'Yeah, right.' Monroe laughed. 'But that's not what I meant.'

'What did you mean, then?' Why didn't he feel quite so confident any more?

'I gotta tell you, for a minute there you had me fooled as well as Jessie. You want to know why?'

Connor didn't say a word.

'Because you fit,' Monroe said, and Connor's heart stopped dead. 'You and your cute little redhead. Daisy, that's her name, right?'

Connor nodded dumbly, trying to pull himself together.

This was ludicrous. Monroe was just trying to get a rise out of him. And it was working.

'She suits you, pal,' Monroe said, swigging his beer. 'Right down to the ground. I'm an artist, I happen to have an eye for these things and I'm telling you. She's the one.'

Connor growled a profanity under his breath, his stomach churning as he tried to see the joke. But why did it suddenly seem as if the joke was on him?

Monroe chuckled. 'Hey, what happened to that irresistible Irish charm, buddy?'

'Why didn't you tell me Jessie and Monroe were friends of yours before we got to the gallery tonight?' Daisy pulled out her earrings and dropped them in a bowl by the vanity.

She'd bided her time, not wanting to bring it up until she'd got a good firm grip on her own emotions. After the shock Jessie had given her it had taken a while.

'Hmm?' he said from behind her, then his hands settled on her waist. He pulled her into his arms, his naked chest warm against her back. 'You looked lovely tonight, you know,' he said, rubbing the silk of her slip against her belly as he nuzzled her ear. 'I may have to hire you for this gig again.'

The comment—and the heat drifting up from her sex at his casual caresses—couldn't have been calculated to ignite her temper quicker if he'd tried.

She turned in his arms, pushed against the muscled flesh. 'It's not funny,' she said, suddenly feeling more hurt than angry and hating herself for her weakness. 'You put me in a really difficult position. Not only not telling me you knew them, but then telling them we were getting married. And leaving me with Jessie like that. I felt awful. You knew I didn't want to lie to people. It wasn't fair.'

He stepped back, but kept his hands firmly on her waist. 'Come on, angel.' He tucked a finger under her chin, lifted her face to his. 'Don't look so upset. There was no harm done. They figured it out quick enough.'

'Jessie didn't. I had to tell her.' She turned away from him, braced her hands on the vanity.

And what Jessie had told her afterwards was still clutching at her heart, making panic clog her throat. Somehow her fantasy had changed tonight and become so much more real, and so much more frightening. She'd kept all the turbulent emotions at bay so effectively this past week, sealed herself off behind a wall of denial and sensation, but now the feel of his hands on hers, that clean, musky, masculine scent had become more intoxicating, more important to her than it was ever supposed to have been.

'I don't understand why you did that,' she said, raising her head to look at his reflection. With his shirt off and his chest bare, he looked as dark and devastating as always, but so much more dangerous now. 'Why did you introduce me to them as your fiancée?'

He shrugged. 'Just an impulse, I guess.' He had the lazy grin in place, but his eyes flickered away from hers as he said it. 'Stop worrying.' He pushed her hair back, trailed his thumb down the sensitive skin of her neck. 'Let's go to bed and forget it.' He pressed his lips to her pulse. 'I've got something much more interesting to discuss,' he whispered, one arm wrapping tight around her waist, his other hand cupping her breast, kneading the swollen flesh.

She moaned. His erection pressed against her bottom through their clothes, triggering the instant, instinctive response at her core. She angled her head to accept his harsh, demanding kiss, gave herself up to the heat, desperate to forget about everything but the feel of his body, the touch of his hands, his lips on hers.

He hadn't given her an answer. She knew that, but did she really want one?

She turned in his arms, encircled his neck with trembling hands, suddenly determined to cling onto the one thing that made sense.

'This is all that matters, angel,' he said, lifting her effortlessly in his arms and carrying her quaking into the bedroom. 'This is all that counts. Remember that.'

Yes. This is all that matters. I'm not looking for anything else.

But even as she threw herself into the moment, even as she chased that glittering oblivion, panic and an unreasonable regret gripped her heart.

CHAPTER THIRTEEN

AS DAISY shielded her eyes to gaze at Belvedere Castle across the meadow, a bittersweet smile tugged her lips. With its fanciful turret and fortress ramparts, the elaborate folly could have been plucked straight out of a Grimm Brothers fairy tale and plopped into the middle of Central Park.

She sighed. No daydreaming allowed. It was their last full day in New York and somehow she'd managed to live in the moment in the last week, keep the doubts and uncertainties Jessie had unleashed at the gallery opening locked carefully away. She wasn't going to blow it all now.

The fact that Connor had turned out to be an expert at living in the moment hadn't hurt a bit. Whenever she'd found her mind drifting to more serious matters, whenever she'd found herself watching him and wondering, he'd found a way to distract her. With a ferry trip round the Statue of Liberty, or a deluxe dinner at his favourite restaurant, or in bed, where he had become an expert in making her forget everything but the heat between them.

But in the few quiet moments they shared, she had a bad habit of thinking about what might have been. If they'd been different people, if they'd needed the same things. She tried really hard not to let her thoughts go there, but right now, with the cartons from their impromptu picnic scattered around them and that damn fairy-tale castle looming on the other side of the meadow, she couldn't seem to stop herself.

After the Governor's Ball tonight and the first-class trip home tomorrow, she would be going back to her real life and, as much as she didn't want to admit it, she knew the thing she'd miss the most, much more than the glamour and the excitement, was the intimacy she'd shared with Connor. He'd be right next door, of course, but as far as she was concerned he'd be out of reach. She had to make a clean break, whatever happened; to let it drift on indefinitely would be suicidal and, anyway, they'd both known right from the start this was strictly a two-week deal.

The sun warmed the floppy hat she'd worn to hide her freckles as she observed Connor stretched out beside her in the long grass, his hands folded behind his head, and his eyes shaded by a pair of designer sunglasses. The hem of his T-shirt had risen up revealing a strip of tanned abdomen above the low waistband of his jeans.

She let her mind drift back to that first night, when she'd yearned to touch his naked body. She knew every glorious inch of it now—and she still had to fist her hands in her lap to stop herself from reaching out and running her palm over that warm, flat, lightly furred belly.

Well, that was certainly disappointing: two weeks of non-stop sexual pleasure hadn't even put a dent in her nymphomania.

She toed her sandals off, stretched her feet out in the grass and watched him. She knew he wasn't asleep, probably just thinking. About what? she wondered. Funny, they'd spent two whole weeks together and yet what did she really know about him? Apart from the fact that he wasn't looking for a long-term girlfriend, he had more charm and charisma than

was feasible and he owned a very successful property de-
velopment company. But as soon as she'd asked herself the
question, a series of pictures flooded her mind like a living
photo album.

The way he'd tucked into his hot dog at Coney Island and
licked the mustard off his thumb with the same amount of
relish as he gave to the meal he'd devoured at a five-star restaurant. The way he'd dropped change into the tin of every
pan-handler and vagrant they passed. How relaxed he looked
in both a designer suit and his favourite faded jeans. The
sound of his terrible off-key whistle in the shower. Or how
he never failed to compliment her on whatever she was wearing, usually before he stripped it off her. So what did that say
about him? Generous to a fault, compassionate with those
less fortunate than himself, definitely not a snob, great taste,
completely insatiable and tone deaf.

But so much more about him was still a mystery. Their
conversations had always been deliberately light and teasing
and superficial. He didn't talk about his past and she didn't
talk about hers. She'd thought that was the way it had to be,
for both their sakes.

But now, with less than twenty-four hours left together, she
wasn't so sure. Because she had to admit she was desperately
curious to know more about him. Ever since she'd tended him
through those hideous night terrors the first night they'd been
together, she'd wondered about him, what had formed him.

She sighed. *Forget it, Daisy. You know what they say about
curiosity and the cat. You'd be better off leaving well enough
alone.*

She heard a shout and looked up to see a father throwing a
ball to his two sons a few feet away. She concentrated on their
game to stop her mind straying into more dangerous territory.

She smiled, noticing the way the older boy kept trying to
push his younger brother out of the way, and how the father

gently intervened. The sight made her heart squeeze. She wondered what kind of father Connor might have made if his last girlfriend had been pregnant after all. She chuckled. He'd probably have a heart attack if she asked him.

'What's so funny?'

She looked down to see Connor watching her, propped up on his elbow, his sunglasses thrown off on the grass and a curious smile on his face. She flushed and tried to think of an innocuous answer.

She nodded across the field to the man and his sons. 'I was just thinking what a wonderful dad he is.'

Connor craned his neck, leaning back on his elbows to watch. Then made a scoffing sound. 'How do you know he's a good father?'

It seemed self-evident to her, but she decided to humour him. 'Because he's being so fair with his two sons. And he really enjoys their company. When I have children, I'll want them to have a father like that. Someone as involved and committed as I am.' The words slipped out on a wistful sigh.

Connor's eyebrows lifted. '*When* you have children?'

'Well, yes.' She blushed, thinking she might have said too much, then thought, *What the heck?* This had been her dream for a long time, why should she keep it a secret? 'I've always wanted a family, a big happy family. In my opinion it's what makes life worth living.'

He watched her for what felt like an eternity, not saying a word. 'Is that what your own was like, then? Your family? Your father?'

The personal question stunned her a little. They'd both been avoiding them so carefully up till now. 'I never knew him.' She shrugged. 'But I was hardly deprived—there was never any shortage of pretend dads.'

His eyes narrowed. 'Pretend dads?'

She gave a laugh, trying for casual but getting brittle instead. 'My mother was the original born-again Bohemian—addicted to the idea of being in love. So she'd fall madly in love with some guy, we'd move in with him and then she'd discover he didn't love her—or not enough. I had a lot of what I called pretend dads as a result.' Why had she brought this up? Thinking about all those men who hadn't wanted to be her father, to be anyone's father, had always made her feel a little inadequate, and very insecure. 'None of them were horrible or anything like that. They all tried to be nice. But they weren't my father—and they didn't want to be.'

'That must have been tough,' he said gently.

His astuteness surprised her and made her feel unpleasantly vulnerable. 'I suppose it was at first,' she said, not sure she could cope with the sympathy in his eyes. 'When I was really little, I used to make the mistake of getting attached to them and then I'd be devastated when they left. But after a while I realised none of my mother's relationships would ever last. After that I forced myself not to get too attached and it was easier.'

Connor sat up, a strange tightness in his chest. She'd just given him an insight into her life he shouldn't really want. He'd been working overtime in the last week to make sure neither of them had too much time to think. He'd nearly blown things wide open at the gallery. And he still didn't know what had possessed him to introduce Daisy as his fiancée to Jessie and Monroe.

So he'd decided that night, when she'd looked so wounded, so unhappy, that the best thing to do was to keep things upbeat and not make any stupid mistakes again. Not to talk about feelings and emotions and any of that serious stuff that might complicate things.

But somehow, watching her now, hearing the hurt when

she talked about all those pretend dads who'd rejected her, he felt the urge to comfort her, to make it right.

He gave his head a rueful shake as he studied her. 'Damn, Daisy, who'd have thought it?' He brushed his thumb down her cheek, felt her shiver. 'Who'd have thought my practical, steadfast little Daisy would be such a dreamer?' He forced a smile onto his lips, desperate to keep the situation light.

She took hold of his hand, pulled it down from her face. 'Why are you smiling?' she asked, and he could see the shadow of hurt in her eyes. 'What's so funny about the fact that I want a family? Just because you don't, it hardly gives you the right to laugh at me.'

'I'm not laughing. I don't think it's funny. What it is, is sweet and incredibly naive.'

'Why naive?' she said warily.

'Because you're looking for something you'll never find. There's no such thing as happy ever after. Your mother didn't find it because it was never there.' He sighed, then nodded at the spot across the meadow where the father was still playing with his sons, the old bitterness assailing him. 'How do you know yer man over there doesn't get drunk every once in a while and take his belt to those boys?'

She drew in a sharp breath. 'Why would you think that?' she whispered, her eyes wide with shock.

He shrugged but the movement felt stiff. 'Because it happens.'

'Your father did that to you, didn't he?' she said softly.

His heart slammed into his ribcage. 'How would you know that?' he said, carefully.

Seeing the compassion, the concern in her face, he wondered why the hell he'd started this conversation.

'You talk in your sleep, Connor, when you're having the nightmares.' Daisy watched his jaw tighten, the cocky smile gone from his face. And her heart bled for him. 'And I've seen the scars on your back.' But how many more scars, she wondered, did he have on his heart?

Jessie had said his attitude to family, to kids, was all mixed up in his past. She knew she shouldn't pry, that she really had no right to pry, but suddenly she just wanted to know. She'd accepted that this had to be a temporary fling, because he wasn't looking for permanent, and she couldn't change that. But suddenly she wanted to know why. Why would he want to deny himself the one thing in life that really mattered?

'Will you tell me about it?'

He gave a half-laugh, but it had a hollow ring that stabbed at Daisy's chest. 'There's nothing much to tell,' he said. 'My mother died. Left my Da on his own with six kids.' His Adam's apple bobbed as he swallowed. 'He came home that night from the hospital, cried like a baby and got blind drunk. And after that everything changed.' He plucked some grass up, rubbed it between his fingers.

She waited, a part of her scared to hear what he had to say, a part of her desperate to know so she could understand. 'How did it change?' she said gently.

He dropped the grass, rubbed his hands on his jeans. 'First off it was no more than a back hand to the head, or a punch now and again you weren't expecting. But then it was the flat of his belt, the heel of his boot, until you passed out. The drink changed him and he couldn't control it.'

Tears spilled over Daisy's lids, but she wiped them hastily away; from the monotone of his voice she could tell he didn't want her sympathy.

'My brother Mac and me, we'd wait at the window, watch for him. Mac would make the tea, and I'd bathe the girls, get them fed and tucked in before he got home. On a good night, he'd be so locked he could barely walk, so we'd feed him and pour him into bed and that would be the end of it.

But on a bad night…' He paused. His eyes met hers. 'That's not happy families, Daisy. That's barely living.'

She cradled his cheek in her palm, desperate to give what little comfort she could. 'I'm so sorry, Connor.'

He pulled away, instantly defensive. 'There's nothing to be sorry for.'

'No child should have to endure that. Not ever.'

He caught a tear on his thumb, wiped it away. 'Don't, Daisy. It's not a bad story, not really. I got out. I made a life for myself apart from all that. A life I'm happy with.'

But it's only half a life, she wanted to say. Couldn't he see that? 'What happened to Mac and your sisters?'

'My…' He stopped, and for the first time since he'd started talking she saw the raw flash of remembered pain. But he collected himself quickly and it was gone. 'The authorities found out what had been going on. We got separated… Fostered and adopted.'

'Did you manage to keep in touch?'

'No. I've not seen them since. But Mac's a movie actor now. Goes by his full name of Cormac.'

'Cormac Brody?' Daisy blinked. She couldn't believe it. 'Your brother's Cormac Brody?' His brother was the Irish actor who'd taken Hollywood by storm in the last few years? Now she thought about it, she could see the resemblance. Both Connor and his brother had the same piercing blue eyes and dark good looks—and that devil-may-care charm. 'But if you know that why haven't you contacted him? Surely his agent would—'

'Why would I?' he interrupted her. 'He's not part of my life and I'm not part of his. I missed him for a while.' He shrugged, his apparent indifference stunning her. 'Just like I missed all of them, but they were better off without me and I was better off without them.'

'But that's not true,' she said, unable to bear the brittle

cynicism in his voice. 'Everyone should have a family. You need them. They're part of you.'

'Daisy, don't,' he said, lifting her chin between his thumb and forefinger. 'It is true. It's the way I want it. Sure, when I was little I used to lie awake nights, praying to Our Lady that my mammy would come back. That my Da would stop drinking. That everything would go back to how it was and we could all be a happy family again. But I learned a valuable lesson. You can't go back, you can only go forward. And you can't rely on anyone. Nothing's certain. Nothing lasts. Life gets in the way, good and bad. Like you got in my way. So we enjoy it while it lasts and take everything we can grab. And that's enough.'

But it wasn't enough, she thought. Not nearly enough. Not for anyone.

He put his arm around her shoulders as they walked back across the park. As the sun dipped towards dusk, giving the fairy castle a golden glow, Daisy considered all the things he'd told her and felt her fantasy collapse and reality come flooding in.

So now she knew. Connor lived in the moment, shunned responsibility and had persuaded himself that family wasn't for him, not because he was selfish, or shallow, or self-absorbed, but because of that abused traumatised little boy who had been forced to grow up too soon, and shoulder a responsibility that should never have been his.

He wasn't scared of commitment, she realised. He was just scared of taking a chance, scared of wanting something that could blow up in his face all over again.

What a couple of cowards they both were.

Because while he'd been scared to take a chance, she'd been so scared of making her mother's mistakes she'd side-stepped, and avoided and denied the obvious all along.

That she was falling hopelessly in love with him.

She bit into her lip, determined not to let her emotional turmoil show as the enormity of what she'd just admitted to herself sank in.

Oh, God, what on earth was she going to do now?

CHAPTER FOURTEEN

As CONNOR stood beside her in a perfectly tailored tuxedo like her own Prince Charming, Daisy let her eyes wander over the magnificent ballroom and began to wonder how much more surreal her life could become. Chandeliers cast a shimmering light on the assembled throng. Women preened like peacocks in their latest designer plumage and men looked important and debonair in their dark dinner suits. The ball was an annual event hosted by the New York Governor for some deserving charity, but according to Connor it was really just an excuse for the state's most prominent citizens to show off.

The necklace he'd given her felt cool against her cleavage, matching the emerald satin gown she'd hastily put together on her second-hand sewing machine a lifetime ago. Daisy took a deep breath, and rested her hand on Connor's sleeve, trying to get her balance. Ever since they'd got back from the park her emotions had been in uproar, her senses reeling. But she had managed to make one important decision this evening. She planned to live the last of her grand adventure tonight to the max. She'd have time enough tomorrow to panic about her wayward heart.

'Daisy, that dress is sensational.'

Daisy turned to see Jessie Latimer, a champagne flute in her hand and a friendly grin on her face. 'Where ever did you get it?' she said. 'Enquiring minds want to know.'

'I…' She hesitated, wondering if it was the done thing to admit you'd made your own ball gown.

'She made it herself.' Connor smoothed his hand over the ruched satin at her hip and hugged her to his side, his gaze darkening with appreciation. 'Not just gorgeous but talented too,' he murmured against her neck.

Daisy could feel the pulse hammering in her throat as Jessie gave her a pointed look over Connor's shoulder.

'That's amazing,' she said. 'Listen, Daisy, I've told my sister Ali all about you and I'd love you to meet her. Actually, it's sort of a mercy mission.' She took Daisy's hand. 'She found out yesterday she's expecting again and she's in a state of shock. I need you to help take her mind off it.'

Daisy acknowledged the little prickle of envy and ignored it. She'd have her big happy family one day. She'd make sure of it. 'I'd love to meet her,' she said, and meant it. A little time spent away from Connor wouldn't necessarily be a bad thing. It might help her get her heart rate under control in preparation for the night ahead.

Connor gave a mock shudder. 'Ali's pregnant again? What's that? Number four?'

Jessie nodded, giving Daisy's hand a tug. 'Actually the doctor said it may be number four and five. She's so huge already. Hence the shock.'

Connor frowned as Daisy stepped out of his arms. 'Wait a minute. Why don't I come over? I can congratulate her.'

Jessie pushed her finger into his chest. 'This is strictly girls only, big boy. Linc and Monroe are over by the bar trying to finesse a couple of beers out of the barman. Go play with them.'

As Jessie led her through the crowd of Manhattan's elite Daisy couldn't resist a glance over her shoulder at Connor. Her heartbeat slowed and her stomach tightened. He still stood where she'd left him, looking impossibly dashing in the middle of the crowded ballroom in his black tuxedo with an irritated frown on his face and his hands thrust into his pockets as he watched her go.

She heaved out a breath. Okay, she was falling in love, but that didn't mean she had to get stupid. All she had to do now was keep the brakes on, enjoy tonight and then confront him tomorrow. See where she stood. Maybe she'd fallen for her romantic fairy tale, but it didn't mean she couldn't still be practical, sensible. Love might be blind, but it didn't have to turn you into an idiot. She still knew what she wanted out of life and, whatever Connor's reasons, he'd made it very clear that afternoon he didn't want the same things. Unless he was falling in love with her too, that wasn't going to change.

'There's definitely something to be said for a bad boy in a tux,' Jessie said quietly, interrupting Daisy's latest strategy briefing.

Daisy's head whipped round. The considering look in Jessie's eyes spoke volumes: Daisy had been staring at Connor for far too long. 'Yes, I suppose so,' she said, trying for practical and getting breathless instead.

'How's it going? We don't have to meet Ali. I just thought you might like a little downtime before the dancing begins. You both look a little shell-shocked. Did something happen?'

She was certainly shell-shocked, she thought. But she wasn't so sure about Connor. She'd caught him watching her, a wary, cautious look in his eyes when they'd been in the cab coming back from the park. That look was the reason she'd decided not to blurt out how she felt. Why ruin the mood before she was absolutely sure? And anyway, she'd wanted to have tonight to add to her memories before it all went belly up, as she was fast suspecting it would. He might need a family, but he didn't necessarily need her. What on earth did she really have to offer him that he couldn't get from a hundred other, much more sophisticated women?

'Don't be silly,' Daisy said, almost choking on the fake bonhomie. 'Nothing's wrong.' Well, not yet. 'This is all just a bit much for a girl from Portobello Road, that's all.'

'Yes, the Americans do excess so well, don't you think?' Jessie smiled back, but Daisy could see she was being kind and letting her off the hook. 'Oh, good grief!' Jessie said, her eyes lighting on something over Daisy's shoulder. 'That woman is a complete menace. Poor Lincoln had to peel her off him ten minutes ago and now she's got Connor in her sights.'

Daisy looked round. All the colour drained out of her face and then pumped back into her cheeks. Wrapped around Connor like a second skin was a pneumatic blonde with a skirt that barely covered her butt and boobs that could poke someone's eye out.

He still had his hands in his pockets, and his body language didn't suggest he was enjoying the encounter all that much, but as the woman leaned closer to whisper something in his ear he took one hand out and rested it on her waist.

A red haze blurred Daisy's vision. 'Who is she?' she asked, her voice calm despite the volcanic eruption bubbling beneath her breastbone.

Doesn't she know he's engaged? she almost added. Then realised her mistake. The molten magma got hotter.

'Mitzi Melrose, the biggest flirt on the planet,' Jessie said. 'Her husband's Eldridge Melrose, billionaire financier, and I don't think he's got what it takes to satisfy our Mitzi if her relentless poaching is anything...' Jessie's voice slowly receded until all Daisy could hear was the buzzing of a thousand chainsaws, her gaze transfixed on her fake fiancé and the floozy.

The Botoxed bimbo was leaning into him now, her pillar-box lips practically touching his ear lobe and her gravity-defying cleavage as good as propped on his forearm.

And, as far as Daisy could tell, Connor wasn't doing a damn thing about it. He'd taken his hand off her hip, sure, stuck it back in his pocket, but he hadn't moved away, had he? She'd never been the jealous type, even with Gary, who'd been an inveterate flirt. Daisy, being the practical, sensible, focussed woman she was, had always thought that possessive women who couldn't trust their partners were creatures to be pitied. But right at this moment she could sympathise with them completely.

She had Connor's ring on her finger. Maybe it was a temporary ring and a fake engagement, but, still, she'd worn it because he'd asked her, she'd let him introduce her to everyone as his bride-to-be and now he had another woman glued to his torso. And if that weren't bad enough, he'd made her fall in love with him, the stupid dolt.

'Jessie, you'll have to excuse me for a minute,' she said, still glaring at her non-fiancé.

'Go for it,' she heard Jessie say with a suspicious lift in her voice. But Daisy didn't have time to process it as she sailed back through the crowd propelled on a wave of righteous anger, the surge of adrenaline making her heartbeat pound in her ears and her skin flush red.

She'd been an idiot. She'd lived in the moment, soaked up every single speck of excitement and in the process lost a crucial part of herself. She was her own woman. And yet, somehow or other, she'd ended up letting Connor call all the shots. He'd got her to New York, he'd got her back in his bed, he'd put his ring on her finger and what had she got? Quite possibly a broken heart, that was what. Fine, she'd deal with that if she had to, but he was not going to get away with pawing another woman in public when he was supposed to be engaged to her. The engagement might be fake, but her feelings were real. She might not have his love, but she intended to have his respect.

His head lifted as she walked towards him, as if he'd sensed her approach, those magnetic eyes fixed on her face and he smiled.

He might as well have pulled out a red bandanna and waved it in front of her nose. What, she'd like to know, was so flipping amusing?

Connor tuned out Mitzi's breathy whisper. His heart pounded as he watched the satin gown Daisy had made shimmer, spotlighting those provocative curves to perfection. He couldn't make out her expression in the muted lighting, but the vision of high cheekbones, fine, alabaster skin and glossy red curls made all his senses stand up and pay attention. His annoyance and impatience dimmed, to be replaced by a rush of longing that he didn't understand—and didn't want to understand.

Even though she was still several feet away he could have sworn he could smell that spicy, erotic scent of hers, and feel the soft swell of her breasts beneath his fingertips.

The truth was, he'd never been a fan of networking, of getting all spruced up and showing himself off. But ever since Daisy had walked out of their bedroom earlier decked out in the ball gown, the green satin hugging her curves and making him ache in some very interesting places, the thought of going to the Governor's Ball and mingling with people he didn't give a hoot about had become considerably less appealing.

What he'd wanted to do was stay in their suite and make love to her for the rest of the evening, then listen to her talk—he adored how she drifted from topic to topic without pausing for breath in that practical, no-nonsense way she had—and then he'd planned to fall asleep with her head pillowed on his chest.

But after all the things he'd told her in the park, he'd been forced to dismiss the idea. He'd let things get too serious again without intending to, telling her things he shouldn't about his past, and then, to top it all, he'd seen the tenderness, the longing in her eyes when he'd put his arm on her shoulders and he wasn't sure what to make of it. She hadn't challenged him about what he'd said, she'd simply accepted it—but he'd been waiting for the axe to fall ever since. For her to tell him how wrong he was for her. For her to throw his past back in his face. For her to demand more from him than he could ever give. But she hadn't done it, and it was making him crazy.

But once they'd been in the limo, her seductive scent tantalising him, he'd finally had to face the fact that he wasn't going to be able to let her go when they returned to England tomorrow as he'd planned. He'd thought that if he sated himself on her during these two weeks in New York, he'd be well over his infatuation by now, but she still captivated him as much, if not more, than she had the first time they'd made love.

She was less than five paces away from him when the chandelier illuminated her face at last. He could see anger and determination swirling in those expressive emerald eyes, and his stomach pitched. Had the penny finally dropped? Was she about to give him the boot?

He clamped down on the sudden surge of panic, the strangling feeling of pain and regret closing his throat. That was too bad. Because whatever was going on between them, it wasn't over. He still had unfinished business with her and if she thought he was going to let her dump him, she'd have to think again.

* * *

'Hi, Connor, why don't you introduce me to your new best friend?' Daisy said sweetly. Sweetly enough to cause tooth decay.

The bimbo had her hand on his lapel now. Daisy's fingers clenched into a fist. She resisted the urge to slug the woman. But only just.

Connor looked momentarily confused, then glanced at the bimbo. 'Oh, yeah, Mitzi, this is Daisy Dean, my fiancée. Do you think you could leave us be for—?'

Mitzi cut off whatever he was going to say with an ear-splitting giggle. 'Your fiancée? You've got to be kidding me.' Her high-pitched voice piped out like Marilyn Monroe on helium. 'You never said you were getting married, sweetie.' She pressed one of her scarlet-tipped talons against Connor's cheek and giggled again before sending Daisy a smile filled with enough malice to make Mussolini look like a pussycat. 'Why, I guess it must have slipped his mind, we were having such a good time and all.' She shoved her expertly moulded breasts forward. 'But then men get distracted so easily, don't they, honey?'

Screw restraint. Daisy wasn't taking *that* lying down. 'Yes, they do.' She smiled sharply. 'Especially when they're being smothered in enough cheap perfume to fell an ox.'

Mitzi's jaw dropped comically. 'Huh?'

'Daisy, what's got into you?' Connor said, gripping her arm and stepping to her side.

She thrust her chin up, willing her bottom lip to stop quivering. 'Oh, I don't know, Connor. Maybe it's that you're wrapped around her when you're supposed to be engaged to me.'

He looked at her as if she were talking in tongues. 'Whoah?'

And she lost it. So this was what it boiled down to, she thought, as her fury—with herself as well as him—raged out of control.

He whisked her off to New York, he told everyone they were a couple, he said things to her she was sure he'd never said to anyone else and he made love to her with a power and a passion that made her lose her grip on reality. But when push came to shove, it had all been a game—at least for him. She was just another of the women he'd charmed into bed.

'You heard me, Connor. Either you respect me. Or you don't. You can't have it both ways.'

'I paid a grand a bottle for this stuff, you little bitch,' Mitzi shrieked.

'Shut up, Mitzi!' he snarled.

'I'm gonna tell my husband about this,' Mitzi squeaked as she shrank back. 'Don't you think I won't and you can kiss that damn deal goodbye.'

'Be my guest, now get lost.' He threw the words over his shoulder, his eyes still fixed on Daisy's face.

The woman flounced off with an audible huff and Daisy became aware of the silence around them. At least twenty pairs of eyes were fixed on their little theatrical display.

'Now why don't you tell me what the hell is going on here?' Connor announced, as if she were a naughty child, completely oblivious to their audience.

Daisy tried to step away from him, humiliation swamping her. But he was still holding her arm.

Oh, God, what had she done? She'd let her anger and uncertainty take over and now she'd made a complete spectacle of herself. But as if that weren't bad enough, Connor was looking at her as if she'd lost her marbles. She felt the tears sting her eyes and pushed them back. It was so grossly unfair. Why did she have to be the one to fall in love?

She bit the sob back. Forget it, she wasn't going to cry over him. And definitely not with all these people watching. 'Let go of my arm. I want to go back to the hotel,' she whispered. 'We're making a scene.'

'The hell with that.' He took her other arm, pulled her close despite her struggles. 'You're going to tell me what you meant. Of course I respect you—how could I not?'

'I'm not talking about this. Not now.' Not ever. It would just humiliate her more. He wasn't going to make her break.

'Oh, yes, you are. I'm sick of waiting for you to say it.'

Waiting for her to say what? But before she could figure out what the heck he was talking about, he clamped his hand on her wrist and started dragging her through the crowd. A sea of heads turned to stare at them both as he marched her out of the ballroom. She'd never been more mortified in her life. But what was worse, much worse, was the thought that he might make her crack and reveal everything—and then she'd be completely at his mercy.

He slammed into the ladies' powder room. The elderly matron busy fluffing her hair in front of the ornate mirror glanced up.

'Why, Connor Brody,' she said. Daisy blinked. Had the old dame just batted her eyelids at him? 'What are you doing in the Ladies' Lounge, you bad boy?'

Connor smiled back, giving her the full blast of his lethal Celtic charm. Daisy barely resisted the urge to kick him. First Mitzi and now a woman three times his age. Did he never know when to turn it off?

'Mrs Gildenstern, it's a pleasure.'

Good God, she'd fallen for the playboy of the Western World. Daisy snorted indignantly, but they both ignored her.

'I need a moment with my fiancée in private,' he said.

'So this is the lucky girl?' the woman purred, fluffing her hair some more and sending Daisy a flirtatious wink. She got up and touched Connor's arm. 'You go right ahead, my boy,' she said. 'I'll make sure no one disturbs you.' Her paper-thin skin crinkled as she grinned. 'But don't you two get up to anything I wouldn't,' she finished as she left the room, chortling like a naughty schoolgirl.

'Sure, thanks, Mrs G,' Connor finished distractedly. He turned to Daisy, all traces of that industrial-strength charm wiped out by a dark scowl. 'Now I want to know what's going on.'

'I don't need to tell you a thing.'

'Oh, yeah.' He pressed her back against the vanity unit, hard thighs trapping her hips, hot hands clamping on the exposed skin of her back and the smell of soap and pheromones overwhelming her. 'Think again. Because you're not getting out of here till you do.'

The warm spot between her legs pulsed hot. She slapped her hands against his chest, and shoved. He barely budged. She glared at him some more. He didn't even flinch.

'I didn't like seeing you paw that floozy,' she said grudgingly. 'But now I'm over it.' *Almost.*

'What floozy? You mean Mitzi?' he said, sounding so astonished the old red rag popped out again and ruined all her best intentions.

'Yes Mitzi. I mean, I know this relationship is a sham. I know we're only pretending to be engaged.' When exactly had she lost sight of that? 'But if you could refrain from smooching with other women in public I'd appreciate it. I happen to have some pride, you know.' Although she'd lost sight of that too somewhere. 'Just because I don't have mile-long legs and breasts that will still be perky when I'm dead. As far as everyone here is concerned I *am* your fiancée and that ought to entitle me to a tiny iota of your respect.'

Now she sounded pathetic too. She wanted to kill him. How had he managed to turn her into a desperate, grasping, needy nutcase that she didn't even recognise?

His scowl deepened momentarily and then his eyebrows

kicked up. 'Jesus. You're jealous,' he murmured incredulously.

'I am not jealous,' she shot back. 'That would make me an imbecile.' Wouldn't it just?

'Yes, you are,' he said, flashing her that megawatt grin. The satisfied gleam in his eyes lit Daisy's temper up like a Chinese firecracker.

'That does it. I'm out of here.' She struggled, but he simply grabbed her waist and held her still. Then his thumbs slipped under the satin of her gown, trailing goosebumps in their wake. She gasped.

'I've got to tell you,' he murmured, his fingers caressing bare skin as his hands wrapped round her, 'you're magnificent when you're mad, angel.' He chuckled, the sound throaty and self-satisfied and wholly male.

Fury engulfed her. She was not going to get sidetracked, not again.

'Don't you dare laugh at me,' she said, 'or I'll slug you.'

She freed her arm and tried to take aim, but he caught her fist in his, laughing as he kissed her knuckles. 'Now, now, angel. Don't get nasty.'

Then she felt it, the solid length of his arousal, outlined against the soft swell of her belly. Heat spiralled from her core and she struggled in earnest. 'No. No way,' she yelped, staring into his eyes and seeing the intent on his face. 'Forget it. We are not making love. If you haven't noticed, we're having an argument.'

'Pay attention, angel,' he said as his clever fingers whisked down the zip on her dress. 'We've had the argument.' The bodice fell away, baring her lacy push-up bra. 'And we're about to have the make-up sex.'

'But we're in the powder room. We can't,' she shouted, frantic and afraid and already so turned on she was sure she was about to explode.

This wasn't possible. It couldn't be happening. She'd never made love in a public place before. 'We can't, anyone could walk in,' she said, her voice rising in panic as he pushed her bra up.

'Don't worry, no one messes with Mrs G,' he said, weighing her breast in his palm.

'But what if Mrs Gildenstern dies of a heart attack?' she blurted out, her voice rising in panic as his fingers played havoc. 'What if the fire alarm goes off? What if the SAS storms the building?'

He fastened hot lips on her nipple, suckled strongly. She choked out a sob as he teased and bit the engorged peak—and every single coherent thought flew right out of her head.

She threaded her fingers through his hair, held on as her head bumped the mirror and she gave herself up to the fireball of sensations.

He lifted her panting onto the vanity unit, brushed his hands up her legs under the billowing satin and plunged his fingers into the heart of her.

'I want you, Daisy. More than I've ever wanted any woman.' He stroked the slick folds of her sex as she bucked against his hand. Then his lips took hers in a kiss so passionate, she could taste his vicious arousal matching her own.

She stared dumbly, her body trembling with need as he pulled the condom out of his breast pocket with unsteady fingers and freed himself from his trousers.

She whimpered as he held her hips, pushed her panties to one side and entered her in one long, relentless thrust. As she clung to him all her thoughts, all her feelings, centred on the exquisite joy pulsating through her. She rode on the crest for an eternity as his powerful strokes took him deeper. She heard his low groan, felt his shoulders stiffen as she took that last wild leap into oblivion.

Her fingers trembled on the damp curls at his nape, her

senses spinning as she listened to the ragged pants of their breathing and her thundering heartbeat, the sounds harsh and uncivilised against the soft strains of music from the ballroom beyond.

He lifted his head and his eyes met hers—determination making the deep blue of his irises glow with purpose.

'This isn't over. Not yet.' His hands stroked her thighs, squeezed. 'You know that, right?'

She could hear the urgency in his voice, the yearning, and her heart swelled with hope. 'I know,' she whispered.

She felt herself plunging into the chasm—but knew she wasn't falling in love any more, she'd fallen.

CHAPTER FIFTEEN

DAISY slept fitfully on the flight home, despite the flat bed, the world-class service and the fact that she was physically and mentally exhausted from the emotional roller-coaster ride her life had somehow become. She couldn't even get a good firm grip on all the 'what ifs' whirring about in her mind, let alone answer any of them.

What if she told him she loved him and he looked angry? What if she told him and he looked bored? What if he thought she was delusional? What if she was?

She resigned herself to the fact that whatever happened she would have to tell him, because the 'what ifs' would drive her completely doolally if she didn't. And then she started stressing over the 'When'. Eventually she fell asleep over Nova Scotia, Connor's hand resting on her hip, knowing that when she got home she would have to face one of the toughest conversations of her life. But she promised herself, whatever happened, she would not wimp out—and she wouldn't let Connor wimp out either. He was going to have to come up with something a bit more substantial than, 'Not Yet'.

* * *

'Wake up, angel. We're home.'

The minute he'd said the H word, Connor felt the little spurt of panic.

Don't be an idiot, it's an expression. It doesn't mean a thing.

He shook Daisy again, leaned down to kiss her cheek. Her lids fluttered open, her eyes fixing on his face. He felt the twist in his chest as he stared into the mermaid green, and the spurt got worse.

Why couldn't he let her go?

He'd been awake during the whole of their transatlantic flight, her lush body curled up next to his, trying to figure it out. She hadn't gone the route of most females and tried to pin him down. That had to be it. As soon as she did the honeymoon period would be over. But a moment ago, when the car had pulled up at the house in Portobello, and he'd turned to see Daisy by his side, he'd begun to wonder if he wasn't in serious trouble. She'd snuck under his guard somehow—and he didn't like it.

'Mmm…' She stretched, giving him a peek of the purple lace of her bra through the buttonholes of her blouse. He felt the familiar punch of lust.

And why did he still want her? All the damn time? Had she put some kind of spell on him?

'Are we home?' she asked around a jaw-breaking yawn.

And there was that H word again. He didn't like it.

'Yeah.' He pushed back, stepped out of the limo. Maybe he needed to get away from her for a while, take a time-out. But even as he thought of letting her go, even for just one night, her hand clasped his as she stepped out of the car and he knew he couldn't do it. The spurt became a flood.

The chauffeur deposited their luggage on the kerb, tipped his hat. 'Would you like me to take them into the house, sir?'

'No, that's grand,' he said, dragging a roll of bills from his pocket and flicking out a tenner. 'Thanks for your help, Joe.'

He watched the long black Mercedes drive away and settled on his course of action. He'd keep her with him for the next little while. He wanted her with him, in his house. But he'd make damn sure she didn't get any closer. She was too close already.

He shoved one of the smaller suitcases under his arm, picked up the two larger. 'Let's take these up to mine. We need to talk.'

She blinked lids still heavy with sleep, her cheeks coloured. 'You know?' she said.

'Know what?' he asked.

Then she looked past him, her eyes widening, and all the pink leached out of her face. The small carry-on bag she carried clattered onto the pavement.

'What's that?' she asked, pointing past him.

He glanced over his shoulder and spotted the For Sale sign. He'd forgotten all about his conversation with the estate agent three weeks ago. He turned back and saw the horror on her face and the sparkle of unshed tears. Something fierce and protective clasped his heart—and not for the first time.

'You're moving out?' she said, her voice so quiet he could barely hear it.

His first instinct was to tell her he wasn't. He didn't want to any more. But the minute the need to calm and to nurture welled up inside him, the panic closed around his throat. What was wrong with him? He didn't want anything permanent. He didn't need the responsibility. He'd had permanent before, he'd had responsibility and he'd failed at it spectacularly. He couldn't risk it again. This was his get-out clause. He couldn't afford to throw it away.

He shrugged, forced himself to ignore the misery in her eyes. 'Sure. But with the market as it is, it'll take a while to sell.' Long enough, he hoped, for him to get over this infatuation once and for all. 'Until then we can continue to enjoy each other. It's been fun so far,' he said, struggling to keep the seductive smile in place.

Daisy felt as if she'd been punched in the gut.

He was selling the house, moving out, and he hadn't even bothered to tell her? And he was looking at her now, his face calm and nonchalant, as if to say, 'Why would I?' It was the same stubborn look he'd had on his face when she'd asked him why he had never contacted his movie-star brother. She looked down at the ring he'd given her and realised just how delusional she'd allowed herself to get.

She gulped down the tears tightening her throat, straightened her spine. 'No, thanks. I'd rather make a clean break,' she said. 'Here.' She tugged the silver band loose and held it out to him. 'I should give this back to you.'

His jaw tightened as he looked down at the ring. He put the suitcases down, but made no move to take it. 'Come on, angel. Don't overreact. This isn't a big deal.'

Maybe not to him, she thought, her heart shattering inside her. Her fingers curled around the ring and she felt the tiny diamonds cut into her palm.

'Actually it is a big deal. Because I've fallen in love with you, you stupid moron.' It wasn't exactly how she'd planned to tell him, but even so his reaction was worse than any she could have imagined.

His mouth dropped open and his skin paled beneath the tan. 'Whoah, what's that now?'

Horrified. He looked horrified. Well, at least she had the answer to her 'What if'.

Biting down on her lips so hard she tasted blood, she lifted his hand and slapped the ring into it. 'It's okay, Connor. It's my mistake. I'll go quietly. I'm not even going to make a scene.'

She thought of all the scenes her mother had made, all the scenes she'd had to witness over the years, and forced the vicious pain back, buried it deep. The only thing she had left was pride—and she couldn't afford to throw it away, because she had a feeling she was going to need it.

She picked up her bag to leave, but he took her arm, pulled her round to face him.

'What's this now? You don't love me. That's rubbish. Since when?'

He didn't sound horrified any more; he sounded angry. He wasn't the only one.

'Don't tell me how I feel. I do love you, Connor. But you know what? I'm not asking for anything in return. Especially as it's pretty obvious you don't want to give it to me.'

She yanked her arm out of his, but he grabbed her back. 'Hold on a minute. You can't tell me you love me then storm off. That's madness.'

'Yes, I can, because you don't love me back,' she shouted, then realised she was making a scene after all. Damn it. 'Well, do you?' she whispered.

He flinched and she felt nausea churn in her stomach.

'I don't love anyone,' he said. 'I'm no good at it.' Was that supposed to make her feel better? 'I don't want this. I told you that.'

She shook her head, the tears choking her. 'I know you did, Connor.' And he had, he had told her. And it was her own stupid fault that she hadn't listened. Or rather, she'd listened with her heart, instead of her head, and she'd got it wrong.

Daisy sighed, suddenly desperately weary, and sick to her heart as well as her stomach.

'Don't worry, Connor. I'll survive. I'll see you around.'

She turned but he called after her. 'Daisy, don't go. Let's at least talk about this some more.'

Didn't he know there was nothing else to say?

She waved over her shoulder. 'I'll be around, maybe later,' she said. Knowing full well that she'd be conveniently absent if he came to call. She'd do whatever she had to do to avoid him over the coming weeks—until he lost interest and moved on to his next conquest—and in the meantime she'd try to repair her heart.

As she walked the few short steps to her home, the sound of her suitcase wheels rolling on the pavement matching the click-click of her heels, she felt her stomach pitch—and refused to look back. She had never felt more bitterly ashamed of herself in her life.

Despite all her care over the years, despite all her caution. She'd got caught in the same foolish trap as her mother—of falling in love with the wrong guy, and hoping against all the odds that he might love her back. And he hadn't.

Connor dropped the suitcases on the floor and slammed the door shut. Well, that hadn't exactly gone according to plan. And where the hell had she got the stupid idea she loved him? It was insane.

He dumped his keys on the hall table, saw the stack of post, left it where it lay and walked down the hallway.

She'd get over it soon enough. Things had got too hot and heavy over the last fortnight. They'd been living in each other's pockets, after all. A little while cooling off would be all for the best. And then they could pick up where they'd left off.

But as he entered the open-plan kitchen, the sunlight pouring through the windows and shining off the polished oak, his gut tightened with dread and the sense of being trapped closed over him like a shroud.

What if she wouldn't come back?

He stared at the bright airy space, the gleaming glass cabinets, and felt as if they were mocking him. He fished the ring out of his pocket, dropped it on the counter top, then gazed out into the garden where he'd first spotted her three long weeks ago.

And for the first time since he'd been a boy, he wanted to pray for something he knew he could never have.

He heaved out a sigh, pushed the ring into a drawer. This was madness. He was just jet-lagged and a little shaken by how devastated she'd looked. But she'd get over it. He'd told her the truth, after all. He didn't love her. He couldn't. He'd always sworn he would never fall in love and that would never change. But he'd get her back, because he wanted her and he knew damn well she still wanted him.

But even as he tried to persuade himself there was nothing to worry about he had the niggling feeling that he'd let something irreplaceable slip through his fingers and there would be no getting it back, no matter how hard he tried.

CHAPTER SIXTEEN

DAISY stifled her tears as she opened her suitcase and saw all the mementoes she'd saved so carefully sitting on the top. The sweetly tacky tourist photo of her in Connor's arms atop the Empire State. The ticket stub from her first and no doubt last Broadway show. A napkin from the Rainbow Room. She also held firm as she folded away the cocktail dress and the ball gown and wondered when she'd ever get the chance to wear them again.

Having showered and changed into her work uniform of jeans and a Funky Fashionista T-shirt, she walked to the stall. Buffeted by the tide of tourists flowing through Portobello Market on a sunny Sunday morning, she ignored the ropey feeling in her stomach and the foggy feeling of exhaustion and still refused to let a single tear fall.

She'd been a fool—that was all. She could cope with this, as she'd coped with every other disappointment in her life. Her throat felt raw now, as if a boulder had got jammed down it, but this wasn't really so terrible. She'd allowed herself to get carried away. When she looked back on this, years from now, she'd see it as a valuable learning experience. Almost certainly.

She sucked in a tremulous breath, returned the wave of a stallholder she knew.

She still had her dream. One day she'd find the right man for her. Connor had never been that man. She'd allowed the stardust and the glamour and the magic of the moment to blind her to the truth. She strolled up the busy thoroughfare, loaded with stalls selling everything from plaintains to paper-chains, crossed her arms over her chest and held in the tearing pain.

She'd get past this, and when she did she'd be able to remember her time with Connor as a dazzlingly exciting and wonderful romantic adventure and nothing more. So a tiny part of her heart would always be lost to him, would always wish that maybe things might have been different, that he might have wanted what she had to offer. But he hadn't and she'd be a fool to think she could change him. Wasn't that the mistake her mother had always made?

As she spotted her stall up ahead, the rainbow of cotton dresses and silk scarves she'd made and designed flapping in the breeze, a small smile quivered on her lips. This was her real life. And she loved it. This was what made her different from her mother. She'd sampled the drug that had driven her mother to find love in the wrong places and for two glorious weeks she'd ridden the high. But she could live without it if she had to. Steady, dependable, reliable was what she needed in her life—and she was the only one who could make that happen.

She stepped up to the stall, a brave smile firmed in place. 'Hey, got a blouse you can sell me?'

Juno's head came up. 'Daisy, you're back.' Her best friend dived round the stall, a welcoming grin on her face and her arms open wide. 'How did it go?'

But as Juno's arms folded around her, the emotions she'd

been holding back so beautifully rose up like a summer storm and burst out of her mouth in a soul-drenching sob.

'Daisy, what is it? What happened? What's wrong?' She could barely hear Juno's frantic questions over the gulping cries ripping her apart.

Juno held on, patting her shoulders, whispering calming words until the sobs subsided, the wrenching pain tightening into a ball of misery. Daisy drew back, scrubbed an impatient hand across her cheeks. 'God, I'm sorry.'

Jacie stared at her over Juno's shoulder, wide-eyed with concern. 'Blimey, Daze. What's the matter? I've never seen you cry like that. Never.'

Juno gripped her upper arms, stood back, her eyes hard. 'He did this, didn't he?'

Daisy hiccoughed, the crying jag not quite done with. 'I fell in love with him, Ju.' A final tear slipped over her lid. She brushed it away. 'What a plonker, eh?'

'Oh, Daze,' Juno said, and hauled Daisy back into her arms for another hard hug. Then she pushed her back, fixed her eyes on Daisy. 'Did you tell him how you feel?'

'Yes, I did. And he doesn't feel the same way,' Daisy said, the admission, spoken out loud, making the depression suffocate her. 'So that's the end of it.' She walked round the stall and accepted Jacie's quick hug.

'Are you sure?' Jacie questioned, ever the optimist.

'Positive,' she murmured, her voice cracking on the finality of it all.

Jacie looked ready to question her some more, but Daisy was saved by a customer eager to buy a shawl.

Juno drew her to one side. 'He's not worthy of you,' she said. 'I thought he was a total scumbag the moment I laid eyes on him. And this confirms it.'

But he wasn't a scumbag, Daisy thought. He was a good man, not the right man maybe, but still a good man. Daisy pressed her fingers to Juno's lips. 'It's okay, Juno. I'll get over him.' She sighed. 'Eventually. We just weren't right for each other. I knew that from the start and I was a fool to think anything else. Anyway.' Daisy paused, blew out a breath. 'He's selling his house, moving on, so at least I won't have to be constantly reminded of my stupidity.'

Why didn't the thought make her feel any better, though?

In fact… She slapped a hand over her mouth as the nausea rose up to gag her.

'Quick, Juno, hand me a bag,' she cried, her voice muffled. 'I'm going to be sick.'

Juno thrust one of the stall's recycled plastic shopping bags into her hand and Daisy lost the contents of her stomach.

'Daze, are you okay?' Juno rubbed her back and took the bag out of her hands. 'Here, I'll go dump this.'

Daisy groaned. She was never ill. The events of the last hour had been fairly shattering, but, honestly, wasn't it about time she started pulling herself together?

'Gosh, Daisy, how do you feel?' Jacie remarked from beside her.

Daisy put her hand to her stomach. 'Not great, actually.' How could she still feel nauseous? She'd thrown up everything she'd eaten in the last twelve hours. 'I guess it's the emotional overload.'

'Either that or you're pregnant.'

Daisy's head shot up. 'That's not even funny, Jace. Not to mention a physical impossibility.' She sighed; at least she hadn't been stupid enough to sleep with Connor without protection.

'Are you on your period, then?' Jacie's eyes dropped to her chest. 'Because your boobs look enormous.'

Daisy glanced down. Her cleavage *was* looking rather

more spectacular than usual, even accounting for her push-up bra. 'It's nothing. I'm due any day now, that's all.'

Wait a minute. When was her last period? In all the excitement of the last few weeks she'd forgotten about it. But... 'What's the date?' she asked.

'The twenty-fifth,' Juno said carefully, having returned from her trip to the bin.

Daisy's blood rushed out of her head and slammed straight into her heart. She couldn't breathe. She wasn't pregnant. She couldn't be; her period was just a couple of weeks late, that was all. Even though it had never, ever been late before. She looked up into Juno's concerned face. 'I can't be pregnant. It's simply not possible. Connor always used a condom, every time.'

Juno frowned. 'You do know they're only about ninety-nine per cent reliable, right? They're not a hundred per cent.'

'I know that, but...' Daisy stopped. But what? 'We never had one break or anything like that.' She couldn't possibly have got pregnant.

'They don't necessarily have to break.' Juno sank down in the chair next to her. Her brow furrowed into ominous rows.

'Of course they do—his sperm can't get through rubber, for goodness' sake.' Daisy jerked a shoulder. 'Not unless it's supersonic or something. Can it?'

'Oh, Daze.'

Daisy swivelled round to see Jacie wearing the same worried frown as Juno.

'What? What is it?' Why were they looking at her like that?

'How late *are* you?' Juno asked gently.

'Only...' She did a quick calculation. Oh, God, she'd been due for over two weeks.

'I think we better get you a home pregnancy test,' Juno

said without waiting for her answer. 'Just to be on the safe side,' she finished hopefully.

'You have to tell him, Daisy.'

Daisy's fingers fisted on the plastic stick, her whole body trembling. She had to be dreaming this, surely. Or having a nightmare. She could not be expecting Connor Brody's baby.

Juno's hand squeezed her shoulder. 'You know that, right?'

'It's not true. Maybe we should do another. There must be some mistake. He'll never believe me if I tell him. I don't believe me.'

'We've done three tests already,' her friend said. 'There's no mistake. And unless it's the immaculate conception, Mr Superstud is the father.' Juno took a weary breath. 'You should go over there now and tell him, get it out the way. Then you can start thinking about what you're going to do.'

Daisy dropped the plastic stick on top of the others in her waste-paper bin, her mind whizzing like a Catherine wheel. The three pink plus signs floated in front of her eyes like something out of a Salvador Dali painting.

'I'm going to call Maya,' Juno whispered, her hand still gripping Daisy's shoulder. 'So you can discuss your options.'

Daisy placed her hand on her abdomen, rubbed. Her heart rate finally calmed down enough so that she could grasp one wonderful, impossible truth. 'Juno.' She looked up at her friend, tears of joy pricking her lids. 'I'm going to be a mummy.'

Tears welled in Juno's eyes too, to match the ones now flowing freely down Daisy's cheeks. 'So you're going to have it?'

Daisy nodded. 'Yes. Yes, I am. I know the circumstances are a total disaster, but I could never do anything else.'

Juno clasped her hand over Daisy's. 'Whatever happens,

I'll be here to help and so will Mrs V and Jace and everyone else you know. And that's a lot of people. You're not alone.'

'I know.' Daisy nodded and sniffed. Why had she ever thought she didn't have a family?

Juno wiped the moisture away, slanted Daisy a wobbly grin. 'Enough hearts and flowers. When are you going to tell Brody?'

Daisy's heart stopped. The moment of euphoria faded to be replaced by a terrible wave of grief. 'I'm not.'

'Don't be silly. You have to tell him. He has a right to know.'

'I can't tell him,' she said dully, the awful reality of what that meant finally dawning on her.

'Are you worried he'll try and make you have an abortion?' Juno said carefully.

Daisy shook her head. 'No, he wouldn't do that.' She stared at her hands, the knuckles whitening as she twisted them in her lap. 'Actually I think he'd do the opposite.' She remembered what Jessie had told her about the pregnancy scare with his last girlfriend. 'There's a core of honesty, of goodness in him. He'll feel responsible and he'll want to do the right thing. I couldn't bear that.'

'But, Daisy, in this case he is responsible. Partly responsible. You didn't get pregnant on your own.'

'But he doesn't want to be a father.' She pictured the way he'd looked when he'd told her about his own family, that sunny day a million years ago in Central Park. 'He had a miserable childhood, Juno. His father was violent, abusive. But he didn't blame his dad for what he did to him and to his brother and sisters. Honestly, when he was telling me about it, reading between the lines, it was like he blamed himself. I think that's why he's so scared of making a commitment. I'm not going to force it on him. I love him, how could I?' she said, placing her hands on her belly.

Juno stood up and paced across the room. 'That is such a load of total rubbish.' She stabbed an indignant finger at her friend. 'Stop being such a martyr. It's not your fault you got pregnant.'

'I know, but I want this baby.' She caressed her stomach, felt the jolt of emotion. 'Whatever the problems, the challenges, the difficulties I'll have to face. This is like a dream come true for me.' Maybe not the whole dream, but a good part of it. 'I think it could well be Connor's worst nightmare.' And then another thought occurred to her. 'Plus, I spent my whole childhood around men that didn't want to be my dad. I know how inadequate that can make you feel. I'm not going to put my own child through that. I couldn't.'

Juno gave a deep sigh. 'Okay, fine, have it your way, Daisy. But I still think you're wrong.' She sat back on the bed. 'And if he finds out, there could be hell to pay.'

'He's not going to find out. He looked horrified after I told him I loved him. I don't think he's going to go to any great lengths to seek me out. Plus he's moving soon. All I have to do is be careful and keep a low profile.'

Juno slanted her a rueful look. 'Yes, and we all know how good you are at that,' she muttered.

CHAPTER SEVENTEEN

'I'LL kill ye little bastards.'

Connor flinched at the slurred shout, scrambled back at the angry thud on the door. The sharp crack as the thin plywood splintered had flop sweat trickling down beneath his T-shirt, stinging the welts from two nights back.

'He means it, Con. He really means it this time,' came Mac's panicked whisper.

Connor flung an arm round his brother's shoulder. 'Soon as he gets in, you go on. Get the girls to Mrs Flaherty's. I'll hold him off.'

They jumped together as another loud crack ripped the air. Connor's gaze was riveted to the tiny latch, hanging by the last two screws. Queasy fear gripped his stomach, the memory of the pain so vivid his muscles tensed, his back throbbed. The thundering in his ears cut out the crash as the door fell forward in slow, silent motion. Connor raised his arms, the thin whimper of Mac's crying piercing the mute terror as the dark shape stumbled towards them. Vicious pain sliced across his shoulder as the belt tore into tender flesh.

Connor bolted forward into darkness, his hands reaching for something that wasn't there.

His chest screamed as he struggled to breathe, his ears ringing with the sound of leather cutting flesh, his shoulders livid with the phantom pain.

He choked down a gulp of air.

Just a nightmare. Just a nightmare. Get a grip, Brody.

Gradually his eyes adjusted to the dim light, saw the plush drapes, the shadows cast by moonlight in the garden beyond. He braced his hands on the bed, let his chin drop to his chest, waited for his mind to adjust, to yank him out of the horror.

But as he waited an eternity to draw that first steady breath the silence echoed around him. The emptiness, the loneliness taunted him.

Why wasn't she here? He needed her.

As his breathing evened out at last he covered his face with his hands, pushed shaking fingers through his hair. Two whole days. Two long, miserable days. And the yearning, the desperation hadn't faded; they had only got worse.

He blew out a breath and finally accepted the truth. He'd mucked everything up.

How could he have been so stupid? What the hell had he thrown away? All this time he'd been running away from the one thing he should have been running towards.

He lifted the sheet, damp with his sweat, settled back into the bed. The residue of the nightmare rippled through him, making his muscles quake.

He shut his eyes and swore that tomorrow he'd make it right. He'd do whatever he had to do, to get Daisy back where she belonged.

'We need to talk.'

Daisy stared in shock as the very last man she'd expected to see, or wanted to see, stood in her doorway.

'Go away.' She went to slam the door.

He slapped his hand against it. 'I will not.' He shoved the door open and strode past her into the tiny bedsit.

'You can't come in here.' Outrage was closely followed by panic. She'd been sick twice already since waking up an hour ago and could feel the stirrings of a new bout of nausea in the pit of her stomach.

'Too bad. I'm in already.' He stood in the middle of the room, his broad shoulders and determined scowl making the small space look a great deal smaller.

'Please leave, Connor. Our fling's over.' She tried to keep the quiver out of her voice. She had to get him out of here, before he saw her vomit. What if he put two and two together? She'd wrestled with what she had to do for two whole days. She hadn't seen hide or hair of him and, while her heart had yearned for even a quick glimpse, she knew she'd made the right decision not to tell him about the baby.

Trust Connor to turn up unexpectedly, though, and ruin her best intentions.

'I've got nothing more to say to you,' she said. 'And this is just embarrassing us both.'

'As if I care about embarrassing,' he shouted back. 'It so happens, I've got a piece to say to you and I'm going to say it. You had your say, two days ago, when you stormed off in a huff. Now I'm having mine.'

'I don't care what you have to say…' She stopped in mid-shout, clasping her hand over her mouth, the sick waves heaving up her abdomen.

He was beside her in a second, gripping her arm. 'What's wrong? You look sick.'

'Get out!' she shouted, then shot out of the room and dashed down the hall to the bathroom.

Connor stood stock-still and listened to Daisy's feet fly down the corridor. So that was the way of it? She loved him so much, he made her retch.

He sat on the bed, dropped his head in his hands.

Damn, what was the matter with him? He was handling this all wrong. You didn't turn up on a woman's doorstep to tell her you loved her and straight off start yelling. What the hell had happened to all the easy charm he'd used on women so effortlessly in the past?

He heaved out a breath. Stood up, hopelessly restless and confused.

He'd be gentle when she got back. She was obviously poorly. Problem was, he'd never done anything like this before and had no practice whatsoever at it. Was he supposed to get down on one knee? Make an idiot of himself? Probably.

He glanced round the small, cluttered room, noticed the fanciful scene she'd painted on the ceiling and sighed.

This could well be the most important moment of his life and he'd mucked it up beautifully. He knew he had a lot of making up to do, after his knee-jerk reaction two days ago, but he didn't have an idea in his head how to do it. What did he know of romance? For sure, he'd talked women into bed before, but he'd never once had to bare his soul to one. He'd spent all morning practising what to say. But in the end he'd got so frustrated he'd come storming in here like a hurricane and blown it completely.

He paced up to her vanity, picked up the little vial of perfume, sniffed. The familiar scent filled him with the same bone-deep longing he'd had in the night, after waking up from his nightmare, and in the past two days as he'd waited like a fool for his feelings to level, to change.

He put the vial down carefully. Scowled when he saw something next to it on the edge of the sink. He picked the small plastic bottle up, squinting at the label.

'Pregnacare Vitamins,' he said aloud. 'What the…?'

'Oh, no.' He heard the pained whisper, looked round to see Daisy standing by the door, a panicked look on her face.

His heart began to pound, but it wasn't panic clawing up his throat as he would have expected, but hope blossoming. Bright, beautiful, glorious hope.

He held the bottle up. 'What are these, now?'

She walked towards him, whipped the bottle out of his hand and buried it in the pocket of her bathrobe. 'Nothing, now go away.'

She turned her back on him, her shoulders rigid with tension, and wrapped her hands around her waist.

He stepped up to her, went to touch her, but pulled his hands away. He wanted to hold her, just hold her for ever. But he knew he didn't have the right. Not yet. The lump in his throat made it hard for him to speak. 'You weren't going to tell me?'

She didn't look round, but her shoulders softened, and he heard her weary sigh. 'Please go away, Connor. Pretend you never saw those. Your life can go on as you want it. And so can mine.'

He rested his hands on her shoulders, unable to hold back any longer, and turned her to face him. She had her eyes downcast but he could see a silent tear running down her cheek. It pierced his heart. He tucked a thumb under her chin, forced her gaze to meet his. 'Is that really how you want it? Don't you trust me? Don't you trust your own feelings?'

She let out a soft sob, bit hard into her lip. 'What if I told you it's not even yours?' she said, desperation edging her voice.

'I'd know you were lying.' He brushed the tear away with his thumb. 'You're a terrible liar, Daisy, you know.' He pressed his lips to hers. 'I love you, Daisy. That's what I came to tell you. Although I've made a mess of it so far. Tell me it's not too late.'

Daisy had thought her heart couldn't feel any more pain, that she couldn't possibly cry any more tears, but hearing him say the words she had dreamed of hearing the last few days and knowing they weren't true felt like the worst pain yet. More tears welled over her lids.

'Don't, Connor. I don't believe you.'

'You're kidding.' He gave a brittle laugh, then frowned. 'I've never told a living soul I loved them before. And now when I do you don't believe me? Talk about Murphy's Law. Why don't you believe me?' He sounded annoyed and exasperated, but then his fingers touched her cheek. The tenderness, the understanding in his eyes shocked her. 'This is because of your mother, isn't it?' he said softly. 'Because she looked for love and didn't find it, you won't believe it when it's standing right here in front of you.'

She searched his face, desperate to believe him, desperate to take what he offered. He was right, her experiences as a child had made her wary of love. But as she looked at him all she could see was his frustration, and his determination.

She drew back, remembering only too well the look on his face two days ago, when she'd told him she loved him. She shook her head.

She couldn't let herself hope for the impossible. She knew the truth. She'd worked it all out, sensibly and rationally. People didn't change. They didn't. Her mother had proved that with every man she'd fallen in love with.

'I knew you'd do this,' she whispered. 'I knew you'd feel responsible. You didn't love me two days ago, and you don't love me now. You don't want to be a father and you don't want me, not really.' She held his forearms, tried to push him away, but he wouldn't let her go. 'I knew if I told you about the baby you'd want to do the right thing. Just like you did for your brother and your sisters. You took a belt for them, Connor. You let him beat you rather than see them get hurt, didn't you? But I'm not going to be another belt. Because that's what I'd be if I let you do the thing that was right for me and not for you.'

He dragged her closer, rested his forehead on hers.

'Daisy, that's so sweet.' He lifted his head and sent her a tentative smile that made her insides feel all shaky. 'But it's also total rubbish. I want you. I need you. I love you. And I loved you two days ago but I was too stupid to see it. And I'm over the moon that by some miracle I got you pregnant.' He cocked his head, the smile widening. 'Although we'll have to have a little talk about how that happened. Because for the life of me I'm sure I used condoms the whole time.' He was grinning at her now. 'And if I can get you pregnant through bonded latex we may have to be a lot more careful if we don't want to end up with twenty kids. But first things first. How am I going to get it into that thick head of yours that I love you?'

She pushed away from him, her anger rising. Why was he making this so hard? 'All right then, tell me why you reacted the way you did two days ago. When I told you I loved you, you looked absolutely horrified.'

Connor swore softly and felt the joy, the hope fade.

So it was all going to boil down to this. He'd have to tell her his darkest shame and hope against hope that she could still love him afterwards. 'Are you sure you want to know this?'

Her lips firmed into a grim line of determination. She nodded.

He let her go, sat on her bed. He'd hurt her, when he hadn't meant to; now he could destroy everything—but it was a risk he'd have to take.

'If I tell you, you might change your mind about loving me,' he said, hoping to give her a get-out clause.

She didn't take it. 'No, I won't,' she said with complete certainty.

He took a deep breath, but he couldn't look at her and tell her, so he gazed down at his hands, fisted in his lap. 'You're right. I took the belt if I could. Mac and me both. But I wasn't being brave, or noble particularly. It was just, they were so little, my sisters, and they loved me. And Mac, he looked up to me, thought I knew all the answers. They all depended on me to keep them safe, to keep us together.' He shrugged, shame thickening his voice. 'But one night, I sneaked out. Maeve Gallagher had promised me heaven the last time I'd seen her. I'd fresh scars from his last drinking session and he'd come home and fallen straight into his bed. I thought they'd be safe, that no harm would come to them. I swear it.'

She sat beside him, put her hand over his. But he still couldn't look at her, couldn't bear to see her contempt at what he'd done. 'But when I got home, there was a commotion outside. The neighbours were crowded about the house. There were lights flashing.' He could still picture it all so clearly even now, hear the murmur of curious voices, smell the scent of peat fires and winter frost and feel the chilling fear that had had him scrambling head first through the crowd. 'The Garda had my Da, he had his head bent, his hands cuffed behind his back. And then I saw the ambulance and Mac.' He gulped down air, tried to steady himself. 'He was lying on a stretcher. He looked so small, his face battered, his arm all crooked. I thought he was dead.' He forced himself to meet her eyes. 'He wasn't dead, but I never saw him again. Him or the girls. I told the social worker I didn't want to. But the truth is I couldn't bear to face them.'

'Why couldn't you?' she asked, her love clear on her face despite all that he'd told her. It gave him the courage he needed to tell her the last of it.

'Because I'd let them down. It was my job to protect them and I'd failed. I didn't deserve to be their brother, not any more.'

Daisy cupped Connor's face in her palms. Seeing the pain in his eyes, the regret, the guilt, she realised she loved this man more than life itself. She tried to speak, but emotion closed her throat.

He gripped her wrists, drew her hands down. 'When you told me you loved me,' he said, 'I was so scared. Scared to love you back. Because after that night, I promised I'd never love a living soul again and risk letting them get hurt. Risk losing them.'

'Connor, it wasn't your fault,' she whispered, the tears flowing freely down her cheeks. 'You were a boy trying to do something even a grown man couldn't do. You didn't let them down. And as long as you love me as much as I love you, you could never let me down either.'

He threaded his fingers through hers, held on. 'I do love you. More than you know. But are you sure that's enough?' he asked.

She pressed her palm to his cheek. 'Of course it is. You silly idiot.'

He blew out a breath, the relief plain on his face as he lent into her palm. 'That's a fine thing to call the man that loves you and is the father of your baby,' he said, emotion deepening his voice.

She smiled, for what felt like the first time in a millennium, and threw her arms round his neck. She clung onto him so tightly she wasn't sure he could breathe.

He chuckled. 'So does this mean you believe I love you now?' he said, his voice muffled against her hair.

She nodded, the joy coursing through her making it hard for her to breathe too.

His arms banded round her waist. 'And there'll be no more doubting it?'

She nodded again, even more vigorously, then whispered, 'I'd like my engagement ring back, now. Please.'

His breath tickled her ear lobe as he laughed. 'I'll think on it,' he said, but she could hear the teasing note in his voice. He lifted his head, framed her face in warm palms, his eyes shining with love. How could she ever have doubted him?

'But first I need you to do something for me,' he murmured.

'What's that?' she asked.

His thumb caressed the pulse in her throat as his hands settled on her shoulders. 'Come home,' he said as his gaze remained locked on hers. 'Come home with me where you belong.'

She thrust her fingers into his hair, brought his lips to hers and gave him his answer in a kiss bursting with love, heat, hope and commitment—and pure, unadulterated joy.

EPILOGUE

'FOR goodness' sake, let me look, you meanie. I've waited weeks already,' Daisy ordered, her fingers grappling with the immovable hands covering her eyes.

'Hold your horses now.' Connor's deep chuckle next to her ear sounded both amused and a bit too smug for her liking. 'I'll let you loose when I'm good and ready and not a moment before. Juno, get the lights,' he shouted past her as his chest pressed into her back. 'There now. What do you make of it?'

His hands lifted and Daisy blinked, the dazzle of fluorescent light blinding her. As the sleek, beautiful lines of glass and wood came into focus through the smell of fresh paint and sawdust she gasped. She slapped her hands over her mouth as tears welled in her eyes and emotion clogged her throat. 'Oh,' was the only word she could utter.

'That bad, eh?' Connor said beside her, sounding a lot less smug.

She turned, bounced up on her toes and flung her hands round his shoulders, nearly knocking him over with her belly in the process. 'Oh, my God, Connor. It's exactly the way I envisioned it. Exactly what I wanted. How did you do it? And how did you do it so fast?'

He'd given her another of her dreams, she thought, her

heart bursting with love and excitement. And this was one she hadn't even realised she'd wanted. In fact she'd needed quite a lot of persuading to start with.

Six months ago when he'd walked into the bathroom after she'd just finished puking and informed her he'd bought her a shop at auction that morning, she'd had the distinct urge to throttle him, if she recalled correctly.

Was he insane? Why hadn't he discussed it with her first? He might enjoy being impulsive, reckless even, but she didn't. How was she going to organise refurbishing a shop? Then manage it and supply it while she was suffering from the worst case of morning sickness known to woman? And how would she handle all the extra responsibility when the baby was born?

But over the months her doubts had faded along with the morning sickness, and the excitement of having her own proper space to display her designs, her own workshop in the back to manufacture them, had built to impossible proportions.

And through it all Connor had been there, by her side. Encouraging her ideas, offering suggestions about the refurbishment, organising the construction, insisting she hire a manager so she could devote her time to designing, overseeing his crew with calm efficiency through all the inevitable hiccups—and on one memorable evening strapping on his tool belt to put up the shelving in the workshop and then letting her seduce him in the newly installed bathroom afterwards.

The experience had brought them even closer together. They weren't just a couple any more, they were a unit, with a shared dream.

In the last month though, with her approaching the end of her pregnancy he'd insisted she stay at home as he and the crew installed the cabinets and counters, finished the fitting rooms and did all the painting and decorating. And she had to admit she'd been a little miffed by his high-handedness. But she still couldn't believe how he had transformed that empty shell from four short weeks ago into the dream come true she saw before her now.

'I didn't do it on my own,' he said, smiling down at her.

'Oh, I know, you must thank all the crew. Are we going to have a proper opening, with champagne? We'll have to invite them all. I was thinking we could have it in a month if we get our skates on and—'

'We'll be doing no such thing,' he said firmly, interrupting her excited babble. He slung his arm round her shoulder and drew her close. 'The grand opening will have to wait a while.' He stroked his palm across her huge belly and she felt the heat right down to her toes. 'You're going to be busy for the next little while, looking after yourself and my child. This place is to be off limits until Junior's out and you're up and about. We'll schedule the opening for July, but only if you behave.'

'But that's ridiculous, that's months away,' she sputtered, starting to feel a little miffed again.

'And Juno here is under strict instructions to make sure you do as you're told.' He winked at Juno. 'Is that right, Juno?'

'Aye aye, Connor.' Juno gave a mock salute, grinning at Connor. The sight warmed Daisy's heart, despite her frustration with the two of them. How could it not?

Connor had gone out of his way to win Juno over since Daisy and he had started living together. It hadn't been easy at first, Juno's hostility towards him making her prickly and tense. But he'd worn her down over time, first getting her to accept him, then getting her to let go of her suspicion of good-looking men, at least as far as he was concerned, and finally engineering an easy friendship between them that had sprung from their mutual love for Daisy.

He treated Juno like a little sister, advising her and looking out for her and teasing her, while she treated him like an older brother, only taking the advice she felt she needed, and teasing him mercilessly right back.

But right now, as Daisy watched the silent communication between them, she was beginning to wonder if they weren't like brother and sister after all. But more like evil twins.

She could feel herself pouting. She hated being ganged up on. 'The baby's not due for two whole weeks.' She scowled at them both. 'Surely I can get a bit done in here before then.' She waddled over to the beautifully carved walnut counter tops, ran her palm lovingly across the smooth, vanished wood. 'We can't just leave it sitting here empty all that time.'

Connor stepped up behind her, wrapped his arms round her enormous waist and hugged her close. 'We can and we will,' he murmured, his breath feathering her ear. 'And from the size of you I'd say two weeks is optimistic, angel.'

She stuck an elbow in his ribs. 'Thanks a bunch. I know I look like a barrage balloon but you don't have to keep reminding me.'

'Stop fishing for compliments.' He chuckled. 'You know right well you're gorgeous.'

Daisy felt herself softening at the compliment. The man's charm was deadly.

He placed his hand over hers on the wood, brought her fingers to his lips. 'There's no rush, Daisy. We've all the time in the world, you know.'

Daisy gave a resigned sigh, the huge rush of love making her chest ache, and knew he'd got her, again. Then she heard a loud choking sound from behind them.

'If you two are going to get all drippy, I'm off,' Juno said, her voice light.

The deep rumble of Connor's laugh reverberated against Daisy's back. 'You best go, then, because drippy's definitely on the cards right enough.'

'You don't have to ask me twice,' Juno shot back, sounding more carefree than Daisy had ever known her. 'I'll be round tomorrow, Daze,' she called across to her. 'To stand guard.'

Daisy leaned round Connor. 'You traitor,' she said and grinned.

'Absolutely.' Juno gave a jaunty wave and left, slamming the shop door behind her.

'Right.' Connor pulled her back into his embrace. 'Now little Juno the killjoy's out the way and I've got you all to myself, there's one other thing we need to talk about. And I want this settled before the baby's born. So you can cut out the delaying tactics.'

'What's that now?' Daisy said in her best Irish brogue, although she had a pretty good idea what he was referring to. After all he'd been banging on about it for months.

'You know full well what. We've yet to set the wedding date.'

'I told you, I don't want to get married looking like a beached whale.'

'And, while you look nothing like a beached whale,' he said, sounding pained, 'I agreed to that bit of fancy, didn't I? You've a few months once Junior's born to get yourself together, but then we're doing it. I found a place in France that would be perfect. It's available for the third Saturday in August. We can party there with all our pals for a week and be back in time for Carnival. I've a mind to book it tomorrow. What do you say?'

She wanted to say yes, there was nothing more she wanted to do than marry this man and claim him as her own for everyone to see. But something had been bothering her for months about their wedding. Something that had nothing to do with her figure. And she still hadn't found the best way to broach the subject.

'I thought you said we had all the time in the world,' she said lamely.

He huffed and turned her in his arms. Keeping his hands on her hips, he dipped his head to look into her face. 'Is there another reason you won't set the date? Because if there is you best spit it out now.'

She swallowed hard, could see the stubbornness in the hard line of his jaw and knew this was it. She would have to say it now, or for ever hold her peace. And that she couldn't do. Connor needed closure on the horrors of his childhood, and he would never have it unless he took this next step.

She took a deep breath. 'I want to contact Mac,' she blurted out. 'I want to invite him to the wedding.'

His eyebrows shot up. 'You… What?'

'He's your brother, Connor. We're having a baby in a few weeks and he'll be its uncle. And when we get married we'll be saying vows that will make us a family for ever. I want him there to witness them with us. Don't you?'

His hands fell from her waist. He looked shocked. But at least he didn't look angry or defensive, which were the two reactions she'd feared the most.

'What…?' His voice broke. He cleared his throat. 'What if he won't come?'

She took his hands in hers, squeezed. 'If he's your brother, he can't possibly be that much of a coward.' She was counting on it. 'You need to forgive yourself for what happened that night—and to do that you need to see Mac again, to make things right with him. He's your family which makes him my family too.' She paused, willing him to understand. 'If you don't want to contact him, I'll accept your decision and we'll never talk about it again. But I had to ask.'

He sucked in a long breath, raised his eyes to the ceiling, and slowly let it out. 'You are the most contrary woman…' he muttered, but there was no heat in the words.

His eyes met hers. 'Okay, you go ahead and contact Mac. But I hope he's ready for what's about to hit him.'

She wrapped her arms around his neck and smacked a kiss on his lips. 'Thank you, Connor. It's the right thing to do, I know it is. And if everything goes well with Mac, we could start trying to trace your sis—'

He slapped his hand over her mouth before she could say another word. 'Stop right there. There'll be no more meddling until we're married, the shop's up and running and the baby's at least five. Do you understand?'

She nodded behind his hand, her heart swelling at the rueful grin on his face. He wasn't mad. He didn't seem upset. He might even be a little pleased about the plan to contact his brother. Everything was going to work out, she was sure of it.

'Now, when I lift my hand,' he said carefully, the mischievous twinkle in his eyes belying the severity in his voice, 'I want you to say you'll make an honest man of me on August eighteenth. No more excuses. You got it?'

She nodded. He lifted his hand.

'Aye, aye, Connor,' she chirped, feeling as if all the happiness in the world had just exploded in her heart.

'And none of your cheek either,' he said, then took her in his arms and kissed her into complete submission to seal the deal.

Three days and fourteen excruciating hours of labour later, and Daisy held another of her dreams in tired arms. As little Ronan Cormac Brody suckled ferociously at her breast, and his father stared down at the two of them, his arm tight around Daisy's shoulders and his eyes filled with awe, Daisy knew she had the happy ever after she'd once only dreamed of in some secret corner of her heart.

Now all she had to do was start living it.

* * * * *

Juno

To Suzy, for knowing when a six-hundred-mile road trip
is not the way to go,

and Daisy, a brilliant author and an even better friend.

CHAPTER ONE

STRUGGLING to control her galloping heartbeat, Juno Delamare scanned the arrivals screen at Heathrow's bustling Terminal Five for details of Flight 155 from Los Angeles. The
words 'In the Arrivals Hall' winked back at her and her heart
stampeded into overdrive.

For goodness' sake, woman. Get a grip.

Juno jammed her fists into the pockets of her newest
jeans—which had a small tear at the knee where she'd been
stacking shelves the day before—and took several deep
breaths. She had to calm down. She was on a mission here,
a very important mission, and she simply did not have time to
have a heart attack—it would put a serious crimp in her plans.

When Hollywood heart-throb Mac Brody walked through
the arrival gate, she intended to be ready—and in complete
control of her faculties—so she could hand him his invitation to her best friend Daisy Dean's wedding and make sure
he agreed to come.

Daisy was marrying millionaire property developer Connor Brody in two weeks' time and she'd set her heart on re-
uniting Connor with his long-lost brother at their wedding.

So Juno had made it her mission to ensure said little brother came whether he wanted to or not.

How exactly she was going to get him to agree she hadn't quite figured out yet. But she intended to give it her very best shot. Daisy had helped Juno put her life back together six years ago—when she'd thought she'd never be able to care about anything or anybody again—and she owed her.

Unfortunately, despite Juno's heartfelt commitment to the cause, when she'd made her secret vow two weeks ago to get Mac Brody to Daisy and Connor's wedding she hadn't given a whole lot of thought to the logistics. But now, as zero hour approached in Heathrow's imposing terminal, the logistics were beginning to choke her.

What if she failed? What if he travelled with a phalanx of bodyguards and she couldn't get near him? What if he refused to take the invitation if she did get near him? And then there was the coup de grâce. When was the last time she'd even approached a strange man, let alone tried to persuade him to do something? Her powers of persuasion were less than nil where men were concerned.

She didn't do seduction—she didn't have the looks, the aptitude or indeed the wardrobe for it. Which meant she would have to appeal to Mac Brody's better nature. But on the evidence so far, he didn't have one.

Maybe she'd never met the guy. Maybe she'd never even seen one of his movies, but Juno had been in Daisy's bright airy kitchen two weeks ago. The morning the letter had arrived... And that had told her all she needed to know about the true character of Mac Brody, Hollywood mega-star and Irish bad boy extraordinaire.

Okay, so he was good-looking—if you went for the tall, dark and dangerous stereotype—but that didn't alter the fact that beneath all that brooding masculinity was a shallow, arrogant, self-absorbed egotist.

Juno's temper rose again at the memory of Brody's callousness.

Daisy had been so excited, so sure the letter would be good news. Only to rip open the envelope and find the wedding invitation she'd sent Brody inside and a note from his agent that stated in one neatly typed sentence that Mr Cormac Brody would not be attending the wedding of his brother Connor and requested that Ms Daisy Dean refrain from contacting him in the future.

The perfunctory note had made Daisy cry, and Daisy hardly ever cried, but almost worse for Juno had been Connor's reaction. He'd slung his arm round Daisy's shoulder and told her not to upset herself so. Mac was entitled to his feelings, they'd no right to pressure him into making a commitment he didn't feel comfortable with and that was the end of the matter. But Juno had watched Connor read the note himself and had seen the sorrow and regret he'd been trying so hard to hide.

What right did Brody have to hurt her friends like that? And worse than that, he hadn't even had the guts to get his hands dirty and contact them himself.

Juno muscled her way through the waiting crowd and folded her arms over the barrier. Ignoring the insistent rat-a-tat-tat of her heartbeat, she studied the stream of owl-eyed transatlantic passengers flowing through the arrival gate. Her mouth set in a grim line of determination. She'd have to hide her hostility towards him if this was going to work. But whatever happened, she was not going to give Brody the satisfaction of seeing how nervous she was—or how much she had at stake—and she absolutely refused to beg.

It would only make the contemptible man feel more superior.

Juno's eyes narrowed sharply as she spotted a tall solitary figure strolling down the concourse alone. In contrast to the other travellers, who were rumpled but well dressed, this guy's clothes were comfortable to the point of being disreputable. Faded denim hung from his lean hips and an ancient LA Dodgers T-shirt stretched across tanned biceps as he lugged a large leather holdall over his shoulder. The matching Dodgers baseball cap had been pushed down so the peak covered his face, but Juno could still see a day's worth of stubble on his chin, and the wavy black hair that touched broad shoulders.

Could that be Brody? She stared, trying to make up her mind. If it was him, he wasn't what she'd expected. With his shoulders hunched, his head down and his fingers fisted on the handle of his holdall, the man walking towards her looked as if he was trying to be inconspicuous.

And it was working. But for his height, which towered at least a foot over her own five feet two, Juno guessed no one would have given him a second glance. But then Juno noticed the way the stranger moved and she knew he had to be Mac Brody. He had the exact same loose, languid gait as his brother, Connor.

She jostled her way through the crowd to head him off at the exit gate—her heartbeat bumping right back up to warp speed.

Keeping his eyes on the grey industrial flooring, Mac Brody blanked out the crowd noise and hitched his shoulder to relieve the knot of tension and fatigue.

He'd never been keen on airports, and Heathrow held some bad memories. The last time he'd been here three years back, the paparazzi had been lying in wait to ambush him. It had been less than a week after his public bust-up with supermodel Regina St Clair—and a mere two days after Gina had sold her story to the press and branded him a coke-snorting wild man who bedded a different woman every night.

Gina's X-rated fantasies might have been funny—but for the fact that a lot of people had believed her and the fallout had followed him around like a monkey on his back ever since. The press had smelled blood that day, and they hadn't let him alone since. He'd never been comfortable exposed to the media spotlight, so it had been a harsh lesson to learn and no mistake.

He'd been mad as hell with Gina at the time. But he'd got over it soon enough. Somehow she'd deluded herself into believing they were in love and he hadn't been paying enough attention to notice. He adjusted the weight of his carry-on bag on his shoulder. Lesson learned. Whenever he dated now, he made it plain exactly what he wanted out of a relationship—and exactly what he didn't want—right from the start.

He glanced up to search the terminal for the exit. Seeing no sign of any photographers or press hounds, he heaved a sigh. He could cope with the paps if he had to, but right now he was exhausted after an eleven-hour flight and back-to-back night shoots during the past week and he didn't need the hassle. Luckily for him, he'd learnt to blend into the woodwork at an early age; people rarely recognised him in a crowd unless he wanted them to.

Spotting the 'Way Out' sign, he changed direction, but as he lowered his head to make for the exit a small figure stepped from behind a pillar straight into his path.

'What the…?' He pulled up sharply to stop knocking the girl down.

'You're Cormac Brody.' Her voice wavered, but the statement was loud enough to attract attention.

'Keep your voice down,' he said, scanning the surrounding crowd. Luckily no one seemed to have heard her.

'I'm sorry to bother you. But I need to speak to you,' she said, polite as you please, but he detected a definite edge. 'It's extremely important.'

'Extremely important, is it?' He'd heard that before. A firm dismissal hovered on the tip of his tongue, but, as his gaze drifted over her figure and then settled back on her face, it refused to come out of his mouth.

Whoever the girl was, she was seriously cute.

The torn jeans and layered T-shirts should have made her look like a tomboy, but somehow they suited her, hugging her subtle curves and accentuating her narrow waist and a pair of small but pert breasts.

Then there was the impact of that pale heart-shaped face to consider.

Not quite green and not quite blue, her round, translucent eyes grabbed most of the attention, but when you added in the soft, carelessly cut cap of dark blonde hair, the clear, creamy skin and perfectly defined bone structure—plus the fact she didn't have a spot of make-up on—he had to admit the effect was striking.

He wondered if she was a fan. And hoped she wasn't.

'What is it that's so extremely important?' He could spare her a moment—after all it was a long time since he'd been this intrigued. 'I haven't much time at the minute, darlin'.'

The doe-like eyes narrowed and she looked even cuter—sort of like Bo Peep in a strop. 'Don't patronise me, Mr Brody.'

He blinked, surprised by the ballsy comeback. No way was she a fan. 'I'd really appreciate it if you'd stop saying my name so loudly,' he said, keeping his tone light, even though this was the second time he'd had to mention it. 'I'm in no hurry to draw attention to myself.' Intriguing or not, she was turning into a bit of a liability.

He glanced past her again to make sure she hadn't given him away and spied the one person he didn't want to see. 'Damn.'

She frowned and began to turn. Throwing his bag down,

he grabbed her shoulders and shoved her against the pillar to get them both out of Pete Danners's line of sight. His nemesis. The same freelance photographer had dogged him like a Rottweiler three years back and he had no desire to repeat the experience.

'Don't look round,' he snapped. He propped his elbow above her head, trapping her body against his to look round the pillar. 'If yer man over there sees me, this trip'll be a misery.'

Juno sucked in a sharp breath, so shocked she forgot to exhale.

What was happening?

One second she'd been staring into staggeringly blue eyes and thinking Cormac Brody was a lot better-looking than he had any right to be and quite as arrogant as she had assumed. The next she'd been pinned against his lean, muscular body.

She got light-headed and remembered she needed air. One breath gushed out and she sucked in another. She could feel every single inch of him. The solid planes of his chest flattening her breasts. The long length of his thighs pressed to hers and the buckle of his belt, outlined against her stomach. The overwhelming scent of minty toothpaste and man suffocated her.

'What are you doing?' she panted, the outraged squeak muffled against his chest.

She hadn't been this close to a man in six years. By rights she should be screaming her head off. But right alongside the shock was the unfamiliar blast of heat that throbbed in every place their bodies touched.

He moved back a fraction, still looking past her shoulder. She took another gasping breath.

'He's gone. Thank the Lord.' The brush of his breath

against her ear lobe had a shudder ricocheting down her spine. 'I owe you one, gorgeous.'

'I—I can't breathe,' she stammered, her teeth rattling.

He yanked off his cap and the bold, unfathomable blue of his eyes fixed on her face.

'What's wrong?'

You're what's wrong, she wanted to yell, but couldn't say the words. She had to stop shaking first.

He bent his head. 'Relax, darlin'.' One calloused palm settled on her neck.

Her breath hitched painfully as he traced his thumb along her chin and then sank his fingers into her hair.

She tried to say something, anything, but all that came out was a choked moan. His hand rested on her nape, holding her steady. 'How about we try this?' he coaxed, his lips so close she could taste the minty scent of his breath.

Then his mouth slanted across hers.

The second those firm lips touched hers, her pulse went haywire—as if she'd been plugged into an electric socket. Shock and something much more potent rocketed through her. Then his tongue slid over her bottom lip and a staggered groan escaped.

She should push him away, her mind screamed. But when her palms flattened against his T-shirt, the muscles quivered beneath her fingers and her hands slid down the hard plane of worn cotton. Her lips parted and his tongue plundered. Fire flashed through her, pulsing in her sex, hardening her nipples—and incinerating the last semblance of coherent thought.

He established a primal rhythm as her mouth opened wider to accept him. Then her tongue duelled with his, tentatively at first but getting bolder as the fire raged at her core. Strong, insistent fingers explored, slipping under her T-shirt, fanning her ribcage and making her buck against him as they caressed over-sensitive skin. Then she felt it. The thick ridge pressing into her belly.

She struggled, trying to wrestle back control of her traitorous body, and he broke away.

'Whoah. That was something else.' His ragged breathing matched her own as he rested his forehead on hers. 'We'd best stop, before things get out of hand.'

Juno stiffened and shrank back as reality returned, dousing the last of the passion like a bucket of ice water.

What had she done? After six years of contented celibacy, she'd snogged a complete stranger in the middle of Heathrow Airport. A stranger she didn't even like.

'Please, could you move your hand?' she said, brutally embarrassed as his thumb continued to rub lazily across her ribs, perilously close to the underside of her breast.

He drew his hand down, rested it on her hip. 'How about we find somewhere we can continue this in private?'

She fumbled with her T-shirt, frantically tucking it back into her jeans as blood surged into her cheeks. Did he think she was a prostitute or something?

He put his finger under her chin, tilted her head back. 'Is there something the matter?'

Of course something's the matter. A nymphomaniac just hijacked my body.

She jerked free. 'N-nothing's the matter,' she stammered.

'You sure?' His brows lowered. 'You're acting a bit strange.'

You don't know the half of it.

'I have to go.' She had to get away from those prying eyes and that harsh, too handsome face, before the nymphomaniac returned.

His hand clamped on her wrist. 'Now wait a minute,' he said with irritating calm.

She tugged, but the warm manacle only tightened. 'I really have to go.'

'You don't kiss a guy like that and then just walk off,' he said, not sounding the least bit perturbed by what they'd just done. 'And what about the extremely important thing you had to discuss with me?'

She opened her mouth to demand he let her go instantly. And then snapped it shut again.

Oh, no. The wedding invitation.

How could she have forgotten about Daisy's wedding? And her mission?

'Please, l-let go of my wrist,' she stuttered, the words trapped behind the boulder of guilt stuck in her throat. 'I have something for you.'

He released her, a sensual smile on his lips. 'I think we already established that.'

Her blush intensified—and her nipples tightened. Damn him. How did he have that effect on her? 'I'm not talking about sexual favours.' She grabbed his wrist and slapped the envelope into his upturned palm. 'It's an invitation to your brother's wedding.'

He tensed and the smile vanished as he stared at the invite.

'It's from my best friend, Daisy, your brother's fiancée,' she added.

His gaze lifted and she thought she saw something flicker in his eyes. But it disappeared so quickly she was sure she'd imagined it.

'I don't have a brother,' he replied, crushing the envelope in his fist.

That was one scenario she hadn't even considered. 'Of course you do,' she blurted out, wondering what on earth had happened between this man and Connor.

He looked completely unmoved. She'd promised herself she wouldn't beg, but after what she'd just done a little begging didn't seem like such a big deal any more. She took a deep breath. 'Please. You have to go. It's really important.'

'Not to me it isn't,' he said with enough arrogance to make her bristle. He lifted the invitation. 'So you can give this back to your best friend and tell her I'm not interested.'

'How can you be so callous?' she asked, before she could think better of it.

'How come this is any of your business?' he shot back, a bitter smile twisting his lips.

She stiffened, stunned by the cold, emotionless tone. 'I told you, Daisy's my friend,' she said, hating the defensiveness in her voice.

'I see,' he said. 'So was the kiss her idea or yours?'

Juno's mouth fell open. She snapped it shut. 'You know perfectly well that kiss was your idea.' What exactly was he accusing her of? 'You know what, Mr Brody.' Forget begging, she'd had about enough of Mac Brody and his titanic ego. 'Just because you're rich and famous it doesn't give you the right to treat your family like dirt. Daisy and Connor are wonderful people—and they deserve a lot better than you.'

'Is that right?' To her fury, he chuckled. 'So if you think I'm such a low form of life, why did you kiss me, then?'

If he didn't stop talking about that damn kiss she was going to slap him. 'I didn't know you then. I do now.'

His lips quirked, apparently immune to the insult. 'But you've yet to encounter the best bit.'

The vivid memory of his arousal had the blush burning in her cheeks. She thrust her chin out, refusing to acknowledge the strange sensation low in her belly. 'I think you overestimate your charms, Mr Brody.'

He laughed. 'But you'll never know for sure now, will you?'

She didn't dignify that with a reply, but she couldn't help hearing his taunting laughter as she marched off.

Of all the arrogant, oversexed, thoughtless jerks.

Juno fumed all the way to the exit doors, her heart pumping in time with her angry strides. She'd been absolutely right about Mac Brody. He didn't deserve a family as wonderful as Daisy and Connor and their beautiful baby boy, Ronan. Thank goodness he wasn't coming to the wedding. What a relief to know she'd never have to set eyes on that infernal man—or his so-called charms—ever again.

Mac's smile died as he watched the girl stalk off. His gaze dropped to the well-worn denim outlining the curve of her bottom. The hum of desire tugged at his groin.

He shouldn't have teased her, but it had been irresistible once he'd seen the way her temper lit up the vivid blue-green of her eyes. Just as the urge to kiss her had been irresistible. He still wasn't quite sure what had happened there.

He'd inhaled the clean, fresh scent of her shampoo, caught the panicked flare of arousal in those enchanting eyes—and his brains had gone south so fast instinct had taken over. The driving need to taste her had consumed him. And once he had, her sweet, innocent response had been so intoxicating he'd lost leave of his senses.

Still, spontaneity was one thing, recklessness another.

He searched the terminal, the crowds now thinning. No sign of Danners or any other celebrity snappers—which was a real stroke of luck. If Danners had spotted him while he'd been indulging himself with the girl, the man could have taken twenty pictures and Mac doubted he would have noticed. He picked up his bag, slung it over his shoulder, then realised he still had the wedding invitation she'd handed him clutched in his fist.

He set off towards the nearest bin. As he'd told the girl, he had no brother any more, no need of family and no intention of going to any wedding. The very last thing he needed was to stir up that whole hornet's nest of emotions. Or the agonising memories that he'd boxed up and forgotten about a lifetime ago.

But as he reached the wastebasket and went to toss the invitation in his hand stilled. He lifted the creased envelope and inhaled the hint of scent she'd left on the paper. Soap and wild flowers. The thrill of sexual attraction shot through him. A thrill he hadn't felt in far too long.

He wanted her. He might as well admit it, as after that kiss there was no mistaking it. She was nowhere near as sophisticated—or as amenable—as the women he usually dated, but somehow she'd captivated him. And he didn't captivate easily.

He stared at the envelope. Maybe her difference was her appeal. With those tomboy clothes, that responsive little body and her prickly temper she represented the one thing he hadn't had in a long while. A challenge.

And he hadn't even found out her name.

Cursing softly, he shoved the wedding invitation into his back pocket.

CHAPTER TWO

SITTING on the tube train as the leafy, suburban enclaves of west London trundled past, Juno replayed in her mind her disastrous encounter with Mac Brody—in minute detail, over and over again.

As she left Ladbroke Grove station twenty minutes later and walked to the bottom end of Portobello Road, she finally admitted the truth. Mac Brody might be an arrogant jerk who made Casanova look like a monk, but he wasn't the only guilty party. She had to take a large part of the blame for this morning's debacle too.

At ten past two on a Thursday afternoon with the market closed, Portobello looked like a ghost town, the empty metal frames of the stalls doing nothing to improve Juno's mood. A couple of confused tourists who obviously hadn't read their guidebook properly loitered next to the darkened window of The Rock 'n' Roller Memorabilia Emporium, but otherwise the street was deserted.

She hurried past the colourful façade of Daisy's shop, The Funky Fashionista, and glanced at the window display she'd spent four hours arranging the day before. Her throat thickened with pride as she admired her handiwork—and guilt swamped her.

How could she have been so reckless and irresponsible? How could she have made such a mess of things?

She rubbed her cheek where Brody's stubble had stung. She knew exactly how. As soon as he'd looked at her, as soon as his lips had touched hers, all her common sense and her good intentions had been burned to cinders in a blast of pure unadulterated pleasure.

Kissing him had been like falling into a sunbeam, making every single cell in her body explode with rapture. But how could her body have picked him, of all people, to respond to with such fervour? A man who had the emotional integrity of a gnat? It was against everything she knew and understood about herself. Against everything she had made herself become in the last six years.

She thrust her hand back into her pocket, turning into Colville Gardens.

Forget about the stupid kiss.

It wasn't important. She couldn't let it be. Mac Brody's dangerous sex appeal and devilish good looks would play havoc with any woman's hormones at a distance of two hundred yards—and she'd got a lot closer to him than that. That was all. Her shocking reaction was simply an accident of chemistry—and geography. An accident of thermonuclear proportions maybe. But still just an accident. It didn't have to mean any more than that. Especially as she never intended to step into Mac Brody's orbit again.

She gave a shaky sigh as Mrs Valdermeyer's bedsit co-op came into view, looking like the poor relation to Daisy and Connor's graceful five-storey Georgian next door.

Right now all she wanted to do was hide out in her room at Mrs Valdermeyer's and spend the rest of her day off catch-

ing up on the shop's bookkeeping and persuading herself this
morning had never happened.

She took the first step up to Mrs Valdermeyer's door. Then
stopped.

'Blast.' The hissed expletive cut the summer afternoon
like a knife.

She couldn't do it. Six years ago she'd promised herself
she'd always face up to what she'd done. This morning, she'd
screwed up and let two people she loved down in the process.

Whatever the extenuating circumstances, she owed it to
Daisy to come clean and then apologise.

'I'm so glad you dropped by.' Daisy beamed a smile over her
shoulder as she led the way down the long hallway of her
home. 'The material for my bridal gown arrived from Delhi.
It's absolutely gorgeous—you have to come and drool over
it with me. '

'Great,' Juno replied, trying to muster some enthusiasm
as they entered the sunny open-plan kitchen at the back of
the house. 'Where's Ronan?' she asked, busy postponing
the inevitable.

'Having his nap. The little terror.' Daisy filled the kettle
at the sink. 'Can you believe it? He woke us up at four this
morning.'

Daisy's eyes lit up as she talked about her son and Juno
felt an odd pang in her chest.

'Enough about He Who Does Not Sleep,' Daisy continued. 'We need to have another talk about your maid of honour gown.' She dropped teabags into a couple of earthenware
mugs. 'There is no way I'm letting you walk down the aisle
behind me in jeans and a—'

She stopped talking abruptly as her gaze landed on Juno.
Her eyes widened. 'What on earth happened to your face?
Is that a heat rash?'

Juno clapped her palms to her cheeks. 'Um…maybe.' How much worse was today going to get?

'Let me go get some salve,' Daisy said.

Juno held a hand up. 'Don't bother. Honestly, it doesn't hurt.' She took a steadying breath, determined to force out her confession before Daisy spotted anything else. 'I've done something reckless and irresponsible and I—'

'Reckless and irresponsible?' Daisy interrupted her. 'You? I don't believe it,' she scoffed. 'You're the most cautious person I know.'

That would be yesterday.

'I met Mac Brody at Heathrow Airport this morning and tried to give him the wedding invite.' She rushed the words, before she lost her nerve completely.

Daisy blinked. 'You met Mac? Connor's brother? But…' She trailed off, clearly at a loss for words.

'I had this stupid idea I could persuade him to come.' Juno twisted her hands in her lap. 'I knew how much you wanted him there. You and Connor and after—'

'Wait, wait,' Daisy interrupted again. 'Go back a bit.'

'Pardon?'

'Are you seriously telling me that you went all the way to Heathrow this morning to meet the handsome, charming and stupendously sexy Mac Brody, movie star? Of your own free will?'

Was that a smile wrinkling Daisy's lips?

'So?'

Daisy giggled. 'So, that's fantastic.' Her friend zipped round the breakfast bar and perched on the stool next to Juno's. 'Now, tell me all about it. No detail is too insignificant.'

'What's got into you?' Juno sensed a trap, but couldn't figure out what it could be.

'Just tell me. Is he as hormone-meltingly gorgeous in the flesh as he is in his films?'

A blush blazed across Juno's chest. 'You can't say that. You're practically a married woman.' Was no woman immune to Mac Brody's charms?

'I may be practically married,' Daisy said, not sounding remotely chastened, 'but I'm not blind, am I? Anyway, it's required that I appreciate him—on a purely aesthetic level—after all, Connor and he are the spitting image of each other.'

The instant Daisy had said it, Juno's mind conjured up a picture of Brody in the moment before he'd kissed her. A picture now branded on her brain for all eternity in glorious Technicolor.

The brutal blush scorched the back of her neck.

The two brothers did look remarkably alike. Mac Brody's features were a little less blunt than Connor's and the colour of his eyes was a purer, fiercer blue, but both men shared the same dark, brooding Celtic beauty. The high, hollow cheekbones, the sharply defined brows, the long, leanly muscled physique and that air of casual danger. So why, apart from Brody's gait, hadn't she spotted the resemblance until Daisy had mentioned it?

Maybe because Connor's looks had never made her heart race or her pulse hammer as his brother's had.

She forced the picture to the back of her mind. She couldn't afford to start hyperventilating again.

'It doesn't matter what he looked like,' she said as soberly as she could manage. 'The point is he refused to come to the wedding, he even said he didn't have a brother and I lost my temper with him and made things worse. I wanted to apologise to you and to Connor. Because there's no chance at all he'll come now.'

'Apologise for what? We already know he's not coming,' Daisy said so matter-of-factly, Juno wondered if her sensitive friend had been taken over by Martians. 'We got that letter from his agent, remember?' Daisy finished.

'I know, I was there. You were really upset.'

Daisy waved the comment away. 'I was a bit at first. But after I'd thought about it I could see I was being overly optimistic thinking he'd come around so quickly. Connor was just as stubborn and misguided when I first met him. After the terrible things that happened to them both as kids, it's no surprise Mac has hang-ups to spare.' Daisy gave a heavy sigh. 'It doesn't surprise me he said he didn't have a brother.'

What terrible things?

The question burned on Juno's tongue but she stopped herself from asking it, and ruthlessly controlled the little spurt of sympathy that went with it. Maybe there was more to the situation between him and Connor than she'd assumed. But Mac Brody had been right about one thing: none of this was any of her business—and she'd got into quite enough trouble already trying to make it her business.

'I'm sure Mac needs a family as much as Connor did,' Daisy continued. 'But it'll probably take him a while to figure it out.'

Juno wondered if the man who had kissed her with such confidence had ever needed anybody. But decided not to mention it.

'But enough about me.' Daisy patted Juno's knee, the spark of excitement returning to her voice. 'What did you think of him?'

'Who cares what I thought of him?' Maybe Mac Brody wasn't as big a jerk as she had thought. Maybe he had his reasons for treating Connor the way he had. But what difference did it make what she thought of the man if she was never going to see him again?

'Juno.' Daisy slanted her a long-suffering look. '*Blush* magazine voted Cormac Brody one of the sexiest men in the known universe last month. We've already established he's completely gorgeous. And, according to the gossip columns, he's currently between girlfriends.' She gave another heartfelt sigh. 'Surely this is one man even *you* could not be immune to?'

The light dawned, and Juno saw the trap Daisy had set opening like a yawning chasm beneath her feet. Ever since Daisy had fallen in love with Connor she'd been subtly trying to get Juno to consider dating again. Juno had pretended not to notice. But as Daisy waited for an answer with an expectant look in her eye the blush blazed into Juno's cheeks.

'Something happened.' Daisy pointed at her triumphantly. 'You're blushing and you never blush.'

'Nothing happened,' Juno grumbled, her scalp feeling as if it had been set alight.

Daisy gasped. 'You kissed him,' she said with frightening certainty.

Juno gaped. What was she? A mind-reader now as well as a Martian?

'That's whisker burn on your cheek, not heat rash,' Daisy announced, her voice giddy with excitement. 'I ought to know, Connor's left me with one often enough. And you met Mac off a transatlantic flight. He wouldn't have had time to shave.'

Not just a mind-reader, flipping Sherlock Holmes.

'It was a mistake,' Juno said, trying to dig herself out of the yawning chasm. 'He had to hide from a photographer and then...' Then what? He kissed her into a frenzy and turned all her brain cells to mush? 'It wasn't anything really.'

'Rubbish,' Daisy said. 'He's the first man you've kissed since Tony. That means it's not just something, it's a mega-ginormous something.'

Juno flinched at the mention of Tony's name. 'This has nothing to do with Tony. I got over him years ago.'

'I know you did.' Daisy grasped Juno's hands, her eyes warming with sympathy, making Juno flinch even more.

'But what about what happened afterwards, Juno? And what about the fact that you've spent the last six years of your life paying penance for it?'

'I don't know what you mean.' Juno tried to pull her hands free, but her friend held firm.

'Yes, you do.' Daisy gave a deep sigh. 'When's the last time you wore a dress?'

'I don't like dresses. They don't suit me.'

'When's the last time you put on make-up, then? Or went out on the town? Or felt the thrill of flirting with an attractive man?' Daisy paused, her grip tightening. 'Why are you ashamed of kissing Mac Brody? The man is every woman's wet dream. Why shouldn't you want to kiss him?'

Daisy stopped talking abruptly, her head tilting to one side. A split second later Juno heard Ronan's lusty wail through the baby monitor.

'I better give him a quick slurp,' Daisy said, pointing at Juno. 'But don't you dare go anywhere. As soon as I've got Ronan settled we're going to have another little chat about your maid of honour gown.' Daisy flashed her a quick grin. 'When I finally meet Mac Brody I'm going to give him a great big hug—for making my best friend realise she's a woman again.'

Juno blew out a breath as Daisy shot out of the room to tend to her son.

As if Mac Brody's kiss hadn't given her enough to panic about, Daisy's heart-to-heart was making her feel like a basket case. Folding her arms on the breakfast bar, she laid her head on her hands and squeezed her eyes shut as she listened to Ronan's cries from the monitor and tried to blank out all the conflicting emotions racing through her head.

Ronan's angry wails turned to indignant sobbing and then cut off completely as Daisy's soothing voice came over the intercom. Juno imagined Daisy sitting in the white rocker by the nursery's terrace doors as she settled her son on her breast—and the strange pang she'd felt earlier tore into her chest.

She jerked upright, realising with horror she was ridiculously close to tears.

What on earth had got into her? Where had that fierce sense of longing come from? That empty feeling inside?

Glancing down at her jeans, she saw the tiny tear in the knee and rubbed her hand over it. She forced down the tears, but the uncomfortable whisper of envy refused to go away.

What if Daisy were right? She'd survived what had happened six years ago, but how could she claim to have triumphed over it when she'd been in hiding the whole time since?

No wonder kissing Mac Brody had been such a shock to her system. After six years of pretending she didn't have a sex drive, he'd demonstrated in one fell swoop exactly what it was she'd been missing. And at the same time brought her face to face with what she'd let her life become. Not just cautious and well ordered, but mind-numbingly dull.

She stared out at the weeping-willow tree in the back garden, noticed the remnants of the breakfast Daisy and Connor had shared together that morning on the patio table. And the little spurt of envy got worse.

She'd sat on the sidelines in the last year and watched Daisy find her happy-ever-after and she'd never even admitted to herself that she wanted one of her own.

Maybe it was about time she took the next step and conceded that survival wasn't enough any more. That dressing like a tomboy and making herself into a nun had outlived its usefulness. Would it really be so terrible to admit that she wanted more than that now?

Daisy hummed Ronan's favourite lullaby over the baby

monitor and Juno felt a little frisson of excitement and trepidation wash over her.

She didn't have to go nuts; she could still be practical and sensible.

But why shouldn't she let Daisy design her maid of honour gown? She'd resisted the suggestion up till now because she'd been scared of what Daisy might come up with. Given Daisy's flamboyant dress sense and her eagerness to get Juno back into the dating game, her caution had seemed perfectly justified at the time.

But it didn't feel justified now. She had to stop being such a coward and start easing her life out of the great big enormous rut she'd driven it into.

And, goodness, if she could snog a movie star in Heathrow Airport and live to tell the tale, surely she could let her best friend design a dress for her. Especially if she made it absolutely clear she didn't want the dress to be too out-there.

Honestly, how bad could it be?

CHAPTER THREE

'DAISY, I…I don't know what to say.' Juno gaped at her reflection in the dressing room mirror, bronze satin shimmering over the curves she hadn't known she had until about five seconds ago. 'I might as well be stark naked. I can't walk into the church wearing this. The minister will have a stroke.'

Daisy laughed. 'The minister will *not* have a stroke.' She cocked her head, considering, then crouched to straighten the hem. 'But he may make a pass at you. He is French, after all.'

The shock had started to wear off, a little, but Juno still couldn't muster the ability to laugh back. 'I have a cleavage,' she whispered in disbelief, astonished at the way the plump swell of her breasts strained against the gown's daringly low neckline.

'I told you hooker underwear had its uses,' Daisy commented. Standing, she gave a contented sigh. 'My job is done. You look sensational.' She smiled. 'But the big question is— how do you feel? Do you like it?'

Juno pivoted on her toes to take another quick look over her shoulder at the way the cut-out in the gown's back plunged tantalisingly close to the upper slope of her buttocks. She took a deep breath and let it out slowly.

She'd never worn anything so beautiful before in her life—or so revealing. This wasn't just out-there, it was over the hill and far away.

She studied the full effect in the mirror again. The bouncy little bob Daisy's hairdresser had fashioned out of her haphazard thatch of blonde curls that morning; the dash of lip gloss and mascara that made her fairly ordinary features look exotic; and her slim figure enhanced by the sleek bronze satin of the gown.

Daisy had made her look and feel sexy for the first time in her life. But did she have the guts to pull it off? When she'd decided to unlock her femininity she hadn't had anything quite this liberating in mind.

'I feel like a different person,' she said truthfully.

'Different good? Or different bad?'

Emotion clogged Juno's throat as her eyes met Daisy's in the mirror. 'Different scared but excited.'

Daisy grinned. 'Excited is good.' She touched Juno's arm. 'And scared is to be expected. You're going to knock them dead.' She plucked a tissue out of her dressing gown and folded Juno's fingers over it. 'But remember, no upstaging of the bride is allowed. And you mustn't cry, or your mascara will run and make you look like a raccoon.'

A giggle popped out of Juno's mouth, the flutter of anticipation making her feel a little giddy. 'Good to know.'

Had she ever felt so young or carefree before in her life?

Juno clutched the bridal bouquet as goosebumps rose on her bare arms and she tried to concentrate on the heavily accented voice of the minister. The fragrant scent of blooming orchids and calla lillies perfumed the air as Daisy held Connor's hand and repeated her vows in a clear, steady voice. The elaborate beading on the bodice of Daisy's wedding dress sparkled in the light from the stained-glass window and made Juno think of a fairy-tale princess.

She smoothed her palm over the bronze satin of her gown and smiled, letting the buoyant feeling intoxicate her. She'd stopped believing in happy-ever-afters so long ago, but being here in this beautiful place and watching Daisy declare her love for Connor made anything seem possible. She sniffed, trying to grab a dose of reality and keep her whimsy in check.

Make-up emergencies aside, she had to control herself. Daisy had worked hard for her happy-ever-after and had found the man of her dreams against all the odds. In her experience men like Connor were rarer than fifty-carat diamonds. She needed to remember that before she got all dewy-eyed. And anyway, getting back down the aisle without falling on her bum in the four-inch heels Daisy had insisted she wear was going to be tough enough. Dissolving into tears would only make it tougher.

She frowned as the minister's musical voice was interrupted by a round of shuffles and coughs and hissed whispers. The hairs at her nape tingled and she had the peculiar sensation someone was watching her. She risked a glance over her shoulder. Most of the congregation were craning their necks to stare at something at the back of the small rural church.

She heard Daisy's quick in-drawn breath at the same moment her eyes focused on the shadowy figure standing by the entrance door. And every last molecule of blood drained out of her head and slammed straight into her heart.

Him? It couldn't be.

She blinked furiously, sure she had to be seeing things. But she wasn't. The man who had been a star player in far too many of her dreams over the last two weeks appeared to be staring straight at her. His head dipped and she could have sworn she felt his gaze rake over her figure.

'Connor, it's Mac. He came.' She heard the delight in Daisy's hushed voice as a battalion of butterflies dive-bombed into her stomach.

'Well, now.' Connor sounded as shell-shocked as Juno felt.

The minister coughed deliberately, a pinched expression on his face at the interruption.

'Excusez-moi, monsieur,' Daisy addressed him in her atrocious French. *'Une momento s'il vous plaît, un personne tres important est arrive. Une momento.'*

She grasped Connor's hand. 'We have to welcome him.'

Juno stayed rooted to the spot, watching as if in slow motion, her heart punching her ribs, as Daisy hoisted up her wedding gown and rushed down the aisle with Connor in tow.

Daisy slowed for less than a second when she reached Mac and then threw her arms around his neck. Juno thought she saw him stiffen as he accepted Daisy's hug, his hand settling on Daisy's back for only a moment. When Daisy finally let Mac go, the brothers shook hands and then Connor gripped Mac's shoulder. Juno couldn't hear a word they were saying above the curious and excited conversations around her, but she couldn't help noticing Brody's rigid posture—so different from his relaxed stance at the airport.

Colour flushed across Juno's sternum as Daisy grasped Mac's hand and led him down the aisle. Tucking her bottom lip under her teeth, she stifled the groan as she watched him approach. She must not let him intimidate her. She wasn't the naïve, inexperienced tomboy he'd kissed and made fun of two weeks ago. She was stronger now and much more sophisticated. Or, at least, she looked as if she were.

'You'll never guess who turned up after all,' Daisy teased as they drew level. 'Juno, I believe you've already met Connor's brother, Mac.'

He'd cut his hair. The thick black locks, now militarily short, only showed the slightest tendency to curl around his

ears. The new hairstyle, together with his clean-shaven jaw
and the perfectly tailored dove-grey linen suit and pristine
white shirt, should have made him look a lot less dangerous. They didn't.

She lifted her chin. 'Hello again, Mr Brody,' she said succinctly, despite the butterflies now having a field day in her
tummy.

'Juno, is it?' His gaze flicked down and her nipples peaked
painfully against her push-up bra. 'The name of a goddess,'
he murmured, the penetrating blue of his eyes as disturbing
as she remembered. 'It suits.'

The minister coughed loudly and Juno started, amazed
she'd forgotten they still had Connor and Daisy's wedding
to finish.

Juno riveted all her attention on the bride and groom as
they returned to their positions, struggling to ignore Mac's
alarming presence. The minister launched back into the wedding service and her fingers clenched in a death grip on the
bouquet. How could she detect the light pine scent of his soap
above the heavy fragrance of the bridal flowers? And what
was he really doing here? Wasn't this the man who'd flatly
refused to come to the wedding only a couple of weeks ago?

After what could only have been a few minutes—but felt
like several decades—the minister declared Daisy and Connor husband and wife. Sweeping his new bride into his arms,
Connor executed a Valentino dip and silenced Daisy's joyous
laugh with an extravagantly sexy kiss. The lavish display of
affection only made Juno more aware of the man standing
behind her.

'That looks like fun.' The provocative whisper at her shoulder cut through the spontaneous round of hoots and cheers
from the congregation. 'How about you and me give it another shot?'

Juno stiffened as his breath feathered across her nape. How

typical. While Daisy had found the man of her dreams, she was being tempted by the Devil incarnate.

Her head whipped round. 'No, thank you,' she said, struggling for composure. 'Once was quite enough for me,' she added caustically. But then her eyes dipped to his mouth completely of their own accord—and she could feel those firm, persuasive lips on hers even though they were standing a foot apart.

'Once is never enough, Juno,' he murmured, her name rolling off his tongue with the intimacy of a caress. She jerked her gaze to his to find those laser blue eyes twinkling with the promise of eternal damnation. 'Especially for you and me.'

She turned her back on him, resisting the urge to hit him over the head with the bridal bouquet. If she didn't know better, she'd think he had gatecrashed Daisy and Connor's wedding just to bait her.

Connor released his wife at last and Daisy held her arms out to Juno. 'I'm so happy, I think I might burst,' she whispered into Juno's ear as she gave her a hard hug.

Juno clung on tight, tears stinging her eyes again. 'You've got the best man in the world,' she murmured back. 'And he almost deserves you.'

Connor's hand settled on her shoulder and she released Daisy to see the brotherly affection in his face she'd come to depend on. 'Now don't go mad there,' he said, drawing her into his arms. 'I might get the idea you like me.'

'Let's not get carried away,' she teased, enjoying the easy camaraderie that had built between them in the past year as she hugged him back.

Connor chuckled as he released her. 'As if I'd dare.'

He reached over her shoulder and she turned to see his hand clasp Mac's. 'It's good to have you here, Mac. It's been too long.' Connor's voice thickened. 'Way too long.'

Mac let go of the handshake first. 'Yeah,' he said flatly.

'You'll come to the reception?' Connor asked, sounding unsure. 'Daisy and I want you to meet Ronan, our son. You'd be his uncle, after all.'

Mac's jaw tensed, a cautious, shuttered expression on his face. 'Sure, wouldn't miss it for the world,' he said after a long pause, but the reply sounded apathetic at best.

An uneasy feeling bloomed in the pit of Juno's stomach, doing nothing to calm the dive-bombing butterflies. She recognised that frigid, closed-off tone; he'd sounded the same when he'd told her he didn't have a brother.

Daisy stepped up to Mac and grasped his hand in both of hers. 'You have no idea how much this means to us, Mac,' she said, the unguarded happiness in her voice making Juno's stomach start to hurt. 'All that matters right now is that you're here.' She grinned. 'And that you've brought an appetite. We have enough fancy French cuisine to feed an army back at the château, so you're going to have to consume your fair share.'

'I'm sure I can choke down a bit,' he replied.

'Connor and I have to get back to greet the other guests.' She winked at Juno. 'So I'll leave you in Juno's capable hands. She can introduce you around and show you how to get there.'

No, she won't.

Juno shot Daisy a horrified look. But as she racked her brain for a suitable excuse Daisy lifted the bridal bouquet out of her arms and whispered in her ear, 'Don't be such a wuss. I'm sure he won't bite.' She stifled a delighted laugh. 'Or not yet anyway.'

And with that Connor and Daisy were gone, swallowed up by the crowd of well-wishers as they strolled down the aisle and out into the early evening sunshine as man and wife.

Juno folded her arms across her waist. She loved the dress Daisy had designed for her, but she suddenly felt naked in it. 'It's only about a ten-minute drive to the château,' she said, not able to meet Mac's eyes. 'I can introduce you to most of the people here and then give you directions.'

He snagged her arm as she made to leave. 'I'll skip the introductions.' His thumb caressed the inside of her elbow, making her pulse jump. 'And I only take directions on set, so I think you'd best show me where it is.' His dark brows lifted, matching the mocking smile on his lips. 'You wouldn't want me to get lost, now, would you?'

I should be so lucky, she thought—her pulse pounding where his thumb stroked. 'Perish the thought,' she said, unable to keep the bite of sarcasm at bay.

He laughed, taking her arm and folding it through his. The fluid movement anchored her to his side—and offered virtually no protection against the muscled strength beneath the tailored linen.

'That's the spirit, darlin'.' He chuckled, the subtle scent of his soap overwhelming as he guided her down the aisle.

She should have pulled away, but she didn't want to let him know how much his nearness affected her. So she concentrated on remembering to breathe and making sure she didn't fall flat on her face in her new heels.

'I've not eaten all day and I'm half starved,' he said casually. Too casually.

She couldn't control the tremble of response. Why did she get the impression Daisy and Connor's lavish reception buffet wasn't the only thing he intended to devour?

The soft summer light gave the evening a golden glow as Mac's flashy sports car turned into the château's driveway behind a queue of other cars. Looking through the thicket of oak trees, Juno glimpsed the baroque French castle standing proud at the brow of the hill. Flowering vines hugged the turrets and balconies and accented a trio of tiered terraces linked by a sweeping staircase. As the powerful car inched closer the main terrace and the ballroom beyond came into view, the throng of guests being served by an army of black-clad waiters brandishing trays of canapés and champagne.

Not for the first time that day, Juno thought of palaces and princes and long-ago pageantry. Daisy and Connor had turned their wedding day into a magical event. She bit back the wistful sigh. Enough with the daydreaming. It definitely was not appropriate in her current circumstances.

She glanced across at the man beside her. In the twenty minutes it had taken them to get from the church to the reception, Mac Brody had been surprisingly subdued. There had been none of the teasing or taunts she'd expected. Probably because he'd been swamped by a crowd of people as soon as Daisy and Connor's carriage had been waved out of sight.

She'd had no idea he was so famous! She rarely went to the cinema—never having had much time for make-believe—and she didn't read the gossip mags either.

But more surprising than all the attention had been the way he'd reacted to it. He'd been patient and charming and remarkably gracious about all the requests for autographs and snapshots, but she'd still sensed how uncomfortable he was. Making her wonder what had become of the big bad movie star who had kissed her with such arrogance at Heathrow.

The tension had eased out of his shoulders once he'd ushered her into his sleek little rented Porsche. But as soon as the château had appeared across the valley his hands had fisted on the steering wheel. As if he were bracing himself for what lay ahead.

Why had he decided to come if this evening was going to be such an ordeal?

Juno's pulse skittered as he reversed the car into a small space under one of the leafy oak trees. Perversely, the glimpse of vulnerability behind his super-confident façade had given her own confidence a nice little boost.

He wrenched up the handbrake. 'We'll have to walk it from here.' His lips tilted as his gaze shifted to her feet. 'You think you can handle all the pebbles in those shoes?'

He was probably used to women who could run a marathon in high heels, but the comment sounded amused not disparaging so she smiled back. 'I should be able to manage twenty yards. If not I'll take them off. You'll have to promise not to tell Daisy though.'

'Why's that now?' he asked, his deep Irish voice shimmering across her bare skin.

'Daisy designed my maid of honour gown. It makes a statement, apparently, which includes the high heels. Without them she'll accuse me of ruining the effect or something.' The babble of information petered into silence. Why had she drawn attention to the frock? It was as if she were fishing for a compliment. Which she definitely wasn't.

His eyes drifted over her figure and her heart skidded to a stop. 'Daisy's mighty talented,' he said as his gaze met hers. 'You look gorgeous.'

Heat pumped into her cheeks and her heart began beating double time as the impact of the softly growled compliment sizzled right down to her toes.

Way to go, Juno. Now you feel like you're stark naked again.

CHAPTER FOUR

WHERE in God's name had she gone?

Mac scoured the main ballroom of the seventeenth-century château for the five thousandth time and took another gulp of his lukewarm orange juice. He glanced at his watch. She'd shot off well over three hours ago as soon as they'd arrived with some excuse about changing her shoes. And he'd not seen hide nor hair of her since. He'd searched the damn château, checking out the two ballrooms—one with an orchestra playing big band music and golden oldies, the other with a famous pop group playing live music for the younger crowd—not once but about three times each. He'd also done several circuits of the outdoor terraces festooned with fairy lights and torches, the lavish banqueting hall where a cordon bleu buffet had been laid out, and wandered aimlessly through the labyrinth of smaller salons. The reception party was in full swing now and the close to two hundred guests were letting their hair down and enjoying themselves. All except for him. He hadn't been this wound up since facing his first opening night on Broadway.

The place was heaving. How could one couple have so many friends and acquaintances? And not one of them seemed to be shy about approaching him and asking after his relationship to Connor. No one, that was, except the one woman he'd come all this way to see.

Pull yourself together, man.

He leaned back against the wall and reminded himself to relax. At least he'd finally got rid of the gaggle of teenage girls who had been stalking him for close to an hour but had been too tongue-tied to say anything.

As he watched the dancers twisting the night away with varying degrees of grace—and waited in vain to catch a glimpse of bronze satin and blonde curls—the question that had been bugging him all evening began to bug him some more.

What had possessed him to come here?

Yesterday evening he'd been at the London wrap party of his latest movie getting an offer he shouldn't have been able to refuse from his beautiful co-star Imelda Jackson. But instead of taking Imelda up on her suggestion of a 'quick, one-night liaison to let off steam', he'd turned her down flat.

He scowled and drained the last of the juice. There was no doubting it any more. The blame for that bit of insanity and his mad decision to come to Connor's wedding lay squarely at the dainty feet of the Invisible Miss Juno.

She'd cast a spell on him and lured him here against his will like some damn siren queen. Ever since she'd kissed him at Heathrow, he'd not been able to get her out of his thoughts. When he'd woken up this morning after yet another erotic fantasy in which she was the headline attraction, he'd known it was past time to take affirmative action.

He didn't obsess about sex and he certainly didn't let women he barely knew invade his dreams. So he'd taken the last in a long line of cold showers, dug out the wedding invite—which he'd somehow forgotten to toss—cancelled his first-class flight to LA that evening and booked a mid-morning one to Nice.

It wasn't until he'd been standing at the back of the little French chapel, though, that he'd realised he'd bitten off considerably more than he wanted to chew. Seeing his brother again had been like taking a solid right hook to the gut and that had been bad enough. But then he'd come face to face with Juno, her slim, coltish figure dressed in some gorgeous bit of fancy that stroked over her curves like a lover's hand. He'd looked into those incredible eyes, felt the jolt of awareness thump him hard in the solar plexus, and he'd known dealing with Connor wasn't his biggest problem—not by a long shot.

She hadn't looked one bit pleased to see him. But just when he'd thought he'd got a handle on her, when he'd felt that connection between them in the car and seen the attraction in her luminous blue-green eyes, she'd done her disappearing act.

Now, after an evening of making pointless small talk with people he didn't know but who behaved as if they knew him, of wandering around like a fool searching for someone who seemed to have vanished—and carefully avoiding his brother and his brother's wife—he felt tense and edgy and seriously pissed off—with himself as well as her.

He should have left hours ago. But he hadn't been able to make himself do it. He couldn't walk away from Juno. Not a second time. Whatever the hell she'd done to him two weeks ago, he needed to sort it out. Tonight. He wasn't spending a moment longer with her dogging his thoughts—especially as he now had the vision of her in that damn dress to contend with.

He dumped his empty glass on the tray of a passing waiter and once more swept his gaze over the crowd. As she was the maid of honour, she couldn't have just vanished. The answer had to be that the woman was trying to avoid him—

which was another new experience. But all he really need do was sit her out.

One thing was for definite, though—once he finally got his hands on Little Miss Juno Whatever-The-Hell-Her-Name-Was she wouldn't be getting away again so easily.

His head stilled as a glimmer of gold caught his eye on the other side of the ballroom. He squinted at the shifting shadows in the entrance lobby and his gaze locked onto the mass of curls sheened by candlelight.

Gotcha.

The embers smouldering in his belly leapt back to life as he wound his way across the ballroom. Oblivious to the bumps and shoves from the gyrating dancers, he kept his eyes peeled on his prey every single step of the way.

'Juno, there you are, thank goodness I found you.' Daisy brushed the wayward strands of hair off a face flushed from champagne and excitement. 'Connor's whisking me away to my bridal bower any minute now.' She giggled, the bubbly sound making Juno's heart flutter. 'As soon as we've got Ronan settled. By the way, where's Mac? Connor's worried he might have left without saying goodbye.'

'Why would he do that?' she asked, trying to keep the guilt out of her voice.

She'd basically abandoned him hours ago and she wasn't too proud of herself. But when he'd given her that look, as if he could see right through her clothing, all the insecurities from their kiss had come flooding back and she'd gone into panic mode.

She hadn't been avoiding him. Well, not exactly.

The plan had been to change into some shoes she could actually walk in and then find him again—after all, Daisy had asked her to look after him and she'd probably imagined the intensity of that look. But once she'd returned from her room, he'd been surrounded by a very persistent group of teenage girls, and after that she'd seen him talking to Daisy's impossibly glamorous socialite friend Joannie. In the end, she'd decided to keep out of his way—he made her nervous and she didn't want to make a fool of herself. So she'd chatted to Mrs Valdermeyer, danced with Jacie's son Cal, had a long discussion with New York artist Monroe Latimer and his wife, Jessie, about modern art and made sure she kept well away from Mac Brody all evening. From what she'd observed he hadn't been lonely, so she had nothing whatsoever to feel guilty about.

'Mac looked as if he'd been hit with a brick when he first set eyes on Connor in the church,' Daisy explained, craning her neck to scan the ballroom. 'Poor guy, I don't think he's quite ready for all this yet.' Daisy's gaze returned to Juno and she grinned. 'Plus, it was pretty obvious once he got a load of you in that dress, he hasn't come all this way just to attend our wedding.'

'How do you mean?' Juno asked, her voice shaking at the shocking bubble of excitement. Mac Brody couldn't possibly have come all this way to see her. Daisy was being absurd.

'Come off it,' Daisy scoffed. 'The look he gave you could have powered the National Grid.'

'Do you really think so?' she said, then realised how ridiculous she sounded. What was wrong with her? She didn't want Mac Brody to look at her like that. Did she?

'Yes, I really do.' Daisy's gaze sharpened. 'Which means that, as I suspected—' she wagged her finger like an indignant schoolmarm '—I did not get the whole truth about that kiss. Exactly how hot was it?'

'Don't be silly,' Juno replied, her pulse rate doing the merengue as her panic button tripped again. 'It wasn't that big a deal.' She should never have told Daisy about that stupid kiss. Her hopelessly romantic friend had blown it completely out of proportion—and now she was starting to do it too.

'I'll just bet it wasn't,' Daisy said, not sounding convinced. Huffing dramatically, she looped her arm through Juno's and dropped her voice to a confidential whisper. 'Ju, baby. However much you may have deluded yourself about that kiss, the point is the man is here now and he's seriously hot and seriously interested. So why are you hiding from him?'

'I'm not hiding,' Juno said, trying to convince herself.

'Yeah, right,' Daisy replied. 'Well, that being the case, why don't you get yourself a glass of champagne and go jump him before someone else gets there first? Everyone's talking about him being here—and if you heard what Joannie Marceau said about him you'd know you have some serious competition.'

Exactly how much champagne had Daisy had?

'I'm not going to go jump him. He's not that interested… And it would be…' She shuddered to a halt.

Jumping Mac Brody would be what exactly?

Insane? Petrifying? Exciting? Exhilarating? Electrifying?

Juno frowned. How many glasses of champagne had *she* had? She couldn't actually be considering Daisy's suggestion. So far she hadn't even had the guts to go up and talk to the man.

'Don't you dare rationalise this.' Daisy shot her a pointed look. 'Sometimes you just have to get back on the horse and go with the flow,' she said, happily mangling her metaphors. 'But one thing I guarantee you, if Mac's anything like Connor in the sack, it'll be a ride to remember.'

Juno felt the flush rocket up her neck.

Right, that was definitely a bit too much information.

'Keep your voice down, Mrs Brody.' Connor's deep Irish accent startled them both. 'There are babies present.'

Juno's cheeks flamed as Connor planted a kiss on Daisy's temple, their baby son, decked out in his pyjamas, balanced comfortably in the crook of his arm. She supposed it was too much to hope Connor hadn't overheard Daisy's grossly inappropriate comment.

Fluttering her eyelashes at her new husband, Daisy didn't look the least bit bothered. 'Goodness,' she said. 'If I'd known you were such a square, I never would have married you.'

Connor banded his free arm around her hip and pulled her into a lopsided hug. 'Tough. It's too late to back out now.' The baby chortled, snuggled between them. 'You've already promised to love, honour and obey, angel. And your son and I have it in writing.'

Daisy laughed, looking like the picture of a blushing bride. 'Did I really say obey? Surely not.'

Juno flushed at the flirtatious words, feeling like an interloper. Which was weird. Connor and Daisy kissed and flirted in front of her all the time. It hadn't bothered her in months. Not since she'd got to know Connor. And anyhow this was their wedding day.

So why was it bothering her now?

'Quick, let go, Connor.' Daisy scrambled out of her husband's embrace and smoothed her bridal gown. 'Don't look now,' she said, peering over Juno's shoulder at the ballroom, 'but something tall, dark and dangerous this way comes.'

Juno knew exactly who Daisy was referring to; she could already feel the heat of Mac's gaze burning into the back of her neck.

Her breath caught in her throat at the sight of him striding through the crowd. Six feet two of leanly muscled and devastatingly sexy male. Cool blue eyes focused on her face with the intensity of a heat-seeking missile. Her pulse rate skidded from merengue to macarena in one frantic heartbeat. He didn't just look dangerous. He looked savage. Making her feel like a rabbit caught in the headlights of an oncoming freight train. Why was he glaring at her like that? And why was it making her feel as if she were about to spontaneously combust?

She kept her eyes on his, unable to relinquish eye contact. Okay, this was not good news, because that wasn't panic making her light-headed, it was excitement.

His steps faltered as he registered who was standing next to her. She thought she saw a flash of alarm cross his face, but by the time he drew level it was gone.

'Hello.' He nodded in greeting, but the single word sounded strained, then his eyes settled on the baby cradled in Connor's arms and he went completely still.

'Let me introduce you to your nephew, Mac.' Connor stroked Ronan's soft curls as the baby's sleepy head drooped onto his shoulder. 'This is our son, Ronan *Cormac* Brody.'

Mac continued to stare at the baby. 'Ronan, is it?' he said at last, the words barely audible over the heavy dance beat from the ballroom. He thrust his hands into his pockets. 'He's a handsome lad.'

Connor gave a heavy sigh. 'We think so.' The sadness and resignation in his voice made Juno's stomach hurt again. Had Mac even noticed the baby's middle name? And why was he being so reserved? It was almost as if he had retreated into his own world.

'And he's exhausted, because it's about a decade past his bedtime,' Daisy said, cutting through the tension with a bright smile. Placing a palm on her son's back, she shot Connor a telling look. 'We should get him to bed.' She turned to Mac. 'We're so glad you came, Mac. We would have liked to see more of you tonight, but we understand if you feel uncomfortable.'

Juno waited for Mac to deny it. Had he been avoiding Daisy and Connor all evening? And if so why? But he didn't deny it; in fact he didn't offer any explanation at all.

Daisy took his hand and gave it a quick squeeze. 'You'll

always have an open invitation to visit us in London. Whenever you're ready.'

'Thanks,' he said at last, his eyes flicking briefly to Connor and the baby. 'It was a pleasure to meet you both, and your lad.'

His tone reminded Juno of the polite, distant way he'd spoken to the guests outside the church. And she knew he had no intention of accepting Daisy's invitation.

After the two brothers bid a stilted farewell to each other and Mac accepted Daisy's quick hug, Juno watched the couple leave. Connor wrapped his free arm around his wife's waist and she rested her head on his shoulder. A band of emotion clutched at Juno's chest. The couple had been as disappointed by what had just happened as she had.

Heartsick for her friends, Juno gathered her courage and made herself ask the question she'd wanted to ask ever since Mac had turned up at the church.

'What made you change your mind? Why did you come?' she asked. He'd hurt Daisy and Connor with his reserved behaviour. Did he even realise that? 'Because it's pretty obvious you don't want to celebrate your brother's wedding.'

His jaw went rigid and his brows lowered over stormy eyes. His face wasn't expressionless any more. In fact, he looked furious. 'You think?' he snapped, the tone brittle with sarcasm.

She opened her mouth to ask what on earth was wrong with him, but before she could get a single syllable out he'd grabbed her wrist and hauled her into the ballroom. He'd shoved his way past several couples slow-dancing in the darkness, dragging her behind him, before she'd got over the shock enough to speak.

'What are you doing?' she stammered, struggling to match his lengthy strides, and keep from being hobbled by the long gown wrapping round her ankles.

Either he hadn't heard her or he didn't care. He didn't even break stride. Shock gave way to temper. People were staring at them. People she knew. And if he didn't slow down she was liable to break an ankle trying to keep up with him. She tried to dig her heels in but he just kept on walking, almost pulling her right off her feet.

Getting more annoyed by the second, she grabbed his hand and tried to prise his grip loose, but his fingers only tightened. They reached the other side of the ballroom and he marched through a set of terraced doors leading onto a secluded balcony. The warm night air hit her skin as he released her to kick the door shut behind them. The sharp slam echoed across the valley and cut the throb of the dance music down to a distant hum.

Her bare back butted against the old stone of the balcony rail as he bore down on her, his dark shape silhouetted by the torches framing the door. Anger and something a great deal more disturbing glittered in his eyes.

A shiver rippled down her spine as she got the sudden impression of a tiger let loose from its cage.

'H-have you gone completely mental?' she stammered, starting to feel unpleasantly like that damn rabbit again.

'How long does it take to change a pair of shoes?' he snarled, his voice dangerously low. 'I've been searching the place for you for the last three hours.'

She sucked in a hasty breath. So astonished at the accusation she didn't have a clue what to say. She could not possibly be flattered. That would be nuts. The wayward emotion flowing through her had to be something else.

'You were supposed to be showing me around, darlin'. Remember? Not hiding from me like some frightened little schoolgirl.'

Okay, that wasn't flattering, it was insulting.

'A what…?' she sputtered. Who the heck did he think he

was anyway? He'd just hauled her across the dance floor in front of everyone like a sack of potatoes. 'You were getting enough attention,' she snapped, regrouping as best she could. 'You hardly needed me there, too.'

'Damn. You *were* hiding from me? What the hell for?' Now he sounded incredulous as well as furious.

Her chin shot up as she fought the blush. 'I was *not* hiding from you, you conceited jerk.' But she had been, and she knew it.

His eyes narrowed and it was obvious he knew it too. The blush got worse.

He grasped her arm, tugged her onto her toes. 'What game are you playing?' He held her chin, forced her face up. 'First you kiss me until I'm so hot I can't see straight. Then you run off. And now you're doing the whole damn thing all over again.' He searched her face with an intensity that had heat flooding between her thighs. 'Stop playing hard to get. There's no need,' he murmured, his lips a millimetre from hers. 'Believe me, you've already got my full attention.'

She flattened her palms against the rigid muscles of his chest, her body shaking. His arms banded around her waist, crushing her in his embrace, his heat burning through the thin fabric of her dress.

'I don't want your full attention,' she said desperately, but the words were breathless and unconvincing, her pulse fluttering like the wings of a trapped bird.

'Is that so?' he said, clasping her neck, sinking his fingers into her hair. 'Why don't you prove it, then?'

She heard her own staggered gasp moments before his lips swooped down in a harsh, punishing kiss. Her fingers fisted convulsively in his shirt, but her lips parted and she surrendered to the powerful possessive strokes of his tongue. A fissure of raw, flaming need cracked open and sent the earthquake racking her body right off the Richter scale.

'Kiss me back,' he urged in a strained whisper.

Her arms lifted and circled his neck, all thoughts of resistance gone as the bone-deep longing, the wild, crazy thrill of exhilaration, fizzed inside her like vintage champagne. Their tongues tangled in a frantic dance. A new unknown power surged through her as he shuddered in response.

He tore his lips away, his breathing as ragged as hers. 'No more games,' he murmured.

He held her cheeks in his palms, his eyes black with desire. 'I came here tonight because I want you. My hotel's in the next valley. If we hurry we should be there in ten minutes.'

She searched his face, harsh with desire, and struggled to make sense of what was happening to her.

Mac had lit a fuse inside her that was about to explode. She wanted him to keep on touching her, to keep on kissing her. She was tired of being afraid. Tired of denying herself the kind of human contact that every woman was supposed to crave. She'd never craved it before. Not even with Tony. But she craved it now. This was the moment she'd been waiting for. The moment when she got to triumph over what had happened six years ago. She had to seize it or she could well regret it for the rest of her life.

So she said the only thing that seemed important. 'I don't have any protection with me.'

'Lord, I love practical women.' He barked out a laugh. 'Don't worry, I came prepared, but the supplies are back at the hotel.'

He stroked his thumbs down her neck and gripped her bare shoulders in hot hands. 'Are you sure about this?'

That he would ask, when it had to be obvious she was already a sure thing, gave her the courage to take that final leap into insanity.

She nodded.

'Thank heaven for that,' he said, grasping her hand and marching back across the balcony. 'Let's get the hell out of here. We've wasted enough time already.'

CHAPTER FIVE

MAC got to the hotel in eight minutes flat, driving the Porsche like a maniac as Juno sat trembling in the passenger seat. The scent of leather and man cocooned her in a world of the senses. She tried to focus only on the physical. The painful throb of her heartbeat, the sharp, heady fragrance of arousal that permeated the car and the rush of the warm night air in her hair as the dark countryside flashed past. She didn't look at him. She couldn't allow herself to think about consequences, about caution or practicality.

But as she rushed to follow his long strides through the hotel lobby and up the stairs to his suite her mind tumbled back to that long-ago summer. What if she were getting in over her head? What if she couldn't handle what was going to happen?

She walked through the door into his suite and forced herself to remember she wasn't that foolish girl any more. She'd grown up. She'd survived the very worst and now she was taking the next step. This night with Mac had nothing whatsoever to do with love or dreams. And everything to do with purely physical pleasure. Tony had stolen something from her all those years ago and now she was going to get it back. And that was all that mattered.

Mac didn't ask her permission, he simply strolled through the suite's drawing room into his bedroom, her hand still clutched tight in his. He hadn't said a word and neither had she since they'd left the château.

Her pulse pounded as he stripped off his jacket and threw it over a chair, then flicked up a switch on the wall. The light dazzled her for a second before he came into focus, looking imposingly masculine and out of place amid the room's fussy antique furniture. Then her gaze snagged on the distinctive bulge in his trousers and she froze.

'What is it?'

Her eyes shot to his face. 'Nothing,' she mumbled, feeling like a naïve fool as a whole new set of doubts crowded in.

What if she was terrible at this? What if she made a mistake? In the comforting shadows of the balcony, with him kissing her, holding her, the physical chemistry between them had seemed so simple, so natural, so right. But now, under the bright lights of his hotel bedroom, with his body so obviously hard and ready, it didn't seem simple any more.

She knew next to nothing about sex. She hadn't made love in six years and the little she remembered about that one brief liaison hadn't exactly prepared her to sleep with a man like Mac Brody.

A man who'd probably had more good sex than she'd had hot dinners.

He placed a hand on her shoulder and she jumped.

'Easy, darlin',' he said, stroking his thumb into the hollow of her collarbone. He pressed a kiss to her cheek. 'Relax. This'll be good for both of us, I promise.' He took her hand, led her to the bed. 'Let's lie down. Take it slow and easy. I'm not going to jump you straight off. I swear.'

She couldn't speak, the rapid beats of her heart hammering against her throat. If only he would jump her. Then she could get this over with quickly, before she lost her nerve completely.

He settled next to her, his long, lean body making the mattress dip.

Pushing her hair back, he nuzzled the sensitive skin beneath her ear. The kiss was barely a whisper, but the sizzle of awareness shot through her, giving her a much-needed burst of courage.

Stay in the moment, Juno. Just stay in the moment.

She reached for his shirt, yanked it free of his trousers with clumsy haste. As he teased her neck with light butterfly kisses her palm explored the hot, muscled flesh, discovering the ridges of his six pack and the thin trail of hair bisecting his belly button. But then his fingers slipped under the straps of her dress, easing the bodice down and exposing the lace at her cleavage. She shuddered, her hands trembling to a halt on his belly.

She didn't think she could do this.

He moved back. Lifting her fingers, he kissed the knuckles. 'Okay, enough of that now.' His voice rasped, the strain clear. 'You look scared to death. What's wrong?'

She swallowed, the tiny bit of courage deserting her. Could he see? Could he already tell how useless she was at this?

'Can we turn the lights off?' she whispered. She didn't want him to see her naked. Her breasts were small, her hips narrow and boyish.

He cupped her cheek, a tenderness in his eyes she hadn't expected. 'No, we can't. I haven't waited two long weeks to make love to you in the dark.'

She opened her mouth to object, but he pressed a finger to her lips.

'Let's compromise.'

He left the bed to turn off the main light switch, leaving

only the pearly glow from the bedside lamp. Even so, panic consumed her as he returned.

This whole scenario had the potential to be a total disaster. Why hadn't she thought it through?

She shut her eyes and braced herself, expecting him to continue undressing her. But he took her hand and flattened the palm against the front of his shirt.

'How about you set the pace?' he said.

Her eyes flew open. 'You don't mind?' she whispered, pathetically grateful for the unexpected respite.

'Why would I mind?' he said, the tilt of his lips full of sexual promise. 'You're going to be doing all the work.'

She gave a small smile back, the pressure in her chest releasing a tiny bit. Maybe this wouldn't be a total disaster.

Her hands trembled as she slipped the small buttons of his shirt out of their buttonholes. With each new glimpse of the tanned, lightly haired torso, she wrestled back a tiny bit of control, another whisper of courage. And slowly but steadily, the well of desire sprang back to life.

He smelled delicious, clean soap and spicy aftershave and the musky scent of man. She opened the sides of his shirt, nudged the starched cotton off broad shoulders. As her courage grew she indulged herself. She investigated the flat brown nipples nestled in the dark curls of hair, heard his muffled grunt as she learned the contours and textures of his heavily muscled chest, the ridged definition of his abdomen. But as the exploration inched lower her fingers slowed and eventually stopped dead on the waistband of his trousers. She couldn't take her eyes off the bulge, which had got a great deal more prominent.

The breath backed up in her lungs. She'd thought she could handle him, could handle what was going to happen between them. But was she really ready to handle *that*?

His hand covered hers. 'Juno, is this your first time?'

She looked up to find him watching her. Embarrassment scorched her cheeks at the perceptiveness in his gaze. 'Of course not. I'm twenty-two years old,' she said, wanting to sound indignant.

'But you've little experience. Am I right?'

Mortification engulfed her. She grappled to pull up the straps of her dress. She had to get away, get out of here, before she made an even bigger mess of things. But as she tried to sit up he grasped her wrist.

'What's this now? Where are you off to?' he asked, sounding both amused and confused.

She tugged on her arm, refusing to look at him. 'You're right. I haven't got much experience at this. In fact I've got hardly any,' she said. What was the point in pretending? She might have matured emotionally since that hideous night six years ago, but that wasn't going to be enough. Not to deal with a man like Mac Brody. 'After all the women you've slept with, you're bound to be disappointed,' she finished, feeling utterly defeated.

So much for seizing the moment. How could she ever have believed this would work? Of course he'd seen through her pitiful charade. Wearing a beautiful dress, putting on a bit of make-up, tottering about in high heels, didn't suddenly make you a sex goddess.

He let go of her wrist and cradled her chin, forcing her to meet his eyes. 'Sweetheart, you've no need to worry about disappointing me. If I was any more aroused at the minute, I'd be doing myself an injury.'

His wry amusement washed away a little of her hurt and humiliation.

He sighed. 'This isn't a test.' His thumb cruised the swell of her breasts, dipped into the curve of her cleavage. 'I'll not be grading you after the event.' Her nipple hardened as his thumb circled the rigid peak through her gown. 'But if you've performance anxiety, why don't I take the lead for a while?'

Suddenly she couldn't breathe. The rasp of his voice seduced her as she concentrated on the lazy stroking.

'I doubt I'm as prolific as you think,' he continued, his clever fingers finding the zip of her dress and giving it a gentle tug. 'But it seems I've got a bit more experience.' The soft swish as the teeth released seemed deafening in the languid silence.

She shivered as he undressed her, pulling the bodice down and baring her to the waist but for her push-up bra. The lace seemed to have constricted around her lungs like a corset.

'Lie back,' he coaxed, tracing his finger in a line of fire down her chest, over the front hook of her bra. 'Let me do the work for a while.' She sank into the pillows as the electric touch sizzled across her abdomen and drew circles around her belly button. 'All you need do is tell me what you like.'

'But I don't know what I like,' she panted out and then bit her lip.

Why had she said that? He'd think she was a moron.

He flashed her a cocky grin, his large palm flattening on her waist. 'Then we're going to have a hell of a time finding out.'

She nodded, not sure she could speak.

'Good girl,' he said, touching his lips to hers as his hand swept up and deftly undid her bra.

She jolted, panic assaulting her as he nudged the cups aside. 'Please, don't.'

She tried to cover herself, but his hands gently bracketed her upper arms, pinning her to the bed. She shut her eyes, her body quivering with acute embarrassment as she felt his gaze on her breasts. She'd always known she wasn't well endowed, but it hadn't bothered her too much. Until now.

'Why would you hide yourself?' The words were gruff with astonishment.

Her eyes opened to see the fierce approval in his gaze. A brutal blush fanned out across her chest. 'They're a bit small,' she whispered.

He gave a soft chuckle, shaking his head. 'Are they?'

Releasing her arms, he cupped her breast in one hot palm. He rubbed his thumb across the nipple and bent to capture it with his mouth. The peak engorged in a rush as his teeth teased and bit softly into the sensitive flesh. She arched into his mouth as darts of fire arrowed to her core.

She panted, her breathing harsh as he feasted on one breast then the other, stroking and kissing and nipping, then drawing the peak into his mouth and suckling hard.

'They're so sensitive, so responsive,' he whispered, his breath cool against her fevered flesh as he lifted his head. 'Don't you know how beautiful that is?'

'Is it?'

He dropped his forehead to hers, sighed. 'Darlin', let's get you naked. I'd no idea you had so much to learn.'

She could hear the teasing note in his voice. And she didn't care. She wanted to learn it all now, and she wanted him to be the one to teach her.

So she lifted her bottom as he stripped off her dress and didn't resist as the final barrier of lacy satin followed her other garments to the floor.

'You're gorgeous,' he murmured, his hands caressing with tantalising slowness—moulding her breasts, sweeping over the curve of her buttocks and stroking her thighs.

Desperation seized her as he delved into the curls between her legs. Heat coiled as his fingers got frustratingly close to her centre and then withdrew. Was he trying to drive her mad? Why wasn't he touching her where she wanted to be touched the most?

'Please… There.' The words choked out as she grasped his shoulders and raised her hips, instinctively seeking that crucial touch.

He laughed, the sound oddly tense. 'Now you're getting the hang of it.'

She wanted to reprimand the smug tone, but then his fingers plunged into the wet heat at last and she couldn't think, let alone speak. She jerked wildly, her nails scraping his back, shocked by the brutal pleasure that twisted viciously inside her. He stroked and rubbed, torturing the pulsing nub, making her sob as her senses rioted, desperate for release.

The broken cry echoed in her head as her body clamped down and then shattered into a billion glittering pieces.

Mac eased his zip down, his erection painfully swollen as it sprang free.

He wanted to make this last, he wanted it to be as good for them both as he'd promised. But watching her climax had lit a fire in his gut that was fast turning to an inferno. For the first time in his life he was in serious danger of losing his precious control. He forced himself to steady his breathing as he kicked off his trousers and boxer shorts and sheathed himself with the condom.

Her eyelids fluttered open and a tentative smile curved her lips, those gorgeous aquamarine eyes all fuzzy with afterglow.

He drew his thumb over the downy skin of her cheek. 'How was that now?'

'Amazing,' she whispered, sounding shocked and happy. 'I had no idea…' she began, then broke off. Her cheeks flushed a bright rosy pink, off-setting the vivid colour of her eyes beautifully.

He let his hand drop. He could actually feel his heart throbbing. He wanted her, with a power he hadn't felt since he had been an untried lad of thirteen, and sex had been the holy grail of his existence.

The irrational thought had a tiny slither of unease wedging itself into the thick haze of lust. He ignored it. She wasn't a virgin. She'd told him so. And neither was he—even if her inexperienced, untutored response had made him feel like a boy again.

'Thank you,' she said. 'Thank you so much. I didn't expect...' She stopped, gave a breathless laugh, the sound sultry and yet unbearably sweet. 'I didn't expect it to be that good.'

Pride surged through him. Pride and something that felt uncomfortably like possessiveness.

'There's no need to thank me,' he said, taking her hand in his and kissing her fingertips. 'As I'm now planning to get my reward.'

'Oh, yes, of course.' She shifted against him, her naked hip brushing his erection as she glanced down. 'I'm sorry, you haven't... Yet...'

She looked both panicked and perplexed and he wanted to hug her. He'd thought she was cute the first time he'd laid eyes on her. She wasn't cute. She was adorable.

He hooked his hand around her waist, tugged her closer. 'How do you feel about round two?' he said, trying to keep the urgency out of his voice. He couldn't wait much longer, but he didn't want to rush her and ruin it.

'If it's as good as round one,' she said with bravado, 'I'm all for it.' Then she slipped trembling arms around his neck.

'I'll do my best,' he said, praying for patience as he grasped her hips and hauled her under him.

She stared up at him, offering herself in a gesture so fearless and so giving he felt something twist hard in his gut.

Ignoring it, he positioned himself at her entrance and sank into her.

* * *

Juno groaned, the pressure immense as the blunt head of
his erection pushed into the slick swollen folds of her sex.
His hands angled her hips, easing his entry, but still it felt
overwhelming. The muscles of her sex clenched, her fingers clutching his neck as a moan escaped her, the pleasure
replaced by a brutally stretched feeling that was too close
to pain.

'Shh,' he crooned, pushing the damp hair from her brow.
'It'll take a minute, darlin'.'

He held still for what seemed like hours but could only
have been moments as she adjusted to the solid length. Then
he moved, her breath catching as he lodged deeper still. The
discomfort dimmed, overpowered by a staggering feeling
of fullness.

She sobbed at the shocking burst of pure pleasure as he
flexed his hips and nudged a place deep inside.

'Now was that good, or bad?' he asked, sweat glowing
on his forehead.

'Good. It was good.' Her voice broke. 'Can you do it
again?'

He chuckled, the sound rich and self-satisfied and tinged
with desperation. 'I'll give it my best shot.'

She wrapped her thighs around his waist and held on for
dear life, bucking clumsily beneath him as the slow, solid
thrusts got stronger, faster and more relentless. Her cries
punctuated his harsh grunts as the bursts of pleasure intensified, rolling into one unstoppable wave.

She rode the crest for an eternity. Exquisite pain, inde-
scribable pleasure crashing over her as she soared through
that final brutal peak into oblivion.

CHAPTER SIX

Juno languished in the last throes of the mind-blowing orgasm cocooned in Mac's arms. Her back cradled against his chest, she could still feel him, semi-erect, outlined against her bottom as his hand covered her breast. His measured breathing brushed her nape.

'So, are you ready now for your marks out of ten?' he murmured.

The wry tone made her lips quirk.

She should have been embarrassed, but she felt so lethargic, so sated, so good about herself it was hard to feel anything but complete satisfaction. She'd done it. She'd finally found out what all the fuss was about, and it had been glorious.

'If it's not at least a nine I don't want to know,' she replied boldly, and basked in his answering chuckle.

'I'm thinking ten out of ten for initiative, five out of ten for staying power.'

She nudged him with an elbow and he laughed, tightening his arm round her waist.

'Now, now, all I'm saying is we're going to have to work on your stamina, darlin'.'

His warm teasing had pride swelling her chest.

They'd been good together, so much better than expected. She might not be the best sex he'd ever had, but she hadn't disappointed him, or herself. To use one of Daisy's analogies, she'd got back on the horse and she hadn't fallen off. And, as predicted, it had been a spectacular ride.

She grinned, snuggled against him and hissed as the aching tenderness between her thighs caught her unawares.

'There now.' He rolled her over and searched her face. 'I hurt you?'

'No, you didn't,' she said, moved by the worried frown. She shifted her bottom and felt the slight soreness again. 'It's just... It's been a while.'

'Damn, I'm sorry,' he said, rubbing his palm on her midriff. 'How long has it been?'

She curled away from him and drew her knees up, feeling a little self-conscious after all. 'A while. That's all.'

He trailed a finger along the curve of her neck, tucked her hair behind her ear. 'There's no need to be embarrassed. You're a beautiful and passionate woman. I'm only curious.' His hand rested on her hip. 'How long exactly is a while?'

She huffed out a breath and considered lying to him, but discarded the idea. Why should she be ashamed? 'Six years.'

'Six...?' The bed bounced as he pulled her onto her back. 'Six years? But you would have been little more than a child.'

'I wasn't a child,' she said abruptly, her heart tripping at the concern in his gaze. 'I knew exactly what I was doing.' She hadn't been prepared for the consequences of her actions, but that didn't matter any more.

'Hell, Juno.' He framed her face, planted a kiss so full of tenderness on her lips she felt a frightening ache around her heart. 'What happened?'

She took his hands in hers, pulled them from her face. The ache getting worse.

She couldn't do this. She couldn't risk falling into any kind of intimacy with this man. What they'd done could never mean anything more than one night of pleasure. She knew that. He was so far out of her league it wasn't even funny. And even if he hadn't been, she knew she couldn't afford to mistake sex for love. Not a second time.

'It was a long time ago,' she said flatly. 'It's not important.'

She lifted the sheet, scooted across the bed, shivering despite the sultry summer heat. 'I'm tired. I ought to go.'

But as she bent to pick up her discarded gown the bed tilted behind her and then long thighs bracketed hers. His arms folded around her waist, trapping her against him. 'Stay.' He let out a slow breath. 'Stay for tonight. No more questions, I promise.'

She should go, but somehow the warmth of his arms, the brush of his breath against the top of her head felt so solid, so reassuring she couldn't make herself say the words.

'Come on, darlin',' he murmured against her ear lobe. 'I won't ravish you again. We both need our sleep. And it's late. Past midnight. You won't get a taxi too easily at this time of the night.'

She watched over her shoulder as he piled the pillows against the bed's ornate headboard. Propping himself on them, he reached out, threaded his fingers through hers.

'Come back to bed,' he whispered, the rough cadence of his voice more addictive than any drug. 'I'll give you a lift wherever you need to be first thing in the morning.'

She gave a huge yawn and he chuckled.

'Lord love it, but good sex is exhausting, isn't it?' he teased, cradling her head on his shoulder and drawing the sheet up to cover them.

'I can't stay for long,' she murmured, another yawn escaping as she snuggled into his embrace.

She couldn't stay the whole night. That would be dangerously self-indulgent. But what real harm would it do to stay for a little while? She knew exactly where she stood. Exactly what this meant and what it didn't. She'd sorted it all out clearly in her mind. And her limbs seemed to have got so heavy, as if she'd been running a marathon. She laid her hand on his chest, took a deep breath of his exquisite scent and felt the steady rise and fall of his breathing beneath her palm.

It felt so nice to be held, just once.

Her eyelids drifted closed as she gave herself permission to enjoy the feeling. For a little while.

He should have let her go. Why hadn't he let her leave?

The question tormented Mac as Juno's head grew heavy on his shoulder and her body relaxed into sleep. He switched off the bedside lamp and glanced down as a beam of moonlight turned her soft curls to a dull gold.

Hadn't he always avoided cuddling after sex? Sharing a bed all night made him feel claustrophobic. So why didn't it feel claustrophobic now? Why did it feel reassuring, listening to her gentle snores and having her body snug under his arm?

And why couldn't he get rid of that picture of her at sixteen, alone and vulnerable, out of his head?

Something had happened to her six years ago, something unpleasant. Why else would she have gone without sex for so long?

But why should it matter to him? And why should he feel responsible?

He'd been careful with her, patient even, though it had nearly killed him. But for some dumb reason he'd still needed to hold her tonight, to keep her with him. To be sure she was all right.

He squeezed his eyes shut, a series of other unsettling pictures from the day intruding on his memory like unwelcome ghosts. Connor and Daisy walking down the aisle towards him, their hands clasped together. Connor's baby son asleep in his daddy's arms. The flicker of fear in Juno's face when she'd caught sight of his arousal for the first time.

He sighed. Was it any wonder he was behaving irrationally? Hadn't he been on an emotional roller coaster the whole day?

Coming to Connor's wedding had been a mistake. He'd known it from the start, but he'd let his libido rule his head and come anyway—and very nearly opened up old wounds in the process. He'd taken advantage of the girl, and used the attraction between them to make sure he kept those wounds well and truly closed. And now he was paying the price.

Guilt. Good old Catholic guilt. That was all this was. He didn't feel responsible for her, he felt guilty about the way he'd used her. Especially once he'd found out how innocent she was.

He inhaled the summer-meadow scent of her shampoo, listened to her breathing and a wry smile curved his lips.

What was he beating himself up for? He'd given her a good time. More than a good time. He was pretty sure he'd given her her first orgasm. She'd even thanked him for it. So what if he'd used her—she'd enjoyed it, hadn't she?

Arousal pulsed in his loins at the memory of how much they'd both enjoyed it.

Down, boy. A repeat performance wasn't the best idea.

He'd be letting her go in the morning with no regrets.

He needed to return to his life and the work he loved. To get back to the clean, uncomplicated solitude of his house in Laguna Beach. And he needed to forget all about Connor and his family, and the girl lying so trustingly in his arms.

But as he fell into dreams she shuddered in her sleep, and his arm tightened around her shoulders instinctively.

CHAPTER SEVEN

JUNO lurched awake to the sound of an overzealous sparrow on dawn-chorus duty, the brilliant morning sunshine blurring her vision, but none of her other senses.

The heady scent of sex smothered the light perfume of the terrace flowers. Goosebumps prickled on her naked skin and a large, rough hand lay possessively on her hip. A low grunt sounded behind her and the hand twitched, sending shock waves rippling through her.

She sneaked a look over her shoulder. And her vision—and all the torrid memories from the night before—came into sharp, vivid focus. Mac Brody lay spreadeagled on his stomach, his broad shoulders and long legs hogging most of the bed and the sheet riding low on his buttocks. His back rose and fell in a steady rhythm. The shadow of stubble on his jaw made him look as swarthy as a pirate, highlighting chiselled cheekbones, but his thick dark lashes were almost boyish.

She shifted onto her back and lifted his hand to place it by his side, being careful not to wake him. She paused, noticing for the first time the nasty scar that slashed from his bicep down to his elbow. Why hadn't she noticed that last night? The hot spot between her legs pulsed hard as she took in the red scratches on the tanned skin of his shoulder blade. Of course she hadn't noticed the scar, she'd been too busy availing herself of his staggering skills as a lover.

Not that she was an expert on such things, but she'd leapt into the lion's den last night and he'd made it the most exhilarating, the most erotic experience of her life. He'd been so careful with her, so patient. Knowing who he was and what he was, she never would have expected such care or generosity.

Edging closer to him, she pressed a light kiss to his cheekbone. He gave a soft grunt, but didn't stir.

'Thank you, Mac Brody,' she whispered, and felt the tingle of tears.

Horrified, she wiped her eyes. What was she doing? She mustn't let herself get over-emotional about their night together. It was only sex—and she had to remember that.

Her heart wedged into her throat. She should never have spent the entire night in his arms. This was just the sort of intimacy she'd been determined to avoid.

They'd made no promises, no commitments. How long was he even likely to remember her name? After all, a man didn't make love like that unless he'd had a lot of practice.

She slipped out of the bed. She'd seized her Cinderella moment and made the most of it. But she'd taken a foolish, self-indulgent risk falling asleep in his arms. She wasn't about to make it worse by hanging around like some star-struck groupie until he woke up.

Having wiggled into her underwear and the heavily creased gown, she gathered up her shoes and crossed the room. She hesitated next to the antique desk beside the door, then picked up a pen and dashed off a quick note on the hotel's letter-headed stationery. She folded the thick white paper, scribbled Mac's name across it, then tiptoed to the bed to prop it by the phone on the bedside table.

Tilting her head, she took one last opportunity to admire

Mac's magnificent body sprawled across most of the bed. And felt the inevitable throb of response.

How could he still look so dangerous when he was fast asleep?

She took a fortifying breath and crept back across the silk carpet barefoot, suddenly eager to get as far away as possible. But as she shut the door the soft click of the lock echoed in some small neglected corner of her heart.

Five hours later, a raucous ring jolted Mac out of a nicely carnal erotic fantasy. Swearing, he kept his eyes shut and groped for the phone.

'Brody,' he grunted into the mouthpiece once he'd finally located the damn thing. 'This better be really good.'

'Mac, why have you had your cell off for two days? And what the heck are you doing in France, man?'

Mac groaned, recognising the harassed Brooklyn accent of his personal publicist, Mickey Carver. 'None of your business, Mick,' he said, his head now throbbing as insistently as his groin. He went to dump the phone, but heard Mickey's panicked plea crackling down the line.

'Don't hang up, Mac. I'm begging you, here.'

He exhaled slowly and brought the handset back to his ear. There was no point hanging up on Mickey. He'd call the management and have them storm the hotel room. 'All right, Mick.' He opened his eyelids and got blasted by five thousand watts of sunshine in both retinas for his trouble. 'But keep your voice down,' he whispered, rubbing his eyes. 'I'm not alone.'

He eased over onto his back and blinked groggily at the indent on the fluffy goose down pillow beside him.

Holding the phone away from his ear, he strained to hear any sound from the en suite. All that greeted him was

Mickey's muffled voice and the rustle of a breeze in the terrace vines.

He frowned. Strange. Where was the woman who had starred in the dream Mickey had so rudely interrupted?

'Hold up, Mick,' he said, interrupting the whining monologue he hadn't heard a word of. 'Can I call you back?'

Mickey heaved an exaggerated sigh. 'Sure. But do me a favour. Next time you decide to rearrange the tonsils of some London shop girl, give me a heads up, will you? I've been fielding calls from the British tabloids most of the night. They haven't quit yet and it's now six in the morning LA time.'

Mac bolted upright, his knuckles whitening on the handset. 'What did you say?' he asked, somewhat redundantly, as he'd heard every word this time—and was having the heart palpitations to prove it.

'The photos are all over the morning papers in the UK.'

'What photos?' Why couldn't Mickey ever get to the point?

'Of you and the shop girl,' Mickey said, sounding taken aback. 'Getting physical on some balcony in France.'

Mac's astonishment turned to fury.

Some bastard had snapped their photo last night. And now that private, impossibly sexy kiss had been served up for public consumption, to titillate people over their morning coffee. A snarled expletive cut the country quiet as his stomach turned over.

'Hey, man. Don't sweat it.' Mickey's voice drifted on as Mac's temper surged out of control. 'They're long-range but you both look really hot. All we need here is our own angle.'

He hated those damn parasites. Why couldn't they leave him the hell alone?

'It'll be great publicity for the European release of *Death Game*,' Mickey wittered on. 'Especially as the girl's British. Hey, she's not there with you, is she?' Mickey's voice peaked with excitement. 'Could I get a quote?'

Mac took a couple of deep breaths. 'No, she's not here,' he growled, suddenly glad of her temporary absence.

He wanted to kill someone and it might as well be the messenger. 'I don't want any damn quotes. Not a one. I've told you before, my sex life is no one's business but my own and if you give a single column inch of mileage to this story you're fired.'

There was a pregnant pause on the end of the line, then Mickey's voice came back on, considerably subdued. 'Understood, Mac. How do you want me to spin it, then?'

Was he hitting his head against a brick wall or what?

'No spin, Mick. No nothing. Tell them no comment and that'll be the end of it.'

Mickey cleared his throat. 'Not quite, man.'

'Why not?'

'They've got the girl's name.'

Damn. 'I'll take care of the girl,' he said and realised he meant it.

Juno would be completely unprepared for what was about to hit her—and he planned to be there to protect her from the worst of it. He decided not to think about the fact that he'd never been the knight-in-shining-armour type before.

He went to hang up and then a thought occurred to him. He brought the phone back to his ear. 'Mick, wait. By the way, what *is* her name?'

He didn't know where she'd popped off to or how long she'd be and he needed to put the wheels in motion. He'd start by booking them a couple of flights to LA to get her out of harm's way.

'Man, you didn't get her name before you nailed her?' Mick's laddish chuckle grated on Mac's last nerve. 'Boy, oh, boy, you're such a player. If I had that kind of power, I'd be hitting on everything that moved too—'

'Shut up, Mick, and give me her damn name,' he snapped,

not liking the renewed spurt of guilt at his publicist's insinuations.

He listened to the rustle of paper before Mickey spoke. 'According to this one she's called Juno Delamare. Works in some dress shop in Portobello Road in West London named The Funky Fashionista and—'

Mac slammed the phone down, having heard all he needed to. Swinging his legs off the bed, he ran his fingers through his hair, scrubbed his hands down his face. He stared out of the open terrace doors, and noticed how high the sun was in the sky.

What time was it? If it was past six in LA it had to be past noon here. After yesterday's emotional roller coaster—not to mention the mind-blowing sex—he'd slept like a dead man.

No wonder she wasn't here. She could have woken up hours ago. She must have headed off in search of breakfast.

His heartbeat evened out for the first time since he'd spotted her empty pillow. He'd have a quick shower and then hunt her down—and tell her how they were going to handle the press.

He stood and stretched, deciding not to dwell on the little resolution he'd made to himself last night to send her packing first thing in the morning. He couldn't let her go. Not after he'd got her into this mess. She'd just have to spend a couple of weeks with him in LA where she'd be safe from prying eyes.

His lips curved as he wrapped the bed sheet round his waist. After the way things had gone last night, he didn't see it being a hardship for either one of them.

He took a step forward, heard the crunch and looked down to see a piece of notepaper snagged under his big toe. It had his name written on it in block letters.

He picked it up and opened it.

His heartbeat skipped up as he read the two short sentences, three times over.

Dear Mac,
Thank you for a memorable night.
Have a wonderful life.
Juno

Astonishment came first.

Unbelievable. She hadn't gone out for a croissant, she'd run out on him.

Swiftly followed by temper. He crushed the letter in his fist.

She hadn't just run out on him, she'd left him a damn kiss-off note.

What exactly did she mean by 'memorable night'? Like he was some convenient stud she could dump when it suited her. And that crack about having a wonderful life. So she'd decided they were never going to see each other again, had she?

He stalked across the room and shoved open the door of the en suite. What gave her the right to decide these things all by herself? And then hare off like some scared rabbit before they had a chance to discuss it.

She could forget that. No woman gave Mac Brody a kiss-off note, especially once he'd decided he didn't want to be kissed off.

Dropping the bed sheet, he whipped back the shower curtain with enough force to rip part of it off the rail. He stepped into the tub, cursing the sight of his morning erection standing proud despite his aggravation.

Wasn't that just fine and dandy?

He switched the shower dial to *Froid* and gritted his teeth. If it wasn't bad enough she'd mortally offended him and done another damn vanishing act, she'd now added injury to her insults.

The frigid water hit him like a slap in the face.

'Wonderful life, my arse,' he growled as he reached for the soap.

CHAPTER EIGHT

JUNO let Daisy's excited chatter and Connor's calm measured responses float over her as the limousine cruised off the Westway and headed towards Portobello.

Why did she feel so out of sorts?

Ever since she'd arrived at the château that morning, she'd felt totally unlike herself. Weary and unsettled, dissatisfied and confused. Of course, it didn't help that her body ached in some very unusual places. Or that her head hurt from fielding Daisy's endless enquiries about why she'd appeared at eight in the morning still wearing her maid of honour gown. Or that their flight had been delayed for three endless hours in Nice airport because of some oversight with the paperwork.

But why couldn't she shake this hollow feeling—as if she'd lost something she could never get back? And why did she keep picturing Mac Brody, the bronzed skin of his back gleaming in the dawn light as she shut the hotel door?

She'd promised herself she wouldn't moon over the man. She couldn't afford to start believing in fantasies. However mouth-watering this one might have been. And yet she couldn't seem to stop herself.

The only explanation was exhaustion.

What she needed was to return to the quiet order of her bedsit, ground herself in real life again and sleep for a week.

A tired sigh left her lips as the pale Georgian terraces of Colville Gardens glided past the car window. Not long now.

'What the hell..?' Connor's startled shout had Juno's drooping eyelids jerking open.

She peered out of the limo's tinted window. How peculiar. A herd of people crowded round the front of Daisy and Connor's house, spilling off the pavement and blocking the road. Then one man with two enormous cameras hanging from his neck broke from the herd and ran towards them. He lifted one of his cameras and fired. The flash of strobe lighting seared Juno's eyeballs like a flame-thrower. By the time she'd refocused the pack of photographers had surrounded the vehicle like ravening wolves.

'We'll have to run for it.' Connor lifted Ronan out of his car seat and cocooned the crying baby against his shoulder. He tapped the partition. 'Jim, get as close as you can and then call the police.'

The chauffeur signalled with his mobile, already dialling the local constabulary.

Juno stumbled out of the car behind Daisy and Connor. The barrage of flashes blinded her as whirring shutter clicks and urgent shouts battered her eardrums. She shielded her eyes from the glare and gripped Daisy's hand as they elbowed their way through the crowd. But she couldn't shield her ears from the questions fired at her like bullets.

'Juno, how long have you known Mac Brody?' 'Is he as hot as everyone says, Juno?' 'You two an item now?' 'Where's Mac? Will he be visiting you in Portobello for another night of passion?'

Her head throbbed and her eyes stung as she and Daisy ran up the steps of the house behind Connor and the baby, flash-bulbs exploding in her face like a demented fireworks display.

She could hear Ronan's high-pitched wailing as Connor shoved open the door, jostled them inside and then slammed it in the face of the media horde.

'What the hell was that all about?' Connor shouted.

'Keep your voice down,' Daisy admonished him. She scooped the distressed baby out of Connor's arms and rocked him.

All three of them jumped when a newspaper landed on the mat and a nose and mouth appeared in the letter slot. 'Fantastic picture, Juno. You sure you ain't got a comment?' a disembodied cockney voice pleaded.

Connor swore and slapped the flap shut as he bent to pick up the newspaper. 'Take this and go to the study,' he said, shoving the paper into Juno's hands. 'I'll wait for the police.' He pulled his mobile out of his top pocket. 'The firm's security can send over some muscle as well.'

Juno followed Daisy and the baby to the study, consumed by guilt.

Why hadn't she thought of the possible fallout from last night? Mac was a famous man. Of course their little tryst wouldn't have remained a secret. And now she'd brought this madness down on Connor and Daisy, on the first day of their honeymoon.

Daisy peeked out of the study window. 'Good grief, they're like a swarm of locusts,' she murmured, her voice ripe with fascination as she let the curtain fall.

'This is all my fault,' Juno mumbled, hideously ashamed.

'Ju, what on earth's the matter?' Daisy hurried over and took her arm. 'Sit down before you fall down.'

Juno sank onto the sofa. Daisy perched beside her as Ronan's cries turned to jerky sobs. Juno's guilt intensified. How could she have been so thoughtless and irresponsible last night?

She stroked a trembling palm down Ronan's curls, his

gulping sobs piercing her heart. 'I'm so sorry,' she whispered. 'Will Ronan be all right?'

'Ronan will be fine,' Daisy said easily. 'He's had a bit of a shock, that's all.' Unbuttoning her blouse, she lifted her breast deftly out of her nursing bra and the baby's mouth latched onto her nipple. His sobs gentled as he concentrated on sucking voraciously. 'You see, all sorted.'

Daisy patted Juno's knee and smiled. 'You can stop shaking now, he's okay.' She nodded at the paper still clutched forgotten in Juno's fist. 'Why don't we see what the fuss is about?'

Juno unfolded the paper on her lap and gawped at the front page.

Underneath the banner headline *'Hollywood Hunk Brody's Night of Passion with London Shop Girl'* was a huge, grainy, colour photograph. Despite the poor picture quality, the image had recognition blazing through Juno like a fireball. Mac towered over her on the château balcony, his dark head obscuring most of her face as his mouth devoured hers. His large hand covered her bottom, drawing her close, while her fingers clutched at his shoulders as she kissed him back for all she was worth.

Daisy hummed. 'Suddenly, the mystery is solved.'

Juno slapped the paper closed, despair and humiliation churning in her stomach. How did you go about explaining the unexplainable? 'I didn't plan for it to happen. He kissed me on the balcony—and we sort of got carried away.'

'I can see that,' Daisy said, a smile lurking at the corners of her mouth.

'This is so awful.' How typical that her big Cinderella moment should turn into a pantomime disaster.

'No, it's not,' Daisy said firmly, easing Ronan off her breast. She lifted the baby onto her shoulder and patted his back. 'Actually, I think it's fabulous.' The smile became a mischievous grin. 'Now, I have two very important questions to ask. Was your night of passion with the Hollywood Hunk as hot as it looks from that photo? And when are you seeing him again?'

The blush that flooded Juno's cheeks had Daisy chuckling. 'Okay, scratch question one,' she said. 'I think I got my answer to that one.'

'I'm not seeing him again,' Juno said firmly. 'It was strictly a one-night deal.'

'Who says? Did he say that?'

'Not in so many words,' Juno said carefully. 'He was still asleep when I left this morning.'

Daisy's eyebrows shot up. 'You ran out on him? A man most women would kill for. Are you nuts?'

'I didn't want to wake him,' she said plaintively. 'I left him a note.' Fine, so it sounded a bit lame now, even to her. But that was hardly the point. 'Anyway, it's academic. He wasn't looking for more than one night—and neither was I.'

It was the truth. Even if her heartbeat did the two-step every time she thought about him. That could only be left-over sexual chemistry—anything else would signal disaster.

Daisy adjusted the sleeping Ronan on her shoulder and gave Juno a look that made her want to squirm. 'How do you know? You didn't wait to find out.'

'I didn't need to wait,' she said deliberately. 'It was understood. I was being realistic.' Wherever Daisy was going with this, she didn't want to follow. Daisy was a bona fide hopeless romantic; she wouldn't know realistic if it hit her over the head.

Daisy held up her palm. 'Don't even think about hiding behind that being realistic baloney. There's a time for realism and there's a time for letting your inner nymphomaniac loose and going completely insane. Having the opportunity for a wild fling with Mac Brody would definitely qualify as the latter.' She sighed. 'I can't believe you let a chance like this slip through your fingers. Forget slip. You just chucked it under a bus.'

'Daisy, don't. It's over and done with.'

Daisy's expression sobered, making Juno feel very, very uneasy. 'Don't do this, Juno. Not now. Not after everything you've achieved in the last couple of weeks.'

'I don't know what you mean.' But she had a bad feeling she did know, and she didn't want to hear it.

'Juno, ever since you met Mac at Heathrow and shared that kiss, I've seen a side of you I've never seen before, and it's been wonderful to watch. Honestly, it's been like seeing a butterfly coming out of its cocoon and learning to spread its wings.' Daisy gave a sad smile. 'Don't you see, you were finally starting to get your spirit back? Just look at the way you wore that maid of honour gown, even though you felt naked in it. And the way you had the guts to spend the night with Mac.' Daisy's tone deepened. 'I bet you were scared to death when you got to his hotel room, weren't you?'

Juno's blush returned full force. 'Maybe a bit. But he was okay about it. Actually, he was pretty amazing really.'

Daisy let out a deep sigh. 'So why did you run out on him?'

'Because I didn't want to make a fool of myself,' Juno blurted out. So it made her sound pathetic? So what. It didn't alter the facts. She couldn't get drawn into another impossible romantic fantasy with a man who wasn't interested. 'For goodness' sake, Daisy, he may be Connor's brother, but he's a movie star. He has women far more gorgeous and glamorous than me falling all over him. I didn't want to have him patronise me and pretend he cared when he didn't. It would have been embarrassing.' And it would have crushed the thrilling feeling of power, of achievement.

She'd discovered something wonderful last night. That the world wasn't going to collapse around her if she took a chance and went with her instincts. Maybe one day she'd even have the courage to go after what Daisy had found and see if she couldn't find the same thing for herself. But if and when she did decide to reach for the stars, she would take it one patient step at a time, assessing the risks carefully as she went. She wasn't going to charge into the unknown, trust to luck and then be forced to spend another six years picking up the pieces of her shattered heart.

'I'm not you, Daisy,' she said. 'And Mac's not Connor, either. I risked everything once before and it was a disaster. I can't do it again. And I won't. Not until I'm sure.'

Daisy clasped her hand, a single tear spilling over her lid. 'I understand, Juno. I really do. You went through something no sixteen-year-old should ever have to cope with. And I would never want you to put yourself through that again.' She scrubbed the tear away with an impatient hand. 'But you have to start trusting your own judgement if you're ever going to be sure of anything again. Don't you see that?'

'Fine, well, my judgement was telling me that Mac Brody was only interested in a one-night stand.'

'You don't know that,' Daisy said, undeterred.

Juno forced out a laugh. 'You're just saying that because he's Connor's brother. You don't know him. Do you want to know what he said to me? Why he really came to France?' she asked.

'I'd love to know,' Daisy said.

'He came because he wanted to sleep with me,' Juno said grimly, feeling guiltier now than ever.

Instead of looking disgusted, Daisy laughed. 'I knew it. I hope you were suitably flattered.'

Juno felt the flush heat her cheeks. Of course, she had been flattered. Ridiculously so. But Daisy was missing the point completely. 'Can't you see how shallow that makes him? He as good as shunned you and Connor and even little Ronan at the wedding reception. You know he did. I don't know how you can forgive him for that so easily.' And how had she?

'You mustn't judge him because of that,' Daisy said, sounding exasperated. 'The situation between him and Connor is complicated. I told you that.'

'I know, I know, you said they had a tough childhood, but that doesn't justify—'

'Juno, listen to me,' Daisy interrupted her. 'They haven't seen each other since Mac was ten years old. Connor is pretty sure he spent the whole of his teens being shunted from one foster home to another.' She let out a heavy sigh. 'I'm not making excuses for him. It really is complicated. And I don't think he's as shallow as you think. He's just careful to guard his emotions.'

Juno closed her mouth. Not sure what to say. She didn't want to think about Mac as a child, unloved and alone. It would make him seem vulnerable again.

'The thing is, Juno, you don't know him either,' Daisy said. 'And the little you did know you liked. I believe you said yourself, and I quote, "Mac was really amazing." Why couldn't you have enjoyed a bit more of that amazing? And got to know him while you were at it? Instead of running off before you gave yourself the chance?'

'You think I overreacted?' Had she overreacted? Had she let herself down? Reverting to her old cut-and-run technique at the first sign of intimacy? Was that why she'd been feeling so empty, so disillusioned ever since she'd crept out of that hotel room? Not because she'd been mooning over Mac, but because she'd taken the coward's way out?

'Maybe a teensy-weensy little bit.' Daisy gave a reluctant laugh. 'There was always the slight chance Mac wouldn't have kicked you out on your bum the instant he woke up.'

'Gee, thanks,' Juno said, smiling despite the crushing feeling of disappointment pushing at her chest. 'That makes me feel so much better.'

The sudden barrage of noise from outside startled them both.

'Quick, hold Ronan and I'll take a look.' Daisy passed the baby to Juno and scurried to the window. 'Maybe it's the police.'

Juno breathed in Ronan's sweet talcum-powder scent, not caring about the police or the press any more. The reporters would leave soon enough when they realised her *'Night of Passion'* with Mac Brody wasn't going to be repeated. The feeling of disappointment got bigger, squeezing the air out of her lungs.

Why had she been such a coward this morning? She'd already taken a chance on Mac—and then she'd totally chickened out. Would it really have been so terrible to stick around? To stand up for herself for a change and see what happened?

Daisy flipped open the curtain and peered out. 'Well, well, well.' Sending Juno a bright smile, she beckoned her over. 'Take a look at this.'

Juno walked to the window, Ronan heavy in her arms as Daisy pulled the curtain back.

Her head spun as she stared at the tall figure taking the steps to Daisy and Connor's door two at a time. With his chin up and his eyes shielded by dark glasses, Mac Brody seemed oblivious to the explosion of camera flashes and shouted questions going off like gunshots around him.

Juno's pulse spiralled out of control as Daisy whispered, 'Maybe Mr Really Amazing's going to give you a second chance.'

CHAPTER NINE

'WE'RE booked on the ten o'clock flight.' Mac paced across the study. Yanking one hand out of his pocket, he glanced at his watch. 'You'd best be getting together whatever you need. We've not long before we have to leave.'

'What flight?' Even though she could hardly breathe, Juno knew when she was being bulldozed.

Mac stopped pacing and looked at her at last. 'The flight to LA,' he announced, as if she had a problem understanding English. 'I'm not leaving you to the mercy of the press. You'll be staying with me for the next couple of weeks, till all this nonsense blows over.'

'Stay? With you?' she sputtered. 'But I can't do that.'

Okay, she couldn't deny the thrill that had made all her nerve endings tingle when he'd stalked into the study. His charismatic presence had sucked all of the oxygen out of the small room as soon as Daisy had excused herself to give them 'a little privacy'.

She'd been overjoyed to see him and pathetically flattered that he'd followed her all the way from France.

But being excited to see him was one thing, completely losing her grip on reality quite another. 'I can't go to LA. I'm managing the shop tomorrow,' she said, trying to bring reason and practicality to a conversation fast spinning out of control.

'Don't be stupid,' he said, as if he were being the reasonable one. 'You won't be able to get near your shop. They'll have the place besieged. They'll stalk you and your customers, scour your bins, stake out your place next door and hunt down your friends until they get the story they want.'

'They can't do that,' she interrupted him, shocked. 'I'll get a restraining order.'

'It takes days to get a restraining order, by which time they'll have made your life a misery. Believe me, I know. I've been in this circus for five years.' He stepped towards her, cradled her cheek. 'Come to LA. I've an estate in Laguna Beach with proper security where they can't touch you. They'll have moved on to their next kill in a few weeks and then you can come home.'

As his knuckle stroked her cheek she stared into his eyes—but the impossibly blue depths were filled with so much sincerity, she immediately smelled a rat. Something wasn't right. He hadn't come all this way to save her from the paparazzi. Surely.

She took a step back. 'Why would you do that? Why would you go to all that trouble? We hardly know each other.'

His lips quirked, one black brow lifting. 'Something we can certainly remedy while you're in LA.'

She swallowed, her mouth bone-dry. 'So you're not really here to rescue me from the press?'

'I am,' he said, the grave statement contradicted somewhat by his sinfully sexy smile. 'But there's no law that says we can't enjoy ourselves while you're there. As it happens I've a few weeks before my next project starts. So I'm in need of a distraction and, it seems, so are you.'

He drew his thumb down the line of her neck; the thrill shot through her like quicksilver and the yearning got worse.

She wanted to go to LA with him, however much she might want to deny it. He made her feel alive and excited in a way she never had before.

She should never have run out on him this morning; it had been cowardly and pathetic. But she had, because there was still some of the frightened, insecure little girl inside her she thought she'd destroyed years ago. Could this be her chance to bury that unhappy child for good? To prove that if she was smart and sensible, kept a clear head and made the right choices not every relationship had to end with a broken heart?

'Define distraction?' she asked, her voice surprisingly steady considering every one of her pulse points was now throbbing in unison.

'Allow me to demonstrate.'

He folded her into his embrace and claimed her mouth with a short, sharp and shockingly erotic kiss. The blissful ache from last night pounded back to life with staggering speed.

When he released her, they were both breathing heavily.

'Does that answer your question?'

She touched her lips, stunned by the force of his hunger and the heat of her own response. She had the answer she needed. This was all about sexual chemistry. Nothing more. They weren't talking about happy ever after here, they were talking about fulfilling a basic human need. A need that, she had discovered last night, Mac was the perfect man to fulfil. But could she keep sight of that and make sure her emotions didn't get involved?

'Last night was only a taster,' he said, his voice husky, his eyes smouldering with erotic promise. 'We've some more memorable nights in our future. Fourteen, to be exact.'

She sucked in a breath. But it wasn't his arrogance that startled her. She'd detected the slightest edge to his voice at the reference to 'memorable nights'. All of a sudden she understood why he'd come after her, instead of the millions of other women he could have chosen as his distraction. The realisation gave her confidence an important boost.

So far Mac had had everything his own way. He'd called all the shots and she'd let him, because she'd been completely blindsided by the passion between them. And that had left her entirely at his mercy.

She needed to have some control over this relationship if she was going to be sure to keep her heart out of the equation. Which meant showing Mac she wasn't a complete pushover.

'This is about the note,' she said as clearly as she could manage while still hyperventilating. 'That's why you're here. It annoyed you.'

How the hell had she figured that out?

While it was far from the only reason, Mac didn't appreciate being read so easily, especially as he'd rehearsed how he would play things all the way from the airport.

Relaxed and charming had been the game plan. He wanted her to know how good the sex would be. He wanted her to know he was doing her a favour. He didn't want her to know how eager he was for her to come to LA—or how much her damn note had rattled him. It would make him look like an idiot.

And the plan had been working well enough, till a moment ago.

Mac forced an indulgent chuckle and lifted a mocking eyebrow. 'Not a bit of it,' he replied, his tone deliberately light. 'It was a nice enough note. Just a bit previous as it turns out.'

Her eyes narrowed and she shook her head. 'I don't believe you. It ticked you off. I can tell.'

How the hell could she tell?

He knew how good an actor he was and he'd given that last statement just the right measure of nonchalance to make it convincing.

'It did not,' he snapped, not even convincing himself now.

'I've become some sort of challenge,' she continued, still studying him as if she could see right through him. 'That's it, isn't it? I'm the one that got away?'

He didn't know whether to be impressed or even more aggravated. No woman had ever seen through him so effortlessly or so precisely before. Given the many ways she'd already mucked up his karma over the past fortnight, though, he settled for aggravated.

He took her arm. 'I've told you already, I don't play games.' Or only games he knew he could win and he was fairly sure he wasn't winning this one. 'It's decision time. Are you coming to LA or not?'

Her brow puckered at the ultimatum and he realised his mistake. He let go of her arm.

What the hell had happened to relaxed and charming? He sounded like an ass. Which wasn't like him at all. He never lost his cool with women, especially when he wanted them as much as he wanted her.

He was on the verge of revising the ultimatum, when she surprised him.

'Actually, I'd like to come.' Her lips lifted in a captivating smile. 'But I've got a few conditions before I can agree to go.'

He tucked his hands into his pockets. 'And what would they be, now?' he said warily. What had become of the tentative girl he'd initiated last night? he'd like to know.

'First of all, we must both agree this is only for two weeks,' she said. 'Once those two weeks are up we go our separate ways.'

He gave a brief nod, not sure why he wasn't more relieved. He'd planned to say the same thing himself, hadn't he? But it still felt strange to have her take the initiative.

'I don't want this interfering with your relationship with Connor and Daisy and Ronan.'

'It won't be a problem,' he said, admiring her loyalty to her friends. She looked so earnest, he decided it wouldn't go in his favour if he pointed out why it wouldn't be a problem. That he had no relationship with Connor and his family and he didn't intend to have one.

She huffed out a careful breath, little pink spots mottling her cheeks. 'This is a bit…' she paused, clasping her hands together '…personal. I hope you don't mind me asking, but I was tested six years ago and…' She paused. 'Well, there hasn't been anyone since. How about you?'

It took him a moment to register what she was asking him. His admiration increased. It was a necessary question in this day and age—especially if she'd ever read any of the rubbish written about his private life in the press. So why could he feel himself flushing?

'I had a test a few years back, for insurance purposes. Plus I always use a condom. And I don't do drugs. Will that do?'

'Okay, that's good,' she said, unclasping her hands and looking so relieved he had the sudden urge to give her a cuddle. She wasn't nearly as tough and savvy as she was pretending to be.

'Anything else?' he asked, running a knuckle down her cheek and feeling better by the second.

The next two weeks were going to be quite an adventure. An adventure without any of the usual risks.

Sure her forthright approach and her perceptiveness might have unnerved him a little, but he was starting to see the benefits. The woman had no angles, no hidden agenda, not that he could see. The thought was so refreshing, it was intoxicating.

That he had no idea what she was thinking, or what she was going to do next, was probably a small price to pay. And anyway, he'd have her all figured out after two weeks. He was an expert at reading people, at studying them, and getting the information out of them he wanted.

Once he knew all her secrets, she wouldn't fascinate him the way she did now.

The nervous smile she sent him intoxicated him even more.

'I'd also like to buy my own plane ticket home.'

Now that was plain stupid. He wasn't agreeing to that one. 'Why would you want to do that?' he asked, exasperated. 'It'll cost a fortune.'

The papers said she lived in a one-room apartment, and he had no idea how much shop girls earned, but she'd be flying to and from LA in first class. He wasn't going to let her travel in economy.

'I've got some savings. And it's important to me,' she said, but he detected a note of uncertainty.

'And why is it so important?' he asked, deciding to take advantage of the little chink in her armour. It was about time he started asserting his own agenda. He was in charge here, not her, and it was probably best she knew it. 'I've already bought the return ticket, so you'd be wasting your money. We both would.'

It wasn't the truth. He'd only instructed his PA to buy Juno a ticket out to LA. Which was quite an oversight now he thought about it. When was the last time he'd dated a woman without already having an exit strategy firmly in place?

It occurred to him at that precise moment she would also be the first woman he'd invited to his home. The house in Laguna Beach was his sanctuary and he hadn't even let Gina stay there overnight, always insisting they sleep at her pad in the Hollywood Hills. He gave a mental shrug. It wasn't significant. Hadn't they just established this was strictly a two-week deal?

'Well, I suppose if you've already paid for the ticket.' She chewed on her bottom lip, still considering. 'I guess that would be okay. I just wanted to make sure I had a ticket home.'

'It's all sorted,' he said shortly, not sure why her persistence was beginning to irritate him. 'Now if you've finished with the demands could you go get packed?' He steered her towards the study door. 'We've a plane to catch.'

And the sooner he got her on it, the happier he'd be.

Excitement, exhilaration and extreme terror all fought for supremacy as Juno rushed down the hallway to tell Daisy her news.

Her mind whirred as she concentrated on the details. She had to arrange cover for her position at the shop, then Daisy would have to help her pack. Daisy could help her select what to wear, so she didn't look like some preposterous tomboy waif when she arrived in LA.

She was taking a huge chance, but it felt right. Because she'd been careful and cautious. She'd staked out her territory and knew exactly how much she was risking. And how much she wasn't. Mac Brody was irresistible, a wicked temptation no woman should ever have to say no to. But if she was practical, if she kept focused, and if she didn't let him walk all over her she knew she could handle this.

The good news was, she was going into this with her eyes wide open. With no delusions and no foolish, impossible dreams waiting to be fulfilled. She had her ticket home and two weeks from now she'd return to her real life with a new sense of purpose and a new sense of herself as a woman. She was curious about Mac and she was excited by the prospect of getting to know him better, but that didn't mean she was going to start fooling herself into thinking he was the man of her dreams. Intimacy didn't have to be a threat, as long as you didn't let it overwhelm your common sense.

She grinned as she thought about the way she'd caught him

out over the note. She'd never felt confident enough to flirt with a man before, but she'd almost been flirting with him.

Who knew it could be so empowering and so exciting? He certainly didn't think she was a pushover any more.

The grin faded as she recalled the weight of his palm on the small of her back as he'd propelled her out of the room. And the way her heart had lurched into her throat when he'd demanded to know if she was coming with him to LA or not.

The bad news was, she had the strangest sensation she'd just grabbed a tiger by the tail.

CHAPTER TEN

JUNO'S keep-things-real plan began to unravel on the first-class flight over the Atlantic.

Luckily she wasn't a complete stranger to luxury travel, having flown down to the wedding in Connor's private jet, so she nobly resisted the urge to squeal when she saw the wide leather seat that folded down into a bed. And her eyes didn't get much bigger than dinner plates when she was handed a glass of champagne straight after take-off. Having Mac's hand settle on her thigh as the plane soared to thirty thousand feet had been more of a challenge. But she thought she'd handled herself surprisingly well, only peppering him with a thousand or so questions about Hollywood and Los Angeles and his home in Laguna Beach before she dropped into an exhausted sleep.

Unfortunately, nothing could have prepared her for the shock of opening her eyes, her mind still groggy from sleep and travel twenty hours later, and finding herself in Mac Brody's home.

She couldn't even remember that much about how she'd ended up in the enormous bedroom suite. After getting through the necessary ordeal of customs and passport control, she'd fallen straight back to sleep on the helicopter flight from LAX down to Laguna Beach. She vaguely recalled opening tired eyes during the journey and being wowed by the sight of the sun peeking over the Southern Californian coastline, then inhaling Mac's tantalising scent and feeling his muscles bunching beneath her cheek as he'd carried her into the house, but that was about it.

She propped herself up on the huge fluffy pillows and stared out of the wall of glass at the far end of the room.

'Good God.'

The whispered exclamation rang out above the sibilant purr of the air-conditioning.

Even spending time in Connor and Daisy's magnificent home in Portobello had not prepared her for living in the lap of this sort of luxury. A wide bleached-stone terrace gave way to the brilliant blue of an infinity pool, its lush lagoon-like feel accentuated by a thicket of yucca palms and exotic potted plants.

Throwing off the coverlet, she scrambled across the thick woollen carpet to get a better look at the eye-popping view.

The house sat perched on a low cliff, the rugged, sun-drenched coastline stretching away round the promontory to afford complete privacy. She placed her palms on the glass and gawped at what she could see of the metal and glass frontage of the house. Stretching onto her tiptoes, she spied the empty cove below the house accessed by a set of stone steps carved into the rocks. Lazy surf pounded onto sand so white it made her squint.

Her breath backed up in her lungs. Kubla Khan eat your heart out. Mac Brody's pleasure dome beat Xanadu hands down.

Then she caught sight of her reflection in the glass. Dressed in a vest-top and a pair of simple white panties, she looked like a scrawny schoolgirl cast adrift in a sea of splendour. The ever-present blush heated her cheeks.

What was she doing here? She couldn't have looked more out of place if she tried!

She took a deep breath. Eased it out slowly.

Calm down.

Staying here for two whole weeks was going to be the biggest adventure of her life. And if she was going to enjoy every second, she simply did not have time for a nervous breakdown.

She glanced back at the bed. Only her side had been slept in. She wondered where Mac had spent the night. She dismissed her disappointment. He'd probably been as exhausted as her. The few times she'd woken up during the flight he'd been busy working on his laptop, so he was no doubt catching up on his sleep. Or maybe he'd gone to work. Even with two weeks before his next project started, he might still have meetings and photo shoots and interviews and stuff like that to do. She doubted movie stars ever had very much free time and she didn't intend to be some annoying little limpet constantly begging for his attention. Come to think of it, she probably wouldn't see all that much of him. Which wasn't necessarily a bad thing, considering how short of breath she got every time she got near him.

She spotted her suitcase by the door. Inside were the array of brightly coloured outfits Daisy and she had ummed and aahed over the day before. She lifted out a lipstick-red retro dress that she wouldn't have dreamt of wearing a month ago—and felt the jangle of nerves retreat a little. Once she looked the part, she'd go and explore the house—if she kept occupied, she wouldn't have too much time to think about how far out of her depth she was.

An hour later, Juno had showered in an en suite bathroom bigger than her whole bedsit. Discovered four other bedrooms, a staggering six other bathrooms, a curved living room with a plasma TV the size of a small cinema screen, a fully equipped gym, a study with what looked like top-of-the-range computer equipment and a library packed full of dog-eared paperbacks, dry literary tomes and enough DVDs to outsource her local Blockbuster.

Exploring Mac's house hadn't quite had the palliative effect she'd been hoping for.

The one thing she hadn't found, though, was any sign of her host. Apart from the series of framed posters in the lobby depicting films of his she'd never seen and the remnants of a hastily eaten breakfast in the kitchen.

She pressed her palms to the waistline of the expertly tailored red dress and stared at the empty bowl. Feeling a lot like Dorothy after she'd landed in Oz.

The gleaming stainless-steel cabinets, inlaid countertops and wardrobe-sized fridge ensured this room was as starkly modern, spotlessly clean and impeccably designed as the rest of the house. She sighed. It was certainly a far cry from the cramped galley kitchen in the bedsit co-op, which she shared with Jacie and her son, Cal, Mr Robertson the seventy-year-old Rastafarian on the top floor and Mrs Valdermeyer and her army of cats. But oddly enough, for all its sleek lines and imposing perfection—and the refreshing absence of cat pong—Mac's kitchen made Juno miss the constant noise and clutter of Mrs V's.

Finding a selection of cereals in one of the cabinets, she poured herself a bowlful and sat down to eat. But as she swallowed the muesli she imagined Mac sitting at the table and eating his breakfast alone every morning and wondered how he dealt with the suffocating silence.

The wave of sympathy was quickly quashed as she tidied both their bowls away into the dishwasher. *Don't be daft, the silence was probably what attracted him to this place.* Peace and quiet was no doubt a precious commodity to a man who made his living surrounded by people. And who said he ate alone here? He probably had a string of women he could invite to sleep over.

The minute the thought entered her head, a vision of all the women he'd shared breakfast with in his luxurious kitchen popped up to illustrate it. And every one of them looked a thousand times more at home here than she did.

She squeezed her eyes shut. *Don't even go there.*

It was way too late to start panicking about Mac Brody's other women. She was here now, not them, and that had to count for something.

She opened her eyes. Maybe a bit of sea air would help keep the nerves at bay.

As she ventured through the sliding glass door onto the terrace the stone tiles warmed the soles of her bare feet. The outdoor temperature had to be a good twenty degrees hotter than London. Despite the salt-scented breeze, her dress stuck to her skin moments after she'd left the air-conditioned cool of the house. She shielded her eyes against the glare from the sun, and spied a movement on the beach below.

A tall, tanned and painfully familiar figure strolled out of the surf and bent to take a T-shirt from the sand. As he rubbed it across his torso Juno's eyes dipped to the lighter strip of flesh across his bare buttocks and the temperature shot up another twenty degrees.

Sweat dampened her armpits and her breathing stopped.

He tugged on a pair of jogging shorts and she managed a shallow breath. Picking up his sneakers, he crossed the beach in long strides, his short hair moulded to his head, the dark locks glistening in the sunshine. She wrapped her arms around her waist in a vain attempt to control the throb of arousal.

Oh, my, the man was at least as impressive as his home.

He stepped onto the terrace and his head came up, almost as if he'd scented her presence. A pair of feral blue eyes locked on her face.

He looked magnificent, the water beading on his chest and running in rivulets down the lean slopes and valleys of his abdomen. Her gaze followed the trickles that dripped from his shorts onto powerful thighs. He looked like a rampant male animal.

And he was all hers, for a little while at least.

She gulped, giddy from lack of oxygen.

'You woke up?' The gruff question had her eyes lifting to his face.

Had she? She was beginning to think this was all some extremely vivid and rather scary erotic dream. She nodded. 'I helped myself to some cereal. I hope you don't mind?'

One dark eyebrow lifted sardonically and a slow, seductive smile spread across his face. 'Juno, you've my permission to help yourself to anything that takes your fancy.'

Her nipples peaked painfully and she took a jerky breath.

She might be a novice at this sort of thing, but she definitely didn't think he was referring to his low-fat, fake-sugar, Swiss-style muesli any more. 'Are you sure about that?' she heard herself say.

His teeth flashed white and his eyes gleamed. 'Absolutely.'

Her heart jumped into her throat and sweat pooled between her breasts. It was a dare, plain and simple, now all she had to do was prove she was up to the challenge.

She took a tentative step towards him, not taking her eyes from his face. Placing her fingertip against her own lips, she took a deep breath and then reached towards him.

He quivered, like a tiger ready to pounce, as her fingertip touched his pectoral muscle, but he didn't move, giving her the sharp burst of courage she so desperately needed.

Her short, neatly trimmed fingernail trailed across his

chest and traced the line of hair down his six-pack. But then she spotted the powerful erection already stretching his jogging shorts and gasped.

He swore softly and hauled her against him. 'Enough of that, you little tease.'

His wet chest dampened the front of her dress, and she shivered despite the heat coursing through her body.

'It's my turn now,' he rasped.

Before she could guess his intent, he stepped back, bent over and hoisted her onto his shoulder.

'What are you doing?' The scent of seawater and man engulfed her as he marched through the kitchen and down the hallway. 'Put me down. I haven't finished my turn yet,' she said, wriggling like crazy as her midriff bounced on the broad shelf of his shoulder.

'Tough,' he said, anchoring her legs with one arm across the backs of her knees. 'You were taking too long.'

His comical frustration had a laugh popping out of her mouth, the heady rush of arousal making her dizzy. He kicked open his bedroom door and dropped her unceremoniously onto the bed.

'So you think that's funny, do you?' he snarled, caging her in as she scrambled up.

He looked so handsome and so determined, excitement gushed and pulsed under her skin.

'Hilarious actually,' she teased as he grabbed her ankle. Who knew flirting could be this much fun?

'That's it,' he declared as he hauled her down the bed and settled over her. 'You are so going to pay for that.'

His mouth covered hers, the kiss going straight from playful to punishing. She ran her fingers through his wet silky hair as he pinned her to the mattress.

He tore his mouth away first. 'Let's get naked before we explode.'

'O-okay,' she stammered.

He grappled with her dress, cursing as he fumbled with the zip, while she gripped the waistband of his shorts, letting instinct take over as she struggled to pull the clinging fabric down flanks knotted with muscle.

His erection sprang out, thick and long and impossibly hard. Her eyes widened and she bit into her bottom lip. Goodness, had it got bigger?

He lifted her face to his. 'Don't panic. I won't hurt you.'

'I'm not worried,' she said, and knew she wasn't. What she was was fascinated. 'Can I touch it?' she asked, feeling foolish when his eyebrows shot up.

He choked out a laugh. 'I told you. You've my permission to help yourself to anything you like.'

'I want to touch it, without you touching me.' It was a bold request. But she knew she'd get sidetracked if she let him caress her. And she wanted to explore his beautiful body, and revel in her newfound power, without fear of interruptions.

He swore softly, then flopped back on the bed and folded his arms behind his head. 'All right. You've about a minute. But be gentle now, I'm close enough to the edge already.'

She still wore her bra and panties, which made her feel even more powerful as she studied him. Everything about him was so incredibly gorgeous—and his naked body was entirely at her disposal. She followed the sprinkling of hair, which curled on the slabs of muscle defining his chest, then thinned to a line down his abdomen. Finally her gaze rested on his magnificent erection. She took her time assessing the rigid evidence of how much he wanted her. And only her.

Heat pounded at her core.

He shifted. 'I hate to rush you,' he murmured, his voice gruff, 'but I've so little blood left in my brain I'm about to pass out.'

She giggled, the feeling of power making her light-headed.

To have him at her mercy was more of a thrill than she could ever have imagined.

She touched the head of his erection. At his sharp intake of breath she glanced up to see heavy-lidded eyes watching her and waiting. Unable to hold back a moment longer, she circled him and drew her fingers down the swollen length.

He hissed and his flesh bobbed violently.

She snatched her hand back, horrified. 'Did I hurt you?'

He chuckled, the sound tense. 'Not in the way you mean, darlin'.' He inclined his head. 'But would you take off the lingerie? I'd be a lot happier if I could enjoy the view while you torture me.'

Despite the cheeky tone, it had been more demand than request. She blew out a careful breath, then got off the bed and unhooked her bra. She let it drop to the floor, then with clumsy hands slipped off her knickers. Heat spread across her chest as she stood before him. Her nipples hardened, stimulated by the air-conditioning and the fierce appreciation in his gaze.

'You're gorgeous,' he said as he took her hand and coaxed her back onto the bed. He dipped his head, looped his arm round her neck as she settled beside him. She could feel the heat pumping off his body, took a staggered breath and tasted sea and sun and the musky scent of man.

He shifted to lean over her, fumbled for a moment, then lifted the telltale foil package out of a drawer in the bedside table. Holding her cheek, he kissed her long and hard, his tongue dominating, exploring and then retreating in a rhythm that robbed her of breath.

As he concentrated on sheathing himself she trailed her fingers down his chest, and cupped the heavy weight of him in her palm.

He drew away and caught her wrist. 'I'm too close, darlin'. We'll have to leave that lesson for another day.'

Drawing his palms down her sides, he moved down the bed, his lips capturing her nipple.

She gasped as his teeth tugged and teased the swollen peak. She writhed, sinking her hands into his hair as his mouth moved lower, his tongue circling her belly-button. The rough, torturous strokes had her breath lodging in her throat and her skin burning hot.

But then he moved lower still, his head no longer within range of her grasping fingers. Pushing her thighs gently apart, he cupped her bottom and placed his mouth on her core.

Juno jerked in shock at the intimate caress. Fire rocketed through her, her body pulsing with a need so fierce she thought she might faint. 'I can't think,' she cried.

His palms rested warm on her thighs as he smiled up at her. 'There's no need to think,' he said. 'Just let go.'

His lips were on her again, branding the heated flesh. She squirmed and struggled against the exquisite torture, but he held her in place, and completely open to him, as his tongue probed and ravished. The shocking sensations sent her senses spinning as the vicious spirals coiled at her core.

'I can't. It's too much. Please stop,' she moaned.

But he didn't stop, his tongue, his lips, his mouth, crucifying her on an altar of ecstasy as she soared over that impossible peak. Her back arched as she sobbed out her release, then collapsed shaking onto the pillows.

She still shivered moments later, shuddering with the aftershocks of the vicious climax when she opened her eyes and saw him smiling down at her, his body poised above her.

'That was beautiful to watch, Juno.'

And unbearably arousing, Mac thought as his erection throbbed against the soft skin of her thigh.

Her face coloured a dark and vivid pink.

'Don't...' He stroked a hand down her cheek as she tried

to look away. 'Don't be embarrassed, sweetheart. You're incredible, the way you respond. It's nothing to be ashamed of.'

'I know, it's just…' She gave a shy smile, which had his heart flip-flopping. 'I can't believe… I've never done that before.'

The amazement, the astonishment in her voice had the brutal ache in his groin twisting harder. He touched his forehead to hers, tried to slow his breathing. He wanted, desperately, to bury himself inside her, to pound away until he'd slaked himself. But, more than that, he didn't want to hurt her. 'Let's wait a minute now.'

'Why? I don't want to wait,' she said.

He cursed quietly, his control faltering. Why indeed?

'All right, then.' He gripped her hips, settled between her thighs and pressed into the slick folds. He heard her breath catch in shock at the fullness of the penetration. He could give her only a few agonising seconds to adjust before he had to move, the tight clasp of her body torturing him. Her fingers grasped the back of his neck and the last thin thread on his control broke. He thrust into her, again and again, spurred on by the pulsing grip of her orgasm.

His own vicious climax roared through him as her shocked sobs of release echoed in his ear. Totally spent, he collapsed on top of her.

'Mac, my leg's gone numb.'

The softly spoken plea yanked Mac back to complete consciousness.

'Damn, sorry.' He lifted off her, flopped on to his back and covered his eyes with his arm. Bitterly annoyed with himself.

He supposed he owed her an apology. He'd taken her like a madman.

To think he'd been up half the night, deciding on a course of action, and he'd blown it already.

All during the flight he'd been brutally aware of her sleeping beside him. He'd made himself work to keep from touching her. Not that he'd got much done, with his ears tuned to every small movement or sound she made. It was madness.

When he'd carried her to the guest bed at four in the morning, he'd been so desperate to wake her and make love to her, he'd forced himself to leave her be.

Surely he could do without her for one night? Show some restraint. She was exhausted and so was he, and, anyway, she was here for two whole weeks. What was the rush?

He'd managed to grab a few hours' sleep in his own bed. But he'd woken up fully aroused all the same. A six-mile jog and a swim in the freezing cold Pacific Ocean—and still the need hadn't gone away.

When he'd seen her on the terrace, that letterbox-red dress hugging her curves and her eyes alight with surprised arousal, he'd stood to attention with no effort at all. Like a boy of thirteen instead of a man in his thirties.

He'd never wanted a woman this much before in his life. It was starting to concern him.

Feeling her hesitant touch on his heated flesh had been a unique kind of torture. But still he'd managed to pull back, had been determined to pleasure her first to prove he could show at least a little of his usual finesse. But her quickfire response, the dewy taste of her arousal had driven him over the edge, and he'd taken her with an urgency that had been nothing short of brutal in the end, despite all his best intentions.

What if he'd hurt her again?

'Are you all right?' He forced the words out. 'I didn't plan to be so rough there at the end.'

She gave a long contented sigh. 'Was that rough? It didn't feel rough, it felt fantastic.'

He opened his eyes to find her smiling at him, her eyes

bright with wonder. The trusting look made his heart stir in a way he didn't like.

There was nothing he wanted more right now than to let himself off the hook. But what did she know about sex? About what she really wanted, or what she deserved? Next to nothing, he suspected. She was probably tender as hell at the moment. He'd taken her too fast, too hard. But she probably didn't realise he could have made it better for her if he'd slowed down, if he'd not been so selfish.

Maybe it was about time he found out about what had happened six years ago. So he could stop torturing himself over it? He didn't want it hanging over him. Making him feel responsible for something he'd had no part of.

'What made you wait so long, Juno?'

CHAPTER ELEVEN

'EXCUSE me?' Juno stammered.

Mac looked so serious, so sombre, his eyes a penetrating icy blue.

'Six years,' he said. 'Why did you wait so long? What happened?'

Realisation dawned. She sat up, tugging the sheet over her breasts, the warm feeling of afterglow gone. 'I'm famished. How about I make us a proper breakfast?'

She scooted over to the edge of the bed, intending to make a bolt for the bathroom, but he grabbed hold of the sheet she was using to cover herself, halting her escape in mid-scoot.

'I want to know what happened. Why won't you tell me?'

Was he serious? She turned to see the determination in the harsh line of his jaw. Her stomach sank. Apparently he was. 'Why do you want to know?'

He let out a slow breath. 'It's been bugging me. I can't seem to get it out of my head.'

'But it was years ago.' She didn't want to talk about her past. Not now she was finally breaking free of it.

He let go of the sheet, moved closer to brush the hair back from her brow. 'You waited six years. And then you chose me. I want to know why.'

'But that's silly, it has nothing to do with you. It doesn't matter any more.'

'It does to me.'

Why was he being so stubborn? So insistent? It made no sense at all. And then she understood, and her stomach plummeted to her toes. This was exactly the indignity she'd tried to avoid. 'If you want me to leave… If I'm not exciting enough for you, all you have to do is say so.'

He swore and grabbed her round the waist as she put her feet on the floor. 'Stop being so defensive. It's nothing like that.' He folded her in his arms, hugging her tight and making it impossible for her to go anywhere. 'You're sweet and surprising and sexy as hell and I like spending time with you. Especially in bed.'

Juno felt warmth spread through her at his easy compliments and wanted to kick herself. How pathetic that she should be so grateful for any scrap he was willing to throw her way.

'So why do you care about my past?' It hadn't been part of their deal. She'd persuaded herself she could handle the intimacy, but this felt like more than she'd bargained for.

His chest rose against her back in a heavy sigh. 'Maybe I'm simply curious, or maybe it's because I'm an actor and knowing people, understanding their emotions, figuring out what makes them tick is part of my job.'

She tried to shrug off his arms, but the hug only tightened.

Her temper spiked. 'I'm not talking about my past just because it's your job to be a nosy parker.'

He chuckled, making her temper spike some more.

'How about I ask you another question, then?' he said, his lips teasing her ear lobe. 'If what happened to you six years ago doesn't matter any more, why won't you tell me about it?'

She stopped struggling, her temper deserting her when she needed it most.

Why couldn't she tell him about it?

'The fact that you're so damn secretive makes it seem like it does matter,' he continued, the teasing note gone from his voice. 'And that's what's bugging me.'

She didn't know what to say to him. It didn't matter, but she still didn't want to tell him about it. And the reason why was simple. She was deeply ashamed of what had happened six years ago. Of how naïve and immature she'd been. And she didn't want Mac to judge her.

Which was ludicrous. This was just a casual fling. Two weeks from now she'd leave his home and probably never see him again. Why should she care what Mac Brody thought of her?

Her heart thumped hard against her chest. Blast. She'd have to tell him about Tony. Because if she didn't she'd be admitting to herself, not only that Tony still had the power to hurt her, but that Mac could too.

'I need a shower first,' she said grudgingly. She felt exposed enough already; she wasn't talking about this naked.

He gave her a final squeeze, then let her go. 'Go right ahead,' he said, sounding suspiciously pleased with himself. 'How about I rustle us up that proper breakfast you mentioned? I've worked up a bit of an appetite myself.'

'All right,' she said grudgingly, her own appetite as good as gone.

Following the smell of frying bacon, Juno stopped in the kitchen doorway and held back a sigh. Mac stood in front of the stove, dressed only in a pair of worn jeans, his T-shirt draped over a chair. He looked like a female fantasy come to life as he transferred bacon onto plates already piled high with eggs and toasted muffins.

Goodness, was it any wonder he'd manipulated her so easily? Just remembering what he'd done to her this morning had made her feel shaky in the shower. The man had the ability to make any woman lose her grip on reality. Once she'd got this humiliating ordeal out of the way she'd make sure she was more careful next time. Pheromones were dangerous things, and Mac had a devastating effect on hers.

He glanced over his shoulder. 'You want to grab some cutlery? It's in the top drawer.'

'Okay,' she said, her mouth going dry. She never would have expected him to cook for her. No man had ever cooked for her before. She pulled the cutlery out of the drawer and pretended not to notice the rapid ticks of her heartbeat. Maybe he'd forgotten what they'd agreed to talk about. The more she'd thought about it, the more it seemed odd that he would even want to know about the girl she'd been. Let alone be interested in discussing it.

He slid the plates onto the table and nodded at one of the chairs. 'Take a seat. We should eat it before it gets cold.'

'I'm impressed,' she remarked, her mouth watering at the lavish breakfast he'd cooked. She sat down and picked up her fork. 'This looks delicious.'

If he wasn't going to mention it, she certainly didn't plan to.

He held up the coffee pot. 'You want a cup?'

'Yes, please,' she said, starting to relax. The salty aroma of the bacon made her stomach growl as she took a bite. 'This beats muesli any day.'

By the time she'd polished off the meal she was feeling almost mellow, sure that he'd forgotten about their agreement in the bedroom.

Seeing he was already finished and nursing another cup of coffee, she picked up his plate. 'How about I wash up?'

'No need,' he said, stretching his legs out and crossing them at the ankle. 'I have a cleaning service. They'll get to it this afternoon.'

'Oh, okay.' She put the plates into the sink.

'What happened to the dress?' he asked.

She looked down at the T-shirt and jeans she'd changed into after her shower. 'I thought I'd go for a walk on the beach after breakfast. This outfit seemed more practical.' And a lot less revealing. After her second shower of the day she'd been feeling considerably less bold.

'That's a shame—the dress was something else.'

She rubbed her hands on the worn denim. Not sure what to make of the little peak in her heartbeat at the casual compliment. She really needed to get hold of her ridiculous reaction every time he said something nice to her.

She tugged on the hem of her T-shirt. 'I think I'll go for that walk now.' The kitchen suddenly felt suffocating.

He smiled, placing his coffee cup on the table as he stood. 'Good idea. We can walk round the point during low tide to the public beach.' He wiggled his eyebrows suggestively. 'They have the best ice-cream stand in LA there.'

She hadn't planned on him offering to come with her. 'I'm sure I can find it myself, if you have something you need to be doing.'

His smile widened as he pulled his T-shirt on over his head. Her eyes were drawn to the play of muscles as his abdomen disappeared behind white cotton.

'As it happens, I don't have a thing I need to be doing right now,' he said.

He slipped his hand into hers as they took the terrace steps to the beach. Squeezed.

'So what was his name?'

Drat, he hadn't forgotten a thing.

She tensed and tried to pull her hand out of his. Mac hung on.

He'd seen how wary she was when she'd walked into the kitchen, and had considered for a moment letting it drop.

But as he watched her eat the breakfast he'd cooked for her he knew he shouldn't. Figuring her out was the first step to getting her out of his head for good. As long as she still had secrets, she'd continue to fascinate him.

Once he knew why she'd picked him, and picked now, he wouldn't feel responsible any more. He was counting on it. There'd be no more guilt trips. And anyway, he'd always been deeply curious about people, other people; it was part of what made him good at what he did.

'Are you really sure you want to hear this?'

He heard the plea in her voice and forced himself to ignore it. 'Tell it like a story. It'll be easier. That's what my shrink says.'

Her eyes went round in her face. 'You have a psychiatrist?'

'Everyone in Hollywood has a shrink. They're like a fashion accessory.' He'd only been the once, and he hadn't told the guy a thing—it had reminded him too much of being in the confessional as a lad—but she didn't need to know that. If he wanted her to open up, it made sense to put her at her ease. 'And confession's good for the soul. Remember that.'

She slanted him a sideways look. 'You don't really believe that, do you?'

Not for a minute.

'Of course I do. I was born a Catholic.' He swung her hand in his and grinned. 'Now tell Uncle Mac everything. It'll make you feel better, I guarantee it.'

She huffed out a laugh, and he knew he had her. 'Oh, all right, then, but I still don't understand why you want to know.' She took a deep breath, shielding her eyes against the sun. 'His name was Tony. I was just sixteen when I met him.'

'How old was he?' He hated the bastard already.

'Older.'

Figured. 'How much older?'

She dropped her hand from her brow. 'I don't know. I never asked him.'

'So how did you meet him?'

'Me and my best mate Candice wanted to see this movie. But it was an eighteen certificate.'

'One of mine, I hope,' he said, trying to keep things light. A shadow had crossed her face.

She sent him a wistful smile. 'No, it wasn't. I've never seen any of your movies.'

He stopped dead in the sand, stunned. 'You've not seen one of my movies? Seriously?'

When her smile widened, he realised how conceited he must sound.

'Yes, seriously,' she said. 'I'm not a big movie-goer.'

'Well, damn, we may have to remedy that,' he said, although he wasn't at all sure he wanted to. There was something refreshing about dating a woman who knew nothing of his public image. Feeling oddly humbled, he took her hand again and walked on. 'So go on now. His name was Tony and he was an old man.'

She laughed again. 'I never said he was an old man. He was just…older. Anyway. Candice and I wanted to get into the movie, so we got all dolled up.' She stifled a small smile. 'Which meant tons of make-up, fishnet tights, short skirts. I don't know what it is about being sixteen and wanting to look eighteen, but you automatically assume you should dress like a prostitute.'

He couldn't imagine her with tons of make-up on. She'd had a little on at the wedding, but she had none on today, and she didn't need it. The colour of her eyes, so striking against her pale skin, her high cheekbones and those plump kissable lips. It would be a crime to plaster loads of paint on such a fresh, beautiful face. She swiped her hair behind her ear in a natural, unaffected gesture, the sunlight catch-

ing the gold in her hair. Did she have any notion at all how
gorgeous she was?

He gripped her hand harder. 'Go on.'

'Tony was there with a couple of his mates. They were all
city-boy types, you know, designer suits, high spirits, full
of themselves.'

He could imagine. The bastards had seen two young girls
and found a way to take advantage of them. The world was
full of users, and the worst were often the best dressed.

'They offered to take us into the movie. Candice and I
were really flattered. We thought we must look very sophisticated, to attract grown men. Tony bought me popcorn and
Coke and put his arm round me. By the time the film was
over I hadn't seen any of it. And I was already halfway in
love with him.'

She gave a self-deprecating laugh, but it sounded unbearably sad to him.

'I gave him my phone number, because he asked. And
over the next few weeks I fell for him hook, line and sinker.
He took me to dinner at a swanky restaurant in Mayfair. We
went for walks in the park. He bought me champagne, and
flowers, and we chatted about everything. He seemed interested in what I had to say and I was pathetically pleased with
all the attention. So when he asked if I wanted to go back to
his place in the Barbican one Saturday, I said yes.'

Mac's gut tightened; he didn't want to hear the rest of this.
But he had to know now. He'd happily kill the bastard, just
out of principle. But he had a sick feeling in his stomach that
he hadn't heard the worst of it.

'When we got to his place, he said all this stuff about how
much he wanted me, how incredible I was, how he'd never
met anyone like me before. And then, he…' She turned to
look at him and for a second he could see the anguish in her

eyes before she banked it. 'I was a virgin and it hurt. A lot. He wasn't anywhere near as gentle as you were—and he was annoyed with me for making such a fuss. He told me to come back when I'd grown up. And that's why I didn't want to do it again. For quite a long time.' She said it matter-of-factly, as if it had happened to someone else.

She shrugged and looked away, the movement so defeated, his stomach ached.

'So now you know what a silly, naïve fool I was.'

'Don't say that.' The words were tight, laced with anger.

Juno turned, stunned to see the barely leashed fury in his face. 'What's the matter?'

He tugged her towards him, rested his hands on her waist. 'Don't say that. Don't even think it.' His eyes searched her face, the deep blue turbulent with emotion. 'You were a child. He knew that and he exploited it.' He held her head, rubbing his thumb across her temple in one slow, gentle stroke. 'Don't ever think it was your fault.'

She shouldn't want his sympathy. His support. His opinion didn't matter. But his words, so forceful, so full of fury on her behalf, made the knot of shame lodged inside her for so long release. And the brutalised child she'd once been was so grateful, the tears clogged her throat.

'Come here,' he murmured as he laid her head against his chest. His open palm caressed her hair, rubbed her back. 'Don't cry, darlin'. He doesn't deserve a single one of your tears.'

They stood together for a long time as she held on to him, breathing in the comforting scent of clean cotton and sea air and listening to the soft rhythmic crash of the surf on the shore and the sure, solid beat of his heart.

She had the sudden urge to tell him the rest, to tell him

all of it. The real horror of what had happened six years ago. But she clenched her teeth and stifled the childish urge to confide more. She'd told him too much already.

Just because he hadn't judged her. Just because he'd been sweet and sympathetic and surprisingly supportive. Just because he was a kinder man than she'd ever thought possible, didn't mean he could ever be the man for her. This didn't change a thing between them.

He lifted her chin. 'You okay now?'

'I'm fine.'

'Good.' He took her hand in his and squeezed hard. 'So how does a chocolate sundae with hot fudge sauce sound?'

'Wonderful,' she said as she squeezed back and willed herself not to care that he'd changed the subject.

But however hard she tried, she couldn't forget how good it had felt to have him hold her when she'd needed it most.

Great going, pal. You just shot yourself in the foot.

Sure, he didn't feel responsible any more, or guilty, or fascinated. After what she'd told him. After the way she'd stood so bravely in his arms, stifling her tears, what he felt was involved. And it bothered him. A lot.

As they rounded the rocks and set out across the public beach towards his favourite ice-cream stand Mac tried to concentrate on chocolate sundaes and hot fudge sauce and licking them off Juno's naked breasts.

He refused to dwell on all the conflicting emotions currently churning in his gut and making his heart lurch into his throat.

He only had one thing to offer her. And that was two weeks of no-strings sex.

So there'd be no more heart-to-hearts, no more delving into her past, no more trying to figure out her psyche. That had been a dumb idea.

From now on he'd be keeping a choke-hold on his curiosity and keeping things strictly sexual—with chocolate sauce on top.

CHAPTER TWELVE

JUNO'S hormones did their usual happy dance as she slipped her sunglasses off her nose and watched Mac stroll across the pool terrace. Returning from his regular morning jog, he looked damp and delicious, his T-shirt and shorts moulded to that mouth-watering physique like a second skin.

Juno swallowed down the boulder of lust lodged in her throat as he walked towards her. After eight days as Mac's house guest, she'd begun to crave that tanned, muscular body and the amazing things it could do to her with an intensity she wasn't sure was entirely healthy.

The last week had been an exhilarating voyage of sexual discovery. Mac wasn't just a skilled lover. He was a master. And she'd been an eager student, lapping up every new experience like a woman who had been dying of thirst.

But he hadn't just proved to be an excellent host in the bedroom. Instead of disappearing for most of the day to do whatever movie stars did, he'd hardly left her side. They'd lounged by the pool, checked out the local art galleries, had quiet meals on the terrace and frolicked in the sea like a couple of kids—nearly drowning each other the day before when he decided to teach her how to surf—as well as making love every chance they got.

That moment of connection on the beach their first day had never been repeated, and she knew she should be grateful for that. Keeping things simple and living every moment to the hilt made sense. She couldn't afford to get involved any more than he could.

Mac lived in a fantasy world, in which beautiful people did beautiful things in impossibly beautiful places. She didn't; she lived in the real world. And once this fabulous voyage came to its inevitable conclusion, she wanted to be able to go back to it without a single regret. She could only do that if she didn't complicate things—or start wishing for things she couldn't possibly have. But it was proving harder and harder as each day passed to keep everything in perspective.

He picked up her glass of lemonade from the arm of her sun lounger. 'So what's Miss Juno been up to?'

'I've been chatting to Daisy,' she said, trying not to obsess over the way his Adam's apple glistened in the sun as he took a thirsty swallow of the icy drink. 'Ronan's cutting his first tooth and she and Connor were up half the night with him.'

He paused before putting the glass down with a click.

'That's tough.' He braced his hands on the sun-lounger, leant over and kissed her, leaving the bittersweet taste of lemonade and longing on her lips. 'You want to join me in the shower?'

He'd avoided the subject, as he always did whenever she mentioned Connor and his family. She tried not to let it upset her. 'I've already had a shower.'

'So have another,' he said, a wicked gleam in his eyes. 'I'll scrub your back.'

More than sunlight warmed her cheeks as she recalled how inventive he'd been yesterday morning when she'd taken him up on a similar offer.

'I better not,' she said with considerable reluctance while her hormones did the hula. 'Daisy's ringing me back in a minute. I wouldn't want to get sidetracked.'

'Oh, wouldn't you, now?' he murmured. His teeth nipped her bottom lip. 'That's a crying shame. Because I'm definitely in the mood...' he paused deliberately '...to get sidetracked.'

'You're always in the mood,' she replied saucily as she gave him a playful shove and acknowledged the delicious spark that always accompanied their banter.

Mac hadn't just opened up a whole new world of sexual discovery for her in the past week. He'd also shown her how to flirt. Teasing and tantalising her until she couldn't resist doing it back. And like his lovemaking, the more she flirted with him, the more addictive it became.

He tapped his finger on her nose. 'Only where you're concerned, darlin',' he said as he straightened. The endearment had a familiar band tightening across her chest.

She chewed on her bottom lip. She still hadn't quite cured her bad habit of taking his casual compliments to heart. The man was a born charmer and she mustn't forget that.

'How would you feel about doing a read-through on a script with me in a bit?' he asked, stretching his neck from side to side. 'I need to start taking character notes before we go into rehearsal next week and, as you're the main reason I haven't, I figure you owe me.'

She shot upright on the lounger, excited at the prospect. He'd talked about his work last night over their meal when she'd badgered him about it, but when she'd asked if they could watch one of his movies together, he'd refused—giving the strange excuse that seeing himself on screen made him self-conscious. She'd tried not to take the obvious lie to heart.

'You want me to read a script with you? I'd love to.'

'Don't get too excited,' he said, an indulgent smile curving his lips. 'You'll probably be bored to death after about ten minutes.'

'No, I won't,' she replied and she knew she wouldn't be. From the little he'd said last night she knew he was passionate about his work. Watching him start to create his next character would be fascinating.

'All right, then,' he said. 'But don't say I didn't warn you.'

She clasped her arms round her bare legs and watched him walk away. The loud ringing of the phone on the poolside table interrupted her perusal of his very nice butt in the damp jogging shorts.

Mac stopped by the phone, reached to pick it up, then paused and pulled his hand back. He looked over his shoulder. 'You want to grab that?' he asked. 'If it's for me, tell them I'll ring them back.'

She leapt up as he strolled into the house. 'Mac, wait.'

He paused at the doorway, raised an eyebrow.

The hairs on the back of her neck prickled, the insistent ringing shattering the mid-morning silence—as well as her peace of mind.

It would be Daisy on the line, which was why Mac hadn't taken the call. She was sure of it.

'Would you wait a minute?' she said. 'I need to talk to you about something. It's important.'

He leaned against the doorframe and folded his arms over his chest, looking mildly amused. 'As always, you have my undivided attention,' he said, his voice rough with innuendo.

Scooping up the handset, Juno interrupted Daisy's greeting. 'Could I call you tomorrow, Daze? Mac and I are in the middle of breakfast.' She quashed the twinge of guilt at the white lie as her friend said her goodbyes.

Placing the handset back in its cradle, she blew out a careful breath. She was overstepping the mark, she knew that, but she couldn't pretend any more that Mac's attitude to Daisy and Connor wasn't a problem.

Why had he behaved the way he had towards them at the wedding? Why was he so determined to have absolutely nothing to do with them even now? And why couldn't he see how much he was missing?

Okay, so their fling was only temporary, and she knew she had to tread carefully, but he'd asked about her past—so, surely, she was entitled to be curious about his. And didn't she at least owe it to her friends to try and get Mac to stop rejecting them?

Mac gave a half-laugh. 'So what was so urgent?' he said. 'After the way you lied to your friend, I'm hopeful it has something to do with showers and getting naked.'

He sounded so confident, so self-assured, but could that really be the case? When he wouldn't even pick up the phone to Daisy?

'Daisy's not only my friend,' she said. 'She's also your sister-in-law.'

He tensed. 'I know that.'

'Do you?'

He straightened away from the doorframe. 'Where are you going with this? Because you've lost me.'

She dragged in a deep breath, squared her shoulders. 'Why won't you talk about them?'

He laughed, the sound hollow. 'I haven't a problem talking about them.'

She clasped her hands together. When Daisy had told her he and Connor had had a tough childhood, she'd been careful not to ask about it, because it had been none of her business then.

But it felt like her business now.

'I know you and Connor were separated as children,' she ventured.

His brow furrowed.

'And that you spent years in foster care as a result.' She soldiered on, finding it impossible to gauge his reaction. He'd looked surprised for a moment and then his face had gone carefully blank. 'But I don't understand why that would make you treat Connor so harshly. Why it would make you behave as if you don't have a brother when you do.'

I can't talk about this.

The panic burned a hole in Mac's gut but he kept the turmoil of emotions off his face. 'You don't have to understand.'

Her big soulful eyes widened at the obvious dismissal. He ignored the stab of guilt. But as he turned to go she rushed forward and placed her hand on his arm.

'Mac, don't. Please don't just walk away.'

He glanced at her fingers. Seemed she wasn't going to let him off the hook that easily. 'What is it you want?' he asked. But he had a bad feeling he already knew.

'The way you're treating Daisy and Connor. It isn't like you. You're not cold or unfeeling. I know you're not. I just want to know why.'

The complete faith in her voice made the burning sensation worse. He should have seen this coming.

Ever since she'd told him about her past, ever since he'd known about that bastard who'd as good as raped her, he'd felt the debt between them but he'd ignored it to get what he wanted. Watching her blossom in his arms, watching her lose her inhibitions had been irresistible.

So he'd rescheduled meetings, skipped interviews, turned off his cell phone and ignored the pile of scripts on his desk he was supposed to be reading to gorge himself on her.

And now here was the reckoning. She was calling in the debt, expecting him to bare his soul in return.

'You don't know me, Juno. You just think you do.'

'What are you trying to say? That you're somehow a bad person? I don't believe that.'

He shook his head. He could walk away now. He probably should. But letting her believe he was a better man than he really was wouldn't do either of them any good.

'You want to know why Connor and I can never be brothers? It's because of what I came from. And what's in me,' he said, feeling as dirty as the sweat drying on his skin. 'Our da was a violent alcoholic.' As soon as he'd said the words he could see the fleshy face, the mottled skin that had struck terror into him as a child. 'He had a particular belt he liked to use when he was really drunk. It had a nice fat buckle.' He formed his fingers into a square. 'About this big.' He kept his gaze steady on hers as he lowered his hands.

She hadn't flinched yet, but she would.

'And every time he went after Connor with that belt, you want to know what I did?'

Juno struggled not to recoil at the bitter cynicism in his voice, or the gruesome picture he'd painted. When Daisy had said tough she hadn't realised it had been that tough.

'What did you do?'

'Nothing. That's what I did. I did nothing,' he said, his eyes dark with memory. 'I'd hear the sickening thud as that buckle cut right to the bone. And I'd do absolutely nothing. Because all I cared about was that it wasn't me on the end of that thing.'

'But what could you have done? You were only a child!'

'There's only three years separates us.' Emotion thickened his accent into a deep brogue. 'And I've not got a mark on me. Not one. While I'm sure Connor has plenty.'

'What about the scar on your arm? How did you get that?' she pointed out, her voice faltering. Why was he punishing himself like this? Surely the villain here had been his father, not a frightened little boy so traumatised by the violence he'd been too scared to fight back.

He clasped a hand over his bicep, rubbed the old wound. 'All right, I'll grant you. That last night wasn't too pretty.' He shrugged, as if what must have been a terrible injury had no significance whatsoever.

Tears pooled in her eyes, slipped over her lids.

'Hey, don't be doing that now.' He caught a tear on his thumb, looking appalled. 'I didn't tell you so you'd feel sorry for me.'

'But what you've told me is terrible.'

'No, it's not. Not any more. I learned to live with it a long time ago,' he said.

Had he? She doubted that. She scrubbed away her tears. It was obvious he didn't want her sympathy. But her heart still ached for the little boy he'd been.

He gripped her shoulders, peered into her face. 'I don't think I'm a bad person.' He tucked his finger under her chin. 'But I am selfish. I look out for number one. And I always have. That's who I am. I'm not interested in playing happy families. With Connor or anyone else.'

He ran his thumb across her bottom lip, the blue of his irises deepening. 'So don't go mistaking me for someone I'm not, darlin'. Because you'll only get hurt.'

Juno studied Mac through the glass as he walked down the hallway towards the bedroom, and realised her careful step-by-step plan had just taken a wild reckless leap into the unknown without her seeing it coming.

Mac Brody wasn't shallow or self-centered. He wasn't his father, and he wasn't to blame for what his father had done to Connor. Whatever he might want to believe.

But who was he really?

And why couldn't she shake the terrifying feeling that

Mac needed her and that she needed him, despite his thinly veiled warning not to get involved?

Daisy had told her she had to start trusting her own judgement. But what if her judgment was wrong? What if Mac wasn't the man she'd begun to believe he was, but just another foolish figment of her overactive imagination? And how much of her heart would she have to risk to find out?

CHAPTER THIRTEEN

'THAT was my agent.' Mac dumped his mobile next to his plate. 'The studio is insisting I go to the premiere of *Death Game* tonight.'

Juno looked up from the delicious lunch of seared tuna she'd been busy pushing around her plate for the last five minutes. She put down her fork and bit back a sigh. She couldn't really ignore the evidence any longer. Ever since yesterday, after Mac had given her that fleeting glimpse into the horrors of his childhood, he'd been restless and tense—and really rather rude.

They'd begun the script-reading yesterday afternoon and she'd been enjoying it immensely, but when she'd probed about how he created his characters he'd called a halt to it without an explanation. And when they'd made love this morning, he hadn't held her afterwards as he usually did, but had disappeared into his office until lunch. So far he'd taken two calls while they'd been sitting out on the terrace and had hardly said a word to her.

She missed the easy camaraderie between them—and his surly behaviour wasn't doing a great deal to get her own cartwheeling emotions under control—but she was trying not to let him get to her, because she had a pretty good idea what the problem was. He regretted what he'd told her. He knew as well as she did that it had deepened things between them and he was probably as confused about it as she was.

If only she knew a little bit more about relationships—and men—this would all be so much easier. But so far the only new thing she'd figured out about Mac was that he was a master of avoidance.

'Is *Death Game* your latest movie?' she asked carefully.

'Yeah. I'm supposed to be promoting it, but I've already rescheduled a couple of interviews and the studio is pissed about it.' He snapped the words, frustration edging his voice.

She put her fork down carefully. Why was he angry with her? 'So it sounds like you should go to the premiere.'

'It makes me look unprofessional if I don't attend,' he continued, as if she hadn't spoken. 'Especially as I'm in LA at the minute.'

That was definitely accusation she could hear. She straightened her spine and held on to her temper. 'If you need to go to the premiere, you should go to the premiere.' Did he think she was going to beg him not to? 'You don't have to worry, Mac. I'm perfectly capable of amusing myself for an evening.'

'You don't get it,' he said, still staring at her. 'I have to take a date with me. No one attends a premiere alone. It makes you look like a loser.'

What was that supposed to mean?

Then she knew and she could feel the blood leaching out of her face. He couldn't take her to a Hollywood premiere. It wouldn't look right, she didn't look right. She bit into her lip, forced herself to stay stiff in her chair.

Don't you dare fall to pieces.

She knew she had no real claim on him, but how could he even consider dating someone else while she was still here?

Had she been wrong about him? Was he really as selfish as he claimed?

'I see,' she said, pleased at the way her voice hardly wavered. 'What are you expecting me to do—give you my permission?'

'I don't need your permission,' he said with a callousness she didn't understand. Why was he being deliberately cruel? 'But don't read too much into it. Okay?'

'Why would I do that?' she snapped back, temper taking over despite her best efforts.

He wasn't going to make her feel inadequate because she didn't fit into his Hollywood lifestyle. She had her own life—she was her own woman—and she wasn't going to let him make her feel like less of a person because of it. She'd allowed herself to get in much deeper than she should have. But what right did he have to punish her for it?

'So who is the lucky lady?' she said, her voice brittle. 'Another of your two-week conquests?'

'What lucky lady?' he demanded, still with that bitter edge to his voice. 'What the hell are you talking about?'

'Fine, don't tell me.' She stood up, threw her napkin down on the table. He was not going to make her crumble. At least not until she was alone. 'It really doesn't matter to me one way or the other.' She wasn't going to let it matter.

He stood up too and grabbed hold of her arm. 'What doesn't matter to you?'

'Who you take to your bloody premiere.' The minute the shout had left her lips, she knew she'd given herself away. Big time.

It did matter. It mattered a lot. And now he knew it did too.

But instead of gloating, or trying to placate her—which would have been far worse—he simply stared. 'Juno. It's you who I'm taking with me,' he said at last. 'Why would I take someone else?'

'Me?' she asked, the huge rush of relief quickly followed by a wave of mortification. What was wrong with her? Why had it meant so much to her? She didn't even want to go. Really. 'But I can't go,' she said in a small voice. 'That would be ridiculous.'

He grasped her other arm to stop her turning away. 'And why can't you?' he murmured. 'What would be ridiculous about it?'

She looked down, the blush burning her scalp. 'It's just…' Why was he making her say it? 'It wouldn't look right. *I* wouldn't look right. I'm not that sort of woman.'

He tilted his head. 'And what sort of woman would that be, now?'

Glamorous. Sophisticated. Beautiful.

'The sort of woman who goes to movie premieres,' she mumbled.

'Juno, you slay me.' He chuckled. 'You don't seriously think they're better than you?'

'Of course not.' Or not exactly. 'But I'd be completely out of my element.'

'And thank God for it,' he said with a vehemence that made her heart stutter.

'I don't even have anything fancy to wear…' she added, a little desperate now. However pleased she was that he'd asked her, did she really want to expose their relationship to any more public scrutiny?

'We'll go to Rodeo, then,' he said easily. 'Get you something fancy. I know a stylist will be able to help.'

Her heart stumbled. Why was he doing this?

He brushed his thumb across her chin. 'The only thing those women can do better than you is show off. And believe me, even in Hollywood, showing off as a life skill is overrated.'

Tears prickled at the backs of her eyelids—and the band

around her heart tightened. He shouldn't say these things. Because it felt like more now, more than it was ever meant to be.

'So will you come to the premiere with me?' he asked. 'I'd be in your debt.'

When he put it like that, what choice did she have? She nodded mutely, her heart thumping in her chest like a sledgehammer. 'I suppose so, if you're sure.'

'I am.'

Mac watched Juno leave to get her shoes and bag and cursed himself for being all kinds of a fool.

He should have taken the opportunity to make up a fictitious date—and told her she couldn't come with him to the *Death Game* premiere.

Ever since yesterday he'd been trying to create some distance between them. For his own good as well as hers. Because she was really starting to scare him.

The way she'd somehow got him to talk about things he'd not told another living soul. The way she'd cried for him when she'd never even cried for herself. The way she still looked at him as if he were one of the good guys, when he'd told her as plain as day that he wasn't. The way she seemed to be able to see right through all the defences he'd constructed so carefully over time and make him need things he didn't want to need.

He didn't just feel involved any more, he felt... Hell, he wasn't even sure what he felt. Which could not be good.

And yet, when his agent had reminded him about the premiere tonight, he'd known instantly he wanted her on his arm—because she would make the whole ordeal that much more bearable.

And as soon as the thought had occurred to him it had annoyed the hell out of him. And he'd taken it out on her.

But how could he have known his irritable invitation would

make her jump to entirely the wrong conclusion? Once he'd seen the crushed expression on her face, he'd felt like the worst kind of heel.

He sat at the table and picked up his cell phone to dial the stylist.

Leaning back in his chair, he crossed one leg over his knee and waited for Juanita Suarez to pick up—and a picture of Juno decked out in another tempting bit of fancy such as the one she'd worn to the wedding formed in his head. Quickly followed by the picture of him peeling it off her.

His irritation dissolved in a haze of lust.

What the hell?

Why shouldn't they have tonight? Why shouldn't he pamper her a little? He'd given her little enough of the movie-star trimmings all his other dates took for granted. And he'd been more than a bit cranky with her since yesterday. It was the least he could do.

Tomorrow would be soon enough to worry about the strange effect she had on him. He'd waited more than a week already. What harm could one more day do?

'Hi, Juanita, it's Mac Brody.' His lips quirked at Juanita's enthusiastic greeting. 'I've a date I want to take to the *Death Game* premiere tonight, and I want to make sure she enjoys it.'

CHAPTER FOURTEEN

MOTHERLY, efficient and expertly groomed, Juanita Suarez took Juno under her wing the minute Mac introduced them, firing enough sartorial suggestions at her to have Juno's mind boggling.

As soon as they got to the glitzy shopping mecca of Rodeo Drive, with its rarefied collection of fashion boutiques and designer outlets, it became apparent Mac wasn't a natural shopper—his eyes glazing over with boredom after less than five minutes.

Juno might once have thought the same of herself. Daisy had always been the design genius behind The Funky Fashionista, but since Daisy had opened the shop Juno had taken her job as manager seriously and had learned as much as she could about fashion for the benefit of the clients. But she'd never had the thrill of putting that knowledge to work for her own benefit. So once she and Juanita had cut Mac loose and the stylist got down to business, Juno found herself marvelling at the dizzying selection of haute couture garments on offer—and getting more and more excited about choosing her own perfect outfit to spend a night on the town as Mac's date.

Maybe there was something to be said for avoidance after

all. She'd been worrying about what was really going on between her and Mac since yesterday and all it had done so far was give her a headache—and kick off an argument about nothing.

When was she going to get another opportunity to dress up like a movie star and go to a Hollywood premiere with one of the sexiest men on the planet on her arm? This would be a story to tell her grandkids one day. She could always start panicking again tomorrow.

'Oh, yes, honey. I love that one on you,' Juanita enthused as Juno stepped out of the dressing room in a flowing off-the-shoulder gown of turquoise taffeta with a beaded bodice. 'The colour's perfect for your eyes. What do you think?'

Juno peered down at herself. The material felt soft and exclusive next to her skin and, while she never would have chosen the dramatic design or revealing cut for herself, she could see it made quite an impact. Goodness, she even had boobs again.

'It's beautiful,' she said. 'But how much does it cost?' Not one of the outfits she'd tried on so far had a price tag, and it was making her a little nervous.

Juanita grinned. 'Aren't you precious?' she said, the condescension sounding pleasant in her laid-back Californian accent. 'Don't you worry about the cost. Mac told me to go right ahead and spend whatever we wanted. And it's always been my motto never to cross an A-lister—especially if I've got my hands on his plastic.' She waved the credit card Mac had blithely handed over before making his getaway.

Juno ran her palms down the luxurious gown. 'I don't feel right spending too much of his money.'

Juanita looked completely nonplussed for the first time since Juno had met her. 'Mac said you were one of a kind—and he wasn't kidding. You're the first one of his dates to say that to me.'

Had he really said she was one of a kind?

'Have you met lots of his dates, then?' The question popped out before she could stop it.

'Quite a few,' Juanita said as she unhooked the gown and helped Juno out of it. 'I used to work for Gina—that's how Mac and I met.'

'Gina?'

'Gina St Clair, the supermodel. She and Mac were an item a while back.'

'Oh.' Juno felt a sinking sensation in her stomach as she tugged her jeans back on. Why had she asked about his ex-girlfriends? She'd promised herself on her first day in Mac's house she wouldn't worry about it. Hearing about all the stunning women he'd dated now would only knock her confidence.

Juanita laughed as she put the gown back on its hanger. 'Sweetie, there's no need to look so miserable. I'll let you into a little secret. But you've got to give me your solemn promise you won't tell Gina I said this.'

'All right.' What was Juanita going to say? And did she really need to hear it?

'Gina fancied herself in love with him. And she hasn't been the first, I'll tell you. Or the last. That man has left a trail of broken hearts through Beverly Hills—and the real tragedy is he hasn't a clue. Women look at him as if he could hang the stars and he doesn't even notice.'

The heat hit Juno's cheeks. Did she look at him like that too?

'He takes them out for a couple of months and then drops them flat,' Juanita continued.

Juno gulped down the ball of dejection threatening to gag her. Where had that come from? She knew her time with Mac was limited. At least she'd never allowed herself to get that delusional. So what exactly did she have to feel dejected about?

'It's all right, Juanita. I know where I stand with Mac.'

'But, honey, you haven't let me get to the best part. I've seen the women in Mac Brody's life come and go. And he treats them all exactly the same. Charming, friendly and totally uninvolved. But you're different.'

Of course she was different. She wasn't a supermodel.

'How?' she asked, sure she didn't want to know the answer.

'He looks at you differently. Like he really sees you.' Juanita winked as she tapped his platinum card to her nose. 'And here's the kicker. He's never once trusted any of the others with his credit card. And there's a saying in Hollywood that I know to be the God's honest truth.' She lifted her eyebrows. 'Plastic speaks louder than words.'

Juno smiled. Juanita's teasing lifting her mood back off the floor.

Whatever was happening between her and Mac, she liked the idea she'd made an impression on him. That he wouldn't forget her too easily.

It seemed only fair—after all, he'd certainly made an impression on her.

CHAPTER FIFTEEN

THE tiny little butterflies that had flitted about in Juno's belly as she'd stood before Mac in her glamorous new outfit and watched his eyes darken with desire had become eagles with ten-foot wingspans by the time their stretch limo slid to a halt in front of the art deco theatre in Westwood.

Mac had briefed her during the long winding drive down Wilshire Boulevard on what would be expected of them once they arrived. But with his hand absently rubbing her thigh through the figure-hugging taffeta, her anticipation levels at fever pitch and his long, lean frame so heart-meltingly gorgeous in the formal tuxedo, Juno had been finding it a little hard to concentrate.

In fact, as he offered her his arm and she stepped out onto the pavement she realised she hadn't heard a single word.

'We'll get this over as quick as we can,' he murmured against her ear as his hand gripped her waist and the camera flashes exploded around them.

He guided her to a wall of people waving autograph books and screaming his name, barricaded behind the main walkway.

'Stay put. This won't take a minute,' he said as he let her go.

It didn't take a minute, it took twenty before he managed

to extricate himself from his fans and come back to her. And during it all Juno could see how stiff and uncomfortable he was, exactly as he had been outside the church in France.

'Sorry about that.' He grasped her hand and gave a curt nod to the security guards who'd been keeping her company. 'Right, let's go see this damn movie,' he said, striding off down the red carpet.

But as they reached the pillared entrance to the theatre, a reporter stepped into their path and shoved a huge microphone under Mac's nose.

'Mac, great to see you here. Charlie Stater for *Good Evening, America*. So *Death Game*'s a new departure for you. What's it like to play the bad guy for a change?'

Mac grasped her fingers and sent the reporter a strained smile. 'Anson's not the bad guy, Charlie. He's misunderstood.'

As the impromptu interview continued and Mac talked about a movie she knew nothing about Juno became aware of the photographers flocking around them. The rapid shutter clicks and endless flashes gradually getting louder and more intrusive.

How did Mac stand it?

'So who's this beautiful vision you've brought with you tonight, Mac?'

She barely had a chance to register the reporter's fawning question before Mac tucked their joined hands behind her back, drawing her against his side.

'This beautiful vision is Juno,' he said before his lips touched hers in a brief but deliberately intimate kiss.

As Mac stepped back, his eyes hot on her flushed face, the reporter's questions, the camera noise, the distant shouts from the crowd faded away, until all she could hear was the rapid pulse of her own heartbeat, thumping in her ear.

Why did she suddenly feel as if this were the perfect time to panic?

* * *

The rest of the reception went by in a blur with Mac introducing her to a host of famous faces whom she was sure she ought to know.

The film turned out to be superb. A fast, furiously action-packed thriller anchored by Mac's central performance.

Juno sat in the darkened theatre and saw yet another side of Mac emerge that she hadn't known existed. He'd immersed himself so completely in the part, the raw emotion etched on his face in the final scene so real and so vivid, he'd become a different person. This was more than talent, she thought. Much more.

After the screening Mac did a series of press interviews with her hand clasped in his. He insisted on introducing her to every reporter. And each time he did, the flicker of panic increased.

By the time they arrived at the after-show party in a Michelin-starred restaurant in Beverly Hills, it occurred to her he'd hardly let go of her all evening. Even during the screening, he'd threaded his fingers through hers and held on.

'So what did you think?' he asked as he whisked a glass of champagne off the tray of a passing waiter and handed it to her.

The question sounded casual, but his eyes fixed on her face and she knew it wasn't.

She remembered how he'd shifted and fidgeted in his seat through most of the movie. He hadn't been lying when he'd said seeing himself on screen made him nervous. The thought was strangely endearing.

She took a fortifying sip of the champagne, not sure she could put her feelings about his performance into words. 'I don't know anything about movies or movie acting. But you seemed so real, like a real person. I totally believed you were capable of killing that man. You looked like you. But I forgot it was you. It was incredible.'

She coloured as the tension left his face and he grinned. Had she made a complete idiot of herself? 'Sorry. Was that as stupid as it sounded?'

'Not at all,' he said, his grin getting even bigger. 'You've just given me the best compliment an actor can ever have.'

'I did?'

'That you believed in the character.'

The pride and sense of achievement in his voice was so genuine, it touched her deeply. 'Your work means so much to you, doesn't it?'

'I've never found a better way to pay the bills, that's for sure,' Mac said flippantly. She was looking at him again in that way she had that made him feel transparent. He wasn't sure he liked it.

'No, I mean, it's not the celebrity or the money that matters to you. It's all about the acting. It's who you are.'

How did she know this stuff? Her intuition was uncanny. And unsettling. 'Yeah, I guess you're right. Acting saved me.'

'How?'

He shrugged. He could tell her this. It wasn't that big a deal—he'd talked about it before in interviews as it was good publicity fodder. 'I made a lot of bad choices as a teenager, ended up in a juvenile detention centre when I was fifteen.'

He took a sip of champagne, and wished it were a beer. How had he got into this again? Baring his soul for no good reason.

'They had a social worker there, suggested I try out for a theatre workshop they were doing. I did and that was it. It was like a drug. I didn't have to be me any more. I could be anyone I wanted to be. And I loved it.'

A small frown formed on her forehead. 'Why didn't you want to be you?'

Now he really needed that beer. No one had ever been

perceptive enough to ask him that before. 'Because I was a little bastard. Not being me was a good thing. Believe me.'

Her frown deepened.

'You're such a brilliant actor, Mac,' she said, the sincerity in her voice making his heart ricochet against his ribs.

Why did this suddenly feel like a very big deal?

'And it's wonderful you found something you're so good at. But you shouldn't confuse being in a bad place with being a bad person. It's not the same thing.'

'Who told you that?'

She smiled, the complete faith in the gesture doing funny things to his insides.

'You did.' She stretched onto tiptoes and kissed his cheek, her eyes warm with approval. 'Acting didn't save you, Mac. Don't you realise, you saved yourself?'

Mac toyed with his second glass of champagne and kept his eyes peeled for Juno's return from the powder room. Tonight had been a much bigger success than he could have hoped. He hated these affairs, but having Juno with him had made the time fly by.

And okay, he didn't know why he'd got so worked up about what she thought of his performance. Plus he wasn't the sentimental type. But he'd got a real kick out of what she'd said about the film and, well, everything.

She was good for him. He liked having her around. Why keep on denying it?

He gulped down a swallow of the sparkling wine, felt the bubbles tickle.

I don't want her to leave. Not yet.

The minute he'd admitted it, the parched feeling in his throat began to ease.

Was that what had made him feel so uneasy in the last

couple of days? Could it be as simple as that? That he just wasn't ready to let her go?

But now he thought about it, it made perfect sense. And the solution was even simpler. Why did they need to put an artificial time limit on their affair?

If they took a couple of months, gave themselves enough time to tire of each other naturally and burn off all this sexual energy—the pressure would be off and the affair could run its natural course.

He finished off his glass of champagne as he studied the door to the powder room across the dining area, the relief intoxicating. He didn't have to worry about how much he wanted her any more. About how much he was enjoying her company.

As soon as she got back he was getting them the hell out of here. They could take the copter back to Laguna and then he intended to indulge the little fantasy he'd been nursing ever since he'd first seen her in that dress.

Tomorrow morning, he'd tell her he wanted her to stick around a while longer. Given the way she responded to him, he didn't expect it to be a hard sell.

'Hello, Mac, darling.'

He tensed, the sultry Southern drawl souring his mood a little.

He turned. 'Hello, Gina. You're looking...' Immaculate, was his first thought as his gaze drifted over the pristine make-up and the blue silk, expertly hung on her tall, angular and emaciated frame. 'Nice,' he finished.

Funny how Juno's small, petite frame and artless style stirred his blood in a way Gina and his other girlfriends never had.

'Nice?' she said, arching one perfectly plucked eyebrow. 'Now there's a word to make a woman's heart flutter.'

He could see the hurt in her eyes and even three years on felt the pulse of guilt.

'I'm not great with words,' he said, annoyed with himself. The woman had all but scalped him in the press. What did he have to feel guilty about? 'Not unless they're scripted for me.' If she fancied an argument she'd have to look elsewhere.

'Oh, I don't know,' she said wistfully. 'You were always very good with words as I recall. But then I always made the mistake of misinterpreting them, didn't I?'

The pulse of guilt increased and impatience flared. 'If there's a reason we're having this conversation, maybe you should get to the point?'

'Actually there is a reason.' She looked down at the champagne stem clutched in her hand. 'I never apologised to you. For the problems I caused. And I'm sorry. More sorry than I can say.'

Her apology sounded sincere and left him momentarily lost for words.

'It's forgotten, Gina. I stopped holding it against you years ago.'

Her head came up. 'You have no idea how ironic that is.'

'Yeah? Why?'

'You were the wronged party and you didn't hold a grudge. And yet I held one against you for years.'

'Why did you?' he asked, his curiosity getting the best of him. He never had understood why she'd found it so hard to move on.

'It's fairly simple, Mac. And I believe I did tell you at the time. I was desperately in love with you. And I was angry that you refused to even try to love me back.'

He shoved a hand in his pocket, her wistful tone threatening to ruin his mood. He wasn't taking the blame for this. Not any more.

* * *

Juno spotted the stunningly beautiful woman with Mac through the terrace doors as soon as she came out of the restroom. Gina St Clair. The supermodel Juanita had mentioned. One of his many conquests.

Who cares if she's gorgeous? It's you he's with tonight.

She repeated the mantra in her head as she made her way through the restaurant's private dining room, trying not to notice how breathtaking the pair of them looked together. Mac debonair and imposing in the dark tailored tuxedo next to Gina, a vision of style and elegance in sky-blue silk. How tall was the woman anyway? At least six feet in her heels if she could look Mac in the eye. And those boobs, what kind of hooker underwear did she have on to make them look so full and perky? It wasn't fair.

She was so busy obsessing over Gina's many assets she didn't take any notice of their body language until she'd stepped out onto the terrace. She stopped dead as Mac thrust a hand into his trouser pocket and angled his body towards Gina, the animated stance suggesting an intimate conversation.

She hadn't planned to eavesdrop. But she couldn't deny the whisper of jealousy.

Was there still something between them?

As Mac's voice carried to her over the tinkle of glasses and conversation she stepped behind a large oleander that sheltered her from view, and listened to every word.

'You weren't in love with me, Gina. You just liked the idea. We looked good together and the sex was pretty good too. But that's all it was.' He sounded irritated and bored.

'I did love you. And you ended up breaking my heart.' The supermodel's voice quivered as if she was fighting off tears, but Mac didn't seem to care.

'Don't be stupid, Gina, there's no such thing as love,' he replied, the flat tone reminding Juno of when he'd spoken to Connor and Daisy at the wedding—of when he'd warned her not to get involved with him. 'Haven't you figured that out yet? And even if there were, it's not something I'm interested in giving—or receiving. And I believe I told *you* that at the time. So if your heart got broken, it was your own fault.'

He said the words without inflection, the complete lack of emotion stunning Juno.

She didn't have to be jealous of Gina; he had no feelings for her. But had he ever had feelings for anyone?

Where was the man who had comforted her so tenderly? Who had confided in her? Who had talked with such candour about his work? And made love to her with such passion? Where was the man who she thought had needed her?

Had that man been real? Or was he just another of the roles Mac was so good at playing?

Juno didn't hear Gina's goodbye, the woman's voice drowned out by the thudding in her ears of her own pulse. Panic closed around her throat as she realised two devastating truths in the space of one single heartbeat.

She'd made the same stupid mistake as Gina. She'd fallen hopelessly in love with Mac Brody.

And it would be her own stupid fault if he broke her heart too. Because she still had no idea who he really was. Or whether he was even capable of loving her back.

CHAPTER SIXTEEN

'WHY don't you tell me what's going on?' Mac shouted into the en suite bathroom. 'Because I'm getting tired of the silent treatment.'

He flung his tuxedo jacket onto the bed, flipped out his cufflinks and waited for a reply. His optimism of less than an hour ago well and truly squashed flat.

Women!

First off, there had been Gina, waylaying him at the party, making him talk about stuff he had no desire talking about and tarnishing the happy glow from his earlier conversation with Juno.

Then Juno herself had got back from the restroom looking pale as a ghost and refusing to meet his eyes—and his mood had hit the skids completely.

He'd done his best to ignore the problem during the limo ride to the Beverly Hills heliport. Hoping that if he said nothing she'd snap out of it. He'd had enough 'deep and meaningful' conversations to last him a lifetime today and he wasn't raring to have another.

But she hadn't snapped out of it.

So he'd clamped down on his apprehension and tried twice

to bring it up on the helicopter ride home. Only to have her give him the brush-off—and then shoot off to hide in the bathroom as soon as they got through the front door.

He dragged the shirt over his head, balled it up and chucked it at the laundry basket, ignoring the tightness in his chest. The white rattan pitched precariously.

'You might as well tell me because I'm not staying out here all night.'

More silence greeted him. Had she gone deaf or something?

Damn it, he'd had plans for this evening. And they hadn't involved showering alone.

Still no reply. He kicked off his loafers. He was fast leaving concerned and perplexed behind and working his way up to annoyed.

Dropping his trousers and dumping them in the basket, he walked into the bathroom in his boxers. And caught her frozen by the shower cubicle, naked, her eyes wide and her clothes neatly stacked on the vanity unit.

The tightness began to ease as he devoured her slim, compact frame, the curve of her bottom and the small but perfect breasts with the large rosy nipples. The blood drained from his head and pumped straight into his groin.

'Do you mind?' She whipped a towel off the rail like a schoolgirl, and covered up all the delicious pink flesh. 'I'm having a shower.'

Right, that was just plain wrong.

'Well, now, it looks like you've got company,' he said, forcing a lazy grin as he padded across the tiles. Whatever had got into her, they could deal with it later.

He'd seen the way her nipples had drawn into hard points as soon as she'd spotted him.

It was way past time they got back to basics.

* * *

Juno tensed, the melting sensation making her knees shake as she stared at the sculpted planes of Mac's naked chest. Then her gaze hit the impressive bulge in his boxer shorts and the melting sensation went molten.

How could he still have this all-consuming effect on her? All he had to do was look at her, with that knowledge, that purpose in his eyes and she got moist?

She couldn't make love to him now, not when her emotions were all over the place. It would be suicidal.

All the way home, she'd tried to focus on what to do, how to deal with the terrifying discovery that she'd fallen in love with him. How to simplify things again and get her practical step-by-step plan back on track. But the subtle scent of his aftershave, the feel of his thigh pressed against hers in the helicopter, had drained her of all her common sense. And she was beginning to see that that had always been the case. Every single one of the decisions she'd made had been influenced by his overpowering effect on her.

She'd kidded herself into believing she was being sensible, rational, when in reality she'd been exactly the opposite. She'd let her inner nymphomaniac loose as Daisy had suggested, and now it had taken complete control of her faculties. She had to try to be practical now. But how could she when her hormones refused to co-operate?

Her fingers fisted on the towel, her back bumping against the glass brick wall of the shower cubicle as he rested his hand above her head. He was standing so close she could see the tiny flecks of grey in his irises.

'If you don't mind, I'd like to shower on my own,' she said, the words strained and breathless.

His palm settled on the side of her neck, making her jump. 'But I do mind,' he said as his thumb glided under her chin, touching the sensitive skin like a firebrand.

She gulped down a staggered breath, felt the long, liquid

tug low in her belly. 'Please, Mac, this isn't a good time.' She couldn't think with his body so close, his scent surrounding her.

He lowered his head, his eyes still fixed on her face. 'So tell me to stop, then.'

The words stuck in her throat as he tugged the towel loose from her numbed fingers and dropped it at her feet.

His mouth covered hers as his hot body pushed her back against the cubicle wall. His chest hair abraded distended nipples and the thick evidence of his desire branded her through the thin covering of cotton as he hauled her against him with one arm.

She bucked as cold water flickered against her side. He'd turned on the shower.

He lifted his head, his lips quirking, determination and arousal darkening his eyes to a rich cobalt. 'Who says guys can't multitask?'

And with that he grasped her waist and lifted her easily into his arms.

'Hold on,' he murmured as his hands gripped her bottom, spreading her thighs wide to accommodate him.

She clung to his neck, her senses rioting as he stepped into the deluge with her wrapped around him. Cool water sluiced down her body, and fire throbbed at her core.

She struggled, trying to free her limbs and her mind from the drugging passion, the brutal arousal. But then her back thudded against the cubicle wall, trapping her against him and the thick, relentless pressure between her legs.

'Don't ever tell me you don't want me.' The light, easy tone had vanished to be replaced by a low insistent demand.

Her hands clutched his shoulders, the broad, muscled sinews bunching beneath her fingers as she tried to find the will to push him back, to hold on to her sanity.

But then he bent his head and pressed his lips to her

neck. Her head fell back, like a flower whose stalk had been snapped at the stem, and her breath struggled out in staggered pants as she surrendered to the inevitable. His teeth and tongue assaulted her senses, sucking and nipping at the pulse point as desire gushed from her core.

'I want you now—are you ready for me?' he demanded.

She nodded, dazed and desperate.

He pulled back for barely a moment, swore under his breath and then the thick head of his erection pushed at the swollen folds. She sobbed, the intrusion remorseless, the whirlpool spiralling out of control as he adjusted her hips and thrust heavily into her.

Fully impaled, she moaned, arousal dimming with the sudden rush of fear.

She couldn't do this. She would lose herself for ever. But she couldn't focus, her senses spinning as all her attention riveted on the intense pleasure.

She hid her face in his throat as his fingers dug onto her hips, adjusting her into position as he began to move. She gasped at the merciless penetration, then he butted that place deep inside, forcing her to climax in a savage rush. Caught in a ferocious undertow, the pleasure faded only to surge back to life, pummelling her as his slow strokes got harder, and faster and more ruthless.

She arched back as he exploded into her on an angry shout and she surrendered to the final furious wave of orgasm.

'Damn it.'

Mac's muttered curse pierced Juno's shattered mind.

Her senses sharpened as he lifted her off him. She stood on limp legs, confused and shaky, as he stormed out of the cubicle.

What had just happened?

The water splashed her shins as she watched him through

the foggy glass. He still had on the drenched boxer shorts, clinging to his buttocks. He braced his arms on the vanity unit, and sank his head down, his shoulders rigid, his stance stiff with tension.

Vulnerability clawed at her. She rubbed her chest with the heel of her hand, her lungs feeling as if they were being ripped out.

Who was he? Had he ever been the man she thought he was?

Moving with care, her thighs aching, her sex tender from the fury of their coupling, she switched off the shower unit. She gathered up the towel and wrapped it around herself. Suddenly desperate to hide her nudity.

'We've a problem,' he said as she stepped out, his voice so rough she had to strain to hear it.

He turned to prop his butt against the vanity unit and fold his arms across his chest.

'What problem?' she asked.

Dread seeped into her stomach like a black bile as his eyes met hers, dark and expressionless. 'I didn't wear a condom.'

'I…' She tried to grasp what he was saying, but her mind could only latch onto the annoyance in his voice.

'You're not on the pill, are you?'

She shook her head and he swore, thrusting his hand through his hair, furrowing the wet strands into haphazard rows.

'When was your last period?'

'I…' She couldn't remember, everything inside her recoiling from the impatience, the temper in the question. 'I'm not sure.'

'Think. It's important.'

Her fingers felt clammy, her heartbeat banging her ribcage. 'I'm due soon. I'm sure I am.'

'We can't risk it.' He thumped his fist on the vanity. 'A

pregnancy would be a disaster. There's a pill you can take, right? To stop it happening.'

The black bile rose up to throttle her as his words hurled her back into memory. To a time, a place, an agony she had sworn she would never revisit. She gulped down the sob that threatened to burst out, pushed back the terrible, churning panic.

Don't go there. Don't ever go there.

She couldn't be that girl again, destroyed, destitute. She couldn't go back to that. Couldn't spend another six years repairing her life. Survival was all that mattered now.

She gritted her teeth to hold back the swell of nausea and willed her mind to cling to the present. 'I'll take care of it.' Her voice sounded as if it were coming from miles away.

She turned to leave, taking that first crucial step back from the abyss. Knowing the only way to survive now was to leave—and to never look back.

'Juno, wait.' Mac shot across the room.

What had he done? This was all his fault.

He'd seen the wariness, the confusion in her eyes when she'd told him she didn't want him and he'd panicked.

But instead of seducing her, instead of stoking the passion between them and waiting for her response, the raw need had taken over and he'd lost control. He'd taken her, claimed her, pounding them both to orgasm, with no finesse and no thought to the consequences. And he'd ruined everything.

'I'm sorry.' He took her shoulders, massaged the chilled skin. 'You're not to blame for this. I am.'

He'd always known he couldn't risk fathering a child. He stared at the backs of his hands, so large and rough against her delicate frame. His father's hands.

She stiffened, making the tremor in her shoulders more

pronounced. 'You're right, a pregnancy would be a disaster,' she said. 'But I'd rather not talk about it now.'

Why did she sound so formal, so polite?

'Let's go to bed,' he said, struggling to keep his voice even as he kissed the top of her head. 'A good night's sleep is what we both need. And we'll sort this mess out in the morning.' If he could just hold her, he could make it right.

She turned, shrugging off his hands. 'I'm really tired. I think I'll sleep in the guest suite.'

And with that she was gone.

He took a step forward, determined to get her to come back, then stopped himself.

Where the hell did he think he was going?

He had to get a grip, to ease off, to give her some space. To give them both some space.

They'd been living in each other's pockets for close to two weeks and somehow he'd let the company, the sense of companionship get to him. Which was exactly why he'd lost leave of his senses in the shower. If this was going to work, he'd have to learn to start backing off. And that meant not giving in to every damn stupid urge where she was concerned.

One night without her beside him wouldn't do any harm. In fact it would probably do them both a great deal of good.

CHAPTER SEVENTEEN

MAC had revised his opinion a fair bit by eight the next morning, having spent a sleepless night tossing and turning in his empty bed.

Something about the way they'd parted had niggled constantly at the back of his mind. He'd been thoughtless and overbearing and she'd had every right to call him on it. But why hadn't she been more angry, more upset with him? She'd been so calm, so controlled, and the more he thought about it, the more it unnerved him.

He had the definite feeling he'd missed something vitally important.

Juno sat at the table, finishing a bowl of muesli as he walked into the kitchen.

'Hello there,' he said, sounding heartier than he felt. 'You sleep well?'

'Yes, thank you,' she said, so politely it made him wince. She didn't look up.

Undeterred, he placed his hand on her shoulder, pressed a kiss to her cheek.

And she shifted away.

Damn it, what was this now? Was she mad with him after all?

He braced himself for the tirade he'd expected the night before, but she kept her head bent over the bowl and carried on scooping up the cereal in careful, precise spoonfuls.

Was she waiting for him to say something first? He sighed. Best to get it over with.

He grabbed the box of cereal, poured himself a generous helping while trying to figure out what to say without making an ass of himself.

'I'll apologise again for treating you the way I did last night. We both got carried away and then I overreacted and went off on one. I'm sorry.'

Her spoon stayed in the bowl. But she still didn't look at him. The niggling got worse.

'There was no need for you to sleep alone,' he pointed out, rather reasonably, he thought.

Her hand lay on the table. He reached over, covered it with his. 'How about we forget it ever happened? A pregnancy's a long shot with you so close to the end of your cycle. And if there is one, well, then we'll deal with it.'

He'd examined the possibility from every angle during the night—as he'd had more than enough time to think about it—and had decided to leave it up to fate. With his past, his heritage, he would never have planned to become a father, but he hadn't been able to get the memory of Connor cradling his baby son out of his head.

In the end he'd come to the conclusion that if by some miracle he'd got Juno pregnant last night, the thought of a little boy or girl with her eyes, her sweet, practical temperament and his tenacity didn't seem like such a terrifying prospect.

She pulled her hand out from under his and it disappeared beneath the table. He felt the tug of annoyance. Surely he'd eaten enough humble pie? He couldn't keep apologising for ever.

'How about we go sailing today?' he said lightly. 'I've a

yacht up at the marina and it's a beautiful day for it.' Just the thought of her in that skimpy yellow swimsuit lying on the polished teak of the bow had his mood improving.

Her chin jerked up and she met his eyes at last. 'I need to leave in an hour. I'm booked on the two o'clock flight from LAX. I've checked out the bus times and I—'

'Whoah.' He leapt up, the chair crashing onto the floor as her words registered. 'You're... What?'

She stood, picked up her bowl. 'I should get back to work,' she said quickly, efficiently as she walked to the sink. 'The weekends are our busiest time. I arranged the flight when I woke up so I could be back on Friday morning.'

'Well, you'll have to un-arrange it,' he said, sure his head was about to explode.

He'd let her go last night. Let her have the time she needed. But he wasn't having this. She wasn't leaving. He wouldn't let her.

'I know it's a few days sooner than we'd planned, but it—'

He crossed to the sink, pulled her round to face him. 'If this is about last night, I'm not apologising again.'

He was beginning to wonder why he'd apologised at all. It seemed she wasn't at all cut up about what had happened. Why did that worry him more?

Her chin came up in a gesture of defiance. 'This has nothing to do with last night. We always agreed this would be temporary. I'm leaving a little sooner than planned, that's all.'

'I know we said that, but...' He trailed off. But what?

She stood in front of him, rigid and unmoved, and yet he could feel his insides roiling like a ship at sea. They *had* said it would be temporary. But somewhere along the line he'd begun to believe it was more. He'd thought she felt something for him. But what if he'd been wrong? What if she felt nothing for him at all?

And as she stood there, unblinking, her chin poking out

and her back ramrod straight, he knew with a startling clarity what it was that hadn't been right last night.

He'd told her a pregnancy would be a disaster—and with barely a hesitation she'd agreed with him. The realisation felt like an arrow shot straight through his heart.

He pulled his hand away as if he'd touched a live flame.

What a fool he'd been. Somewhere in the last ten days, he'd come to believe she thought well of him, that she thought more of him than he'd ever thought of himself. But she didn't.

He stiffened, the pain an echo of the crushing feeling of rejection that had dogged him throughout his childhood. A bitter reminder of all those people who had taken him in, but had never wanted to keep him.

'If that's the way of it, I guess I can't stop you,' he said as placidly as possible. 'I'll have my PA arrange transport for you to LAX. There's no need for you to be taking the bus.' He put just the right note of indifference into his tone.

He was an actor. He could do this. He had his pride. And that was all that he had now.

She said nothing, her eyes downcast.

'It's been fun, Juno.' And that was all it was ever meant to be. When had he lost sight of that? 'Have a wonderful life.'

He threw her own words back at her as he made himself walk away.

For if there was one lesson he'd learned as a lad, it was simply this.

Never let them know you care.

'Are you all right, honey? You don't look too good.' The check-in woman's pristine make-up hid a homely face full of concern.

'I'm fine, really.' Juno managed a weak smile as she took the boarding pass in trembling hands. If she could just get on the plane before she broke down, she knew she'd be able to survive this. 'But thank you for asking.'

She boarded in a daze, desperate not to think about anything. But the horror of her final moments with Mac kept replaying in her head.

There's no such thing as love.

That was what he'd told Gina. And he'd meant every word. He'd never needed her. That had all been some infantile fantasy that she'd created to justify needing him.

He'd warned her not to make him into something he wasn't and yet she'd insisted on doing just that. How could she have been so stupid? How could she have fallen in love with a man who could never have loved her back?

She'd wanted to tell him how she felt. Had even harboured some foolish, last-ditch fantasy during the long restless night that if she told him of her feelings he would declare his undying love in return. But optimism had never been her strong suit and his cold dismissal once she'd told him of her plans had doused the last flicker of hope.

Her heart wasn't just broken, it was shattered, humiliated. Telling him she loved him this morning—and hearing what he'd told Gina—would only have humiliated her more and made it that much harder to pick up the pieces and move on.

The tears trickled down her face as she stared out of the tiny window at the vast geometric sprawl of Los Angeles. As the plane dipped into a turn she caught a glimpse of the jagged coastline and the plateau of the Pacific beyond. She imagined Mac in his magnificent glass and steel house by the sea—no doubt ready to move on to his next conquest. She wanted to be angry with him. To shout and scream and rail against the pain.

But as the jumbo's engines surged, lifting it above the clouds, the anger she wanted to feel refused to come. All she felt was devastation, and a crippling sense of loss.

He'd told her she would get hurt. Why hadn't she listened?

CHAPTER EIGHTEEN

'DAISY'S absolutely right, you look dreadful.' Dr Maya Patel's capable voice did nothing to sooth Juno's misery, or the feeling that she'd failed herself and everyone around her. 'Why don't you tell me the symptoms and I'm sure we'll be able to cure whatever ails you?'

Only if you have a cure for self-pity.

It had been four weeks since she'd come home. Four weeks since her 'fabulous adventure' had turned into a complete disaster. A complete disaster that she knew was entirely of her own making.

So why couldn't she snap out of her self-pity?

She'd thrown herself into her work at the shop, making sure she had no time to dwell on the situation. She'd handled the inexplicable burst of tears when she'd had her period on her first day back. She'd deflected the flood of calls from tabloid reporters trying to persuade her to sell her story until they'd dwindled to a mere trickle. And she'd weathered the storm of emotions when a poster from the movie she and Mac had seen together had been pasted up on the huge billboard at the end of Portobello Market.

But, despite all her best efforts, the impact of what had

happened kept catching her unawares. She'd lost weight, she couldn't sleep, she was still bursting into tears at the most inopportune moments and she'd even thrown up several times in the last few days.

She'd turned into a self-indulgent misery guts and she was starting to hate herself.

And, as of yesterday, she had Daisy on her case too. Once Daisy had arrived back from her honeymoon, she'd taken one look at Juno and immediately booked her a GP's appointment.

Of course Daisy had probed about what had happened with Mac, but Juno had been too humiliated to tell her the truth, insisting she just had a bit of a virus. In fact she'd been so convincing, she'd begun to wonder if maybe she did have a virus.

She hoped so, because she couldn't allow herself to mourn something that had never been real a moment longer. 'I think I may have a stomach bug.'

Maya nodded sagely. 'You look exhausted. Have you been having trouble sleeping?'

'Yes, a bit.'

'Mood swings?'

She nodded. How did Maya know that?

'How about your waterworks? Do you need to go to the toilet a lot at the moment?'

'Actually, yes, I suppose so.' Was the woman clairvoyant?

Maya propped her elbows on the desk, steepled her fingers. 'Right, then, I think we should start by doing a pregnancy test.'

Juno coloured, feeling the now all too familiar sting of tears. Of course, everyone knew about her two-week affair with Mac; it had been reported in most of the papers. But seeing the compassion in Maya's eyes only made her feel more inadequate and more depressed. 'I'm not pregnant, Maya. I can't be. I've had a period since…' She stared at her lap.

'Since I got back. And we didn't.' She hesitated. 'We were careful.' Almost all of the time.

'Let's just say you're humouring me, then,' Maya said firmly.

Juno sighed and nodded. What was one more humiliation to add to all the others?

'It's positive,' Maya said gently, staring at the on-screen print-out. 'You're pregnant.'

Juno sucked in a breath, feeling as if an articulated lorry had slammed into her chest. 'That... That's not possible.'

'I'm afraid it's very possible,' Maya replied, swivelling her chair round, the sympathy in her gaze making Juno feel nauseous. 'The period you thought you had was most likely just spotting. Was it very light?'

'I don't... Yes. I suppose,' she stammered, her mind numb. She'd had twenty minutes to wait for the test to be administered and the results to come through, but she'd remained calm. This at least was one calamity that couldn't happen.

And now it had. Tears flooded over her lids.

Maya rushed around the desk and pulled her into her arms as the first sob burst out. 'Juno, love, don't worry. We can sort this out,' she said, abandoning the doctor-patient etiquette and stroking Juno's hair like the friend she was.

'I can't deal with this now. I can't,' she whispered between the jerking sobs, tears dripping onto the hands clutched in her lap.

How could this have happened? Was she being punished? For making the same terrible mistake twice in her life? For falling in love with a man who didn't really exist?

'I'm calling Daisy. You're not dealing with this alone.' Maya framed her face in warm hands. 'What you need is a good night's sleep. As soon as you've got that done we'll take the next step and talk through all the options. Okay?'

'Please don't tell Daisy,' she blurted out.

How could she face her friend? How could she face Connor with this news?

'That'll be your decision,' Maya said carefully. 'But you're going to need a lot of support in the next few weeks, possibly months, and Daisy's a fantastic person to have in your corner. '

Juno nodded meekly. Knowing Maya was right. However hard it was going to be to have to admit how witless and irresponsible she'd been, she needed her best friend more than ever now.

And then another thought occurred to her. And the lorry crushed her ribcage.

'Am I…?' She paused, tried to breathe through the fear. 'Am I going to have another miscarriage?'

She didn't feel miserable any more, she felt utterly destroyed.

'There's no reason you should.' Maya walked back to her desk and sat behind it, her doctor's hat back on. 'Lots of women have miscarriages and then go on to have viable pregnancies. But as soon as you're ready we can give you a thorough examination, find out how the baby's doing and talk through the possible risks.' A small smile curved her lips. 'So you've already decided to have this baby?'

Juno's body began to shake. 'I don't know.'

But she did know, which only made the whole situation a thousand times worse.

Could she really risk putting everything she was—everything she hoped to be—on the line again? And could she survive what she'd been through six years ago, if it all went horribly, hideously wrong a second time?

CHAPTER NINETEEN

'Ju, THIS is madness. You've got to tell Mac. Not doing so is not an option.'

Juno stared at Daisy across the breakfast bar, her mouth firming into a stubborn line. She'd been preparing herself for this argument for the last forty-eight hours, but she still didn't feel ready to deal with it.

As expected, Daisy had been the Rock of Gibraltar ever since she'd arrived at Maya's surgery two days ago armed with a comforting hug and a sturdy shoulder to cry on.

She'd whisked Juno back to her house, insisting she stay in the guest bedroom for the rest of the week. She'd pampered her and cajoled her and calmed the worst of her fears. Then, after she'd coaxed out most of the story of Juno's disastrous adventure in La-La Land, she'd helped her to begin rebuilding her confidence and her courage.

Daisy had convinced her that having the baby was a no-brainer if that was what she wanted to do in her heart. She'd held her hand through the exam Maya had given her. She'd fed her, bought her enough pregnancy vitamins to stock a supermarket and embarked on a series of pep talks about not retreating back into her shell and not blaming everything that went wrong in her life on herself.

When Juno had woken up this morning with the dappled shade casting sunny shapes onto the luxury furnishings of Daisy and Connor's spare room, for the first time in a month she'd felt able to cope with everything that had happened to her and much better able to face what the future might hold.

But the one thing Juno had refused point-blank to talk about was Mac. And Daisy had respected her wishes, until she'd broached the question that Juno had been dreading a minute ago.

She didn't know what to say to convince Daisy to drop it.

Daisy as usual took her silence as a challenge. 'I hate to do this, but I'm forced to point out at this juncture that you said the exact same thing to me when I fell pregnant with Ronan. I didn't want to tell Connor and you said I had to. And while I hate to say this even more,' she added with a soft smile, 'you were right.'

'This is different,' Juno murmured, staring at her half-eaten bowl of muesli. Trust Daisy to hoist her with her own petard.

'How is it different? Doesn't Mac have a right to know he's going to become a father too?'

Juno shook her head. She hadn't wanted to tell Daisy this.

It had hurt terribly to hear what Mac had said on their last night together—because it had reminded her so forcefully of what Tony had said all those years ago when she'd told him she was pregnant—but at least Mac had been honest and made it absolutely clear he had no desire to father a child with her. The reasons why hardly mattered now.

'If I told him, he would expect me to have an abortion. And as I've decided not to, I don't see much point in telling him.'

'How could you possibly know that?' Daisy demanded.

Juno looked up to see her friend's horrified expression.

This was exactly what she had wanted to avoid. She had no desire to make Mac look bad in front of his family. Maybe, one day, he'd want to contact Daisy and Connor again, and she didn't want to sour the relationship.

'Because he told me so.'

'Are you sure?' Daisy didn't look convinced.

'Yes, I'm sure.' Or sure enough. He hadn't loved her the way Connor loved Daisy. So why should he want her to have his baby?

Daisy blew out a breath. 'I find that incredibly hard to believe. But even so, how on earth do you propose to keep it a secret?'

'He won't contact me again.' Of that one thing she was absolutely sure; that vain, foolish hope had died a death days ago when she'd received no word from him. 'And I don't think he's going to contact you again either. If he does I'll handle it.'

Would he want to have a relationship with the baby once it was born? The question had plagued her ever since she'd made the decision to try and carry the baby to term. She'd eventually come to the conclusion that the answer was certainly no. He didn't believe in love. And he'd told her he wasn't interested in playing happy families. How much more conclusive proof did she need?

'What about the press?' Daisy said. 'What if they find out?'

'They've moved on. No one's contacted me in over a week. As long as there's no sign of Mac I have no celebrity value.' Which was one major plus.

She settled her hand on her stomach. Make that two major pluses.

'I have to move on, Daze. I have to handle what I can control and forget about the rest. Having a healthy baby is all I care about at the moment.' It was all she could allow herself to care about.

Mac was her past. The baby was her future. And right now she had to concentrate on not panicking herself to death. On getting through the first three months of this pregnancy safely, so she could start to get excited about the prospect of becoming a mother.

Daisy gripped her hand, squeezed hard. 'I understand that. But we do have one other major problem on our hands.'

'Which is?'

'What Connor's going to make of all this when he gets back from Berlin this afternoon. He and Mac were hardly on speaking terms when Mac took you off to LA. I'll be honest and tell you we had a bit of a row after you'd gone to the airport. You know how overprotective he can be.'

Juno huffed out a breath. Connor was another thing she didn't want to think about. The business trip that had kept him out of the way for the last two days had been one small blessing in the massive mess she'd made of her life.

'Do you want me to talk to him?' she asked. Would nothing in her life ever be simple or straightforward again?

Daisy patted her hand. 'It's okay, you've got more than enough on your plate. Leave Connor to me. But I'm just warning you, I can't make any promises.'

Juno sighed. She didn't expect promises any more.

A full twenty-four hours without having to deal with any major emotional upheavals would be more than enough.

Mac trudged up the steps from the beach and glanced at the pedometer on his wrist.

Ten miles. He'd run ten miles, pushing himself to the limits of his endurance after another sleepless night. And he still felt like crap. Usually the endorphins kicked in and gave him at least a small lift as he showered and changed and got ready to drive to the studio for rehearsals. Rehearsals that so far had been a total disaster. He hadn't been able to find the character, not even a glimpse of it, for the first time ever.

Over the last week he'd been running further and further every morning but the exercise wasn't doing the trick any more.

Stepping onto the terrace, he lifted his sodden T-shirt to wipe his dripping face. And paused to stare at the sun-lounger where Juno had often lain in the shade to welcome him back from his jog. He cursed quietly and let the T-shirt drop.

Who the hell was he kidding? The aching pain, the loneliness hadn't got any better in the month since she'd left him. If anything it had got a great deal worse. The house that had once been a sanctuary had become a prison. Everywhere he looked he saw her. In the pool in that damn yellow swimsuit. At the breakfast table eating her morning muesli. In his bed and in the shower, her lithe body responding to his touch. She was like a ghost, taunting him to try and forget her.

It had got so bad he'd even toyed with putting the house on the market this past week. But what would be the point of that? The memories would still be there, dogging him wherever he went. He didn't need a new home. What he needed was her.

But each time he'd picked up the phone, intending to call her and demand to know why she'd left, he'd kept coming back to their final parting—and he hadn't been able to do it. Maybe it was pride, more likely just the survival instinct that had been bred into him as a lad, but he'd needed her to come to him. For the first few weeks he'd even fostered this stupid daydream that he might have got her pregnant and she'd be forced to contact him. But it hadn't happened.

He slammed into the kitchen and opened the fridge. Grabbing a bottle of mineral water, he rolled the chilled plastic against his forehead. As he leaned back against the countertop his eyes fixed on the chair in which she'd been sitting the last time she'd had breakfast with him.

The hum of the air-conditioner was the only sound to break the silence. The empty silence that had started to suffocate him.

'Stop being such a damn coward, Brody,' he snarled into the deathly quiet.

Unscrewing the cap, he gulped down the water and then lobbed the empty bottle into the trash. She wasn't coming to him, so he'd have to go to her.

He strode through into the living room and went to pick up the phone, then jerked his hand back when the ring tone blared out. The silly little spurt of hope that it might be Juno was ruthlessly quashed. Hadn't he just got over wishing for the impossible?

He grabbed the handset and shouted into the receiver. 'Brody here, who is this?'

'It's Connor.'

The shock of hearing his brother's voice was so great he was momentarily struck dumb. 'Connor?'

'Yeah, your big brother, remember me?'

He heard it then, the brittle sarcasm, but the hope overcame his usual caution.

'How's Juno?' he asked, not even attempting to disguise his eagerness for news.

He didn't care why his brother was calling or even if the guy hated his guts. Connor lived right next door to the woman who he had just this second admitted to himself meant more to him than breathing. This had to be fate finally doing him a favour, surely.

Connor laughed, the sound harsh. 'That's rich. How is she? How the hell do you think she is?'

'I don't know how she is,' he said through gritted teeth. 'That's why I'm asking.'

So Connor had good reason to despise him. So what? He didn't have time to go into that now.

'What was it all for, Mac? Just tell me that much.' The edge had gone from Connor's voice to be replaced by sadness. 'Was this some kind of payback? Did you want to punish her because you couldn't punish me? Because if that's the case, she never deserved to become—'

'I've not a single clue what you're talking about,' he interrupted with a panicked shout. 'Has something happened to Juno? Just tell me how she is, damn it.'

He was sweating like a pig, the phone slipping in his grasp. Visions of all kinds of imagined carnage running through his mind.

'Yeah, something's happened to her,' Connor said, the hint of bitterness now layered with resignation.

'What? What's happened? Is she sick? Has she been hurt?' If he had to ask again he was going to climb down the phone line and throttle Connor himself, brother or not.

'I'd say she's both,' Connor replied. 'She's pregnant, with your child. Which she's decided to have even though she's scared to death. And she—'

Mac slapped the phone onto its cradle, cutting Connor off. He'd not heard much after the second sentence anyway.

Juno was pregnant, with their child, and she hadn't told him? She'd be at least a month gone by now—and yet she hadn't once thought to pick up the phone? Did she think so little of him, then? He forced the anger forward to dull the pain. He didn't care what her reasons were any more.

She was his. She always had been. He should never have let her cut him out of her life in the first place. And he'd be damned if he'd let her cut him out a moment longer.

CHAPTER TWENTY

'WHERE'S Juno?' Mac hurled the question at Connor as soon as his brother opened his front door. 'The old girl next door said she's staying with you.'

He pushed past his startled brother but was stopped in his tracks by the irate shout that followed him down the corridor. 'Get the hell back here. You'll not come barging into my home without an invitation.'

He turned to see Connor stalking towards him in his stockinged feet, his face furious.

Great! Fantastic! He'd spent a good part of the last eleven hours on the red eye from LA nursing a blistering headache and letting his anger stew. If his brother was spoiling for a fight he was more than happy to oblige.

'I don't need your invitation to speak to the woman who's carrying my child.' He ground the words out. Whatever issues his brother had could damn well wait.

'Think again,' Connor shot back, the steely determination in his face brooking no argument. 'She's not here.' He shoved a door open and pointed inside a darkened room. 'Now stop shouting, get in there and calm the hell down or you won't get to speak to her at all.'

Sure he could feel the steam pumping out of his ears, he stalked into the room Connor had indicated. What right did his brother have to treat him like a sulky child? As soon as he got Juno's whereabouts out of the sanctimonious bastard he was going to give him both barrels.

'Sit down,' Connor ordered, pointing to the leather couch.

Mac folded his arms and stood his ground. 'Say what you've got to say and then tell me where she is.'

'Sit the hell down, before I throw you down,' Connor shouted back.

His hands bunched into fists until his knuckles whitened. But after a second's debate, he cursed loudly and sat on the sofa. Beating the crap out of Connor wasn't going to help him find Juno. More's the pity.

'So what is it you want?' he snarled, then realised he sounded like a sulky child.

Damn it.

'I want to know what kind of man you are. That's what.' Connor sneered, his eyes narrowing. 'I want to know what kind of man has unprotected sex with a woman, then doesn't even have the decency to find out if he's got her pregnant or not.'

It wasn't like that.

He wanted to yell back, the injustice of Connor's accusations making his head throb and his stomach revolt. But the guilt that had followed him around for most of his life choked the words off in his throat.

'You know what kind of man I am,' he said, his voice cracking. 'Do you think I don't know what you think of me? What you've always thought of me, ever since we were lads together in that stinking hole. You think I'm a selfish, irresponsible bastard. I get it.' He sunk his head into his hands, to release the screaming tension in his shoulders.

Anyone who said confession was good for the soul didn't know what the hell they were talking about.

'I'll grant you, that was true then,' he continued, forcing the words past lips dry as a desert. 'But it's not true any more.' He raised his head to meet Connor's eyes. 'I want Juno back. I think I'm in love with her.' He blew out a breath, the words taking him by surprise. 'That's why I'm here.'

It took him a moment to realise the contempt in Connor's face had turned to astonishment.

'You think I blame *you* for what happened? When we were kids?'

'I know you do,' he replied. 'That's why it was your wife invited me to the wedding and not you.' Why was Connor prolonging the agony?

'Mac, that's ridiculous.' He sat down, settled his hand on Mac's shoulder. 'I never thought any such thing. I always thought it was me to blame. If I hadn't gone out that night. If I hadn't been so determined to keep it all a secret. We could have got help. I could have stopped him.'

'But you told the social worker you never wanted to see me again after we were split.' Could it really be true? That his brother didn't hate him after all?

'Because I felt so ashamed,' Connor replied. 'I saw you that night on the stretcher, unconscious, your face all bruised and bloody, your arm cut up and bent out of shape. I couldn't get it out of my head. You were my little brother, barely ten years old. I should have been there to protect you and I wasn't. It crucified me for years.' Connor shook his head, the bitter regret in his voice releasing something black and ugly inside Mac and setting it free at last. 'Until I met Daisy and she made me see, it wasn't our fault, it was his and the things the drink did to him.'

He pulled Mac into a brief one-armed hug.

'I should have told you years ago. And you're right, it

should have been me invited you to the wedding,' he murmured against Mac's ear before letting him go. 'But I was too much of a damn coward. I'm sorry, Mac.'

Mac saw the genuine love in Connor's eyes and realised he'd found his brother again. In fact he'd never even lost him. He drew in a sharp breath through his nose. Perilously close to making an idiot of himself.

'Apology accepted,' he murmured. 'But we best stop this now, or we're going to start weeping all over each other like a couple of girls. And I don't know about you, but I've an image to protect.'

Connor chuckled. 'Don't give me that—you're an actor. Don't you cry all the time?'

Mac raised an eyebrow. 'Keep it up, pal, and I'll have to hurt you.'

Connor just laughed, the low amused sound reminding Mac of their relationship as boys. Connor always determined to look for the best in everything and him always brooding about what would go wrong. He'd missed having him in his life.

Connor stood up and walked to his desk. 'Now we've had our Kodak moment—and established the fact that you know how to cry like a girl,' he said lightly, 'we need to talk about Juno.' He propped his butt on the desk and crossed his legs at the ankles. 'So you love her, do you? Are you sure about that?'

The anger and temper kicked back in at the careful question. But it wasn't directed at Connor any more.

'I know it took me far too long to figure it out. But yeah.' He nodded, more sure of himself than he'd been in years. 'Yeah, I do. And I want to put things right. But it's kind of tough when I don't have a clue whether she loves me back or hates my guts. She didn't want to tell me about the baby, and that's not making me feel too hopeful.'

'Don't look at me.' Connor shrugged. 'I can't tell you whether she loves you or not. Daisy had to hit me over the head with how she felt before I got the picture.' He paused. 'But there are a couple of things I know that you don't. According to Daisy she's been miserable since she got back from LA, so she's certainly not indifferent to you.'

Mac was fairly sure that wasn't a glowing endorsement, but right now he'd take it. 'What's the other thing?'

'What do you know about a guy called Tony?'

The deep-seated anger that had smouldered ever since he'd first heard the name leapt into flame. 'That the guy raped her when she was only sixteen. And that I'd like to hunt him down and strangle him with my bare hands.'

'You and me both,' Connor said grimly. 'Daisy told me the story, but there's a fair bit more to it than that. Which may explain why she didn't tell you of the baby. Juno's smart and capable, but she's also much more fragile than she appears. I guess you know you're the first guy she's been with since him?'

Mac could feel himself flushing as he nodded.

'Don't underestimate how big a point that is in your favour. She trusted you, Mac, and that counts for a lot after what she's been through.' Connor reached round and grabbed a pen and a notepad from the desk. He drew a few quick lines, made a couple of notes, then tore off the page and handed it to Mac. 'She's over at the store at the moment. Here's a map. It's not hard to find from here.'

Mac took the page, stared at the roughly drawn street plan. He wanted to see her again, desperately, but he was starting to realise healing the twenty-year rift between him and Connor had been the easy part. He stood and folded the note into the back pocket of his jeans. 'Thanks.'

'Get her to tell you the rest of it, Mac. But hold on to your temper, for God's sake. And be honest with her about how you feel.' He gave a wry smile. 'It'll be good practice for dealing with my new niece or nephew when they arrive.'

Mac nodded and strode to the door, the thought of the baby and Juno and the enormous mess he had to sort out if he was going to set things right making his head hurt again—and his heart pound.

'Mac, one more thing,' Connor called after him.

He glanced round with his hand on the doorknob.

'Put in a good word for me when you're finished. Juno's going to murder me when she finds out it was me who blew the whistle on her.'

'Forget it, big brother,' he said, trying to find some small scrap of humour to ease the tension. 'After that crack about me crying like a girl, I'll be setting her on you myself.'

CHAPTER TWENTY-ONE

JUNO took a sip of the fennel tea that helped to steady her stomach and typed the next line of numbers into the calculator.

Who would have thought she'd ever enjoy doing a VAT return? She pressed her hand to her stomach and took a deep breath of the pleasantly musty air. She hadn't puked once this morning, and, while doing the bookkeeping in the haphazard mess of Daisy's workshop probably wasn't ideal, being back at work had been a major boost. As Daisy had refused point-blank to let her go front of house on a Saturday, which was always their busiest day, she'd settled for number crunching in the back room and was finding the monotonous, methodical work surprisingly soothing.

Life was finally starting to look up. She'd had the baby's heartbeat checked this morning at Maya's surgery and had been able to count off another day towards her three-month mark and the point when she could start making plans for her and the baby. And the sun was shining through the tiny window, making the dust motes glitter.

All she had to do now was focus on achievable goals and let everything else take care of itself. Maybe she'd never been destined to have a happy-ever-after with the man of her dreams, but if she was very lucky she might have something every bit as good in eight months' time.

She heard the door open. 'Just a minute, Daze,' she said as she typed the last of the August suppliers' receipts into the calculator.

'You should have told me about the baby.'

Her head shot up at the deep, husky voice—and all the breath sucked right out of her lungs.

'What are you doing here?' she whispered. Surely she had to be hallucinating.

He stood by the door, his tall, broad-shouldered frame in worn jeans and a Cal Arts T-shirt making the cramped room look even smaller.

'I came to talk,' he said calmly, his eyes raking over her face, the intense blue making her breath catch. 'Among other things.'

He stepped towards her, but she shot out of her chair and moved back. 'Go away. I have nothing to talk to you about.' She couldn't go through this, not again. The yearning, the longing and the knowing it had never been real.

'That's nonsense and you know it.' He skirted the table and she retreated another step, backing into a rack of dresses pushed against the wall.

'Why don't we start with why you walked out on me?' he said as he continued to bear down on her. 'And then we'll move right along to why you didn't tell me about our child.'

'Why would I?' she said as a rage that she hadn't even known was inside her rose up to batter her chest. 'Why would I tell you about a child you don't want?'

There could only be one reason he was here. One reason he'd flown all the way from LA. The sickening realisation had fear sprinting up her spine.

She tried to dash past him, trapped and desperate to escape. But he stepped into her path and wrapped an arm round her waist. Hauling her into his arms.

'You're going nowhere until you explain that statement,' he said, holding her easily as she tried to struggle free.

She lifted her fists, pummelled his chest. 'I'm not having an abortion. You can't make me.' Tears blurred her eyes, the fear growing like a tempest.

'Juno, stop it, it's nothing like that.' He took the blows and tightened his arms until her attempts to hit him became futile and she struggled uselessly in his embrace.

'I won't do it. I won't. Leave me alone. I hate you,' she cried out.

But it wasn't Mac she saw any more, it was Tony, the sneering contempt, the smug indifference on his face. And then the last of the rage, the fury, drained to leave nothing but bone-melting exhaustion, bitter sobs racking her body.

'Shh, Juno, don't take on so.' His voice seemed to come from a great distance away as he lifted her. He took the seat she'd vacated and cradled her limp body in his lap. His hand brushed her cheek, pushed the hair back from her face. 'I never told you to have an abortion. And now you've fallen pregnant, an abortion is the last thing I want.' He covered the hand fisted in her lap.

She shifted, trying to get off his lap, but his arms held her in place.

'You told me to take the morning-after pill,' she said. 'What's the difference?'

He cursed softly and gave a heavy sigh. 'Ah, hell. That was a stupid knee-jerk reaction, said in the heat of the moment. Don't hold it against me now.'

'Why would you say it if you didn't mean it?'

His eyes flicked away.

'I'd always believed I could never be a father. That I might have the same thing inside me, the same weakness my own father had.' He hesitated. 'But now I can see how foolish that was.' He looked back at her, squeezed her hand. 'I want to be a father to this baby. Do you believe me?'

Seeing the truth in his eyes, she felt emotion swell in her chest. 'Yes.' She huffed out a breath, resigned to telling him the rest. 'But there's a good chance there might not be a baby.'

'Tell me what happened, Juno,' he said gently, brushing his thumb across her cheek. 'Because I've a feeling it wasn't only me you were fighting a moment ago?'

Her bottom lip trembled perilously. She supposed she owed him this much. She'd accused him of something he'd never really said. 'I got pregnant,' she said simply. 'After… After the night with Tony.'

'I see,' he said. 'That's not all, though, is it?'

She shook her head, wondering when he'd become so perceptive.

'My parents were furious. They wanted me to get rid of it. Said I'd made a foolish mistake. And I had.' She gulped the tears down, determined not to cry. This had all happened so long ago. Wasn't it about time she got over it? 'But I couldn't do it. I moved out, I wanted to prove them wrong. I got a room at Mrs Valdermeyer's. I had all these silly dreams. I would have the baby and Tony would be overjoyed and tell me he loved me and…' She swallowed; it all sounded so idiotic now, like a little girl playing house. 'I went to his work to tell him. He was furious, told me if I was pregnant I better get unpregnant. He picked up the phone to arrange an abortion, and I just ran off. I never saw him again.'

'That bastard.' She could hear the sympathy and anger in his voice, drew strength from it.

'Two days later, I had a miscarriage. A spontaneous abortion, that's what the doctor called it. It was for the best, I understand that now. I wasn't mature enough to have a child.

But it seemed so final, so cruel at the time. As if the baby was made to suffer for something I did.'

'Juno.' He sighed, threading his fingers through hers. 'Don't do that now. Don't punish yourself for something that you had no control over.' A lopsided smile tugged at his mouth. 'It screws you up. A very wise young woman made me realise that a while back.'

As she sent him a weak smile she felt the last traces of guilt leave her heart. Until all that remained was the distant ache of grief for the child she'd lost.

He rested a palm on her midriff, warming her through the thin cotton of her dress. 'So what does the doctor say about this little one? How careful do we have to be?'

The 'we' had her pulse skittering, but she pushed back the spurt of hope. One thing she'd promised herself in the last month was that she wouldn't yearn for the impossible. Just because he cared about the baby, just because he wanted to be a part of its life, didn't mean he wanted anything more.

'Maya says everything's progressing normally. She seems pretty confident. Once I get to the three-month mark, we'll know for sure.'

'So that's good news, right?' The spontaneous grin made his dark, handsome face look impossibly boyish and the pang of longing squeezed her heart.

She nodded and climbed off his lap, desperate for distance. She still loved him, so much, but she couldn't let it cloud her judgement again.

He stood behind her. 'So where do you think you're off to?'

She turned to face him, determined to focus on the reality, not the fantasy. 'I can email you, when I have my antenatal check-ups,' she said, sweeping her hair behind her ears. 'How long are you planning to be in London?' When he said nothing, simply stared at her, she hurried on. 'I have my first ultrasound at ten weeks. If you like I could give you a schedule. Although the first one's probably not worth coming all the way from LA for.'

A schedule? What on earth was she on about?

Mac frowned, sure he'd slipped into an alternative reality. Hadn't they just established that they were going to be doing this together? As a couple?

'There'll be no need for me to come over from LA as you're coming back with me.' Her mouth had dropped open but he soldiered on. Surely she would see this was the obvious solution. 'Luckily the whole cast is in rehearsals at the moment, so the director can work round me for a week or so. If that's not enough time for you to settle things here, we could maybe make a short trip back before shooting starts in October? But you'll not be travelling alone. And that's final.' On some things he intended to be absolutely firm.

'I'm not moving to LA. My life is here.'

He huffed out a breath. He supposed he could negotiate. If he absolutely had to.

'I'm not meaning to be a dictator about this. But I'm under contract and my current project is shooting in the US, so it makes sense for us to be based there for the next six months. But after that I'm a free agent. I've no more projects I'm committed to. And I'm at a place in my career where I can call the shots.' He placed his hand on her crown, stroked it down her hair, enjoying the soft silky texture and feeling positively magnanimous. 'We can move back here before the baby's born. I could buy a place in Daisy and Connor's street if that's what you want.'

In fact the idea had considerable merit now he'd thought of it. He and his brother had a fair bit of catching up to do.

She ducked out from under his hand, but instead of looking pleased, and grateful, she looked upset. 'Who said we were going to be living together?'

The question threw him completely. 'Of course we will be. What else would we do once we're married?'

'Married?' she all but squeaked. 'I never said I'd marry you. In fact you haven't even asked me!'

'True enough.' He grasped her hand and pressed a quick kiss on her knuckles. In his eagerness to get things sorted he'd missed a fairly important step. Luckily it was easily remedied. 'Will you marry me, Juno?'

She tugged her hand loose. 'No, I will not,' she shot back so succinctly he knew he hadn't misheard her.

'Why the hell not?' he said back, his head throbbing again. Why was she being so damn contrary? 'I love you and you love me. And you're having my baby. What else would we do but get married?'

She looked as if he'd slapped her, and suddenly his good mood plummeted into the abyss. Once she'd told him the horror story about Tony and her miscarriage, once he'd explained why he'd said the things he had and apologised, the relief had been enormous. He'd just assumed that everything would be okay, that she must love him, that their parting had all simply been a hideous mistake.

But had he put two and two together and made five?

What if she didn't love him after all?

And did he have the guts now to lay his feelings bare, knowing they might not be returned?

'You love me?' Juno quashed the desperate surge of hope, of love. Was it true, or was this just another role he was playing? For the baby's sake? 'Since when do you love me?'

'Since...' He paused, raked a hand through his hair. 'Since for ever, I guess. It's always been there, I was just too stupid to see it.'

Well, that wasn't exactly convincing.

'But it's been over a month and you never contacted me.'

A miserable thought struck her and she felt as if her heart might be breaking all over again. 'How did you know about the baby? Was it Connor? That's why you came, wasn't it? Because Connor told you I was pregnant.'

She saw the guilty knowledge in his eyes and wanted to scream. If only it could have been true. If only he could have loved her. But she wasn't going to live a lie. Not ever again.

And next time she saw Connor, he was a dead man.

'This never meant more than great sex to you,' she said, when he didn't respond. 'I heard what you said to Gina. I know you don't believe in love.'

His eyes narrowed and instead of the shame she'd expected to see, she saw annoyance. 'So that's what the silent treatment was about that last night?' He didn't sound too pleased about the discovery. 'I never said that to you, I said it to Gina. And if you hadn't been sneaking around and listening to what wasn't meant for you to hear you wouldn't have known of it.'

He wasn't putting this on her. 'That's not the point.'

'Grand! Well, how about this for a point?' He stepped forward, forcing her back into the dress rack. 'What I said to Gina's no bearing on anything. I would have told her I was gay if it meant she'd stop pestering me.' His eyes swooped down her frame. 'And while I'll admit that the sex has certainly been great between the two of us, and I plan to have a lot more of it...'

She felt the liquid heat pool between her thighs at the husky promise.

'It's only a small piece of what I feel for you. And another thing. I'd decided to come before Connor rang me.'

'But it still took you a whole month to do it!' she said, aghast at his gall. How naïve did he think she was? She straightened her spine. Faced him down. 'Don't patronise me. I'm not some sad, pitiful little creature you have to pretend you're in love with, Mac.'

His jaw dropped; he didn't look annoyed any more. He looked astonished. 'Er, hello? Since when have you ever been sad or pitiful? You're the strongest, smartest, most resilient woman I know. And every damn time I tried to patronise you, you wouldn't let me get away with it. So you're not holding that against me now.'

Good grief. Her heart stuttered and stumbled.

Was it possible he really did love her?

Delivered in that curt, irritated voice with not one ounce of his usual charm and eloquence, the surly compliment had to be the most convincing she'd ever heard. And the most wonderful. But even better than that was the feeling of power, of entitlement that gripped her. He never had patronised her. It was the truth. Because she'd never let him.

He was the most charismatic, the most gorgeous, the most overpowering man she'd ever met and yet they'd always dealt with each other as equals. He'd challenged and provoked her and driven her completely nuts—while liberating her body, and setting her spirit free.

'You really *do* love me?' She still couldn't quite believe it. Did she really get to have her dreams come true?

He swore viciously, not exactly the epitome of anyone's dream man. 'Haven't I just got through telling you as much? Now stop mucking me about and tell me whether you love me back.'

She saw the vulnerability in his eyes, heard the exasperation and uncertainty in his tone, and all the love and longing and joy she'd tried so hard to hold back cascaded through her like a river in full flood.

Thanks to all the tragedies and traumas they'd had to face in their lives, all the insecurities they'd carried around with them, they'd put each other through hell.

But now, at long last, they'd found their way to heaven.

She flung her arms around his neck. Clung on. 'Oh, Mac, I don't just love you, I adore you.'

His rigid shoulders relaxed as he wrapped his arms around her waist and lifted her off her feet. He buried his face against her neck, blew out a staggered breath. 'Thank you, God.'

He sounded so relieved, she laughed.

He lifted his head and pinned her with a dark look. 'It's not one bit funny. You just took ten years off my life.'

'Sorry,' she said, not feeling remotely apologetic. 'Will I ever be able to make it up to you?'

His hands massaged her bottom, pulling her tight against the hard evidence of his arousal. 'Well, now,' he said, the sensual tone turning her knees to jelly. 'Give me a minute and I'm sure I'll think of a fitting punishment.'

But as his mouth lowered to hers and her fingers curled into his hair…

Daisy burst through the door.

They jerked apart.

'Mac, you can't come barging in here. Juno's not ready for this,' she panted, shooting Mac an accusatory look. She turned to Juno. 'I'm so sorry, Ju. I was at the deli picking us up some lunch. I didn't know he was here. Are you okay?'

Juno was momentarily speechless, never having had the chance to feel like a naughty schoolgirl before.

'She's fine. In fact, she's ecstatic,' Mac announced crossly as he hauled Juno back into his arms. 'Now scram, sis.'

Juno let a giggle slip out at Daisy's astonished expression.

'Oh, my goodness.' Daisy clapped her hands, her eyes shining with glee as her brain finally processed what she was seeing. 'You two made up! This is phenomenal.'

'It'll be a lot more phenomenal when you get lost.' Mac's disgruntled reply sounded for all the world like an annoyed big brother.

Daisy lifted up a hand in surrender as she scurried backwards out the door. 'I get the picture. I'm scramming. In fact, I was never even here.'

The door closed on a muffled thump, the sharp click of the lock echoing in the small space.

'Now where were we?' Mac murmured, lowering his head for a second time.

Juno pressed a finger to his lips, struggling to grab hold of a little sanity amid the tidal wave of joy. 'We can't make love in here,' she gasped, the thrill racing up her torso making it hard for her to breathe. Let alone resist. 'It would be…' What? 'Really impractical.'

'Darlin',' he drawled, nipping her fingertip, 'that practical nature of yours was the first thing I fell in love with.' He chuckled, his questing fingers flipping up the hem of her dress and slipping beneath the waistband of her knickers. 'But you'll have to trust me on this.' He cupped her buttocks. 'Sometimes impractical works every bit as well.'

Twenty-five glorious minutes of pure pleasure later, and she had to concede he had a point.

EPILOGUE

'HERE, let me.' Connor took the flower out of Mac's trembling fingers in the musty quiet of the church's antechamber. 'Calm down, man. You look as if you're about to be shot, not marry the woman of your dreams,' he said as he threaded the flower stem into the buttonhole of Mac's wedding suit. A smile curved his lips as he pinned the flower into place. 'I thought no Hollywood star worth a damn got stage fright.'

'Ha, ha,' Mac said, not amused by the smug tone. He brushed damp palms down the fine linen of his suit, the nervous gesture doing nothing to ease the apprehension tying his guts in knots. 'I don't get stage fright.' Or at least he hadn't until now. 'That's for amateurs.'

But he was an amateur at this, he thought miserably. He'd had seven months to prepare for this moment and he still felt scared to death. What if he wasn't any good at being a husband? Being a father? As he'd watched Juno's small, delicate body ripen with his child over the months he'd been on a merry-go-round of pride and excitement and bone-numbing terror. How would he live with himself if he failed at the only thing that would ever really matter in his life?

He took a shallow breath, tugged on the shirt collar that was threatening to cut off his air supply.

'So what's the problem, then?' Connor said quietly, the smug tone gone. 'You're not having second thoughts, are you?'

Mac gave a half-laugh. 'Are you kidding? I need her so much it hurts.'

And that was the problem, right there.

At Daisy's insistence, he'd had to spend the night without Juno in his arms for the first time in seven months and he hadn't slept a wink. He'd tried to sneak in and see her this morning, but Daisy had shooed him away from the château suite with some rubbish about it being bad luck. And now here he was a nervous wreck for the first time in his life. He wanted to put his fist through a wall but knew it wouldn't help.

The only thing that would calm his nerves was seeing Juno walking down that aisle towards him and knowing he deserved her.

'What if I muck it up?' he muttered, more to himself than Connor.

'All you have to do is stand there and say I do,' Connor replied easily. 'Just be glad you're not the one has to wear the frock and walk down the aisle in five-inch heels. And, rest assured, I'll give you a good solid kick if you forget to speak at the relevant moment.'

Mac forced a half-hearted smile, grateful for Connor's attempt to lighten his mood, even if it wasn't working.

The last time he'd wanted something this much, he'd been ten years old lying in a hospital bed, alone and scared and in pain and desperate to have someone there to care about him. He hadn't got what he wanted then.

'I'm not talking about the wedding,' he mumbled. 'That's the easy bit. I'm talking about the marriage. What if I muck *that* up? What if I make a mistake? What if she decides she doesn't love me after all?'

It was his greatest fear and the minute he'd said it he felt as if he'd exposed a part of himself he'd never intended to expose. But Connor didn't laugh or crack a joke or make fun of him, he simply gave his head a rueful shake.

'You're not going to muck it up, Mac. You're a good man, and you're going to be a great husband and a great father. Just watching you with Ronan is proof of that.' Connor rested his hand on Mac's shoulder. The reassuring weight eased the tension in Mac's stomach for the first time in months. 'Juno is happier than I've ever seen her. She believes in you—and with good reason.' Giving Mac's shoulder one last squeeze, Connor lifted his hand. 'All you've to do now is start believing in yourself.'

Mac swallowed, the sweat drying on his palms at the complete conviction in Connor's voice.

Juno believed in him. She trusted him. Amazing as it seemed, it was true. He let his mind wander back over the last seven months and thought about how she'd shown him she loved him, so many times, in so many different ways.

When she'd grabbed his hand and pressed it to her belly so he could feel the baby kick as they'd been sitting on the beach in Laguna one lazy Sunday this spring. When she'd told him not to be a pompous idiot and then seduced him in the shower a month back after he'd voiced his concerns about their continued lovemaking in her condition. When she'd flung her arms around his neck and demanded he carry her over the threshold the morning they'd moved into the house round the corner from Connor and Daisy's. And when she'd laughed delightedly as he'd pretended to stagger with her in his arms while he walked into their new home.

The look of steady, abiding love in her eyes every one of those times and a million more was the only thing that mattered now. So long as he focused on that, he'd be able to figure out the rest.

'Okay. No more panic attacks, I swear,' he said, letting out a deep breath and feeling as if a ten-ton weight had been lifted off his shoulders. 'Thanks for the advice.' He smiled at his brother.

'Not a problem. It's all part of the best-man service,' his brother said, smiling back.

The loud chimes of the chapel bell ringing the noon hour interrupted them.

'Damn it.' Connor glanced at his watch. 'Is that the time already? We better get you out there.' He patted his pockets and pulled out the twenty-four-carat-gold bands Mac had bought seven months back as soon as Juno had accepted his proposal. 'Great, right, we're all set,' he said, slipping the wedding rings back into his breast pocket and wiping his brow with the back of his hand.

Mac chuckled as Connor hustled him out of the antechamber.

'Calm down, Con,' he said, his confidence returning as they walked into the tiny French chapel where he had once ogled Juno in her maid of honour gown. 'No best man worth a damn gets stage fright, fella.'

He laughed as Connor cursed and shoved him into position at the front of the church now packed to the rafters with Hollywood A-listers and market-stall holders alike, all dressed in their best to wish the happy couple well.

Mac crossed himself, clasped his hands together and looked over his shoulder, eager for Juno to make her entrance. He just wanted to get this over with now so she'd be his for ever.

A satisfied smile curved his lips and he sent up a silent prayer of thanks.

Damned if he wasn't going to have a wonderful life after all.

* * *

'I still can't believe you insisted on doing this when you were eight months pregnant. It's completely mad,' Daisy remonstrated for about the twentieth time in the last ten minutes. She stood up, propping her hands on her hips. 'Right, you can take a look now,' she said, whipping the sheet off the cheval mirror in the church rectory. 'But I'm taking no responsibility whatsoever if you expose a nipple while you're walking down the aisle.'

Juno took in her reflection and laughed. Daisy's cream silk creation flattered her ripening figure with sleek, simple lines but dipped so low at her cleavage she blinked. 'Oh, God.' She clasped a hand over her mouth to stifle a giggle. 'I see what you mean.'

'I did warn you your boobs would get enormous,' Daisy said, and huffed out a breath. 'I still don't understand why you and Mac couldn't wait until after the baby was born. It would have been so much simpler.'

Juno turned to her friend and gripped her hand, the grin she'd been sporting for a good seven months getting wider by the second. 'Not for us,' she said simply. 'You know how nervous Mac's been getting in the last few weeks.' She felt emotion tickle the back of her throat at how desperately he'd been trying to hide it. 'He'd have gone into a complete tailspin if I'd made him wait a minute longer. He practically had a fit as it was when I told him the church wasn't available till April, way back in October. He would have kidnapped me then and there if I'd even hinted we wait until after the birth.'

The memory of how desperate he'd been to get them safely wed still had the power to make her heart quicken.

Daisy stifled a giggle herself. 'Having seen the look on his face this morning when I told him he couldn't see you, I guess you have a point.'

The bells of the noon hour rang out across the small vestry.

'Oh, dear,' Daisy said, the teasing tone turning to conster-

nation. 'I had to promise Connor we would not be fashion-
ably late, so he wouldn't have to physically restrain Mac from
storming down the aisle to get you.' She gave an apologetic
smile as her eyes dipped to Juno's cleavage. 'But that means I
won't have time to find some lace to preserve your modesty.'

'Don't be silly,' Juno said, still smiling. 'The dress is gorgeous. And if the worst comes to the worst and I end up
flashing the minister we'll just have to hope he doesn't have
a heart attack or Mac really will kidnap me.'

They both laughed.

Daisy sobered first. 'God, Ju.' She clasped Juno's hands
tight, tears sparkling in her eyes. 'I'm so proud of you.'

'Why?'

'Remember how panicky you were at the prospect of wearing that maid of honour gown when we were last here? Since
then you've blossomed into the beautiful butterfly you were
always meant to be. And it's all your own doing.'

'No, it's not. It's Mac's too,' she said, sniffing back tears of
joy. 'Anyone can be beautiful when they know they're loved.'

As she walked down the aisle towards the man of her dreams
and saw the love shining in his eyes—and the flare of arousal
as his gaze drifted to her cleavage—her heart soared. How
could any one heart feel so full and not burst? she wondered.

A week later, sore and exhausted after a demanding twelve-
hour labour, Juno had her answer as she watched her husband of eight days hold his tiny baby daughter in his arms
for the first time.

'So what do you think of her?' she whispered, her voice
weary, her heart full to bursting again.

His eyes met hers over the bundle cradled so carefully
against his chest, his gaze filled with pride and awe and un-
conditional love.

'You did well, Mrs Brody. She's the most gorgeous baby in the known universe.' A single frown line wrinkled his brow. 'Although I may have to give you both a lecture on not missing your cue.'

She laughed, recalling how frantic he'd been when he'd woken up in the middle of the night to find her panting through her first contractions, three whole weeks early.

'I'm sure I'll do much better next time,' she teased, and watched the colour drain out of his face.

'Now, now, let's not get ahead of ourselves,' he said forcefully. 'It's going to take a considerable time for my heart rate to get back to normal after this little one's arrival.' But then he glanced down at his daughter and grinned. 'But at least Daddy'll die a happy man, won't he, darlin'?'

Juno sighed as she sank into the pillows and her husband settled next to her with a besotted smile on his handsome face.

Her heart soared into the stratosphere, but still didn't burst—and she realised why.

I guess you just get used to being this happy.

* * * * *

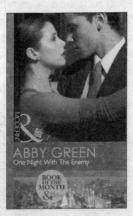

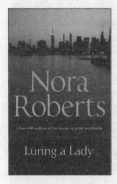

Rules are made to be broken this summer!

Midsummer madness has gone to everyone's heads…two new arrivals have blown into Glenmore and life at the hospital looks like it could get tricky for Flora and Jenna.

So, it's time to set some rules.

Flora's summer is simple, avoid kissing Connor MacNeil.

Jenna's summer 'Why I shouldn't fall in love with Dr Ryan McKinley' list is a little more complex…

It's so difficult to be good when temptation is right on the doorstep. But rules are rules.

Can sparkling summer flings ever turn into forevers?

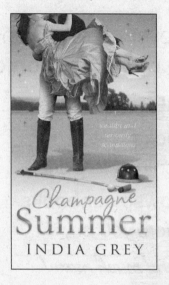

Tamsin's ready to spend her summer relaxing, until Alejandro—the man who nearly destroyed her reputation —comes back into her life. Now his world of champagne and scandal awaits her once again…

Sarah's summers are about spending time with her little girl. She never has a chance to think about herself. Until an encounter with a film director turns her life upside down and thrusts her into the exciting world of glitz, glamour and gossip pages.

www.millsandboon.co.uk